Mud and Glass

Laura E. Goodin

ODYSSEY
BOOKS

Published by Odyssey Books in 2017

www.odysseybooks.com.au

A Cataloguing-in-Publication entry is available from the National Library of Australia

ISBN: 978-1-922200-86-0 (pbk)
ISBN: 978-1-922200-87-7 (ebook)

Cover design by Rachel Roberts

This work is dedicated to Dr Van Ikin, who in his selflessness, skill, and pursuit of knowledge exemplifies the best of academia.

Chapter 1
Celeste Becomes Involved

Pace held the insect in a pair of tweezers, bringing it closer to my face.

'Hey, Celeste, see that blue patch on its head?' she said. 'It's supposed to be shaped like a comma, and it isn't.'

'Pace, for God's sake, I'm a geographer, not an entomologist!'

In theory, Pace was a geographer too. But her curiosity was white-hot and all-consuming. I don't *exactly* trail meekly behind her—I'm pretty smart myself—but keeping up with her does add a certain spice to life.

Pace placed the bug gently back into its plastic box and picked up the next one.

'This one's bizarre, too. See?' She held that bug up to my face as well.

'Yeah, look at that, whaddaya know,' I said after a glance at the bug. I turned back to my own work: poring over a hundred-year-old thesis on the Miraculous Mud Flats of Purple Bay. Rivers were my thing. The Purple River was, in my opinion, the finest of them. The Miraculous Mud Flats alone were worth a lifetime of study. Miraculous because they shifted with each tide to make fabulous, otherworldly patterns that glittered when the tide was out. People came from across the globe to see the spectacle—it was Purple Bay's only real industry, apart from a bit of fishing, and Purple Bay University, an institution of somewhat faded glory.

I was not immune to the beauty of the Mud Flats, but they fascinated me for many other reasons. Not least was the fact that they hadn't expanded into the bay by more than a few metres in a hundred years of observation. Meticulous observation at that—Millicent Strudthorne, the author of the thesis I was reading, had been a brilliant obsessive-compulsive, and my own research was reaping the benefits. Clearly, something was wearing the delta away about as fast as the river was depositing it.

'Hungry?' said Pace as she examined another bug.

'I've sworn off eating bugs, ever since that time in tenth grade when Toni Comiski found a roach in her locker and—'

'Yes.' Pace and I had both attended St Basilissa's, and her memories were as vivid and uncomfortable as mine.

'Anyway, yeah, I could do with some lunch. What did you have in mind?'

Pace took a grocery bag out of her desk drawer and slid the tray of bug boxes across the desk to clear a space. She took out a half-loaf of bread, a jar of peanut butter, and two bruised apples. 'How's this?'

I looked in my bag: no food, but five dollars I'd forgotten I had. I waved the bill in the air. 'My dear Hypatia, today we eat like lords!'

'On five dollars? And don't call me Hypatia.'

'Ice cream after the peanut-butter sandwiches, then.'

'Deal.' She took a huge mouthful of bread and peanut butter. 'How are the Mud Flats going?' she said indistinctly.

'Okay, I guess. My buddy Millicent measured and tracked like a mad thing, but I can't see any patterns—nor, by the same token, any anomalies that might give me a clue. The data is all just … hissing static.'

Pace shrugged and focused on eating her sandwich. When we were finished, we left our windowless office and emerged into the spring afternoon.

A moment later I wished we'd stayed inside. Jasper Smith-Fennel was running across the quad to catch up with us. At one point he'd been helping Pace with her research, but on a field trip there'd been an unfortunate interaction involving a mug of hot coffee and a trowel, and he'd come to the brutal realisation that she'd never love him. Words had been said, and shots had nearly been fired. I blush to say that I saved the day by knocking Jasper to the ground and flinging the gun into the bushes. But Pace had decided not to press charges, and Kortnoz had gone along with her decision, so here he was, still—and interminably—working on his PhD.

'Hey, Jasper,' said Pace wearily. I said nothing at all, which seemed to suit him.

'Halley over in Entomology wants to know where her bugs went. What do you need them for, anyway? You're a *geographer.*'

'I'm an *academic,*' she said. 'I *like* learning things.'

'Yeah, well, I'm an academic, too, but I don't go poking my nose into other people's research areas and making off with their experimental livestock.'

'Jasper, the day you learn that calling yourself an academic doesn't automatically make you one will be a happy day for us all. Now, go proofread your references or something, will you?'

That was a bit mean. Jasper had a reputation for the appallingly inconsistent style of his references; it was the cause of many a smug chuckle down at the pub preferred by those with PhDs. With a hissy little intake of breath, Jasper flounced off.

The line at the ice-cream stand was long; this was the first really warm day we'd had in a while. In front of us, two baby-faced undergrads were frowning as they talked.

'So *I* said, "I can't believe you're actually asserting that the Franckholm Hypothesis applies to the acoustics of human speech," and then *he* said, "Just who's the professor here, Danny?" and then *I* said, "Well, you're the one standing at the front of the room, I guess that's going to have to do." And that's when he told me I'd been dropped from the course.'

I tuned out. Undergraduates' complaints were old news.

Soon it was our turn to order. 'A cup of macadamia-chilli, please,' said Pace. She liked her desserts to put up a fight.

'A cup of caramel-apple, please,' I said. I didn't.

'Sorry, we're out,' said the work-study kid behind the counter.

'Oh, go on, live a little,' said Pace. 'Have the macadamia-chilli.'

I bristled at the challenge in her voice. 'All right, I will,' I said. 'Make that two cups of macadamia-chilli.'

We sat in the shade of a nearby tree, tears coursing down our cheeks as we ate the ice cream.

'Good batch,' gasped Pace. I didn't think my throat would work anymore, so I didn't even try to reply.

It took a few minutes after the last mouthful for me to risk speaking. 'I'm still not sure I see the appeal,' I said as I dragged my sleeve across my still-streaming eyes.

'You know you're alive,' said Pace.

'You know how I know I'm alive?' I said. 'I ask myself: alive or dead? And every single time so far, I've answered: alive. Really, it's not all that hard to determine.'

Pace's phone rang. From the way her face lit up when she saw who was calling, I knew it was Kortnoz. I decided that would be a good time to wander over to the recycle bin and throw out our empty ice-cream cups.

When I got back, Pace was bouncing around like a kid. 'Let's go, let's go! Ty needs us to help with some field work!'

'I can't. I have pages and pages of Millicent Strudthorne's mud-flat observations to wade through, no pun intended. You go.'

'He was specific. He needs two people to help.'

'Bring Jasper. It'll make his day.'

'Please, Celeste! What kind of geographer turns down field work?'

I felt myself starting to weaken. A bird sang in the tree over-head and a sudden soft breeze cooled the last of the chilli tears on my face.

'Okay. I need to get my gear from the office, though.'

Back in the office, I reached between the two filing cabinets to get my field pack. It was grey with dust, and several spiders swung anxiously from it on long cobweb streamers. I dusted the pack off, and tossed the spiders and cobwebs back behind the filing cabinets. I checked the contents: compass, notebook, pen, pocketknife, headlamp, batteries, whistle, jacket, water bottle, first-aid kit, harness and carabiners, helmet, emergency food bar.

I went to the water fountain to fill the bottle; by the time I got back, Pace had checked her own pack. Hers was far more worn than mine, but conscientiously repaired and cleaned. Pace filled her water bottle, then we were off to Kortnoz's office.

Kortnoz and Pace shared a quick kiss, then he said, 'Celeste! Thanks so much for agreeing to help today. I'm desperate to retrieve this find!' He smiled, a brilliant, exuberant smile. At moments like this I could see what Pace saw in him.

Kortnoz heaved his pack onto his shoulders. It was twice the size of mine, full no doubt of various gauges and meters. He was a bit of a gear freak.

His four-wheel-drive was parked in the lot near the Visual Arts building. It was often mistaken for some student's sculpture project, because it was dented and scraped, and usually encrusted with dozens of different colours of mud in abstract layers and forms. I knocked a dried blob of dirt off the door handle, wondering where Kortnoz had managed to find blue mud, and got into the back seat.

Kortnoz took us out along the coast, away from my beloved Mud Flats and out to where steep sandstone cliffs dropped a down to the sea. The sound of the waves was raw and exciting, and the foam splashed and sparkled against the blue sky and bluer water. I was glad I'd agreed to come with them.

Kortnoz pulled off the road onto a grassy headland and stopped near the cliff edge, and he and Pace got out and started setting up an anchor point.

The four-wheel-drive was parked nose toward the cliff, and Kortnoz wrapped a tape sling around the bullbar and closed the two ends of the loop in a heavy carabiner as big as his hand. Then he got a big wooden beam out of the back, lay it across the front of the tyres, and pounded a couple of small pickets in front of it to help wedge it in. I found it all a little alarming: what was he planning on bringing up from the bottom of the cliff?

'Celeste!' Kortnoz beckoned me back to the four-wheel-drive. He held a small box. 'Turning the knob in this direction is "lower". It's got a limit on it, so even if you slip and top out the knob, we'll never go fast enough to flatten when we land. This way is "raise", and it's also limited. To stop, just zero the knob again. Yank the cable out as a panic stop. I mean, emergency stop. I know you wouldn't panic.' Another smile.

Kortnoz went to get his pack out of the back seat. He set it down and started sorting through the contents, leaving some things on the back seat, keeping others.

'Hey, Pace,' I said, 'this wasn't exactly the impulse expedition you made it sound like. What's going on?'

Pace leaned close, her face eager. 'I probably shouldn't tell you,' she said quietly. 'Just act surprised when Ty does. In a small cave at the bottom of the cliff is a metal box about as big as a couple of loaves of bread. That's what he's bringing up.'

'So he needs a reinforced anchor, a winch, a backup lifeline, carabiners as thick as your arm, and two assistants to bring up something smaller than a bag of groceries.'

'Uh-huh.'

Kortnoz walked to the front of the vehicle and attached a thick steel plate to the big carabiner, then hooked two more carabiners into holes around the edge of the plate. Those would be for his and Pace's lifelines.

'I don't suppose this has anything to do with geography,' I said.

'*Everything* is geography,' said Kortnoz. It had been his mantra back when I, an overawed undergraduate, had sat in on his seminars, and we had all adopted it in a rush of hero worship. (One particularly irritable young woman on my freshman-year dorm floor would pound on the bathroom door and call out, 'Is *that* geography, too, Celeste?')

Kortnoz handed me one of the radios. We turned them on and I walked a few metres away to do a radio check. The signal was fine, and the battery was fully charged.

Pace checked Kortnoz's harness and helmet. He grunted as he put his pack on, and walked heavily to the edge, Pace following. I started the winch and brought the end of the wire rope to them as it unwound. They threaded the lifelines through their descenders, took hold of the wire rope, and, with a pair of cheery waves, disappeared over the edge.

A few minutes later, Pace's voice came on the radio. 'Okay, Celeste, you can stop the winch. It's going to take a few minutes to get the box secured.'

'That's fine,' I said, and sat down to enjoy the day. The only sound I could hear, apart from the waves, was the distant pulse of a helicopter. Sometimes being a sidekick was okay.

The helicopter was getting louder. I looked around: there it was, a few kilometres back along the coast, toward Purple Bay. It was flying fairly low—not too far above the level of the cliffs—and it was definitely heading this way. Stupid hotdog pilots, marring a nice day like this with their flying tricks. I started to get uneasy; it was staying alarmingly close to the cliff. From here it only looked like a hand's breadth between the rotor and the rock. The noise continued to grow. I peered into the cockpit, squinting against the glare off the glass—was that—was that a *rifle*? My heart pounded, and I scrabbled to get under the four-wheel-drive. I heard shots, and bits of grass and dirt flew up around me. Then the noise of the helicopter receded. I fumbled for the radio and called Pace.

'Did you hear those shots?' I had to shout over the noise of the helicopter, which sounded like it was returning. 'Get into the cave and stay there.'

'It's too small, we can't both fit.'

'Then you stay there and get Kortnoz to find another cave.'

'There isn't one! Ow, Ty, no, I'll stay outside. Ow! All right, quit shov—'

I risked poking my head out a few centimetres to peer at the helicopter. No markings of any kind, not even a registration number on the fuselage. It moved away from the cliff edge and dropped straight down, obviously following the line of the ropes.

I heard more shots, then there was a flash I could see even in broad daylight, and a massive bang. The helicopter rose above the cliff again and wheeled back toward Purple Bay. On one side of the fuselage, toward the tail, was a large hole with scorch marks around it. Hell's bells, did Kortnoz have a bazooka in that pack?

'Winch us up, quick!' Pace said over the radio.

'Right.' I had no time to catch my breath. I crawled out to where the winch control was lying in the grass. I slowly turned the knob.

'Firewall it, Celeste!'

'Right!'

I twisted the knob all the way. I felt a lot better a moment later when I saw Pace and Kortnoz pop up above the cliff edge.

'Slow, now!' shouted Pace, and I backed the winch off to crawl speed. They guided a black metal box up over the edge, clambering up after it as the winch dragged it close to the vehicle.

The three of us just managed to stagger with the box to the back of the vehicle and heave it in. I resumed my place in the back seat while Kortnoz started the engine and Pace did a last-minute sweep to make sure we hadn't left any gear behind. Finally she, too, got in.

'Dr Kortnoz?' I said as we started driving. My voice was shaking. 'Did you know you were risking all our lives?'

Kortnoz pulled the vehicle over and twisted in his seat to look at me. 'I promise you, I didn't know they'd been monitoring me.'

'Who?' My voice cracked. 'Why are you so *calm*? Why aren't you calling the police?'

'I can't risk it getting out that we've found the box. It's the missing piece to a lifetime of research. It's my shot at the Delmarva Geography Prize. It's the answer to a question that has haunted humankind for centuries: who wrote the Littoral Codex, and what does it mean? And once the cops know—well, a lot of other people will know. And it's not time yet.' Pace nodded in support.

The Littoral Codex—the ancient book so impenetrable that in three hundred years nobody had even figured out what language it was in before research had ground to a frustrated halt. It had been variously proposed that it was the solution to the quest for a unified field theory, the gateway to alternate universes, the secret to making a great meat pie, whatever you wanted most to know.

After a moment I said, 'Get real. The key to the freaking Littoral Codex just happens to be hidden in a cave that you just happen to find that just happens to be conveniently close to Purple Bay University. You don't think someone's pulling your leg?'

'There have been stranger coincidences in academia,' he said solemnly over his shoulder. 'Remember how Grady Turkle discovered the Turkle Group of antibiotics because he hadn't cleaned out his fridge while his wife was away on business? And what about Sharwa Haddad, who got caught up in a minor avalanche in the Pillar Mountains, and while she was digging herself out, found the snow cave of the last surviving speaker of the presumed-extinct language she'd been studying for twenty years? And then there's—'

'That's okay, Ty, you don't have to justify yourself,' said Pace with a savage look at me. 'You've been right so many times before.'

'Who are the helicopter people, anyway?'

'I'm pretty sure it's the Littoral League, led by Dr Honeycott.'

'Norella Honeycott? Impossible,' I said flatly. 'She died in a hang-gliding accident last year,' I said.

'Staged,' said Pace. 'To free her from university life so she could pursue her real passions.'

'And those would be?' I said.

'First, the secret to the Littoral Codex, and second—' Kortnoz paused, then said miserably, 'me.'

Chapter 2
Celeste Gets a New Student

Three days later was the first day back to classes after spring break. I still ached from our efforts to wrestle the box into the back of Kortnoz's four-wheel-drive and, after a hair-raising trip back to Purple Bay where it sounded (and felt) like the vehicle's back end was dragging on the road surface, into the safe in Kortnoz's basement.

I also ached because this Monday morning class was my least favourite: Intro to Geography. Two hundred itchy undergrads, only one or two of whom had even a spark of genuine interest in the subject. I wished I could get away with using a megaphone and a cattle prod. I was sure I'd get better results, but there were those pesky student welfare regulations.

'All right,' I sighed as I walked into the cavernous lecture hall. 'Did everyone do the readings?' Undergrads do reserve readings over spring break? Fat chance.

'Dr Carlucci?' said one young thing. 'The library was closed over the break.'

'Was it?' I said sceptically.

'Yeah, they said it was because the ceiling tiles were growing predatory mould and it wasn't safe.'

'Predatory mould.'

'I saw what it did to the head librarian,' said someone else, and shuddered.

Well, it wasn't as implausible as some of the excuses they came up with. 'All right, has the library been sorted out yet?'

Some nodded and muttered, 'Uh-huh.'

'Then you have an extra week to turn in your summaries.' A few of them gave surreptitious gestures of triumph, which I ignored.

'Dr Carlucci?' In the glare from the open doorway stood a shadowy figure. 'I've just transferred into your class.'

It was Danny, the kid from the ice-cream line the other day. Four or five of the undergrads groaned; a few more put their heads in their arms. One or two even turned around and said, 'Aw, piss off, Danny.'

He walked up to the lectern and handed me the paperwork. All was in order: the late-transfer clearance, the change-of-major form, the apologetic note from his academic adviser: 'There's nothing I can do. Please just try to cope.'

'All right, Danny, find yourself a seat.'

I started my lecture—the characteristics of population movements in pre-industrial societies—but a moment later Danny had his hand up.

'Yes, Danny?' More groans from around the room.

'Dr Carlucci, will you be presenting an exhaustive list of the factors that influence population dynamics?'

I smiled sweetly. 'Well, why don't you just listen to the lecture and find out?'

'It's just that, well, my time is valuable, and—'

'Thank you, Danny. You may stay or go as you please. But I will be expecting you to turn in excellent work that complies with all the assessment criteria regardless. Am I making myself clear?'

His eyes narrowed and he nodded. I spent the rest of the hour lecturing jauntily and hoping Danny would, in fact, walk out.

At the end of the lecture, as I was gathering my notes, I heard two of the undergrads talking quietly.

'Did you hear how she talked to him? She's so brave! And she doesn't even have tenure yet.'

'I wonder if she knows what she's gotten into?'

'Oh, she *has* to. Everyone knows about Danny.'

What, Danny the axe-murderer? Danny the evil genius with a nuclear cannon in his dorm room? I didn't think so.

When I got back to the office, I was surprised to find Pace already there. She tried every year to avoid teaching before noon. One semester she'd had to teach at eight o'clock due to an unfortunate double-booking of the lecture hall between her Geography and Media seminar and Intro to Pantomime I. Her hands had shaken for three solid months, and to this day she couldn't be trusted around anyone from the Department of Dramatic Arts.

She looked up from her computer and frowned. 'You look annoyed.'

'Oh, someone just transferred into my Intro class and he's already trying my patience. Remember that obnoxious undergrad from the ice-cream stand the other day?'

'Yeah, what a dweeb. Too bad.'

One of the teaching assistants stuck her head in the door. 'I'm really sorry to hear, Dr Carlucci.'

'Hear what?'

'Danny Snotnose Wexler.'

'Has everyone heard of this kid but me?'

'He's been chucked out of nearly every department in the university, but the word is he can't be thrown out entirely, or we lose hundreds of thousands in charitable donations.'

'From his parents, I'm assuming.'

'Uh-huh. I hadn't thought one family could *be* so rich, but there you have it. Well, sorry again. Bye.'

Pace looked at me with raised eyebrows.

My stomach sank a bit more when the phone rang. Sure enough, it was the head of the Earth Sciences School, who spent five minutes explaining that young Danny only needed an understanding mentor to blossom.

I sighed. 'I'll do my best.'

'Thanks, Celeste. It means a lot. And it will be remembered at tenure time if you can get him through.'

I reflected as I hung up that he'd left the obvious corollary unspoken: it would also be remembered if I *couldn't* get him through.

I considered ranting to Pace, but before I could get started, she said quietly, 'Ty wants to have a look at the, the stuff tonight. Want to come and help? Eight o'clock.'

'Um, sure,' I said, mostly out of years of habitually agreeing to Pace's plans.

The phone rang again. It was my mother, who worked over in Personnel.

'Honey, is it true? Do you really have that Danny Wexler in one of your classes now?'

'Yes.'

'Oh, my. You know he's been—'

'—kicked out of nearly every department, yes.'

'Well, I'm sure you know how to handle it. But let me know if you need any help, will you, sweetie?'

'Sure, Mom. Thanks. Love you.'

'Love you, too.'

Pace had a strange expression on her face. 'All these years, and you still get along with your mother.'

'All these years, and you still don't get along with yours.'

'I used to watch her pick you up at the gates of St Basilissa's, always smiling, always glad to see you.' She stared vacantly for a second, then shook herself. 'Anyway. When do you see Danny again?'

'Wednesday. Then Friday. Then every Monday, Wednesday, and Friday until the final exam. Maybe there's a break in there for study days, but that seems too far away to be real.'

'You probably need something to cheer you up. What do you think of this?' She reached into a desk drawer and brought out a small, battered book with a stained cover. *My Time on Purple Bay, a Reminiscence* by Millicent Strudthorne.

I took it from her eagerly and began to turn the pages. I had to be gentle, as time had done some damage. 'Pace, this is fantastic! Where did you find it?'

'Oh, there's a little bookshop in Beggar's Pit, not many people know about it.'

Beggar's Pit was the oldest, and by far the nastiest, neighbourhood in Purple Bay. But drunks and punks never bothered Pace much. She gave off powerful vibes, particularly when there were books to be browsed.

'When do you need it back?' I asked.

'What? No, it's yours. I'm giving it to you.'

I felt my eyes start to prickle, but Pace wouldn't thank me for crying. I pulled myself together and started reading the book. Every page was a treasure trove of wit, insight, and terrific illustrations that Millicent had done herself.

'Celeste?' The voice sounded far away. 'Celeste? Don't you have to teach another class soon?'

I jumped. Pace was right, it was nearly time for my eleven o'clock. I was always eager for this one, though: Advanced Riverine Geography. Flooding, levees, erosion, siltation, bridges, shipping, emergency management, travel and tourism, agriculture—rivers *were* civilisation.

I managed to put the book in my desk drawer and head out to the class. At least there would be no Danny: the students were all hand-picked by Kortnoz. He'd let me teach it because of my research specialisation, but he kept a close eye on how the dozen or so students progressed.

Today was the start of their in-class presentations. Nicki and Ricky—housemates, sweeties, and research partners, so inseparable their friends called them 'The Ickies'—were up first.

'We decided to study the braiding on the delta of the Purple River,' said Nicki. 'We overlaid satellite photos from the last ten years and morphed them to produce this animation.' She played the animation and I watched, mesmerised, as the channels split and merged, split and merged, grew, diminished, and disappeared, only to form again.

'We correlated the configurations with rainfall and with the value of the Krasnian dollar versus the Northern dollar, with a cross-reference to the Krasnian gross domestic product. We found that when the Krasnian dollar is weak relative to the North Kras dollar, Krasnian goods become relatively cheaper than Northern goods, and therefore more in demand—particularly in North Kras, but in other countries as well. Krasnian manufacturing increases, which increases discharge of waste water and by-products into the Purple River. Rainfall has some effect on the rate of change in the braiding patterns, but the main determinant is the level of Krasnian manufacturing activity. This, ultimately, is controlled by the strength of the Krasnian dollar, and is positively correlated with increases in gross domestic product.'

'Very impressive,' I said. It occurred to me that I had an opportunity here. 'Let's run that animation again, and see if we can detect any increase in land area.'

I stared hard as the animation ran. The edge of the delta fluttered like a curtain in the breeze, but never extended further in any lasting way. I looked extra hard at the photos of an anomaly there'd been a few years ago when Purple Bay had started to silt up. The sediment load and the turbidity of the water had dramatically increased for two months, but these photos showed no actual advance in the delta. *Why* wasn't the delta growing? Aliens, behemoths, big cosmic steam shovels, anything?

'That's odd,' murmured Nicki.

Ricky glanced at her, then mimicked her expression. 'Yeah, that's odd,' he said.

'How far back can you get these satellite images for?' I asked Nicki.

'I don't think they go back much further than that.' She bit her lip. 'Sorry.'

'No, no, not a problem. I was just curious, that's all. Good work, you two. Now, who's next?'

* * *

Pace was out when I got back to the office. There was a note on my whiteboard: 'See you at eight.' I looked over at Pace's desk at the boxes of bugs. She'd put a few drops of water and a tiny piece of lettuce in each box.

I took out Millicent's *Reminiscence* and resumed reading. She'd loved Purple Bay, loved the river from headwaters to delta. Sure, she was a bit … overly dedicated about the measurements, and about the way her laundry was done, about her breakfast, her clothing, other people's clothing, adherence to traffic laws, the number of pages in each day's newspaper, how many times she brushed each tooth. But hey, it was that kind of attention to detail that made her the researcher I could never be. I had no idea how such a meticulous person could ever have gotten involved in a scandal, but the rumours were persistent, if vague: some said she'd been involved in an illicit liaison with a student, some that she'd embezzled university research funds, some that she'd falsified research results and sabotaged colleagues' work.

Me, I'd already been involved in several, not least the time when I'd stolen Pace's research and published it. Oh, I'd had noble intentions (I thought I was saving the Purple River by making the research public when Pace had been too timid—I should have known *that* was impossible). Still, the fallout had been pretty bad—reprimands, the postponement of my tenure application by two years, and the very stern dictum that 'One more mistake like that, Celeste, and we'll have to let you go.' Tenure, or unemployment and disgrace—there was no middle ground. And no matter how careful I was, it still might end in disaster, now that I had Danny Snotnose Wexler to worry about. The loose cannon, the unknown quantity, the fart in the library.

The rest of the day moved past as sluggishly as a reed-choked stream. I ate dinner—toast and orange marmalade, because it was two days before payday (a hamburger and a beer, which was what I really wanted, would have to wait).

Finally, it was time to take the bus over to Kortnoz's. I walked the last two blocks to his house, and knocked on the door. The pinpoint of light from the peephole flicked to dark, then bright again, and Kortnoz opened the door.

'Thanks for coming over,' he said.

'No problem.'

'Would you care for something to eat?'

Department chairs got paid better than we did. The coffee table was covered in plates and bowls: chips, vegetables, bread, dips, chocolates—chocolates!

'Wow, thanks, Dr Kortnoz.' I ate as fast as I could without actually burying my face in the dishes. He watched me with an awed expression on his face, but didn't say anything. He probably remembered what it was like to earn a non-tenured professor's salary. Maybe it's better in some other university in a parallel universe, but at Purple Bay they did their best to wring more than their money's worth out of you.

'Celeste,' said Pace, 'didn't Sister Genesia have a few words to say about your mealtime decorum?'

'She's not here,' I said with my mouth full.

After a while, when I no longer felt the sharp little rodent teeth of hunger in my stomach, I picked up a piece of chocolate and sat back on the sofa. I noticed, somewhat guiltily, that it was the last piece, and realised I must have eaten all the rest. I'd make it up to Kortnoz sometime. When I, too, had tenure.

'Shall we head downstairs?' said Kortnoz. Once in the basement, Kortnoz opened the safe, and he and Pace worked hard to pull a rollered shelf out, upon which was the box. Kortnoz put a brace under the front of the shelf. Then he and Pace lifted the lid.

Inside were five pieces of glass or polished quartz about as big, and as thick, as my hand. They were smooth, rather than faceted, and gave back the light from the room in a soft glow. Each was a different colour: purple, red, yellow, green, and a smoky grey.

'That's what was so heavy?' I said.

'The box is what's heavy. Thick panels of lead, protecting

these—the filters!' said Kortnoz rapturously. 'If you look at the pages of the Codex using these filters, the secret writing appears!' He sobered. 'That's what I think, anyway.'

'And nobody's done a spectroscopy on the Codex this whole time and figured this out?' I said.

'The Codex isn't in a museum. It's in the keeping of the Praxicopolis family.'

'Those nutbags? How'd they get hold of it?'

'They bought it in a surreptitious deal about thirty years ago,' he said. 'The National Museum was just about to fold, and they offered enough to keep the museum going for generations. The director agreed to the sale if the Praxicopolises signed a lengthy list of agreements having to do with allowing access to scholars and other legitimate researchers. All of which they instantly broke. The whole thing was hushed up, and everyone just assumed the museum had removed the book to a super-controlled environment "for its preservation".'

'So,' I said, 'all we have to do is keep these glass blocks safe, find enough money to buy the Codex back from the Praxicopolises, keep it safe long enough to find an expert in ancient Krasnian languages who can decipher the hidden text, get the expert's translation verified by another expert, write up the findings, get the paper peer-reviewed, and publish it to international acclaim and the benefit of humanity across the globe. And manage, the whole time, to keep from getting killed in some sort of tragic and horrible way.'

There was a moment's silence.

'Yup,' said Kortnoz.

'Easy,' said Pace.

'We're geographers, you do remember, right?' I said. 'Not archaeologists, not linguists. Geographers.'

'Everything is geography,' Kortnoz and Pace intoned together.

Still, I had to admit that their enthusiasm was grabbing me. Pulling this whole plan off meant we'd be making very big news, which in turn meant a pretty good crack at the lecture circuit. Speakers' fees were one of the few ways a reputable academic had of making a decent living (the disreputable ones had found a few other ways). And I was not entirely immune to the lure of fame, I'll confess it now. We all have our flaws.

'What's the first step, then?' I asked.

Pace answered; of course, they'd been discussing this on their own. 'It's no good asking the Praxicopolises; they've refused dozens of requests for access to the Codex. We need to start by researching the family, looking for some kind of leverage we can use.'

'They don't live in Purple Bay, do they?' It wouldn't exactly be their kind of town, what with the crime, the boisterous tourists, the shoddy and decaying Opera House and the shoddy and decaying musicians who hung out there, and the hopeless sports teams. Really, the Miraculous Mud Flats were the only draw, and the Praxicopolises had never shown an interest as far as I knew.

'No, they live up in the mountains, about five hours' drive away.'

'I guess the Net is the best place to start, since we can't talk to them.'

The Infonet had been around for about ten years, and we'd all quickly gotten used to consulting its gathered wisdom for every random musing and research question. Like any large, chaotic system, it occasionally produced collaborations of stunning beauty along with the noise. President Kim-Hatton kept threatening to shut it down, as it 'widened the gap between the regular folks and the geeks'—of course, her solution was to drag the geeks back rather than help the regular folks catch up. I couldn't wait for the next election, so we could see the back of her. The good news was, the Infonet *was* so big and chaotic, even a president had no way of squashing it all at once.

'How much time do you have over the next few days?' said Kortnoz.

'A bit,' I said reluctantly. 'I've got Millicent Strudthorne's thesis to finish going over, and that's taking a lot longer than I'd estimated. Then there are mid-terms to grade, and pretty soon it will be time for the losers in Intro to start panicking and I'll have to extend my office hours to cope.'

'You're too soft with them,' said Pace. 'Do what I do, give it to them straight. "You're stupid, lazy, ignorant, and self-centred. If you ever show up in a geography class again, I'll make sure it's the worst experience of your academic career."'

'I can't do that. I'm not tenured.'

'We all know why *that* is,' muttered Pace, who, to be fair, really was trying her best to get over the whole unpleasant research-theft incident.

'Hey,' said Kortnoz gently, putting an arm around her shoulders. 'That's over now.' She rested her head against his cheek for a moment.

'And, what's with sticking me with Danny Wexler?' I said, to change the subject.

'What?' Kortnoz was genuinely surprised. 'The Board Chair's snotty little son? Is he an undergrad already? I remember him as a five-year-old nightmare. One evening she and her husband— Dan Wexler senior, the one who runs all those newspapers and television stations—brought him to a reception for some overseas scholars. It took maintenance three days to bring the room back to usable condition. A few months later, one of the scholars came out with a book: *The Myth of Krasnian Civilization*. Two entire chapters were devoted to Krasnian child-rearing customs. It did wonders for tourism, but who wants to be famous for having children who are considered by the international emergency-management community to be individual natural disasters?'

'So you didn't set me up?' I said.

'No, of course not, I'd never do that to any of my faculty members. Someone must have gone over my head. I'll see if I can sort it out in the morning.'

'Thanks,' I said. 'But if you want me to find time to do that Net research, I'd better head home.'

'Ty, can I borrow your car to give Celeste a ride home? The buses don't run all that often, and it's starting to get dark.' Another unexpected kindness from Pace. Maybe her relationship with Kortnoz was having an effect.

'Keys are over there. Thanks, Celeste. It'll be worth it, I promise.'

'Sure, Dr Kortnoz. See you tomorrow.'

As soon as we got in the mud-caked four-wheel-drive, Pace said, 'We involved you today because we needed a third person. Ty thinks you've learned your lesson, but you'd better not go trying to steal *his* research.'

'I—'

'That's all I'm saying about it.'

We spent the rest of the trip in silence.

Chapter 3
Celeste Finds Out More About the Praxicopolis Family

The next day I didn't have to teach until one o'clock, so I spent two hours looking for references to the Praxicopolises. There was no shortage, but I quickly learned I could group pretty much all of them into three main categories: Gee, aren't they rich; gee, aren't they reclusive; and gee, they could work on their people skills a little. I started to look for anything outside these categories. Site after site, index after index, and nothing I hadn't seen on a dozen or, as the morning wore on, a hundred other sites. It was as though they all came from one Praxicopolis Ur-Text, repeating each other's assertions and embellishments back and forth. President Kim-Hatton had nothing to worry about: the Net was doing very little to educate anyone.

Glumly, I logged off and went outside for a walk. The beautiful spring weather was holding, but it did little to improve my mood. When I got back, it went from glum to startled to annoyed in a moment: Danny was waiting outside the door.

'Hello, Danny.'

'Dr Carlucci, I was wondering if I could talk with you for a minute.'

I said blandly, 'Sure, Danny, come on in,' and opened the office. I gestured to the chair next to my desk, but he grabbed Pace's chair and spun it around to sit facing me.

'Now,' I said, as cheerfully as I could manage, 'how can I help?'

'You may have heard some unfortunate stories about me.'

I saw no reason to reply to this.

'Haven't you?' he said in sudden accusation.

I made myself keep smiling. 'Why, yes, Danny, I have. And, frankly, so far you've done nothing to convince me that they were exaggerations.'

'Well, they are. I'm perfectly happy to play by the rules and work within the system. Whatever you've heard, no one has ever accused me of cheating or lying.'

'I believe you,' I said. Nobody so obnoxious would have the kind of smooth-talking technique you'd need to pull that sort of thing off anyway. 'So …?'

'So as long as you play fair, so will I.'

'Danny,' I said carefully, 'are you implying that I wouldn't play fair? Like what, that I'd … deliberately grade your papers low or something?'

'It's happened.'

'Has it occurred to you that maybe you were actually doing substandard work?'

'Impossible. My IQ's been tested by the most robust instruments known. I'm brilliant.' And he said it not belligerently, as I would have expected, but almost pleadingly, like a little kid.

A thought struck me. 'Danny, tell you what: if you can make up the work of the first half of the semester in the next two weeks, I'll assign you a special research project. That should—' *(keep you quiet)* '—give you something more at your level to work on. What do you say?'

'An entire half semester's work? In two weeks?' He was back to his brusque, obnoxious self.

'You're brilliant, remember?'

'Mm, yeah. Okay, deal. What's the special project?'

'I need to find out the locations of the populations both directly and indirectly affected by the media outlets owned by the Praxicopolis family.'

He frowned, then shrugged. 'Okay. Can I start now?'

'I don't want you to get too scattered. You focus for the next two weeks on catching up, then I'll give you the full research brief. Oh, and, Danny—'

He'd been about to stand up, but paused with his hands on the arms of Pace's chair. 'Mm?'

'I play fair, too. Always. Got that? Good. See you in class tomorrow.'

He left looking a bit bemused. I wondered if anyone had ever seen his obnoxious behaviour for what I was starting to think it was: a plea to be taken seriously. I remembered feeling like that as an undergrad—hell's bells, I sometimes felt like that *now*. Poor, snotty Danny. Really rich, with no social skills. If he moved to the wilderness and stopped answering emails, he could be a Praxicopolis. I wondered if they were all brilliant, too. Cagey, certainly, according to all the sources.

I went back to the computer and, on a whim, did a search for all sites containing 'Praxicopolis' and 'Wexler'. There were three: the Census Bureau, which didn't count because it listed everyone in Krasnia; the Purple Bay University Alumni Club, again not much of a lead; and the Purple Bay Community Orchestra. I clicked on that one, and found that the biography of young violin prodigy Danny Wexler listed his teacher as Angelo Praxicopolis. I wondered if Angelo knew his name was on the Infonet.

I searched for sites containing 'Praxicopolis' and 'Angelo', 'Praxicopolis' and 'violin', 'Praxicopolis' and 'music', 'Praxicopolis' and 'teacher'—only the single Community Orchestra site, again and again. It was the only mention of Angelo. Renegade? Deceased? I had no way to know—except through Danny.

I ate the lunch I'd brought in: a cheese sandwich and a carrot. I thought longingly of the chocolate I'd had the night before at Kortnoz's. If we solved the Littoral Codex—chocolate every day! Breakfast, lunch, and dinner! It was a good thing the thought of that made my mouth water; it meant I could manage to chew and swallow the slightly stale bread. I wouldn't throw it out unless it were actually mouldy.

I was just getting my notes together to go teach my one o'clock when Pace stormed in and threw her pack onto the floor with a savage whipping motion.

'What's wrong?'

'Nothing,' she snapped.

'Just asking,' I said, and left. This next class, Geography of Art, was all right as far as it went. What it was *supposed* to be about was how various factors of proximity, landforms, and interaction between cultures affected the development of particular artistic styles. What it usually degenerated into was a debate on the obvious patriarchal characteristics of mountain ranges and how they combined with societal prejudices and domination patterns to produce works that were clearly the crying out of imprisoned and overwhelmed expressions of the subjective reality and if you weren't in collusion with the oppressors you'd see it yourself, don't you read the newspapers, it's happening all around us *right now*. My main job was to make sure the self-appointed oppressed didn't haul off and slug the unsuspecting oppressors, who were usually wistful, underfed kids who kept forgetting to shave (the boys) and change their shirts (all of them).

The Ickies were in this class, too, unfortunately, because *he* irritated the piss out of me and *she*, while clearly competent, made me want to shake her and bellow, 'I don't care what he's like in bed, ditch him now!'

I lectured for nearly the full hour and a half, then started asking the students about the readings assigned in the syllabus for the week. It soon became clear that Nicki had read them closely; Ricky managed, as usual, to mimic her responses convincingly enough to make it only just possible he'd glanced at the readings himself. Most of the others had made a barely passable effort. Once I got tenure, maybe they'd let me teach graduate students. I couldn't wait.

After class, Pace was still in the office, and still in a foul mood.

I took a risk. 'Sure I can't help?' I asked. Pace was typing furiously, her nose only a few inches from the screen.

'The bugs, the bugs!' she said. 'They want my bugs.'

'I thought they wanted *their* bugs,' I said. 'Which you borrowed without asking because they were busy and you didn't want to disturb them.'

'Details,' she said. 'I tried to tell them about the markings on the bugs' heads, and that I needed to breed a few more generations to determine whether this was a chance aberration due to environmental factors or a true genotypical change. They refuse to listen. Oafs. Philistines. *Administrators.*'

She pushed herself away from the desk. 'You're a *geographer*,' she mimicked in a thin, nasal whine. 'Bugs are for *entomologists.*' She dropped back to her own voice. '*Everything* is geography, *everything*. If these bugs are mutating due to something in their environment, in other words because of where they are and what human beings are doing there, that's a geographical issue.'

'Okay,' I said. 'Hey, did you know that one of the Praxicopolis family was a violin teacher?'

'Really?' she murmured. Then, as she realised what I'd said, she looked up and said, 'Which one?'

'Angelo.'

'Angelo,' she said pensively. 'Papa Praxicopolis had four sons and three daughters, and I'm pretty sure Angelo was one of the sons. Is he still teaching?'

'Doesn't seem to be. Do you think he's still alive?'

'He'd only be in his seventies, so maybe he is. Maybe he just got tired of teaching. God knows I sympathise.'

'Hey, you know what else? Danny Snotnose Wexler was one of his students.'

'*That's* interesting. So young Danny has hidden talents, does he?'

'Don't know, I've never heard him play. Maybe he sucks. How did you find out about the four sons and three daughters? They've got the lowest Infonet profile of any rich people on earth. Lots of opinions about them, but almost no personal details. It's driving me nuts.'

'Last semester, when Ty and I started doing some research on the Codex, we read a lot of old issues of the *Backwash*. There's plenty in there that never made it onto the Net.'

'You're telling me you actually believe something you read in the *Backwash*?' The *Purple Bay Backwash* was the city's only daily newspaper, and the only media outlet within a couple days' drive that wasn't owned by the Praxicopolises. Even though it had no competition, its owners were obsessed with raising circulation figures, and usually resorted to dubious journalism and hysterical editorials to do it. Sadly, it kept working.

'I've got a new helper on our Codex project, by the way.'

'Celeste! I can't believe you told—'

'Calm down, I didn't tell him anything except that I had an extra-credit research project for him, plotting the footprint of the Praxicopolis empire.'

Pace looked at me dubiously. 'Who is it?'

'Danny Snotnose Wexler.'

'Angelo Praxicopolis's violin student. Uh-huh. Good one.'

'Well, I didn't know that until after I'd set him the project. And I couldn't unset it. So let's see what he turns up. Maybe his connection to the family will end up being a positive.'

'Maybe the moon will do a tap dance in my linguini.'

'You're very pessimistic for once.'

'Those thugs in Entomology are after my blue-headed bugs. How am I supposed to feel?'

'Can't you take them home or something? Then Entomology'd need a warrant. And maybe the bugs would like a change of scene. If you're waiting for them to breed, I gotta say this isn't the most romantic place I can think of.'

'Oh, I don't know …' said Pace vaguely, and got that look on her face that she got whenever she was with Kortnoz.

I abruptly decided to change the subject. 'So what else can you tell me about the Praxicopolises? No point in my wasting time finding out stuff you already know.'

'Not much. You may have to go out and do some more field work—you know, interviewing people who know them, or knew them. Only one of Papa's seven children seems to have had any kids of her own. Camellia had a daughter, named Opal. There was a big party when the kid was born, covered extensively on the *Backwash*'s society page, and a bit of coverage when the kid's father died. And that's pretty much it. After that, they stopped appearing. Anywhere. In print or in person. I suggest starting with the retirement homes. You don't have any more classes today, do you? Didn't think so. Off you go!'

'What, today? What about my own research?'

'You've got all semester to write that paper.'

'You've got all semester to solve *your* little puzzle.'

'What, the bugs?'

'Your *other* little puzzle.'

'Did our brush with death the other day not impart a certain sense of urgency?'

'If I don't publish, I don't get tenure. If I don't write, I don't publish. If I run around playing superheroes with you and Dr Kortnoz, I don't write.'

'But if we do play superheroes, you get tenure, you get lectures, you get fame beyond your wildest dreams. Why don't you head on over to the University Park Retirement Home? Lots of old academics there, still sharp as a tack. They're bound to remember something. And if you hurry, you'll still have tonight to work on your Mud Flats research.'

I sighed, put a notebook, some pens, and Millicent Strudthorne's *Reminiscence* in my pack, and said, 'All right. But if all this backfires and I don't get tenure, you and Kortnoz can pay my rent and feed me.'

The Mud Flats research would be the slow and steady way to tenure—that and putting up with students who irritated me and administrators who annoyed me as much as they did Pace. Solving the Codex was the fast and dangerous route: glorious and pyrotechnical, but far, far riskier. As I walked to the nearby neighbourhood of University Park, I decided I was going to try to juggle them both. Screw it up, and it was back to my high-school job of quality control at the thumbtack factory.

When I arrived at the retirement home, I walked up to the front desk.

'Hi,' I said to the receptionist. 'I'm Dr Celeste Carlucci, and I'm doing some oral-history gathering as part of my research over at the university. I was wondering if any of your, um, guests, clients—'

'Inmates?' suggested a voice from a nearby hallway.

'Residents,' snapped the receptionist, with a venomous look off to his right.

'Thanks—if any of your residents would like to chat with me.'

'Go ahead, they're all of sound mind and retain the ability to give informed consent,' he said casually.

'You'd like to think that, wouldn't you?' said the 'inmate' in a thin voice that could have been male or female. A gaunt, wrinkled figure with wispy hair and dark skin hobbled into the lobby. 'It means you don't have to think about us or take care of us or anything, you selfish prick. You and all the rest of them.'

The receptionist flapped a hand lazily towards each of us. 'Dr Carlucci, meet Dr Garrick. Dr Garrick, Dr Carlucci. You can start with him. There's a lounge just up the hallway. Coffee is in the next room up from there.' And he turned back to his book.

I walked over to Dr Garrick and shook his hand. 'Please call me Celeste,' I said.

'And you can call me Dr Garrick. Show some respect. It'll make you stand out around here.'

We shuffled down the hallway to the lounge. 'Can I get you a coffee?' I asked.

'Not on your life. Stuff looks like swamp water and tastes like burnt toast. And it gives me the shits.'

We sat down on the sofa. 'Is it really that bad here?' I asked. 'You sound kind of unhappy.'

'Nooooo! I just complain for something to do. I've always been a complainer. First I complained to my academic adviser. Then when I got a teaching job I complained to my department chair. When they promoted me to department chair, I complained to the Dean. Pretty soon the Dean stopped listening, so I complained to the board. They wised up to me pretty quick as well, so I started complaining to the media. *That* wasn't such a good idea, but I already had tenure so they couldn't fire me. What they did do was stick me in an administrative position, the sadistic bastards, and let me rot there complaining to all the other career whiners. Finally my kids put me in here because *they* were sick of my complaining. That lazy little twerp at the front desk is paid to just sit there—thing is, he's not allowed to get up and leave, so I can make him earn his salary a bit by complaining to *him*.'

'Wow,' I said. 'Why not just … not complain?'

'Old habits die hard.'

'I'm actually here to see if anyone here can tell me anything about the Praxicopolis family.'

'Boy are you in luck! Practically everyone in here has a beef with them.'

'Why's that?'

'Just guess an answer out of the air, and chances are someone in here will claim it. Todd Strudthorne, for example—'

'Any relation to Millicent?'

'He's her grandson. Don't interrupt me. Todd Strudthorne was just on the verge of patenting a microsurgery technique that would have benefited millions and oh by the way would have made him rich. One night his lab was burgled and the computer stolen. Mysteriously, the backups were wiped in a freak electromagnetic pulse. The university investigators blamed a thunderstorm that somehow went unnoticed across the length and breadth of Purple Bay. Strudthorne knew, though. He'd been all through school with one of the Praxicopolis boys, and he knew the Praxicopolis style. Of course, the invention was patented by a

Praxicopolis front company a few months later.'

'So who else?'

'I'm bored. It's no fun talking without complaining. You come back this time tomorrow and I'll have lined up three or four people to give you their whole sad stories in a hideous, quavering, geriatric chorus of complaint. How will that do you?'

'Just fine, Dr Garrick. Thanks for all your help.'

'Aw, knock it off. I know what you're after. You've got the lean and hungry look of someone who wants tenure bad. Lucky for you I have sympathy for a poor, dumb PhD who can't play the game properly. Speaks well of you, in fact—only the really *devious* ones get tenure with no problems. Everyone else has to do their best to navigate the corridors of hell with a compass that always points to "Get stuffed".'

I walked home feeling like my head was full of gears that weren't quite meshing. Everything I heard or read these days was reminding me of everything else I'd heard or read, but not in any way that made sense. Just lots of random words flashing across my brain: phrases I'd heard or read, bits of half-formed thoughts, nothing I could grab onto and *understand*.

My apartment was a haven of quiet and solitude. It was only the one room, of course, but I kept it fairly neat except for the bookshelves. My window had a view of the university campus and, far away, the sparkle of the Mud Flats in the afternoon sun— which was why I'd taken the apartment. I couldn't see more than just that glimpse, but it was enough to inspire me when I felt discouraged and overwhelmed. Like now.

Dinner was a bowl of cereal, and my evening's entertainment was a few more chapters of Millicent's *Reminiscence*.

> The next day, Prudence and Hancock stopped by. Prudence honked, 'Oh, Millicent, making those tedious measurements again! And on such a lovely day! Why do you not simply enjoy the Mud Flats? Why must you

understand them?' Hancock added, 'Why, yes, Millicent—the world is full of utterly incomprehensible things to be enjoyed! Why, look at my lovely Prudence! I don't understand her in the slightest, yet I find her very enjoyable indeed!' And he gave a loud laugh like a cascade of rubbish bins. 'Oh, Cockie,' giggled Prudence.

You see, fair reader, what I was up against.

I sure did. Human nature hadn't changed much in a hundred years. Millicent was rapidly becoming not just my research subject, but my hero. I wondered if she'd ever gotten tenure. Based on what I was reading, I doubted she'd been 'devious' enough. I grinned again, remembering Dr Garrick, then stopped suddenly, thinking, how come all the really cool people are either dead or dying?

And with that depressing thought, I turned out the light and went to sleep.

Chapter 4
Celeste Broadens Her Academic Horizons

Wednesday morning, Intro to Geography. I reviewed the previous lecture and took up today's topic: how industrialisation changed population-movement patterns, and the effects of the change.

Danny kept his mouth shut—maybe my strategy was working. At the end of the lecture, he came up front.

'Hi, Danny. I appreciate your not interrupting today.'

'That's—that's okay, Dr Carlucci.' He looked genuinely surprised for a second. 'I started working on the project yesterday.'

'Well, you were supposed to concentrate on catching up, but if you think you can handle it, I guess I should let you try. Have you come up with anything yet?'

'I've started mapping the footprints of the Praxicopolis-owned radio and television stations. That's going to take me a while—there are tonnes of them, and they're all pretty high-powered, they reach nearly everywhere.'

'That's a terrific start, Danny. Can you keep me updated as you go along? I'm also interested in any manufacturing interests they may have, although it's probably impossible to find those out. But either way, thanks. It looks like this may work out for both of us.'

I gathered my papers and went back to the office. It looked like it was going to rain later. Rats, I hadn't brought my umbrella. What kind of geographer doesn't pay attention to the weather report?

In my mailbox was a note from Jasper. 'Call me. It's important.' I crumpled it up and threw it in the recycle bin.

I unlocked the office door, sat down, and tried to focus on

Millicent's thesis. I decided to enter some of her data points and generate a graph, to see if any trends became more obvious. I turned my computer on and waited for it to boot up. As soon as it did, a message popped up. Oh, hell, it was from Jasper. I closed it without looking at it, then checked my email. Sure enough, an email from Jasper, which I deleted unread.

'I need to talk with you,' said Jasper from the doorway. 'Now.'

I did not invite Jasper to sit. 'Well?'

'I know we haven't been getting along, exactly, but I need to ask for your help.'

'If it's about Celeste's bugs, you're out of luck.'

'It's not about the bugs!' His voice was suddenly high and distressed.

'What, then?'

'You're the only person in the department who'll understand.' I doubted it, but nodded for him to continue. 'I need to get hold of some research.'

'So? That's your job.'

'It isn't published yet.'

'Email the researcher.'

'I want to steal it.'

'Get out.'

'But—'

'What are you, stupid? If I screw up like that again, I'm out on my arse. Get out. We never had this conversation.'

'But it's Dr Kortnoz's research!'

'Is that supposed to make a difference? Get out.'

'He's ruining everything!'

'I thought that once myself. I was wrong. So are you. Get out.'

A minute after he left Pace came back in with a cup. 'I saw Jasper stomp off. What was the big deal?'

'He wanted me to help him steal some research.'

'You're joking. How insensitive, not to mention dumb, could he be? Did he say whose? And why?'

'Dr Kortnoz's. And I didn't let him stick around long enough for the why. Or even the what.'

'I wish he'd just finish his PhD and go. You don't think he's still in love with me, do you?'

'Of course he is. That's why he keeps after you about the bugs. But this is something separate. At least I think so. He said something about Dr Kortnoz "ruining everything".'

'That sounds familiar.'

'*I* was trying to be altruistic,' I said, perhaps a bit defensively. 'In the cause of greater knowledge. Jasper isn't the altruistic sort.'

'You can say that again.'

'So … does Jasper know about the project? What other research could he be wanting to steal?'

'Ty's been very careful. The three of us are the only ones involved.'

'Except for the people in the helicopter. They're pretty involved, them and their guns.'

'Oh, will you get over that? Occupational hazard.'

'For an academic?'

'If you're the right *kind* of academic. Say, how did your trip to the retirement home work out?'

'I'm going back this afternoon. Ever hear of a Dr Garrick?'

'Ty's mentioned him a few times. Bit of a whiner, apparently, but his complaints always made sense.'

'He and I talked for a bit yesterday, and he said most of the people in there have some sort of grievance against the Praxicopolises. Sabotage and stealing patents were the two he mentioned at the time. He's getting a few people lined up for interviews today. He seemed to relish the idea.'

'Don't you feel funny, a geographer doing investigative journalism?' Pace grinned, and waited for me to say it.

'Yeah, yeah, everything is geography. Happy?'

'Smug, and that's nearly as good.'

I ate my lunch and went to teach Advanced Riverine Geography, holding my backpack over my head to keep the rain off. For an hour I managed to forget about Jasper, Danny, the helicopter, the guns, the Praxicopolises, and the damned Littoral Codex and just listen to the rest of the students' presentations. They were good, I was happy. Life was okay.

Which was why I was completely unprepared to see both Jasper and Danny walking towards me from different directions when I left the classroom. Time to disappear. I hurried around the corner of the building and went into the last place I figured they'd look for me: the Department of Dramatic Arts.

In all my years at Purple Bay University, I'd never been inside. I wasn't much for plays. If sarcasm, wailing, despair, and swear words were what I wanted, I could always just sit in on one of Pace's sophomore seminars.

I walked along the hallways. In practice rooms and tiny performance spaces painted black, emotional undergrads howled and writhed. They were dressed in black as well, every one of them, head to toe, so sometimes it was hard to figure out where all the noise was coming from.

'The lights!' shrieked one, in a voice that swooped up and down like a siren.

'Bobby, it's not you. I have to … find the deeper me,' said another.

Further down the hall I heard, 'When the oppressed realise that bureaucracy places paper-and-red-tape fetters on their acquiescent and apathetic limbs …'

Oh, for God's sake.

Towards the end of the hallway, through the open door of a classroom, I heard someone saying, 'Oh, for God's sake.' Feeling an instant kinship with whoever it was, I lingered. A few more minutes in the building to throw my pursuers off the scent wouldn't hurt either. I peeked through the doorway.

Someone about my age, so I assumed he was an assistant professor of some sort, was looking at an abashed trio of undergrads. He was holding up one finger and wagging it as he talked.

'You see how stupid this finger looks? Do you ever actually

see anyone making a point by sticking their finger up in the air like this? No? Neither have I. Except on stage. For some reason every actor goes through a phase where they pick up these stupid, forced, fake idiosyncrasies. If you do it again, any of you, I'll fail you. No negotiation. No mercy. Got it?'

They nodded, looking scared. One of them caught sight of me outside the door. The professor noticed the look, and came to the door.

'Can I help you?' he said with a bit of asperity.

'Oh, no, sorry. I was just … I just … I agree with you about the finger thing, by the way. It drives me nuts.'

His expression changed to wicked amusement. 'If you've got a minute, why don't you come in and watch this gang do their scene? A bit of objective feedback might do them good. Are you an actor?'

'Oh, God, no. I'm a geographer.'

'Wow, really? I've never met one of those. Take a seat! Okay, guys.'

They exchanged nervous glances, but got into position, the two young women standing centre stage, the guy off to the side.

'How are we going to keep him from finding out?' said the young woman in the grey shirt.

The other one started to raise a finger, then pretended to scratch her nose in thought instead. 'I know!' she said at last. 'We can get Trevor to bring him on a wild goose chase!'

Enter the guy. 'Did I hear my name?'

Apparently, the two female characters were trying to organise some sort of surprise for an off-stage boyfriend, and their dorky pal Trevor was supposed to play the red herring. The scene went on for way too long, like a bad situation comedy, and finally the professor said, 'Curtain.'

He turned to me. 'Well?'

'Um. Who wrote the script?' I said, as neutrally as I could.

'The department chair.'

'I don't suppose Trevor turns out to be an alien or a spy or something interesting, in disguise?'

'No,' said all four, sadly.

'It's … it's not a particularly riveting scene, is it?'

'No,' they chorused again.

'You did a good job of not pointing,' I said to the one who'd scratched her nose.

'Thanks.'

There didn't seem to be a whole lot else to say after that.

'Thanks for letting me watch.'

'That's okay,' said the guy. 'It'll be more of an audience than we get on opening night.'

'Don't people flock to the department chair's plays?'

'No,' they all said.

'What if you, like, doctored the script a bit?'

'She'll be there. She comes to every performance.'

'But once she hears all the cheering and takes her bow, she might not have the guts to admit that it wasn't what she wrote.'

'It's risky,' said the professor. 'It could get us in real trouble.'

'Tell her beforehand that you're requesting a few slight changes, which will be small enough that she can only agree. And then later you can say, "We knew you'd want to keep polishing the script along those lines, but you were so busy." Every department chair likes to be noticed for being busy. Then, on opening night, thunderous applause!'

They thought about it for a few seconds. 'I'm game,' said the grey-shirted woman.

'Me, too,' said the guy. 'Anything would be an improvement.'

'Well,' said the other woman, 'I guess we haven't got that much to lose.'

'I do,' said the professor. 'I haven't got tenure yet.'

A fellow-sufferer! 'You know, I'm in the same boat, and I have to say I'm getting a little seasick. Maybe *we* should rock that boat instead of letting it make us spew!'

'That was some metaphor,' he said. 'I'm Russ Gartner.'

'Celeste Carlucci.' We shook hands.

'If I change this script, what are *you* going to do to rock the boat?' His students started to look hopeful.

I felt suddenly reckless. 'I'll … I'll make sure Danny Wexler gets exactly what he deserves.'

'Danny Snotnose Wexler? Are you stuck with him now? Wow, you're brave. Okay, deal. You give Danny exactly the grade he deserves, and I'll make this script into a masterpiece.'

'Disclaimer: Danny is pretty smart, and I actually don't mind him all that much.'

'Not yet, you don't.'

'But do we still have a deal?'

'We do. Do we have a luncheon engagement tomorrow?' His students nudged each other and smirked.

'We … we do. See you in the quad at noon.' Good thing the next day was payday.

'Oh, by the way,' he said as I was about to go. 'We all have to agree not to talk about this. If the chair finds out, we'll have to stick to the original script. And no one wants that. Do we?'

We all shook our heads vigorously. Russ smiled then, and the thought crossed my mind that maybe Kortnoz's smile wasn't anything to write home about after all.

I walked out of the Dramatic Arts building feeling like I'd just been filled with helium and springs. Better yet, I'd shaken Danny and Jasper off my tail. And the rain had stopped, just in time to head over to the retirement home.

Dr Garrick was waiting for me in the lobby, which meant I didn't have to deal with the receptionist. I noticed it was someone different; if all the residents were like Dr Garrick, they'd have trouble holding on to staff.

'Come on,' he said. 'I know where we can get better coffee.' He took me to the elevator, and we went up three floors. 'Drusy Kelso has a cappuccino machine that her kids gave her as a guilt present.

One of those really fancy ones, looks like a torture device. You haven't had coffee until you've had Drusy's coffee.'

Dr Garrick knocked on one of the apartment doors. Sure enough, as the door opened, a wave of coffee aroma swirled into the hallway and made me weak at the knees. A tiny woman, her hair fuzzy and white, her skin smooth and olive, stood in the doorway.

'Dr Drusilla Kelso, Dr Celeste Carlucci,' said Dr Garrick.

'Why so formal? I'm Drusy, sweetie, and I'll call you Celeste if you don't mind. If I forget your name, you'll tell me again, won't you? Of course you will.'

Inside the apartment were another half-dozen people, all drinking coffee except for one, who was slugging diet soda directly out of a large bottle.

'Everyone,' said Drusy. 'This is Celeste, the one researching the Praxicopolises.'

'Praxies! Boooooo!' yelled several of them. One made a loud farting sound, which I was hoping was just a derisive raspberry.

'I brought a recorder,' I said, 'but if you'd rather, I can just take notes.'

'Roll the tape, I'm not afraid!' said a wizened man crouched over his cane. 'It's way past time for that!' The rest of them shouted agreement in their reedy voices.

'Okay, then,' I said. I put the recorder on the coffee table and switched it on. 'Start talking!'

They all started at once. Drusy banged her coffee mug on the table. 'One at a time!' she hollered. 'Ruby! You first!'

A prim woman sitting on the sofa cleared her throat in the sudden silence. 'My name is Dr Ruby Chen,' she said clearly in the direction of the microphone. 'Fifty years ago I was a graduate student at Purple Bay University, Department of Communications. The Praxicopolis media empire was just getting started: two local radio stations and a community newspaper. My research uncovered that the Praxicopolises were using intimidation and blackmail to acquire a string of weekly newspapers within an hour or so of Purple Bay. Nasty, nasty work. In one case, one of Papa Praxicopolis's sons got a newspaper owner's teenage son drunk, then tied him up and threatened him with every kind of torture known to humankind. Nothing could ever be proven, of course, but the owner sold up within the month. The boy ended up with severe emotional problems.'

The others murmured, 'Terrible, awful, shocking.'

'Camellia, one of the Praxie daughters, married an insurance executive,' said Drusy. 'Made his life hell, apparently. He was found one morning in the gutters of Beggar's Pit, knifed to death but still clutching a bag of pornography. His body had been stripped of any identification, and Camellia waited four days before she bothered reporting him as missing—four days, she let his body lie on a slab. My husband was devastated—he'd been his best friend from school.'

'Bruce, the bald one, he sure knew what he wanted, didn't he?' said one of the women on the sofa. 'He wanted to be remembered as a great benefactor. Oh, sorry, I'm Nancy Wilhelm, former chair of the Department of Anthropology, Purple Bay University. Anyway, he decided he could look like a great guy by giving a lot of money to the university. But he put so many conditions on it that research has been stifled for two generations. "Contracts of tenured faculty must include a clause of loyalty to the university and its governors." "A Praxicopolis must be present at all evaluations of PhD dissertations." We fought for months, but the war was already over before it began. The university has never been the same.'

'Angelo, the youngest one, though, he was different. He was a musician, wasn't he?' said the man hunched over his cane.

'Yes, violinist,' said a few voices.

'He started out teaching under an assumed name, because nobody would send their child to a Praxicopolis,' said Drusy. 'But it leaked out eventually. Probably one of his vicious siblings blew his cover. By that time enough people had gotten to know him that they shrugged and said nobody picks their family.'

'Where are they all now?' I asked. 'Are they still alive?'

'That kind never dies,' said Dr Garrick. 'They just hang around for spite.'

'Oh, wait, didn't one of them cark it a few months ago?'

'No, that was that guy who used to have sex with goats, wasn't it?'

'Somebody loathsome, anyway.'

'The world is going to hell.'

'It certainly is.'

Drusy brought over a platter of cookies, and I helped myself as I listened to them talk. I didn't know how useful this was going to be, but I was already making plans to track Angelo down.

'So,' I said to the room at large. 'There were Camellia, and Bruce, and Angelo …'

'And Pablo, and Frank, and Lucille, and …'

'… and Dahlia, wasn't it?'

'I thought it was Deborah.'

'No, definitely Dahlia.'

'She's the one who sued my cousin the restaurateur because she found a hair on her fried Bay snapper. Bankrupted him. I must be getting old. Of course it's Dahlia, not Deborah.'

Pretty soon their conversation got more general, then downright vague, and I sensed many of them were getting tired. I was a bit tired myself from trying to listen to three or four conversations at once.

As soon as there was a bit of a lull, I said, 'Thanks so much, everybody. I have to head back—those mid-term papers don't grade themselves!'

They all gave sympathetic chuckles as I gathered up the recorder and my notebook, and a few more cookies. Drusy noticed, and tipped all the remaining cookies into a plastic bag for me. She waved away my thanks.

'Lenny said you don't have tenure yet.' I must have looked puzzled, because she added, 'Lenny Garrick. You just take these, I'm sure you can think of a good use for them.'

'Thanks, Drusy. If I have any more questions, can I give you a call?'

'You can come over for dinner if you want! How about Saturday?'

'I'd love to—thanks again!'

'Six o'clock. You know we old folks like to eat early.'

'See you then.'

Everyone called out their goodbyes, and I saw myself out.

If that was what being an ageing academic was like, I was looking forward to it.

Chapter 5
Celeste's New Friend Proves His Worth

I usually devoted Thursday mornings to research, but I was too edgy to do more than enter a few columns of Millicent's figures into the spreadsheet. I fidgeted, played computer games, rearranged the pens in my drawer, cleaned out the long-neglected recesses of my backpack, and fidgeted some more. Realising I was useless for any real work this morning, I took out Millicent's *Reminiscence*, which I'd taken to carrying everywhere.

> The research goes badly. The figures refuse to reveal to me any clues as to why the sediment disappears as quickly as it's deposited.
>
> There is, however, one intriguing anomaly. During the month of August, the sediment did extend slightly to form a bar that persisted into early September before it, too, was eroded. I've written to Foster, who is doing field work at Alarm Bay this year, to see whether a similar pattern held true further east. I don't hold out much hope for useful information, however; Foster is not a meticulous person. His desk is always in disarray, and I have no idea when the last time was that his shirts made the acquaintance of an iron, nor his hair of a comb.

I raised a hand to my own, somewhat unruly, hair. At least my desk was neat. Maybe Millicent would have cut me some slack. I remembered seeing a comb in one of the pockets of my backpack, and thought that, considering I actually had a date in less than two hours, I might make a bit of an effort with my appearance.

I dragged the comb through my hair, the pain reminding me why I didn't do this very often. I was struggling with a particularly large and stubborn knot when Pace walked in.

'Oh. Have a date today?' she said.

'Yes, as a matter of fact. Ow.' The comb suddenly ripped downward, the knot trapped in its teeth like a horrible black insect.

'Love hurts,' she said, and switched on her computer. A minute later, she swore.

'What?' I said as I rubbed my aching scalp.

'An email. Never mind. Not your problem.'

'The bugs again?'

'No, Entomology seems to have given up for the moment. You can always outlast an entomologist, it just takes more time than you'd think.' But she said nothing more about the email.

My hair conquered, I returned to the *Reminiscence*. August. An anomaly in August … I sent an email to the Ickies (I knew whichever I sent it to, they would both read it) asking them to see if they could get more data for the July-to-September period of the year they were studying in detail. I wanted to get a much more precise view of the delta—a frame per day at least, preferably two.

'So,' said Pace, 'what have you found out about the Praxicopolises?'

'They're all nasty. Except for the one who taught violin. He seems to be the family disgrace—a decent guy. Did you remember signing an oath of loyalty to the university and its governors when you got tenure?'

'They told me it wasn't binding.'

'Yeah, well, I wouldn't be too sure. Bruce Praxicopolis made the university write it into all the contracts, and according to my sources, he doesn't seem to be the type to leave loopholes.'

'So, what's loyalty mean? I do the best research I can in an attempt to bring honour and glory to the university. I teach as best I can, in an attempt to bring along the next generation of researchers who will attempt to bring honour and glory to the university. See? All good for the university. Very loyal of me.'

'What if the governors tried to make you change your research topic, or fiddle with the results, or sabotage someone else's research?'

'There's enough of that going on already. What's the difference?'

'The difference is,' I said, 'that once you sign the contract, they can throw you in jail if you don't do what they say.'

'That's crap,' said Pace casually. 'Besides, hasn't happened yet to anyone I've heard about. Well? Who's the date?'

'Just someone I met when I was walking around campus yesterday. A fellow-sufferer in the non-tenured wilderness.'

'Is he smart?' That always mattered more to Pace than 'Is he good-looking?'

'Seems like it. A bit too soon to tell, though.'

'What department?'

I choked. If Pace knew he was from Dramatic Arts, she'd make my life hell.

'Oh, one of the humanities or other, I can never tell them apart. Literature, rhetoric, creative writing, painting, sculpture—all a hideous blur of mournful people dressed in black and talking about themselves. Russ was wearing a blue shirt yesterday, though, so I'm hoping he's different.'

'Blue! What a rebel. Is he good-looking?' Pace was human, after all.

'He has a nice smile.'

'That *is* important,' she said, and looked thoughtful.

'Hey, your artiste, he's not in Dramatic Arts, is he?'

'Oh, sorry, I've got to go. I just remembered I have to go see my mom about some stuff. I'll see you after my one o'clock.'

'Wait, I forgot to ask. Can you come over to Ty's for dinner tomorrow night? You can catch us up on anything you've found.'

'Sure,' I said, gathering up my backpack, the notes for my one o'clock and the *Reminiscence.* 'You can give me some clues as to what to ask next. I'm having dinner with someone named Dr Kelso over at the retirement home on Saturday. Maybe I can ask her some more questions.'

'Wow, Drusy Kelso? Is she living there? She was Ty's professor for one of his electives, I can't remember which one. He mentions her from time to time—she was famous for her lavish end-of-year parties for her students. Apparently she was quite a cook.'

Two free dinners in a week, one of which with a famous cook—life was good.

I hadn't planned on seeing my mom today, but we hadn't talked in a few days, so why not? She was always glad to see me, just as she'd been all my life. Okay, I felt a bit guilty for using her to escape Pace's scrutiny. But she wouldn't mind—probably think it was funny.

The Personnel building was all the way across campus, but the weather had cleared up since yesterday, and it was a pleasant walk.

'Hi, Mom,' I said when I got to her desk. 'I just came over to say hello, and to take a break from Pace.'

'Yes, well, glad I could provide an excuse,' she said. 'Are you sure she's a good friend for you to be spending time with?' Mom had said variations of this sentence to me every week for the past fifteen years.

'We've been through a lot together. And she did eventually mostly forgive me for—'

'Least said, soonest mended,' she said quickly. Mom didn't like to talk about unpleasant things, such as my shaming the Carlucci-Golden family the way I had. Sometimes I wished she'd just yell at me and get it over with.

Mom's boss appeared at my shoulder. 'Beatrice, can I ask a favour? Oh, hello, Celeste. Long time no see.'

'Hello, Ms Toller.' Strictly speaking, I could have called her by her first name, but I'd known her since I was eleven and, as with Kortnoz, I just couldn't bring myself to do it. Besides, she'd given Mom a bit of a rough time back when my disciplinary hearing was going on, and I would have felt like a hypocrite had I appeared more friendly toward her than I actually felt.

'Beatrice, I need you to cover for me at the Admin meeting Monday at nine. It's over in their conference room. Okay? Thanks.' She smiled sweetly and walked away.

'Does she ever actually wait for a reply?' I said once she was out of earshot.

'She hasn't yet. Funny, though.' Mom stopped.

'What?'

'Well, she usually enjoys going to those meetings.'

'You're joking.'

'Sadly, no. "I like to know what's going on," she says. Do you have lunch plans, by the way?'

I felt myself blush, just as I used to do when I was fifteen and Mom asked me how my date had gone. 'I … yeah, sorry.'

'What's his name?' Mom sighed.

'Russ.'

'Russ what?' she said in a singsong voice.

'Russ Gartner,' I said in the same voice.

'Oh! Over in Dramatic Arts. He's a very nice young man. Except that …'

'Mom, *what*?'

'You know why he hasn't got tenure yet, don't you?'

'It didn't come up in conversation, no,' I said, a tad frostily.

'He refuses to sign the contract. It's been in the media and everything, or else I couldn't talk about it. He's only still here because the case has gone to court, and they can't fire him yet. The administrators don't want to pay someone to teach his classes while he sits at home, so he still comes in. I'm told the students are very fond of him.'

'Why doesn't he want to sign the contract?'

Mom beckoned me close. 'No one is supposed to talk about it, but there's a clause in there where you agree to be loyal to the university.' Her voice went even quieter. '*And its governors.*'

'Oh, that,' I said conversationally. 'Pace says it doesn't mean anything.'

'Pace has a very narrow focus.'

'No, Mom, she's always taking on new research projects. About everything under the sun.'

'But she doesn't know anything about *people*.'

I tried to think of something to say, but couldn't.

I was still leaning over Mom's desk; she took the opportunity to kiss me on the forehead.

'I'd love to chat some more, sweetie, but I've got to get back to work. Have a lovely lunch. But keep your head, all right? I know how you get.'

'Aw, *Mom*,' I whined, just as I had said at fifteen when she'd given me the same admonition. We both laughed, but I could tell she was serious.

I stopped by the bank machine to withdraw the cash I would need for lunch. I checked my watch: about an hour to go. I found a bench and took out the *Reminiscence*.

> Today I did my measurements in the rain. I prefer it: no tourists inquiring about my business, no tiresome university students on their way to and from the beach. I stood in the midst of the thousand braided streams, tarnished silver in the dull, grey light, listening to the whisper of the rain and the cry of the marsh birds, and gloried in my solitude.
>
> I thought, once, that I saw something out to sea, a light flashing violet, just once, but there was no ship or dirigible or airplane. I forgot about my measurements and stood, one hand on the adjustment knobs of my theodolite, staring at the horizon. I saw the flash four more times, each time a different colour: red, yellow, green, and a flash that looked smoky grey through the rain.

I tell you this here, fair reader, and not in my schol-
arly writings, because I can prove none of it, and
nothing but stone-cold fact has a place in academic
research. The rush of curiosity is merely the catalyst
for discovery, not discovery itself. Without proof, I can
consider these flashes nothing but a symptom of eye-
strain and overwork.

I saw nothing more for several minutes, and returned
to my measurements.

There was something about that description that was both-
ering me … reminding me of something. Colours. The colours!
They were the same as Kortnoz's glass tablets!

I had absolutely no idea what that meant, but at least I'd have
something intriguing to report to Kortnoz at dinner on Friday.

The thought of eating made my stomach snarl. Was it time to
head to the quad yet? Nearly. I was hoping the walk across campus would help me calm my jitters.

It sort of did, but whatever calm I'd gathered disappeared
instantly when I saw Russ waiting for me at the fountain in the
quad. He smiled when he noticed me walking towards him, and I
wondered if, hungry as I was, I'd be able to eat lunch at all.

'You're early,' he said.

'So are you. Aren't actors always supposed to be late?'

'If you are, after a while you stop getting gigs.'

We walked together toward the campus food court, just off the
quad. 'Burger, pizza, healthy stuff, or deep-fried stuff?' I said.

'Can we afford the pub? I'd like a beer with my burger.'

'Today's payday—let's go for it. It'll mean rice and beans next
week, but I can cope.'

'Me too. I take it that means you don't have tenure either.'

'Oh, haven't you heard of me? I'm Celeste Carlucci, who got a
two-year holding pattern for stealing her best friend's research.'
Might as well get it over with. I looked sideways at him, waiting

for his expression to change. It did, but to amusement. I hadn't been expecting that. 'How come you're not filled with contempt?'

'Because now I'm remembering the story, and as I recall, you stole it because you thought you were saving the Purple River.'

'Well, yeah, that *is* what I thought. Most people don't believe me, though.'

He laughed in a cold way that scared me a little. 'If you'd been stealing research out of malice, they wouldn't have given you the holding pattern, they'd have recruited you for the board of governors.'

'And here's me thinking it was my altruism and virtue that saved my job,' I said uneasily.

'Not at Purple Bay. I'm surprised your altruism didn't make them fire you right away. You must be doing some other research that they really want.'

'I never thought of that. I'm researching the Miraculous Mud Flats, and who cares about that except for me and Millicent Strudthorne?'

His face lit up. 'You know about Millicent?'

'Sure, I plough through her data every day, looking for patterns and anomalies. And my friend gave me this.' I took the *Reminiscence* out of my bag and showed it to him. 'How do you know about her?'

'My grandmother was one of her last students before she retired. Grandma said she'd never had such a demanding professor, but it was an experience that shaped the whole rest of her life.' He handed the book back.

'Was your grandmother a geographer?'

'No, a painter, but she was interested in all kinds of things. "*Everything* is art," she used to say.'

We found a table in the pub; eating early had its advantages. 'What would you like? I'll go up and order while you save the table,' I said.

'Just a cheeseburger and an ale, thanks.' He handed me some money for his order.

I was only a few steps from the counter when someone bumped into me from behind, hard enough to make me stagger.

'Hey!' I said. Suddenly I felt an arm around my shoulders and, at the same time, a cold, sharp edge against the right side of my neck. My left arm was seized in a painful grip.

'Let's go, out the door,' someone said quietly.

'What are you, nuts?' I said, but the edge pressed against my neck. The pain made me panicky, but I forced myself to stay still.

'Who are you?'

'Let's *go*, stupid.' He started to push me toward the door.

Maybe I could trip him, or grab his hand and yank it away from my neck before he had the chance to cut me badly. I tried to keep my mind clear, to wait for an opportunity. One thing was for sure: I would be no safer wherever he was taking me than I was right here.

I felt him turn around as if he'd been startled, and used that moment to yank his hand away from my neck. He turned back to me, but I heard a horrible crack, just as his head slammed into my cheekbone. I cried out, and he dropped to the floor.

I looked through the water streaming from my eyes to see Russ, breathing hard and trying to flex his hand.

'Security!' he yelled. 'You, behind the counter, call Security!' My attacker stirred, and Russ kicked him hard in the stomach. 'Stay there, you.'

Russ looked at my cheekbone. 'Sorry—you're going to have a terrific shiner. I didn't know his head was going to rebound just that way. And—he nicked you with the blade, but it's not much of a cut. Keep an eye on this guy for a second, would you?' He took some napkins from the dispenser on the counter and handed them to me before resuming guard duty. 'The cut is right there.' His fingertip brushed my neck and, even though I was starting to shake and feel nauseated, the touch still felt very nice. I pressed the napkins hard against my neck.

'How did you know he was trying to kidnap me?'

'No actor is going to admit that an audience is just walking out of her own accord.'

'I don't think I'm hungry anymore.'

'Me neither.'

'Here's your money.'

He took it with his left hand, then yelped and switched it to his right. His knuckles were already swollen and bruised.

'Are you all right?' I said.

'Well, it didn't hurt at the time, but holy hell, it's sure starting to now. As soon as Security gets here and takes our details, we'd better go to the infirmary and get checked out.'

'I've got to teach a class at one o'clock, I don't have time for that.'

'We'll just stop in for a minute and see if they think that cut needs stitching. You can't wait more than an hour or two before it stops being an issue and you end up with a big, bulging scar on your neck.'

'Okay, okay. Here's Security, anyway. Tons of 'em. Wow, I wonder what the kid behind the counter told them. They're outfitted like they're after Godzilla.'

The one thing the administrators at Purple Bay University did spend a fair bit of money on was campus security. After the Add-Drop Riots about twenty years ago, the few universities that could afford it built up their own in-house shock troops. In theory it was to control campus crime, and I suppose I was glad enough of that, but I also could imagine what things would be like for any students who decided to hold a rally or picket the administration building.

Russ and I watched them handcuff my attacker and take him away. We gave our details and our stories to the senior officer, and told her we were going over to the infirmary.

'You want one of my people to come with you?' she said, as if more attackers might be waiting to ambush us.

'No, thanks,' I said.

'You sure?' said Russ.

'Yeah. Thanks.'

Russ and I went over to the infirmary, where he got a cold pack for his hand, and I got a bandage for my neck and another cold pack for my cheekbone. Each of us also got a foil strip of mild painkillers.

'You know,' I said when we were on our way out, 'everyone who sees us together is going to assume you belted me.'

'Oh. You have a point. Maybe you should give me a black eye so that at least it looks like you gave as good as you got.'

I smiled, which made my face hurt.

'Hey,' I said after a moment. 'Thanks.'

'Hey,' he said gently. 'You're welcome.'

'I have ten minutes to get to my next class.'

'I'll come with you.'

'That's okay, thanks.'

'I'd feel better if I did, if it's all the same to you.'

'Okay, then, sure.'

'Plus … I like being with you.'

I blushed and couldn't think of anything to say. The rush of blood in my cheeks made my face hurt again, and I could feel my pulse in the bruise over my cheekbone.

As we walked, Russ said, 'Do you have any clues as to what all that was about?'

I thought hard. No, I couldn't tell him yet, not before I checked with Kortnoz. 'I think I do, but it has to do with some confidential research I'm involved with. I'm really sorry, but I can't say anything more. I know you got hurt because of me, but …'

'No, it's okay. I'm just relieved he wasn't a disgruntled former boyfriend. I'd really have to watch my back then.'

With a shock that made my stomach jump, I realised what he was saying. I couldn't help smiling then—grinning, actually— even though it hurt a lot. Russ glanced over to see my expression, then grinned too. This was turning out to be a very interesting day.

We got to the classroom door; I was a few minutes late after all, and all the students were there.

'What's this one?' whispered Russ.

'Geography of Art.'

'Mind if I sit in?'

'No, go ahead.' I took the cold pack off my face and walked in. Everyone gasped.

'You'll probably hear it from the grapevine, but I was attacked earlier today. The assailant is currently in the custody of Campus Security, who I'm sure will be conducting a thorough investigation. However, it's a good idea to walk with friends and avoid the more isolated parts of campus. Okay, today's topic is the beginnings of the Infonet and the rise of location-independent artistic collaboration.'

I delivered the lecture, waiting in vain the whole time for the painkillers to kick in. 'Okay, questions?' I said when I was done.

Nicki raised her hand, and Ricky looked uneasy. 'Dr Carlucci, I would disagree that artistic collaboration can be location-independent.'

'Okay, Nicki, tell me why.' I liked it when they disagreed with me, as long as they were polite about it.

'Well, you can't have a—an orchestra concert on the Infonet. The synchronisation would be off. And you can't have a play over the Infonet. How would the actors interact quickly enough? How would they gauge audience response?'

'That's a very good point,' said Russ, then stopped. 'Sorry, I'm just observing. Sorry.'

'No,' I said, 'go on.'

'Okay,' he said, and cleared his throat a bit bashfully. 'I think it's important to think about the nature of each project individually. If you make the distance and discontinuities *part* of what the art is exploring, that can make the work very exciting and relevant. Don't try to force an Infonet performance to be what it isn't. And don't stop it from being what it is. Each medium has unique characteristics that the artist can cherish and use to push in to new territory. Don't you think?'

'Have any of you not decided on a topic yet for your final project?' A couple of them raised their hands sheepishly. 'Well, you might want to consider a location-independent artistic collaboration, along with an evaluation of the advantages and constraints that the format imposed on the project with respect to some of the principles of geography we've been looking at.'

A few looked pensive, and Nicki was positively glowing. I saw her nudge Ricky and whisper; he looked even more glum than usual. Uh-oh, trouble in paradise, I thought. Maybe this relationship would self-destruct after all.

'We're pretty much out of time for today,' I said. 'See you all on Tuesday.'

As they were filing out, one of the students said, 'You're Dr Gartner, from Dramatic Arts, aren't you?'

'Yup.'

'Cool,' said the student, and nodded.

'Thanks,' said Russ, and nodded back.

'How did you get to be the cool prof?' I asked.

'I answered a want ad. What have you got on for the rest of the day?'

'I was going to do some more work on my Mud Flats research.'

'I think it would be better if you took it easy the rest of the day. I know that's what I'm going to be doing.'

'You don't have any classes to teach?'

'I mostly teach in the mornings, if I have a choice. Gets it over with.'

'What's your research area?'

'Location-independent, Infonet-facilitated artistic collaboration.'

'No way!' I blushed again, and my cheek pounded.

'No, it's good, you did a great job on that lecture.' I looked at him sceptically. 'Really, you did. Did you consult Smith and Turbano?'

I nodded. 'And Ruiz. And Shui *et al.* And ...' I stopped.

'Yes?' he said, clearly trying not to laugh.

'And Gartner,' I muttered. 'But not Russell, it was Graham.'

'That's my dad. Taught me most of what I know.'

'So the Gartners are an academic dynasty.'

'Like the Strudthornes. Yup.'

'I don't see anything in the *Reminiscence* about Millicent's love life. How did she get to found a dynasty?'

'She was married before she started the *Reminiscence,* but she never said a word about her husband. Even to her favourite students, like my grandmother.'

'Was his name Strudthorne?'

'She never said. Apparently the only reason she mentioned him at all was that her son, Talbot, was getting a hard time at school from some bullies who were implying that his mother had never bothered to marry. And even he only mentioned his father once, to a *Backwash* reporter. He ended up regretting it, because the *Backwash* spent the next two years trying to confirm whether Talbot's parentage was Millicent's secret scandal.'

I suddenly realised Russ had been staring at me. 'Well?' he said.

'Uh, well, what?'

'Are you going to go home and rest now?'

'Oh. Maybe. I want to stop by my office and check for mail before I go. And I have to phone my mom, so she hears about our little mishap from me first.'

'Then do you promise you'll go home?'

'Yes. I promise.'

'What if you get attacked again?'

'They're not going to try twice in one day.'

'Why not?'

I didn't have an answer.

'I'd feel better if I could at least walk you to the bus stop.' We both knew people without tenure couldn't afford cars or taxi rides.

'Okay, but like I said, I want to stop by my office.'

'Let's go, then.'

Russ and I went to my mailbox, which I was thrilled to find empty. So was the office, mercifully. I phoned my mom. She spent five minutes trying to persuade me to stay with her and Dad that night, and another two or three asking me if I was *sure* I was all right. By the time I was done, I'd lost my chance to escape: Pace came through the door just as I hung up the phone.

'Oh, hi. Is this the lunch date? Hell of a lunch break, what is it, nearly three?'

Then she noticed my face, and the bandage on my neck. That black eye must have looked dramatic by now. It certainly *felt* dramatic.

'What … the … hell,' she said.

'I got attacked. These are battle wounds. Russ helped me fight them off. Security has the guy in custody.'

'Russ?'

'Oh. Russ Gartner, Pace Garoux.'

Russ looked impressed. 'Pace Garoux, as in Hypatia?'

'Don't call me that,' she snapped. 'Honestly, Celeste, don't you brief people at all before they meet me?'

'I didn't think you'd be here.'

'Where did you get attacked?'

'The pub on campus.'

'What a stupid place to attack someone. And why you? Oh. Never mind.' She turned to Russ. 'So, how do I happen to be so famous?'

'Weren't you the one who discovered the fault up in the Purple Mountains that opened up into an active lava pit?'

'Yes, that was me. What department are you in?'

I cleared my throat. 'Well, I'm just going to check my email, and then Russ is going to walk me to the bus stop.'

'I'm sorry, Russ, what were you saying?' said Pace, with a sideways glance at me.

'Dramatic Arts.'

I buried my face in my hands, but it hurt too much and I had to emerge. Pace was staring at me with a funny look on her face.

'Dramatic Arts,' she repeated.

'Yup,' said Russ cheerfully.

'But you know about faults and lava pits.'

'I read a lot. An actor should have a good range of general knowledge.'

'You don't do … pantomime, do you?' Pace said.

Russ laughed, startled. 'Well, not for a living, no. There are some aspects of pantomime that are useful for young actors to practice, of course, such as fine motor control and harmonising movement and expression to communicate emotion, but—'

'All right. Celeste, if he ever gets stuck inside an invisible box or pulls an invisible rope or walks into an invisible wind in my presence, he can just keep walking.'

'All winds are invisible,' said Russ. Uh-oh.

'Don't talk to a geographer about weather,' she snapped.

I decided to skip checking my emails. 'My headache is getting a little worse, Russ. Maybe we should go now.'

'Sure,' he said.

Once we were out of the building, I said, 'Sorry. Pace has got a temper. But she's been a good friend, and she's mostly forgiven me for stealing her research.'

Russ swapped sides as we walked so he could hold my hand. After all we'd been through, I saw no reason not to encourage this, and moved in to walk slightly closer. It occurred to me that meant that he had hit the attacker with his left hand—he was left-handed. Why was that suddenly interesting to me? Why was *everything* about him so interesting?

As we waited at the bus stop, he said, 'I don't want to walk away just yet. Please, could I ride with you on the bus? It's not to protect you or anything patronising like that. At least, only a little. Mostly the liking being with you thing.'

I was starting to get used to that idea, and I was starting to enjoy it, even though I knew Pace was going to give me all kinds of static tomorrow. I took a long, appreciative look at Russ's face, which was looking more handsome to me by the minute, and his shoulders, and … I was going to start drooling in a minute if I didn't get a hold of myself.

'I'll take that look as a yes,' said Russ. He leaned in to kiss me, but I flinched as his lips touched mine.

'Sorry,' I mumbled. 'Face hurts.'

'Serves me right for knocking the guy's skull into you. It's okay—I'll wait.'

If I'd blushed before, that was nothing to how I felt when he said *that*, his voice low and intimate. I hoped my knees wouldn't give way.

The bus arrived, and we sat down, leaning into one another.

'This is my stop,' I said as the bus approached my apartment building.

'I actually live back the other way, closer to Beggar's Pit.'

'Yikes.'

'Oh, it's not so bad. Most of the time. In fact, I'll probably walk back, it's such a nice day.'

We got off, and he walked me to the door of my building.

'You know what?' he said.

'What?'

'We never did eat lunch. In an hour or two I'm going to be starving. Why don't I use that burger-and-beer money and get us a pizza and bring it by at, say, five? Meanwhile, you can make a cup of tea, lie down, and read a good book. I know that will help you feel better.'

That sounded like the best idea I'd ever heard. 'Pepperoni and pineapple, please,' I said, and took my wallet out to give him my share.

'No, I get special rates at a pizza place back near campus, because the guy who runs it is my freshman-year roommate's brother's best friend.'

'Wow, that's convoluted.'

'Most of life is.'

Chapter 6
Celeste Discovers Something About the Ickies

I woke up at five to the sound of someone yelling my name. Out of habit, I brushed my hair back from my face, and swore as the pain reminded me that I had a savage black eye.

'Celeste! Let me in!'

'Shut up!' hollered someone from one of the other apartments.

'But the pizza will get cold!'

'I'll make your pizza cold! Shut up already!'

I hurried to the window and opened it to see Russ below, holding a pizza box. He saw me leaning out.

'It is my lady, O, it is my love! O, that she knew she were!'

'Russ, for God's sake!'

'She speaks: O, speak again, bright angel! for thou art as glorious to this night, being o'er my head, as is a winged messenger of heaven …'

'Just a minute, just a minute!'

I closed the window, pushed the buzzer to let him into the building, and opened my door. He bounded up the stairs and into the apartment.

'How come you're so chipper?' I said. 'Shouldn't you be suffering post-traumatic stress or something?'

'It'll probably catch up with me later. No point in going looking for it. Are *you* all right? You slept right through the doorbell. Hungry?'

'Surprisingly, yes.' Russ set the pizza on the table. 'I don't have much to offer to drink, I'm afraid,' I said.

'Ah-hah!' he said, and took off his backpack. 'Problem solved.' He brought out a bottle of wine.

'Russ—'

'Robbed a bank,' he said, and winked.

'Oh. That's okay, then. I don't have actual wine glasses, but I suppose it's not all that crucial.'

'Not to me. I once went on a date with someone who spent way too much time criticising the shape of the wine glasses. Really, I don't know what she was expecting at Mooey's Burger Barn.'

I got a couple of glasses. Russ poured the wine and we started devouring the pizza. I was glad he'd gotten a jumbo-sized one.

'Hey,' he said with his mouth full. 'What about *your* post-traumatic stress?'

'I've been friends with Pace for fifteen years. I never get to the point of *post*-trauma.'

'She's a bit of a legend around campus: the parachuting incident, the flood in the governors' parking lot, that time when she flew the nomadic tribe in from the North Kras steppes and almost started a war—'

'Well, who knew it was illegal to export North Kras ponies? And the tribespeople wouldn't come without them. It was a bit of a job getting them onto the plane, too, I have to say. And the ponies were even worse.'

'So you've been there for these exploits. How come the only thing I've ever heard about you, then, was during your hearing? And even that just got minimal coverage, mostly in the campus newspaper.'

'Oh, I'm just the sidekick. That's one of the things that shocked Pace so badly when I stole her research. It was pretty much the first time I'd done anything independently. So, tell me about acting.'

He handled the change of subject smoothly. 'I've been an actor all my life, starting in preschool. My family, most of whom are artists of one kind or another, were thrilled. "Thank God he didn't end up in computers," I heard my mom saying the other day to my aunt. "Or accounting," my aunt said. I think they actually shuddered.'

'I thought your dad was a geographer. That's not artistic.'

'It is, the way my dad does it. Actually, he's more artist than geographer. Doesn't cope well with administrators. Didn't you wonder why he doesn't teach here? He and my mom just live a half hour outside of Purple Bay.'

'Okay, I'll bite. Why not?'

'He decided to strike out on his own when he realised that the loyalty clause in the tenure contract wasn't just about letting them know when you wanted to go on sabbatical. They wanted to direct his research into, well, profitable areas.'

'How come you let yourself in for the same problems, then?'

'I'm trying to bring down the system from the inside.'

'Are you serious?'

'Absolutely.'

'And your dad thinks this is a good idea?'

'Are you kidding? He's never been prouder of me. He says he only wishes he'd had the guts at the time.'

'So what's he do, if he's not teaching?'

'Consulting. Businesses are always keen to find ways to do location-independent collaboration. He's doing quite well. Which makes my mom happy, because she doesn't have to worry so much about selling pieces and getting shown.'

'A painter, like your grandmother?'

'Sculptor. It makes the family home a bit crowded, but her stuff is really good. At least, I think so.'

'What plays have you acted in?'

'Oh, just about everything. Comedies, satires, absurdist plays, classics, children's theatre—that was an experience. I had to dress up as a head of lettuce. Good thing actors learn early to have no shame.'

'What kid on earth is interested in a head of lettuce?'

'I was the villain.'

'Evil lettuce.'

'Yup.'

For some reason I found that unbelievably funny. I laughed, then I tried to take a breath and couldn't. A horrible, panicky feeling swept over me. Suddenly I was crying, sobbing. I looked for somewhere to put my pizza down so I could go get a tissue or something, but all I could think was that I'd gnawed on it already and I didn't want to put it back in the pizza box because that would be rude. And that made me cry harder.

I heard Russ get up and go into the kitchen. He came back with a plate, and I put the pizza down. Then he handed me one of the napkins he'd brought along with the pizza. He pulled his chair over next to mine and sat down, putting his arm around me.

'That's a relief,' he said.

I blew my nose and said, 'What?'

'I wasn't quite sure how you coped with something like being attacked. Or realising the truth about lettuce. I'm not sure which is more traumatic, to be honest.'

'The lettuce. Definitely the lettuce. Trips to the supermarket will never be the same.'

'Here. Have some wine.'

'Wow, that's a very nice wine.' I took another healthy sip.

'You're not on the painkillers at the moment, are you? Because maybe I shouldn't be giving you wine in that case.'

'Nope. I fell asleep before I could take another dose. How's your hand doing, speaking of pain? It *looks* horrible.' The knuckles were swollen, and a big purple blotch covered most of the back of his hand.

'Thanks. No, it's okay, as long as I remember not to use it much. Using the computer tomorrow is not going to be fun.'

The rest of the evening passed without another breakdown on my part. We talked, mostly about people we both knew at the university, but also about our research, our students, our parents, President Kim-Hatton ('I once heard a media conference where she actually said that universities were choking the life out of industry by stealing the generation's best minds for useless academic research'), and ice-cream flavours. I contended that toffee banana macadamia was the best; he preferred chocolate marshmallow. At least we'd never fight over who got the last of the ice cream, I caught myself thinking, and blushed again. I wondered if I'd always blushed this often, or if I just noticed it now because it made my cheek hurt.

To my intense embarrassment, I yawned.

Russ said, 'That reminds me, it's getting late and I have an eight o'clock class tomorrow. Plus that script to revise.'

'Do you think you can actually pull that off?'

'Can you teach Danny Snotnose Wexler?'

'Sure I can. I suppose it would be unwise to tell you he reminds me a little of myself.'

'Really?' Russ sounded shocked.

'Yeah, except I have better social skills.'

'I'll say. Listen, will you be okay?'

'You've been terrific, Russ. I'll be fine. Even though we finished the pizza *and* the wine.' I looked forlornly at the box and bottle, both empty.

'Or maybe *because* we finished them. Can I come by your office and say hi tomorrow?'

'Sure, I'd like that. I teach Intro at nine—' Russ made a sympathetic noise—'but I'm back in my office from about ten-fifteen until I teach again at one.'

'See you then.' He kissed me very gently on the forehead—not at all the way my mom did—and left.

* * *

I lay awake for quite a while, grinning stupidly. I didn't even care that it sort of hurt.

The next morning the black eye was truly appalling, and the

skin around the cut was an angry red. It was going to be an ordeal trying to teach two hundred easily distracted kids when I looked like I'd just lost the lightweight title.

Sure enough, they took more than a minute to settle down when I walked into the classroom. When there was finally a moment of relative quiet, I explained about being attacked and hoped that would be the end of it.

The lecture was uneventful, aside from being my usual scintillating exposition of the fundamentals of geography. I spent the last ten minutes questioning randomly selected victims about the reserve readings; many of them had actually done them since Monday, which both stunned and gratified me.

After class they thronged around me.

'Dr Carlucci, did you know the guy who attacked you?'

'Dr Carlucci, how did you get that cut? Did he have a knife?'

'Dr Carlucci, have you ever studied martial arts?'

To all the questions I steadily replied, 'Sorry, it was upsetting. I'd really rather not talk about it' while pushing my way towards the door.

Just outside the doorway waited Danny.

'I've gone through the syllabus and I'm pretty much caught up.'

'Wow, Danny—that was in less than a week. You're pretty sure you understand the concepts?'

He nodded.

There was something funny about how he was looking at me. Maybe he was upset by the injuries. 'It's okay, Danny, the doctor at the infirmary said these were minor injuries. I'll be fine.'

'It's just …' He swallowed. 'No, that's good. That it's not serious. That's good.'

'Thanks.' I was touched.

'I just wanted … to tell you that I can start making some real progress now. On the other project.'

'Great. Can you give me weekly summaries of your findings? Say, every Friday starting next week?'

'No problem. Well, gotta go. See you.'

I watched him scurry away. He seemed strangely twitchy today, not the swaggering boy I'd first noticed in the ice-cream line. Something was worrying him.

* * *

Russ was waiting outside the Geography mailroom.

'Hello,' I said.

He said nothing, just embraced me gently and gave me another one of those forehead kisses that were not in the slightest like my mother's.

After a long, delicious moment he stepped away. 'I can't hang around, alas! But I was hoping you'd be free sometime this weekend for a walk or a visit to the museum or something.'

'Saturday at ten, museum steps,' I said.

'See you then!' And he walked away with a bouncy step that made me smile.

'Aren't you embarrassed?' said Pace, who'd been in the mailroom the whole time.

'Not in the slightest.'

'I would be.'

'This from the woman who brought the entire Krasnia Day parade to a halt with her "Spirit of Krasnia" costume.'

'I felt a statement needed to be made, that was all. Was it my fault they had no sense of irony?'

'How long were you in jail that time?'

'Three days. The food wasn't bad.'

My mailbox was blessedly empty except for another note from Jasper, which I threw out without glancing at it. Pace and I walked back to the office, and she unlocked the door.

We both halted in the doorway. The office had been trashed. Papers were everywhere. The computers were missing. And Pace's bugs were squashed on the floor.

'Where's your stuff backed up?' Pace asked in a harsh voice.

'On the server.'

'Well, there's that at least.'

I stepped carefully into the room. Some of the papers were pages torn from Millicent's thesis. It was destroyed. I had no idea whether there was another copy anywhere, or whether it had ever been scanned.

'We'd better get Security over here,' said Pace. 'Don't touch any-thing.'

We backed out and closed the door, and Pace took out her phone and dialled Security.

A few minutes later, the same team that had taken my report in the pub showed up at our office. The officer in charge did a double take when she saw it was me again.

Her team went to work taking photographs and trying to get fingerprints.

'You two had better find somewhere else to work for now. We're going to be a while. We like to be thorough,' said the officer in charge in a voice I found chilling.

'I've got to go to the library and try to explain about Millicent's thesis,' I said as Pace and I walked along the hallway. 'And then I've got my one o'clock to teach. What time should I show up at Dr Kortnoz's for dinner?'

'What?' said Pace.

'Dinner. Tonight. You and Dr Kortnoz invited me. Remem-ber?'

'Oh. Yeah. Seven.'

I was stunned to see two shiny tracks from Pace's eyes to her jawbone.

'You okay?' I said gently.

'My bugs.' And she turned away. 'That was sick. Whoever did this is sick.'

I knew better than to say anything comforting. Instead, I just said, 'I'll see you tonight, then.'

'Yeah.'

My stomach jumped unpleasantly at the thought of facing the head librarian to tell her that what might be the only copy of Millicent's thesis was now destroyed.

I took the elevator to the top floor of the library building and knocked tentatively on the head librarian's door. 'Dr Maher?'

She looked up from her computer. I was shocked to see a patch of swollen, greyish dots on her face and arms. I remembered one of my students talking about the predatory mould: 'I saw what it did to the head librarian.' If this was how the damage looked a week later, I didn't want to think about what she'd gone through.

She smiled, then winced, as I did. 'Hello, Dr Carlucci. Please excuse my appearance. But it looks like you've had a bit of a tough week yourself. We can suffer together. I'm sure you heard about the predatory mould.'

'And I got attacked in the pub yesterday. And today my office was broken into. That's why I'm here. I'd borrowed a thesis. Millicent Strudthorne's thesis. And ...' I started to feel the same way Pace had at the thought of her poor squashed bugs.

'And it's damaged,' she finished for me.

I nodded and tried not to cry. 'Torn to bits. Security has cordoned off the office, so I can't even try to see how much is missing or irreparable.'

'They have, have they? That's interesting. This gives them a very good excuse to go over the office pretty thoroughly, doesn't it?'

'Are you saying they engineered the break-in? Dr Maher, you *are* joking, aren't you?'

'It's not the first time something like this has happened, is all I'm saying. Don't despair about the thesis yet. There may be a scan in the National Library, or a duplicate in the Strudthorne papers, down on the third floor. You may need to pay for the scanning and reprinting, I'm afraid, as the destroyed copy was signed out to you. I know it's unfair, but there's not a lot we can do about the insurance rules.'

I gulped. Well, it would just mean beans and rice for a while longer, that was all. And if I ever did find out who did it … I was shocked at the visions of violence that writhed before me.

'I appreciate your coming right to me,' said Dr Maher. 'I'll put the word out for another copy. And if we notice anyone taking a sudden interest in Millicent Strudthorne and her work, we'll keep an eye on them.'

'Wouldn't that violate, I don't know, librarian-patron confidentiality?'

'Only if we told you—or Security, or the governors—who it was. But if we think someone's a risk to the integrity of the collection, well, who's going to blame us for watching a bit more intently?'

'Thanks, Dr Maher. You're terrific.'

'Oh, I'll call in a favour one day, don't you worry. I keep track!'

'I'm okay with that—just let me know what I can do for you.'

'Thanks. Say, why did you come to me, and not the thesis-collection desk?'

'It's … too weird. Everything is too weird. I just had a feeling you'd want to know.' I met her gaze. 'There are other things going on, too, aren't there? Not coincidences. They're linked.'

'Dr Carlucci, one thing librarians all know is that *everything* is linked. Everything. It's the first lesson of the first class in every library-science degree.'

'I sort of meant, in a more immediate and unnerving way.'

'Yes, well, in this case that's also true.'

'I don't suppose you can clue me in on any of it.'

'Librarian-patron confidentiality.'

'I see. I have to go teach now. Thanks for all your help and understanding. Take good care of those mould wounds, okay?'

'I will. And you—don't you go getting involved with just any old book. Make sure it's worth the trouble.' And she looked hard at me.

She knows, I thought. Kortnoz has told her about the Littoral Codex and the glass tablets. I thought Pace said it was top secret.

I had a pretty hard time concentrating during Advanced Riverine Geography. The students were all very concerned about my damaged head, which was touching. The Ickies had brought me a big plastic tub full of homemade cookies, and that nearly drove me to tears. Ricky handed them to me, and said proudly, 'I made them myself. It's the first time I've ever made cookies. I asked my grandma to email me the recipe. I hope you like chocolate chip.'

'They're my favourite,' I said with real feeling. 'Thank you so much! And thank your grandma for me.'

'Me, I'm hopeless in the kitchen,' said Nicki. 'But Ricky is a natural. He only started cooking this year, and everything he touches turns into fantastic food!'

I looked at Nicki closely. Sure enough, her face was just a bit fleshier than it'd been at the beginning of the semester. I was starting to understand why she stuck with Ricky. Just about everyone has some kind of special talent or other, something that makes them exactly the person you need at exactly the right time.

That made me think of Russ, which was always nice, but distracting. With a mighty mental effort I started the lecture, and managed, just, to speak coherently for most of the allotted time. A few minutes from the end it all became too much and I sat down.

'Sorry, guys. It's been a rough couple of days. Tell you what: Nicki, what have you and Ricky found out about the July-to-August period of your data?'

They looked at each other nervously.

'Well, we had a preliminary look,' said Nicki.

'But it's kind of weird, so we think the data might be, like, screwy or something,' said Ricky in his usual precise way.

'Would you be able to bring the photos in on Monday? I think we could spare a few minutes out of the class time to look at them.'

'Sure, I guess,' said Nicki.

'Sure, yeah,' echoed Ricky.

The other students all looked intrigued and eager. Teaching

this group made up for all the dolts and dullards in Intro.

'Let's call it a day, then,' I said. 'And thanks again for the cookies.' I offered to share them with the class, but, God bless them, they all refused to take even one.

I went straight home from class. I figured maybe I could get a couple of hours' sleep, which I desperately needed, before going over to Kortnoz's. I carefully set the alarm for five-thirty and changed into pyjamas, then I retrieved the tub of cookies out of the depths of my pack and took out a cookie. I bit into it.

It was like a big chocolate monster was giving me huge, enthusiastic hugs. It was like the sudden realisation that someone had found out what birthday present you wanted the most *ever* and sent it to you as a surprise.

'Oh, wow,' I murmured, my mouth still full of cookie. 'Oh, wow, oh, wow.' I wasn't sharing these with anyone. I swallowed the first cookie and instantly began on another. At this rate, I reflected, it wouldn't be long before sharing them would no longer be an issue.

I slowed a bit after the fourth cookie. The fifth one I ate at an almost civilised speed, then realised I was starting to feel just a bit sick to my stomach and should probably put the cookies away. Feeling wistful, yet anticipating the joys to come when I had cookies for breakfast the next morning, I put the lid back on the tub and climbed into bed to take a nap. I was starting to like this sleep-in-the-afternoon thing.

Chapter 7
Things Start to Get More Complicated

I awoke at the sound of the alarm, and with a craving for cookies that puzzled me until I remembered the marvellous plastic tub and the treasures within. I managed to leave them alone while I got ready to catch the bus to Kortnoz's place. I didn't want to spoil a free dinner.

It was dark by the time I arrived. I rang the bell and waited. And waited. Then I knocked and waited some more. Then knocked harder. Sometimes Kortnoz could be vague, and Pace was rattled after the office break-in. Maybe they'd just forgotten, and headed out to get some dinner on their own. I took a piece of paper out of my notebook, wrote a sorry-I-missed-you note, and pushed it through the mail slot. Then I went to get the bus back to my neighbourhood.

I got home to find a note in Pace's handwriting sticking out of my mailbox.

'Damn, you've already left. We're on the run. We're leaving something for you in a place of great significance to you and me. Please go get it and find somewhere to hide. But don't rush—people will stare. By the way, was that cookies I smelled from your open window? One, keep your window locked, what are you, nuts? And two, they smelled fantastic. Save some for me, will you?'

I was pretty sure the something was the glass tablets, and the 'place of great significance' was that lava pit up in the mountains. I rubbed my wrists, remembering how the ropes had hurt and the heat had stung.

I dangled over the lava pit. 'Jeez, Pace, what did I ever do to you?'

But I knew. There was a paper in the *Journal of Applied Fluvial Geomorphology* with my name on it. And the research was hers.

'You were never going to publish!' I gasped. 'You kept wanting to run the models "one more time"!'

'It's too early! We know the sediment is alive, but we don't know its intentions.'

'INTENTIONS!' I screamed. 'It's SEDIMENT! It hasn't got any intentions except to float down the river and silt up the delta. The sediment isn't the problem!'

Pace knew what I meant. Dr Kortnoz had disappeared just after Pace had defended her dissertation. Not long after, the sediment load in the Purple River had increased fivefold. I had a theory that Kortnoz was at the headwaters, stirring up trouble as well as sediment.

'Pace, I can publish a retraction! I—I'll use my fellowship money to fund the field research you and Jasper need to finalise your data. And I'll run the sims for you with my server time. I swear it.'

Pace was tempted. She picked up a rope with a vicious-looking hook on the end, whirled the hook around her head, and flung it out, jerking back on it to snag the rope I hung from. She pulled me roughly over to the side of the pit; I raised my knees just in time to avoid slamming my face into the rock. She stepped backwards, dragging me up, and I wriggled my legs and body onto the ledge. Pace cut the cords on my wrists, and I stood.

I shook my head to clear the memory. Pace had a weird sense of what was appropriate. But I was damned if I was going to risk going up there at night. Even with a headlamp, the approach was treacherous. If it was a safe hiding place, it would still be safe between now and morning. Besides, anyone driving up that way in the dead of night was bound to attract attention. During the day I'd be just another hiker or photographer or loony university researcher. God knew there was no shortage.

I'd have to phone Drusy and cancel our dinner plans. I looked up the number for the retirement home.

'Purple Bay Retirement Home, how many I help you?' said the bored work-study kid on evening shift at the front desk.

'May I speak with Dr Kelso, please?' I said. I heard a click when Drusy picked up.

'Hi, Drusy. Sorry to bother you, but I'm afraid I need to cancel our dinner plans for tomorrow.'

'Oh, Celeste, thank God you phoned! You're not going, you know, *out* tonight, are you?'

Had Pace told *everyone* about the Littoral Codex research?

'No, I didn't want to risk a fall in the dark. You know how clumsy I am.'

'You need to come and see me. Let's let our dinner plans stay the way they were.'

'Are you sure we don't need to make them any earlier? Like, lunch plans? Breakfast plans?'

'Oh, no, dinner's fine. A few hours either way—well, time's all the same to us old folks, you know that. You just do what you were going to do tomorrow. In fact, why don't you spend the whole day out? Pack a few things and just leave in the morning. I'll see you as we planned—don't be late, or I'll start to worry you stayed home and got distracted and forgot about this old lady.' Her voice sounded high and tense. Suddenly I figured out why.

The Littoral League. Drusy was trying to tell me they'd found out where I lived and were planning to ambush me at my apartment.

Suddenly I really, really didn't want to spend the night here. I called my mom.

'Hey, Mom, can I crash with you and Dad for a night or two? There's … a lot of noise in the neighbourhood these days, parties and stuff, and, what with all the stress recently, well … I hope it isn't too much trouble.'

'No, not at all. Would you like me to come and pick you up?'

I wanted my mom. And it would save me nearly two hours waiting for the bus and taking it across town.

'Yes, please, Mom.' My voice shook.

'Hang on, sweetie, I'll be there soon.'

Drusy thought I was safe here until tomorrow, but I couldn't be sure. What would they think was worse, drawing attention by making lots of noise on a Friday night, or trying to get me in broad daylight?

I packed a few days' clothes and the plastic tub of cookies, and made sure *Reminiscence* was in my backpack. Then I sat to one side of the window to wait for Mom. I saw headlights pass the building a few times. Then one slowed down before picking up speed again. I turned the lights off.

It was an eternity before I heard the sound of my mom's car. I hadn't known I could pick it out of a million other cars. I was out into the hallway in a second. I had a panicky moment fumbling with the keys before I managed to lock the door, then I ran down the stairs and out to Mom's car.

'Hi, Mom. Thanks for picking me up,' I said as casually as I could.

'No problem, sweetie.'

We drove through the darkness. Mom sniffed. 'Do I smell cookies?'

'Yeah.' I steeled myself. 'You want one?'

'Oh, I shouldn't. But yes, please.'

It was a wrench, but I gave Mom one of Ricky's cookies.

'Oh, my,' she said with her mouth full. 'Your father must never have one of these. Ever.'

I heard the yearning in her voice, and, because this was my

mom, gave her another cookie. I gazed mournfully at the diminishing pile in the plastic tub.

'Thanks, sweetie. These are fabulous. I suppose it would be overly optimistic to ask if you made them.'

'It would. One of my students wanted to cheer me up for getting attacked.'

'Tell them they should be a chef, not a geographer.'

'I wonder if there's such a thing as a geographer-chef.'

'Well, sweetie, I'm afraid you'll never know first-hand. Would it kill you to learn how to make scrambled eggs? I worry that you're going to starve.'

'As long as there's toast and marmalade, I'll cope okay. Besides, I hate scrambled eggs.'

'You do? But I made them every morning for you before school.'

'I … know.'

Mom glanced over, and I shrugged. To salve her feelings, I offered her another cookie. Then I had to have another. To keep her company. The tub was nearly empty. I told myself I could always ask Ricky to make another batch.

Mom parked on the street, so Dad could leave with his boat at dawn for his Saturday morning fishing. His job was stressful—he worked as a planner in the Purple Bay city government. ('Everything is planning,' he was fond of saying.) He craved the quiet of the more isolated shores of Purple Bay at sunrise. While the fishing was best just at the edge of the Mud Flats, he preferred the deeper waters and gentle, sandy beaches to the east, the opposite way from the cliffs where Kortnoz had found the glass tablets.

Home was as it had always been. I relaxed just breathing in the scent I remembered: a combination of the cleanser my parents used in the bathroom, the laundry soap, the flowers in the window boxes, the spicy cooking my dad preferred (his family was ethnically North Kras), and, just faintly, the smell of pine resin that wafted in from the forests in the nearby foothills.

'Thanks again for letting me stay,' I said. 'Hey, is Dad home?'

'Yes,' called my dad from the living room. 'Hello, Mousie! Come on in and give me a hug.'

'I'm not as mousey as I used to be.'

'So I hear. I hear you're fighting off attackers single-handed.'

'No, I had help.'

'Oh?'

'A very nice guy. Named Russ. I'm going to the museum with him tomorrow.'

'Woo-hoo, now that's what I call a steamy date! What goes on behind the dinosaur exhibit, huh? Huh?'

'Pete, knock it off,' said Mom. 'You'll make her self-conscious.'

'It's okay, Mom. I've been walking around for a couple of days with a really attention-getting black eye. I'm sort of getting over being self-conscious.'

Mom brought out a plate of cheese and crackers and carrot sticks, and I sat down to watch television. Dad was watching a documentary on the customs of North Kras.

After a few minutes I said, 'Why are you watching this, Dad? Your family still does most of this stuff. It can't be news to you.'

'Just a bit of cultural affirmation, I guess. Also, I want to keep my eye on the media. If I detect a systematic campaign of racial and cultural slurs, hoo boy, won't I be on the warpath!'

'Have you noticed any slurs yet?'

'No, but I can't afford to get complacent.'

'Dad, you were born here!'

'Speaking of getting attacked, did I tell you I used to get beaten up in school for being a Northie?'

I was appalled. 'You're joking.'

'Nope. And I don't trust the Praxicopolis media dynasty as far as I can throw the nearest repeater. If it will boost ratings or circulation, and hike up the cost of advertising, they'll run it. Including racial slurs. There was a big market for them back forty years ago, when the Krasnian economy was in the pits.'

Chalk up one more against the Praxicopolises. I was starting to feel a bit emotional about bringing them down.

'Let me have a look at the damage,' said Mom, and leaned in close. 'Wow. They weren't exaggerating.'

'Who weren't?'

'A couple of your students. I walked past them today on my way to the quad and heard them talking. "Dr Carlucci sure got busted up," one of them said. And the other one said, "Sure did." Not exactly witty and urbane chitchat, but I was interested because you're my daughter.'

'Well, geographers aren't always noted for their party personalities.'

'Then one of them said something a bit strange. "I hear she's mixed up in some kind of bizarre illegal research project, and they were trying to shut her up." I'm assuming those are just rumours?' Mom looked at me keenly.

'For the most part, yes,' I said. 'Pace and Dr Kortnoz are doing some research on some old documents. You know how Pace is, her nose into everything. I was helping them recover some of the originals. I guess the whole project was trickier than Pace thought. I think she's stepping on the toes of some established researchers in the field. You know how they get. "You're a *geographer*. Go and research *geography*".'

'But everything is geography, I know, I know,' said Mom wearily. 'You *all* say that. I can't help thinking it's just a way to give yourselves permission to go stomping all over other people and their research. Maybe it would be better if everyone were a bit more respectful, hm?'

'Sure, Mom,' I said. 'Is the spare room okay for me to use?'

'What, you mean your room?'

'It's not mine anymore. I moved out, remember?'

'You'll always have a place here. And a good thing, too, isn't it?'

'Yes. Thanks. I mean it.' And I gave her a hug, then gave my dad one too. 'I'm really bushed. It's been kind of a hectic few days. Do you mind if I just go up to bed now?'

'Not at all. Good night, sweetie.'

'Night, Mousie.'

'Good night. I'm leaving in the morning to go to the museum, and then I have a dinner date with a friend at the University Park Retirement Home, so I'll be back tomorrow night.'

'See you then, sweetie.'

That was the last good night's sleep I was going to get for a while.

Chapter 8
Dinosaurs Play a Small Part

I'd set my watch and my phone to wake me at eight. I was out of the house and walking toward the bus stop by eight-thirty. The eight-forty-five bus into the centre of Purple Bay would give me plenty of time to get there by ten.

The museum was a block or so from City Hall. It was one of the most beautiful buildings in Purple Bay—in fact, it had always been my favourite. It was made of sandstone, and the edifice was carved into breaking waves and mountain ranges and rivers and forests. There were fish instead of gargoyles (although the gnaw-fish could pass for either). Brightly coloured banners hanging out front advertised the current travelling exhibits and gave the place a festive feeling at odds with the cool, staid, green-marble darkness within.

I was early. Ordinarily I'd probably just sit and relax in the sunshine and watch people go by. Today I was too edgy for that. The only thing I could think of to do while I sat on the steps waiting for Russ was to take the *Reminiscence* out of my pack and start reading.

Can't people think of anything besides the Littoral Codex? It's been the sole topic of conversation for weeks. It's just an old book of philosophy, but people are convinced it holds the key to all enlightenment or some such foolishness. There are three separate projects right now trying to decode the wretched thing—that's research money that could be better spent on figuring out real issues with real consequences, such as where the silt of Krasnia is off to. If it's being taken away and used for some reason, I want to know by whom and for what. And how. That's a tremendous load of mud to make off with.

I guessed some things never changed. I was near the end of the *Reminiscence*—if Millicent ever found out the answer, she'd have to tell me about it sometime in the next twenty pages. I wondered if there was a Volume II.

I checked my watch—four past ten—and glanced up and down the footpath. I saw Russ, and felt an adolescent rush of giggly joy. I'd have to get *that* under control.

'Sorry I'm late,' he said as he reached me.

'Within acceptable parameters.' We went into the building, the security guard checked my backpack for any instruments of mayhem or vandalism, and we turned into the first gallery: dinosaurs. I remembered what my father had said, and blushed.

'What's up?' said Russ. 'You're blushing.'

Crap. 'Nothing. Maybe I got a bit of sun outside.'

We wandered from skeleton to skeleton, imagining Krasnia as it had been when they'd been living beasts crashing through the Krasnian swamps. The Purple River had been a quick and lively mountain stream, the delta nothing but a rocky gap in the cliffs where the river tumbled over stone and sand to get to the ocean. I wondered if the dinosaurs had thought that their daily problems were all-consuming and eternal. And here we were, so many millions of years later, with our own all-consuming and eternal problems. And we didn't even know what theirs had been. That's how all-consuming and eternal any of us, or our problems, were.

'Hey, look here,' said Russ. 'Isn't this a photo of your friend Millicent?'

The placard read, 'Noted geographer Millicent Strudthorne is pictured here next to the tetraceratops skull fragments she discovered in the Miraculous Mud Flats during field work for her doctoral dissertation.' 'Dr Strudthorne, well-respected in the academic community for her analysis of the formation of the Mud Flats and their effect on the patterns of human settlement in the region, discovered the fragments as she was sampling silt depths at the mean high-tide level. She famously remarked to a *Backwash* reporter at the time of this photo, "For God's sake, can't we get this over with? The sooner I can hand this rubbish over to the Palaeontology department, the sooner I can get back to work."'

The photo showed a severe woman who may have been in middle age—it was hard to tell from these older photos—wearing the same sort of clothes for field work that I preferred: long, loose shorts with lots of pockets, a long-sleeved shirt, again with lots of pockets, and a broad-brimmed hat. She was wearing enormous gumboots, which were coated in mud nearly to the top, and standing next to a pile of what looked a lot like the sticks and weed that got left on the Mud Flats by the tide every day. I would have to take the museum's word that that was a tetraceratops skull.

'That's her, all right,' I said. 'Boy, she was cranky *all* the time.'

'Maybe "focused" is a better word than "cranky".'

'You're very diplomatic.'

He gave me the knee-buckling smile. 'Thanks—I've worked hard at it. It smooths the career a bit. You have no idea how sensitive actors can be. And the techies! Rule one of successful theatre: respect the techies.'

'Geographers can get pretty snippy, too, actually. Maybe it's anyone who cares about what they're doing. Human nature.'

'I'd like to think we can rise above it and be nice to each other. You get better art that way.'

'And better geography, frankly.'

We moved into the Undersea Realms exhibit. The gallery was lit by a dim, rippling aquamarine light—a nice effect. Russ took my hand and we walked through the near-darkness, looking at enormous jellyfish and huge underwater plants. They should be waving in the currents, but they were frozen in an eerie snapshot moment. I couldn't help wondering if they moved when no one was looking, then started to imagine I'd *seen* something move out of the corner of my eye as we passed each display. I was jumpier than I thought.

It was the same in the Mammals exhibit: did that lion's tail just twitch? What was that behind those trees? Gemstones wasn't quite so bad—rocks don't move by themselves, even my subconscious knew that—but Ancient Civilisations was creepy, with all those sarcophagi and mannequins.

'You okay?' said Russ, after the thousandth time I'd turned around to make *sure* I hadn't just seen something move.

'I guess I'm just a little jumpy. Getting knifed sometimes affects me like that.'

'What, you've been knifed before?'

'Joke.'

'Oh. Hey, before we move on to Stars and Planets, how about we get a coffee?'

I checked my wallet. 'Sure, okay. I wouldn't mind sitting down for a while.'

We went to the museum cafe and got coffees. I'd had some toast and cereal at Mom and Dad's, so I would be fine until lunchtime. I looked at my watch. Oh, it *was* lunchtime. I heard Russ's stomach growl.

'Hm,' he said. 'Hungry?'

I remembered what I'd seen in my wallet. 'I'll be okay, thanks.'

'I did some voiceover last month and they paid me. Let me get you something. No, really, listen: "By the time you think you need a lawyer, it's already too late," he said unctuously. "Talk to us today—get a jump on disaster."'

I had to laugh. 'You bottom-feeder! Who wrote that crap?'

'The senior partner. It's better than the steaming, rotted silage the department chair puts in her scripts.'

'How's that going?'

'Well, I'm an actor, not a writer. But … I think I'm making progress. It's now improved to being abysmal. If I stick with it, don't let myself get overwhelmed, I may be able to make it just barely watchable.'

'Yikes.'

'How's it going with Danny Snotnose Wexler?'

'Honestly? I don't know what everyone's problem has been. He's working hard, keeping his mouth shut in class—for some reason, I think he's decided he likes me.'

'Tell him you've got a boyfriend.'

'Have I?'

'Would you like one?'

'What, you mean you? Yeah, all right.'

We both grinned idiotically.

'So,' he said after a moment. 'What would you like for lunch?'

'Wow, what would I like for lunch … Oh, I'm so unprepared. It's an honour just to be nominated. Um, provolone and pesto on focaccia, toasted, please.'

'Sure thing. Won't be a minute.'

I watched my boyfriend go up to the counter and buy me a lunch. Remarkable.

Suddenly I got that something-moving impression again. Ridiculous—this was a cafe at lunchtime, it was buzzing. Of course people were moving. But this was something else, something … not right. I decided I'd turn around next time *before* I got the feeling. Steady. Steady … *now*.

It was that weedy little menace Jasper Smith-Fennel. I couldn't mistake him. Nobody looked like Jasper, lucky for them. He saw me looking straight at him, sneered, and left the cafe. He was tailing me.

I stared, seething, for quite a while at the spot where Jasper'd been.

When Russ got back with the sandwiches, he frowned and said, 'What's wrong?'

'I think I've got a stalker. One of our graduate students. He was involved in the events that led up to my hearing, and we did not end up on good terms. To put it mildly.' I'd knocked him down, disarmed him, thrown his gun away, and beaten him up, to be precise.

'So … he's stalking you because he hates you.'

'Basically.'

'Pretty mixed-up guy.'

'Again, to put it mildly. He actually asked for my help the other day. To—get this—steal some research.'

'I guess he thought that since you'd already crossed that line …'

'That was altruism!'

'I know, I know! I'm your boyfriend, I'm on your side, remember?'

'Oh yeah.'

'Are you going to report him?'

'He hasn't threatened me, or come to my apartment, or anything I could actually interest the police in. He's just unpleasant.'

'Can't you report him for conspiring to steal research?'

'Are you kidding? Who'd take me seriously on a charge like that?'

'I would.'

'You're not on the board of governors.'

He laughed then, and I was surprised at how bitter it sounded.

I was dying to know more about him and the governors. 'Why do you laugh so sardonically? Does the battle not go well?'

'I'm doing my best to line up more voiceover work, if that tells you anything.'

'What, before the chair's play is performed? Can't she pull some strings for you so you can finish out the semester at least?'

'I sure hope so. I'm going to need at least that long.'

'How are you going to do it?'

'I already care too much about you to put you in the middle of that.'

I would have argued if I hadn't felt the same way about him. After all, I hadn't told him about the Littoral Codex, had I? But what was he going to think if I went into hiding? I had to tell him *something*. I waited until we were mostly finished eating.

'Russ? You know that research I told you about, that I'm helping Pace and Dr Kortnoz with? I may need to head out of town for a few days for some field work on that.'

'Who's going to teach your classes?'

'Dr Kortnoz will line someone up, I'm sure.'

'When will you be back?'

'I don't exactly know. Just a few days, I hope.'

'You'll be careful, won't you?'

'Probably not.'

'I appreciate your candour. I'd appreciate it even more if you stayed safe. This is the same research that nearly got you kidnapped, after all.'

'Want to go look at the Hall of Stars and Planets?'

'Are you changing the subject?'

'Yes. *And* I want to look at the Hall of Stars and Planets.'

He sighed. 'Okay. Will I have to get used to this?'

'To what?'

'To worrying about you?'

'My folks never have.'

'Maybe your mom and I should have a talk, see if we can figure out some way to keep you out of trouble.'

'She's already tried just about everything. And the nuns at St Basilissa's nearly brought in an exorcist.'

'Saint who?'

'She's the patron saint of chilblains. No, really, you can look it up. It's the high school Pace and I went to. Stop laughing!'

'I don't even know what a chilblain is.'

'Well, if you get 'em, ask St Basilissa to help you out.'

I couldn't concentrate on the stars and planets. I was already worrying about my dinner with Drusy. She knew something, that was for sure. But was it going to help me, or get me into more trouble?

Without thinking, I turned to Russ and buried my face in his neck.

'Whoa, simple field work shouldn't get you this upset,' he said as he hugged me.

'Sorry,' I mumbled.

'That tickles.'

I took my face out of his neck. 'Sorry again.'

'Can I come with you?'

'*What*?'

'Wherever you're going. On your field work. Can I come, too?'

'Russ, please. I'll be back in a few days.'

'You'd better be.' His hug tightened, then released.

We stayed at the museum about another hour, but I don't think either of us was paying too much attention to the exhibits. If you'd asked me, 'What do you think it would be like to go on a date with a new boyfriend while death was hanging over your head and you had way too many nasty secrets to keep?', I'd have said it didn't sound like a really fun time. But what it did was make me feel like Russ had always been a friend and ally. It wasn't an entirely bad feeling. I wanted to know what it would be like to spend time with him once all this was over and things were calm and happy again. Then it occurred to me, had things ever been calm and happy?

'What time do you need to be going?' said Russ.

'Just this afternoon, or off on the field work?'

'I meant this afternoon, but both, I guess.'

'I have to meet someone for dinner at six. After that, I don't really know.'

'Is this dinner date better-looking than I am?'

'Yes, actually, and smarter, and in her eighties. A friend at the University Park retirement home, so don't get insecure.'

'Every actor is insecure. Why do you think we become actors? Hey, if I might never see you again, which I'm getting the impression you think is a possibility, can I at least hang out with you until your dinner date?'

'Seeing as I might never see you again, that would be okay with me.'

'Has your stalker been following us lately?'

'Um, I don't think so, why?'

'I was hoping to put on a show. Actors put on shows.'

'Geographers don't—' I started to say, but then I had to stop talking because Russ and I were in the middle of a kiss that just wouldn't stop. Passers-by snickered, and one or two clucked disapprovingly.

'Hope that didn't hurt,' he murmured after a while.

'Nope, my face feels better. Everything feels better, in fact, after that.' Which was why I kissed him again.

For years I'd tagged along with Pace on one adventure after another. I'd agreed to help with the Littoral Codex because Pace had asked me. Even stealing Pace's research had been a reaction to her decisions, her actions. But as I stood there kissing Russ, I suddenly wanted something that had nothing whatsoever to do with Pace. For the first time in fifteen years, I didn't give a damn what Pace thought.

It was a sweet, sweet moment, where Russ, and wanting Russ, and being wanted by Russ, took up my entire world. Then I remembered Pace and Kortnoz were in danger. And whether I owed them loyalty or not, they were still important to me. And they were counting on me. They trusted me.

Well, I'd just made a decision. This was the very last time I was going to get dragged into Pace's personal dramas. I was tired of being a sidekick. As soon as this particular drama played itself out, I was declaring myself an independent agent.

Russ and I walked to the river as the afternoon light slanted, golden and gentle, across the water. We listened to the kayakers calling and laughing to each other, watched the barges lumber by out in the dredged channel, dodged skaters and cyclists on the paved riverside path. A few kilometres to the south we could see the Miraculous Mud Flats sparkling like foil ribbons in a breeze.

'I love this river,' Russ said.

'Why?'

'Because of all the stories. A river, especially a river with a city clinging to it, means stories. And telling stories is the great genius of humankind.'

'I'm different, I guess. I love the river for its … its power, its persistence, the way it changes from source to mouth, but it's always itself. If there were no humans here to live the lives that made the stories, I'd still love this river.'

'Then you wouldn't be here either.' Russ laughed.

'Details.'

The light turned from golden to glowing red. We'd walked most of the way to University Park.

'Welp, time for my dinner date,' I said as briskly as I could.

'I know bad acting when I see it.'

'Yeah, maybe, but if I cry you might not want to be my boy-friend anymore.'

'No, you're right, no one likes a whiner. Wait, here, let me write down all my contact details. If the line is busy, it's my agent with the deal of a lifetime, shouldn't take that long to negotiate, just try back in a minute. Okay? You'll call me? As often as you can? And when you get back?'

He'd written three phone numbers, an email address, an instant-messaging screen name, and a postal address.

'I'll call,' I said. 'I'll keep calling. I'll call some more.' On the part of the paper that was blank, I wrote my number and my parents', tore it off, and gave it to him. 'That one is Mom and Dad, and it's just for emergencies, real ones. I don't want my parents worried over something trivial.'

Another kiss, and we parted. I kept glancing over my shoulder to watch him as I walked to the retirement home and he walked toward the bus stop.

There was a different receptionist this evening—so far, no two the same. 'I'm here to see Dr Drusy Kelso,' I told her.

She smiled pleasantly, which was a surprise, and said, 'I'll just let her know you're here.' A minute later she said, 'Go on up, Apartment 358. You know how to get there?'

'I'll be fine, thanks.'

Drusy welcomed me in. The apartment was full of the smell of good food, and I hoped I'd be able to eat it. It might be my last hot meal for a while.

'Sit down, honey, we'll talk while we eat.'

I sat at the dining-room table and Drusy dished up two plates of noodles and stew. After the first bite, I ended up having no trouble at all eating steadily, even after Drusy started talking.

'That Hypatia—oh, you'd better not tell her I called her that, she's got a temper! Pace is what she prefers, isn't it? Well, she's a bit of hot pepper, isn't she? I don't think Tyrone knows even now what he's gotten himself into!' She chuckled. 'They're off hiding, as I'm sure you know. They gave me a full briefing before they went, because they knew you were coming over here. Very clever. I wouldn't have thought either of them was that devious.'

'They both did get tenure.'

Drusy chuckled. 'True. But you can call it deviousness or you can call it survival tactics. Right now it's survival. They explained to me about the glass tablets, and how they want to decipher the Littoral Codex. Very admirable, but they're not the only ones. They told you about the Littoral League?'

'And its leader, Dr … what was it?'

'Norella Honeycott.'

'She's got the hots for Dr Kortnoz, he said.'

'It's a little more complicated than that. Yes, she has, as you say, the hots. But she's also more than a little unbalanced. He does not reciprocate her hots, so to her that means he's the enemy.'

'Even though she's in love with him.'

'Even though. And because he's the enemy, she wants to thwart his research, because—since she loves him—she knows that's the way to hurt him the most. And she's desperate not only to stop him deciphering the Codex, but to decipher it herself. She set up the Littoral League fifteen years ago, just after she got her PhD, as a focal point for research about the Codex. She figured, in what looked like altruism at the time, that if everyone pooled their research, they could succeed more quickly and with more robust results.'

'Or … she could have her fingers into everyone's research, keeping secrets where she wanted to so as to get a jump on every-one else.'

'Yessiree,' said Drusy. 'By the time most of the researchers caught on, it was too late. She stopped getting new people in, but she twisted the ones who stuck around, and they now function as … what's the word?'

'Henchmen.'

Drusy smiled. 'For a geographer, you're certainly good with words.'

'Are you a geographer too?'

'No, I used to teach economics.' I couldn't help it—I winced. My two semesters of economics were the worst experiences of my undergraduate years. Even if you counted the time Pace decided she could get double the benefit from our senior-year Practical Geography field work by combining it with her ninjutsu club's annual intensive training camp. To this day, Neil Funk had the scars on his backside from a throwing-star exercise that got wildly out of hand, and he still hyperventilated whenever he saw ads for martial-arts movies. Economics had been worse.

'Oh, now, don't be like that. Economics is fascinating—it offers windows of understanding onto whole vistas of human endeav-our. You might even say *everything* is economics.'

I let that go past. 'So why did Pace and Dr Kortnoz have to hide now? Why not last week, when we recovered the glass tablets?'

Drusy frowned. 'Honeycott may have thought of a way to get

the Praxicopolises to give her access to the Codex. The timing is a little suspicious—right when the tablets are recovered, the Praxies decide to become selfless and virtuous? Still, it's the only thing I can think of. If there's access to the Codex, the tablets become very valuable indeed. If there isn't, they're just pretty pieces of glass.'

'There are five of them, all different colours. How does it work?'

'There is a form of secret writing where, if you look at the text through a specific filter, you can discern marks obscured by the ordinary writing. You'd have to talk to a physicist like Mark Durakovic, up on the fifth floor here, for the details. Optics isn't his field, but he's a dabbler, and probably knows as much about it as anyone you'll find at the university these days. I imagine it has to do with which filter you use, or perhaps there are five different sets of secret writing to look at, one with each filter. Or you pick two filters. Or three. Or swap them around. You can see that even *with* the glass tablets, it's going to be a huge job to understand the Codex.'

'How would Honeycott persuade the Praxicopolises to give her access to the Codex? Maybe she's as nasty as they are, but that's not going to mean they want to be buddies.'

'Blackmail?' said Drusy.

'If they could be blackmailed, you'd think they would have been by now. There's clearly no shortage of people who loathe them.'

'Maybe they finally left one loose end for someone to unravel. Maybe someone can finally prove something.'

'What good am I going to do if I'm hiding, too, though? How am I going to find anything out? How am I going to—'

'Just for a few days. That's all. We'll sort out what Honeycott is doing and how we can protect you.'

'Who'll teach my classes?'

'Geography … that would be Lenny Garrick.'

I choked. Let him loose on my Intros? And if he and Danny so much as sat in the same room together, the universe would self-annihilate. And he'd tear the poor Ickies to bits. 'No,' I said. 'Maybe we can find another way.'

'The finest geographical mind this century has seen? Don't be silly! They'll love him! His students *always* loved him. You ask Tyrone.'

'I just don't want to trouble him. He's retired. He deserves a break.'

'Are you kidding? He's been aching to rummage around in young minds again. "I'd put things in order," he says. "Turn 'em into *real* geographers."' She imitated him so well that I gave a startled laugh. 'That's settled, then,' she went on. 'Lenny will teach for you. We can find your schedule on the department website. Don't worry, he'll do fine. You won't recognise your students when you get back. Where's your bag, by the way?'

'At my parents' place.'

'Hm. You'll have to go back there tonight anyway, or else they'll worry. I know how parents worry—I caused mine a few nights of lost sleep in my day. Tomorrow morning one of our friends will come by at, let's see, eight o'clock to pick you up and take you where you can get that package. Then she'll bring you to a safe hiding place we know of. That will buy us a few days to try and make a plan.'

My head was spinning. While Drusy got out the cake and made the coffee, I wrote my parents' address and phone number on a piece of paper. Drusy set my coffee in front of me, then rummaged in a drawer until she found a cell phone.

She handed it to me and said, 'Now you keep that phone off most of the time, do you hear me? Just turn it on once a day to check for messages. If that. Less chance you'll be tracked that way. And leave your own phone at your parents' place.'

I nodded. Despite myself, I was finding this kind of exciting. I felt guilty, because people I loved were worried about me, people I cared about were in danger. But all the same there was a pounding thrill to it all. I hated to think it, but I was becoming more like Pace every day.

No, I thought an instant later. Pace makes her own decisions. I'm still being ordered around by everyone. Getting in trouble and making trouble are two entirely different things.

'Now, how are you going to get home, honey?'

'I usually take the bus. There's one every hour along University Avenue that goes right near my parents' place.'

'At least there'd be witnesses if anyone tried anything. And no log of the address, like there'd be with a taxi. I hate to say it, but that's probably best. In which case, you should leave soon. I'll ask a couple of our more ambulatory residents to wait with you at the bus stop, all right?'

'I … no, it's okay … um … yes, please,' I said. 'Yes, I'd like that. Thanks.' Celeste the Brave with her Fighting Octogenarian Bodyguards. But I knew it was only common sense not to wait at a dark bus stop by myself.

Drusy made a few quick phone calls, and we sipped the last of our coffee until there was a knock on the door. Drusy stood on tiptoe to squint through the peephole, then opened the door. Three people I remembered from the other evening bustled cheerfully in. They told me their names, which I instantly forgot, but it didn't seem to matter, as they kept up a jovial chatter that meant I didn't have to talk much.

I stood up and got ready to go. 'Thanks, Drusy. Thanks for all your help.'

'That's all right, honey. Anything that pisses the Praxies off and undermines the board of governors is a good day's work! Plus, I like you. I can get enough of your friend Pace, I have to say, but you're a very different person altogether.'

'Pace is smarter.'

'Maybe she is, maybe she isn't. But you've got something she hasn't got.'

'What's that?'

'Real courage.'

'Huh?' Pace was the most reckless person I knew.

'When things get bad, and they probably will, you'll see what I mean.' She gave me a hug with fragile arms and placed a quick, dry kiss on my cheek. 'You take care, now, honey. You take care. We're doing our best on our end, you remember that. You've got helpers all over Purple Bay that you don't even know about. The Praxicopolises have their empire—well, so do we.'

I had no idea what she was talking about.

My three escorts and I shuffled the two blocks to the bus stop. They could sure talk. I could still hear them inside my head when I was miles away and the bus started to climb into the foothills near my parents' house. I pushed the stop-request button at my usual place, and walked the last ten minutes doing my best to be alert without looking furtive. Nothing draws attention like looking furtive. Pace had told me that once in sophomore year when she needed someone to help her carry the books she was borrowing from the department chair's office. While the department chair was out of town on a conference. And the only way to get them was to pick the lock. It's not easy to look nonchalant when you're picking a lock, but Pace managed it.

My parents were reading when I got home. That was a relief. I'd been afraid I'd find them barricaded in the bathroom because Littoral League henchmen had surrounded the house.

'Have a nice time, Mousie?' said Dad.

'Yes, thanks.'

'Is he a good kisser?'

'Pete, *stop* it,' said Mom.

'As it happens, Dad, yes, he is.'

Mom made an exasperated sound and picked her book up again.

'And dinner was good?'

'Yes, it was terrific. Most of the people at the retirement home— in fact, I think all of them—taught at the university at one time or another. It's a blast to talk to them.'

'Have times changed?'

'Not to hear them tell it. They had the same worries I've got. If I ever have grandkids, and they want to be academics, I'm sure they'll have the same worries, too.'

'There's optimism for you,' said Mom sourly.

'Anything on television?'

'Kim-Hatton's address,' said Mom in the same sour voice.

'You're not watching it.'

'We're not just not watching it, we're actively avoiding it,' said Dad. 'Who elected her, anyway?'

'Uh … like mostly everyone,' I said. 'That's what "elected" means.'

'Krasnia is going to the dogs. I'm sure my parents didn't foresee Kim-Hatton when they emigrated. If they had, they'd have gone somewhere else entirely. Like the middle of a tundra somewhere. And herded elk.'

'Yeah, Dad, you'd have been happy growing up on the elk ranges.'

'You bet I would.'

'But you wouldn't have met me,' said Mom. 'No way would you catch me milking an elk.'

I debated telling them that, in fact, elk aren't herded at all, reindeer are. But I knew from experience that would set my father off on a long-winded speculation on how you could make elk-herding work if you really wanted to, and what you might do to domesticate an elk, and how you would acquire rights to the land, and where you'd put the infrastructure to transport all your elk-herding-related products. He was a planner, that's what planners did. But I was sort of not in the mood.

The bus ride had taken long enough that I could plausibly plead fatigue and head upstairs. I packed my bag and backpack for the morning and went to bed, where I tossed and turned until about midnight.

It wasn't much later than that when I awoke, panting and terrified. Someone was pounding on the door.

Chapter 9
Celeste Discovers What Lies Beneath the Surface

'All *right*, all *right*,' yelled my father, adding some choice words in the North Kras dialect as he thumped downstairs. 'What?' Then his voice dropped, and I couldn't make out the words anymore. A moment later he came back upstairs. 'Mousie? Someone downstairs says it's an emergency with your friend Pace. She says please hurry and get dressed.'

I stood up. 'Thanks, Dad. Who is it?'

'Dr … um … Maher, I think she said.'

The head librarian?

'Could you please tell her I'll be ready in a minute?'

'Sure, Mousie. Hey—are you going to be all right? This is all getting a little scary.'

'I'll be fine, Dad. I may have to go out of town for a few days to help Pace, especially if she's sick or something, in a hospital somewhere. Right now I don't know enough to give you any firm schedules, but I'll be back soon. Okay? Is Mom awake?'

'How could she not be?'

'As soon as I'm dressed I'll come in and say bye.'

I turned the light on and Dad pulled the door shut behind him. At least now I didn't have to worry about sleeping through the alarm.

Once I was dressed, I knocked on my parents' door. 'Gotta go. Thanks again for letting me stay. I'll call you as soon as I know what's going on, okay? And I'll be back in a few days, like I told Dad.' I gave them each a kiss. They murmured goodbyes and stared after me with wide, worried eyes as I left.

Dr Maher was standing on the porch. 'Come on, we've got to head up into the mountains.'

'I thought it would draw too much attention if we went in the dead of night. Weren't you supposed to show up at eight in the morning?'

'We're running out of time. Ty got a text message to us, God knows how. The Littoral League is getting close to discovering them—the safe house they'd been at two nights ago was broken into. We can keep moving them, but only for so long. The good news is, it's a very effective misdirection to keep the League from noticing where you and I are going.'

'You know where the lava cave is?'

'Pace gave me the coordinates before they went underground.' She pointed at the luminous screen of her satellite-navigation module. 'This is top of the line, it will get us as close as the road goes. After that I've got a portable unit that's nearly as good. And, of course, you've been there yourself.' She winked, and I assumed Pace had told her the whole story.

'Um, in daylight, and on the way up I was hogtied on the floor of Pace's back seat. Come to think of it, I was fairly rattled on the way back, as well. You'd better not count on me for precision navigation.'

'We'll just have to do our best, then.'

'Footing's pretty treacherous, I do remember that much. It's not going to be fun in the dark.'

'It won't be fun for pursuers, either, and they won't have the advantage of *knowing* it's treacherous. In the zeal of pursuit, they might sprain their ankles or something equally convenient.'

The ride up the mountains in Dr Maher's little car was nerve-wracking. I thought a dozen different times that she'd scraped the bottom right off the fuel tank as we bumped along rutted fire roads and stony tracks. Dr Maher, however, looked like she was having the time of her life. The light from the dashboard showed her teeth bared in an exultant grin, and she wrenched the steering wheel around with an abandon that I found almost frightening.

At length we got to the point where the track was too narrow even for a car as small as Dr Maher's. She turned the engine off, reached behind the seat, and handed me a flashlight, taking another herself. She got out a backpack and put it on once we were out of the car.

We stepped meticulously over the jagged rocks and pushed through the underbrush that nearly blocked the path. It was horribly, frighteningly hard to do both, knowing that one misstep could mean a nasty fall. Maybe very nasty.

The path was steep, and between that and the tension, I was starting to get seriously out of breath. 'Dr Maher!' I called softly. 'Wait!' I doubled over for just a second.

That second was all it took for someone to dart out of the darkness and tackle me. My flashlight rattled back down the path as I fell. A sharp agony of heat consumed my wrist and forearm, but I had to ignore it. There was just enough moonlight coming through the branches overhead to tell the difference between my attacker and the darkness. With the hand that didn't hurt I found his head and slammed my palm into his face over and over. I must have gotten him a good one to the nose, because he cried out and his grip on my waist loosened. I worked one knee up between us and shoved outward to get myself some space, then lined up with his head and kicked hard. He collapsed to the ground and was silent.

I stayed on the ground, too, wondering when the adrenaline would wear off and my arm would *really* start to hurt. Boy, would I have a lot of explaining to do when I got back: first the black eye and the cut throat, and now a broken wrist and God only knew how many cuts and scrapes I was too revved up to feel yet.

Dr Maher appeared out of the brush. The whole fight must have taken less than ten seconds. 'God, I'm sorry,' she said. 'I thought you were right behind me. Who's this joker?' She pointed her flashlight at his face. 'You pounded him pretty good, by the looks of that nose.'

I got slowly to my feet and went over to look at his face. 'I have no idea.' I'd had the wild idea for a second it might be Jasper, but he already knew I could take him in a fight. Besides, I suspected Jasper was afraid of the dark.

Dr Maher took some cord out of her pack. She tucked one of the attacker's arms close to his ribs, rolled him over the arm onto his side—'No need for him to suffocate, and it's easier to tie him up this way'—and bound his hands and feet.

'Right,' she said briskly when she was done. 'Let's get your flashlight and go.'

'What about him?'

'They'll be back to get him before morning, I expect. Who taught you to fight?'

'Pace.' I made my way back down the path a few steps to where my flashlight was still shining. I picked it up in my good hand and joined Dr Maher.

'Why doesn't that surprise me?' she said. 'By the way, please call me Joan. Formalities are nice, but they waste time in situations like this.'

'What if there's another henchman?'

'They would have been there to back up the first one. Obviously he thought you'd be an easy mark. He must have been trailing us for quite a while, waiting for a moment when we'd get separated. I'm so sorry about that. Really.'

'Don't mention it,' I said, although I was actually more than a little peeved. I'd been all set to go blindly where she led, and she'd already made a mistake that could have ended my life. How come I never got the infallible mentors?

'Are you all right?' she asked me. Finally.

'I think my wrist is broken, but aside from that I'm okay.'

'Let me see.'

I held my arm out gingerly. It was already swollen and bruising.

'Can you move your hand at all?'

I tried, and nearly blacked out. 'Um. No.'

She reached into her pack again—what was that thing, a gateway to another dimension?—and got out a first-aid kit, from which she took an elastic bandage. 'It won't take the pain away, but at least it may immobilise the wrist enough for you to function, and to keep it from getting worse as you walk along.' I shone my flashlight on the injured hand, and bound up my wrist as tightly as I could stand it. Slightly tighter, in fact, but I had to admit it hurt less. She pinched one of my fingertips and watched it turn from white back to pink. Apparently that happened quickly enough that she was satisfied I wouldn't get gangrene before we could get to a doctor.

And we started back up the path. It had been challenging before; now, I was shaking and depressed as the adrenaline seeped away, and only had one hand to push branches aside and help me scramble up the rocks.

The path led to an opening in the mountainside. We squeezed in, and I remembered the last time I'd been here. The steady red light was the same, as was the sudden heat. I shone the flashlight up to the roof of the cave: yup, there was the hook—bolted to the roof by some lunatic a century or more ago—from which I'd dangled over the lava. I shuddered. To this day I don't know whether Pace would really have let me drop into the fiery depths.

Joan was already poking around, looking for the tablets. I started doing the same, looking behind and under rocks and shining the flashlight into crannies. I was slightly taller than both Pace and Kortnoz, so I would probably be able to reach it wherever they'd put it. Unless he'd boosted her up.

I swung the flashlight beam up and slowly across the walls

above my head, trying to make out some sort of scratch or scrape that would show where they'd left the tablets. Pity the dry heat made the cave unsuited for moss or lichen; they would have clearly shown the marks from anyone climbing up.

Wait—there. A smudge of dull black right about shoulder height. Right where the tip of Pace's boot would have scraped against the rock if she'd been standing on Kortnoz's shoulders. I looked up: a tiny hole, partly obscured by an outcropping, so high up that Joan would have to stretch even if she were standing on my shoulders. Great.

'Joan—over here. You'll have to stand on my shoulders. I'll do my best to give you a leg-up, but I've only got the one hand working.'

Luckily the wall was rough, and Joan managed to climb up using a combination of holds in the rock and bits of my anatomy. I stood as steadily as I could, but she wasn't small, and my legs shook. I felt like a weightlifter staggering around with a bus held overhead. It was a very long few seconds before Joan said, 'Got it!'

The tablets were in a tote bag that I recognised as one Pace had picked up at last year's Krasnian Geographic Society convention. The slogan, 'See the World with Geography!', and the cheery cartoon globe mascot, made me more irritable than ever. Joan pushed the straps onto her shoulder—the bag instantly made her a lot heavier—and climbed down.

'Let's go,' I said. 'They're going to start wondering what's keeping our hog-tied friend back there. And there's nobody guarding your car.'

'True enough.'

We picked up our flashlights and headed down the path. It was maddening to go carefully, but it was just as dangerous going down as it'd been coming up. And Joan was struggling to manage the bag.

When we got to where we'd left the attacker, we saw the cords in pieces. Someone had come and cut him loose.

'Uh-oh,' said Joan.

'Is there a Plan B?' I said.

She got two guns out of the backpack and waited for me to turn my flashlight off and put it in my pocket before handing me one.

'I don't know how to work one of these,' I whispered frantically. 'What if I blow my own head off?'

'It's not mysteries of the ancients,' she snapped. 'You have a PhD, work it out. Just keep your finger away from the trigger until you know you need to shoot something.'

Not far from where the path opened out, Joan held up a hand. She turned her flashlight off and we stood still for several minutes, listening. 'Cover me,' she murmured, and started walking toward her car. *Cover* her? I didn't even really know what that meant; I'd only ever heard it on television.

I heard a twig scrape along a nylon jacket—a sound I'd heard a million times on hikes, no mistaking it. But neither Joan nor I were wearing nylon. I turned in the direction of the sound and fired, aiming what I hoped was too low to actually kill anyone.

'Run for the car!' yelled Joan, and I did. We got in, and she turned the key. For a terrifying instant the car wouldn't start. She tried again, and then we were bouncing down that track like a kid's toy bounces down the stairs.

It was only when we'd gotten onto the main road that Joan spoke. 'I'm going to take you to one of our safe houses. You can stay there for a few days. I hope.'

'Isn't this all just a bit melodramatic?'

'Ask Pace and Ty. They're the ones with bullet holes in their car.'

I remembered with sudden clarity how it had felt to cower underneath Kortnoz's four-wheel-drive as the helicopter hovered a few feet away.

'What am I supposed to do while I'm holed up? I only have one book with me.'

For some reason that made her laugh. 'You'll see.'

Just outside of the city, she pulled over and made a phone call.

'Fifteen minutes,' she told someone.

Once we were actually in town, I realised she was taking the back streets around to the northern entrance to the university.

'Someplace on campus? Doesn't seem very isolated. Or safe. I'm an academic, I'm *supposed* to be on campus.'

'That's the irony,' she said. She parked in the lot near the gymnasium. 'Here, put this jacket on. And tuck your hair into this hat.' She took a large, floppy jacket and a hat, also floppy, from the floor of the back seat. She put on a wig of long red hair and a pair of enormous glasses and said, 'Have you got your stuff? Okay, let's go. And remember—don't look sneaky or nervous. Walk like you own the campus.' We got out of the car and she grabbed the tote bag, one of the flashlights, and her pack-that-had-everything before locking the doors.

The parking lot was only dimly lit—another cost-cutting measure, no doubt, but for once it worked in my favour. We walked around the side of the gym to where the enormous wheelie bins sat on the blacktop like a bunch of cows lying patiently in a field. Joan squeezed in behind one of them and ducked down. I heard a metallic scraping, then she stuck her head up and waved me over. I pushed myself between the bin and the brick wall and saw that she'd moved a rusty metal plate that I would have taken for the access hatch to the water pipes or something. There was a tunnel behind it. Of course. Of course there was.

A minute later I heard some scuffling and grunting, and two people climbed out. It was now pretty crowded behind that bin.

Joan handed the wig and the glasses to one of them, and said, 'Give the hat and jacket to Marnie.' I handed them over, and they put the disguises on.

'Let's go,' said Joan. 'You first, so I can slide the plate back. You might need to take your pack off and push it ahead of you for a while.'

The other two shoved past us as politely as they could and headed toward the parking lot. The whole swap had taken about a minute.

The tunnel was so cramped I couldn't even crawl on all fours. I had to drag myself forward with my elbows, and do my best to raise each knee up enough to give a little push without jamming my butt against the roof. And at each move forward, I had to push my backpack and gym bag ahead of me. My wrist was incandescent with pain. The tunnel was metal-lined, and the din hurt my ears.

I counted one hundred and forty-seven awkward and painful 'strides' before the floor of the tunnel suddenly stopped and my bags dropped to land with an echoing thud somewhere below. If my hips hadn't still been wedged against all four sides, I would have tumbled onto my face after them.

'Go on,' urged Joan. 'It's only a half-metre drop. You can reach the floor from where you are.'

Sure enough, I could just put my one good hand down and brace my weight on it until I could finally free my knees and land like a frog on the floor. I scurried away so neither Joan nor her bags would land on me.

I heard her land with an 'oof', then I heard the zipper of her backpack. A moment later she snapped the flashlight on. We were in a room about the size of a shipping container—in fact, it looked quite a bit like a shipping container in every respect, except that I couldn't figure out why you'd need a tunnel into a shipping container.

'Where is this?' I asked.

'Did you notice the tunnel was sloping downwards?'

'No, I had other things on my mind.' I sounded sullen, even to myself.

'I know—sorry. We'll get you a doctor soon. We're under the football field.'

'Is this, you know, it? Are we there?' I hoped not.

'No, just a breather.'

'Not more tunnels, not like this one, please.'

'It's easier from here on.' I gave her a dubious look.

'What was that swap for, back at the bins? In case someone checked the security cameras?'

'You're getting the hang of this,' she said approvingly.

'What will they make of that one-minute gap when we were all snuggled behind the bin?'

'Drug deal, of course.'

Great. Security now had a video of me doing what looked a lot like a drug deal. And they already knew I got into fights, and that I had something in my office that was desired by the sort of people who break into offices.

I stood up and tried to stretch the cramps out of my arms and legs. I hadn't accomplished much by the time Joan said, 'Time to move on.'

I hadn't seen a door, not even a trap door, but Joan reached up and fiddled with a bolt on the wall, then stooped down and did the same with one near the floor. With a clang and a high, screeching wail, a bit of the wall slid aside as she pushed. At least this time the passageway looked big enough to walk in, if we doubled over.

Feeling resigned, I put my pack on and picked up my gym bag. The excitement I'd felt at Drusy's was long gone—fear, pain, fatigue, and a growing awareness that it would soon be breakfast time had seen to that. I hunched over and went into the passage after Joan.

In the light of Joan's flashlight, I was stunned to see doorway after doorway open off the tunnel on either side. This was an absolute labyrinth—and all beneath the university grounds. Who knew about this? Why wasn't it even *hinted* at in the stories the undergrads told each other during pre-dawn study breaks?

My Inner Geographer, who'd been cowering from all the stress, emerged, and I said, 'Joan, we're on the coast. On the very flat, very silty coastal plain. The nearest competent rock strata are several kilometres away. How is all this staying dry? How does it not cave in or slip into the sea?'

'Celeste, for God's sake, I'm a librarian, not an engineer.'

These weren't primitive tunnels. People had gone to a great deal of trouble to build them properly—people with detailed knowledge of engineering, geology, and project management. The tunnels were way too old-looking to have been built in this century, but without more clues—artworks, writing, something that told me more about the builders themselves—it was impossible to guess how old they actually were.

We walked for quite a while. I was just adding aching feet and back spasms to my list of complaints when we turned off into another passage.

'Not long now,' said Joan.

She stopped in front of an ornate metal door with a sculpted brass handle. Here was my clue, but I couldn't place it in any particular Krasnian style.

'Go ahead,' Joan said, bouncing a little on her toes, as if she were waiting for me to open a present she'd brought me. 'Go on in. They've unlocked it for us.'

I pushed the handle down with my good hand and pushed against the door with my shoulder. Then I just stood in the doorway, staring.

I was on a balcony, looking down into a room the size of a small church. It was lined with carved and painted bookshelves: dragons, pirate ships, clouds, horses, knights, castles, minarets, jungles, deserts, pagodas, weavers, sculptors, kings, queens, farmers, hunters, hawks—all lively with bright colours and gilt and inlaid jewels, all wonderfully made. The light from dozens of frosted-glass globes spread warmly and steadily through the room, making the jewels and gilt glow. Galleries lined with brass railings went along every wall, and every alcove held hundreds of books. Down below, the floor was mostly covered by a dozen huge, heavy, dark, wooden tables; I could glimpse carpets and mosaics of red, gold, blue, and green on the floor between them. I looked up: the ceiling was painted in a dark, night-sky blue, with silver stars. The room smelled wonderfully of paper and glue and varnish and dust.

I turned to look at Joan, my eyes shining. 'Don't tell me this is my safe house.'

'Uh-huh. You say you only brought one book? No problem.'

'Do I sleep under one of the tables?'

'I'll show you. There's an office just off the main reading room that's been fixed up with plumbing and everything.'

'Where is everyone? A place like this, shouldn't it be full of researchers? Or tourists?'

'Even members of secret organisations have to sleep sometime.'

We started walking along the gallery toward an enormous staircase, which, like the galleries themselves, was richly carpeted.

'What secret organisation?' I said. 'And who vacuums this place?'

'Need-to-know basis,' she said. 'If I could tell you, I would, because I think you'd be a fantastic asset to what we're doing. But I can't right now. Down one flight and duck under the stairs to the left.'

I slid my good hand down the banister as I went down the steps. The wood under my fingers was solid and comforting.

Under the stairwell was a plain door, out of place in all this opulence. It was unlocked, and I went into the room. After the glories outside, it was stark, utilitarian, like a freshman-year dorm room. Twice as big, though, luckily. It had a simple bed, a desk with a phone on it, and a chair. One wall had a door, which I opened: toilet, sink, and shower. The bed was already made up, and a towel, washcloth, and bar of soap were waiting in the bathroom.

'Let me make a phone call, and see if we can get a doctor here right away to look at that wrist.'

I tried to say I'd be all right, but just then my wrist emitted a throb of pain that felt like hot pokers drilling through it.

Joan picked up the phone, which must have automatically

connected somewhere, because she didn't dial. 'Joan Maher here. Is Dr Compton still in the complex? Could she please come down and check out a possible broken wrist? Yes, in the guest room. Thanks.' She hung up. 'Hopefully she won't take long. Meanwhile—' She frowned. 'Do I smell *cookies*?'

'Oh!' I looked in my backpack. Sure enough, the plastic tub was still there. I guessed, after all the trouble she'd been through on my account, I should offer one to Joan. I opened the lid: there were only two left. Feeling resigned, I held the tub out to her.

'Thanks.' She took a bite and her eyes widened. 'Where did you *get* these? They're incredible.'

'One of my students made them. He should probably switch majors to food science, I'm thinking.'

We were still savouring the cookies when there was a knock on the door.

'Who is it?' called Joan. Very sophisticated security system, that, I thought.

'Dr Compton.'

Joan opened the door.

Dr Compton said, 'Right, now, let's have a look at that wrist. Yours, is it? Do I smell cookies?'

'We ate them. I'm Celeste Carlucci.'

'Oh, I know. Here, sit on the bed. Let me take that bandage off. Did you do this, Joan? Nice job, very neat.'

The moment the bandage loosened, the pain increased a hundred times. 'Sorry,' said Dr Compton, 'but I have to have a look. Can you move your hand at all?'

'Not without shrieking.'

'Hard to tell if it's broken or not without an x-ray, but I don't think so. I'll give you a brace for it until we can look at it properly tomorrow.' She took a brace out of her bag; it went from the top of my palm down to my elbow, and was tight enough to hold my entire forearm rigid. 'Here are some painkillers. Don't go overboard, you should stay alert.'

What was that supposed to mean?

She put her things back in her bag and stood up. 'Try and get a few hours' sleep, okay? I'm going to do the same myself. Good night, or rather, good morning.' She shut the door behind her as she left.

Joan said, 'An x-ray is one of the things we'll get taken care of tomorrow. Or, as Dr Compton points out, today.'

I didn't bother with the painkillers; the brace was really helping and Dr Compton had a point, I didn't want to get any foggier than I already was. I kept eyeing the bed, wondering when Joan would say, 'Why don't you just catch up on your sleep, Celeste?'

Instead, she said, 'I suppose you want to know more about Ty and Pace.'

'Are they all right?'

'They were when I left to get you.'

'That's all I need right now, thanks.' The pillows were plump and the sheets were white.

'Hungry?'

'I will be. But I'm okay now, thanks.' I ran my hand over the comforter: soft and light and fluffy. Undoubtedly warm.

'Need a book?'

'Not at the moment, thanks.' I sat on the bed. The mattress gave just a little. Perfect.

'Something to drink?'

'Goodnight, Joan. Thanks so much for everything.'

'Don't you want to look at what Pace left for you in the lava cave?'

That did interest me enough to postpone sleep for another few headachy minutes. Joan put the tote bag on the table and took out a wad of plastic the size of a brick. It was layers of plastic bags, and Joan took a distressingly long time to work them off, one by one. Finally she revealed the tablets, just as I'd remembered them.

'Yup,' I said. 'That's them, all right.'

Joan seemed disappointed. 'Just … glass blocks. A little heavy for their size, maybe, but that's it.'

'*Special* glass blocks,' I said, and yawned. 'Now I need to sleep.'

'These are probably as safe with you as they'd be anywhere else,' she said. 'As long as you lock the door behind me. Pick up the phone when you wake up, and it will automatically connect you with the office. We've got someone there all the time.'

'Thanks,' I said, and yawned again. When Joan left I bolted the door. I had only just enough energy to brush my teeth, take my clothes off, and turn back the bed before I collapsed onto the mattress. It was as good as I'd thought. Perfect mattress. Had to get a mattress like this for myself one of these days. Maybe when I got tenure …

Chapter 10
Sleep Is the Least of Celeste's Worries

Hunger woke me. I ignored it long enough to shower and dress, then picked up the phone and heard a rattling dial tone that went on until a cheery voice said, 'Hello? Is that Dr Carlucci?'

'Yes. Who've I got?'

'It's me, Dr Carlucci! Nicki! Isn't that cool? They told me you were in the guest room!'

I nearly dropped the phone. 'Um, I thought it was supposed to be a secret that I was here.'

'Oh, that's okay. I'm part of the organisation. My family's been in it for generations. Ricky doesn't know. I had to tell him that sometimes I need to go help out an elderly relative. *Sort* of true. And it's really cool to be able to get help with my papers and research. All combined, the people here know pretty much everything.'

Just then my stomach growled. 'Wow, Nicki, this is an amazing coincidence. By the way, do you know how I might get some breakfast?'

'I'll be there in a few minutes to take you to the canteen. It won't be really fancy, but there's tons of food and most of it's okay, except for the sausages. They look pretty dicey to me, although Dr Maher ate a whole plateful and seems fine.'

'Thanks, Nicki. I'll wait for you here.'

I wanted to find out more. Maybe Nicki would let slip more than Joan had. I was Nicki's favourite professor, after all. At least, I assumed I was, although I hadn't distributed the student feedback forms yet this semester. Every now and then there was a real surprise: the combative, surly student who ended up giving you all fives and writing in the comments section how you changed their life, or the sweet, smiling little thing who never said a thing in class but panned you viciously. One year someone stapled a worm to one of Pace's evaluation forms.

I noticed there was a key next to the phone. I checked: it was for the door into the library. I stepped into the space under the staircase and locked the door behind me. I passed the time until Nicki came and got me by staring at the carvings. You could hide anything in a place this big and elaborate. Why hadn't Pace just brought the tablets here?

It hit me like the beat of a huge drum: Pace didn't know about this place. Someone was trusting me with information they didn't want Pace and Kortnoz to have.

I knew something Pace didn't.

Nicki startled me; the carpets on the stairs had muffled her footsteps. 'Hungry?' she said.

'Completely.'

She took me through a door a few steps past the staircase and into a hallway—a real one, not a damp, dirty, cramped passageway, I was happy to see. After a minute or so I started to smell food, and my stomach growled again, loud enough to make Nicki grin.

'Not long now, Dr Carlucci.'

The canteen was all stainless steel and glass and steam. 'Damn, I left my money in the guest room,' I said.

Nicki gave the response I was hoping for. 'Oh, no, Dr Carlucci, you don't *pay* for the food. You're our *guest*. Please help yourself.'

I was having quite a good run of other people feeding me. Pity I had to be fleeing from mortal peril to get it. I loaded up a plate with bacon, potatoes, grilled tomatoes, fruit, and danish and sat down to devour them. It didn't take me long.

Nicki watched in awe. 'You *were* hungry.'

'I had a rough night last night. And I don't have any of Ricky's cookies left.'

'Aren't they amazing? He's not much of a conversationalist, but boy can he cook!'

I decided circumstances were informal enough that I could ask diplomatically. 'It doesn't seem like the two of you have a lot in common, do you?'

'Oh, you know. He's very sweet. And he's smarter than he looks, he really is.'

I concentrated on eating my breakfast so I wouldn't have to respond. Ricky's mid-terms in both classes had been disasters. His papers were slightly better, but I knew why that was.

'You're the one who really seems to love geography, though,' I said after I'd eaten a few mouthfuls.

'Oh, I *do*,' she said, beaming. 'It helps you understand so many different things—history, art, economics ...' She took a deep breath. '*Everything* is geography!'

I couldn't help smiling, but it was a wry smile. I'd once been that bubbly and idealistic. Now I was on the run, busted up, tired, and in danger. Maybe I should have become an accountant.

'Now what?' I said, as I stood up to bring my plate to the rack.

'Um, I don't know. They didn't tell me that. I guess you can just, you know, hang out. Look at the books in the library. The card catalogue was destroyed about eighty years ago in an bizarre incident involving large amounts of wine, a disgruntled teaching assistant, and a flamethrower. So you never know what you'll find in there, it's always an adventure.'

'Nobody's re-catalogued it? Ever?'

'It would take too long, and the books are still sort of in order. Most of the people in the organisation can only get away for a few hours in a week, sometimes less, and there aren't that many of us to begin with. Speaking of which, I should probably be getting back. Spending Sundays with my aged aunt is only plausible for a few hours. Then Ricky starts to get lonely.'

'You don't feel that's a bit … clingy?'

'Tonight he's making crispy shredded beef with orange sauce, steamed dumplings, and mango sorbet.'

'Ah.'

'So—would you like me to show you back to the library?'

'Yes, please. This time I'll leave breadcrumbs.'

'It gets like that. There are no maps, obviously, can't risk it. I guess you'll have to memorise your way around.'

We started back down the hallway. 'Nicki … what is this secret organisation?'

'Well, we're not supposed to talk about it, but I can tell you that the librarians at the university are just the coolest. That's all I can say, though. Otherwise I'll get into trouble.'

Rats.

'Are your family librarians, then? Are they disappointed you're a geographer?'

'They're just happy I didn't end up like my brother.'

'And how did he end up?'

'He got a job in university admin. Working for the board of governors.'

'Wow, really? That would be unnerving, to have someone from the board always in the house.'

'Oh, he moved out last year. There was a big scene. I think my parents are still upset, to tell you the truth. So geography is just fine by comparison. Funny, though.'

'What?'

'He hasn't said a word to me, not an email, nothing, since he moved out. But just the other day he phoned me up, asking how the studies were going. Who my professors are. What they're researching. Asked me about you, in fact.'

'What, by name?'

'Let me think. No, just "your geography professor". But you're teaching both my geography classes this semester, so who else could he have meant?'

'Mm.'

'I didn't say much. I've never really liked him. Not since he flushed one of my dolls down the toilet because I wouldn't do his math homework for him. Well, here we are,' she said, opening the door to the library. 'You'll be okay?'

'Yes, this will be great, thanks.'

'Lunch starts at twelve. Do you want someone to come and get you? I can leave a message at the office.'

'No, thanks. I think I can find my way to the canteen myself now.'

'Okay, then. Have a good time!'

'Thanks, Nicki. Hope dinner goes well.'

'Oh, it will!'

The door closed behind her. I let myself into the guest room and used the toilet, washing my hands as best I could without getting the inside of the brace soaking wet, then started my exploration of the library.

Most of the books looked to be more than a hundred years old, bound in faded cloth and scuffed, dusty leather. They were still shelved by subject area, although, despite Nicki's optimism, quite a few had gotten out of order over the years. I walked past shelf after shelf of biography and history. I went up one floor: literature, music, and drama (I wondered, with a giddy swoop in my stomach, what Russ would say if he could see this place, these books). Up one more to chemistry, biology, astronomy, geology. Eventually I found the geography section.

I skimmed the shelves, looking for 'Strudthorne.' I was nearly through geography, just one alcove from the start of palaeontology, when I saw it: a copy of Millicent's thesis. Unlike the copy I'd borrowed from the university library, which was commercially bound, this was hand-bound, and labelled in neat script on the spine in gold ink: *An Inquiry into the Rate of Advancement of the Miraculous Mud Flats of the Purple River.*

I sat down on the floor, back against a pillar, and opened the thesis. Good God, this was the original manuscript—the entire thing was written in an exact, regular hand. Millicent's, I figured. What I read next left no doubt. On the inside of the front cover was written:

> Fair reader, you hold in your hands the only true, full, and unaltered copy of my research. The board of governors compelled my adviser to edit the results, and it is the edited version that was filed with the university and state libraries. Tell no one that this copy exists, or they will destroy it as well! I must trust you, fair reader, to use what you find here without revealing its source. Confirm my measurements for yourself, publish the research as your own. That is my legacy to you, and my secret plan to thwart the governors. I, who will have no voice by the time you read this, will speak through you. I must fight the governors, even from the grave, and you will be my champion. Together we can advance the cause of justice. Courage, fair reader—courage!

Holy smokes. I turned to the data tables that I knew I would find in the back. There they were: row after row, column after column of freakishly neat figures. I recalled my own haphazard writing. Sorry, Millicent, I thought. You've got a pretty slack champion. But I'll do my best.

On a hunch, I started checking the figures for August. The copy from the university library had shown no anomaly, but the *Reminiscence* had been very clear: in August, and only in August, the delta had grown, and in September it had receded to its prior limits. Yes! There it was!

Had enough time passed that I could make Millicent's research public? I remembered Nicki saying how her brother had been asking about her geography professor, and I shuddered. No, the governors were too attentive. I would have no chance to repeat the measurements if I drew any more attention to either myself or Millicent's research.

But August was months away, and I had a suspicion that time was growing short. Pace and Kortnoz had forced the governors' hand—or the Littoral League's, which had drawn the governors' attention, same thing. The answers now depended on what the Ickies could dig up from the satellite photos.

I turned back to the beginning of the thesis. I needed to read the whole thing—the real thing. I ached to have the 'official' version so I could do a side-by-side comparison, but I'd have to rely on my memory. I'd spent long enough poring over it that I was pretty sure I could pick up major discrepancies, but it was the details that I wanted.

I went back to the guest room and got a notebook and pen out of my backpack. I would probably be more comfortable just sitting there at the desk, but I returned to the geography section because I'd quickly grown to love the library and didn't want to lose a minute of sitting amongst the books and the carved shelves.

I started taking notes on the things I noticed. A sentence, key to understanding Millicent's conclusions, that I didn't remember seeing before. A paragraph that read much more smoothly without the awkward qualifiers there'd been in the other version. Slowly, a very different picture was building up.

Because Millicent had spent hour after hour, week after week on the Mud Flats, she'd begun to notice small differences, things the casual visitor would never pick up. One morning she'd noticed a wide channel that was sharp-edged, straight, with mud ploughed up and crumbling along it as it dried in the sun. In an hour or two, when the tide rose again, it would have been as soft and sodden as the rest of the countless channels.

'In the absence of any other explanation, I conclude,' she wrote, 'that human intervention is a significant—and perhaps the only—factor in the failure of the delta to expand during the survey period.'

I hadn't remembered *that* from the other version, that was for sure. Human intervention. I read on. Millicent thought someone was dredging up the sediment as soon as it was deposited—filtering it, *looking* for something, then dumping it far out into Purple Bay so that they wouldn't keep looking through the same particulates over and over. The furrow in the mud, she thought, might be from dragging replacement equipment toward a waiting rowboat.

Why did the activity stop in August? Humans took vacations in August, at least in Krasnia. Universities were on break; even summer session was over by then. Lots of people were out enjoying Purple Bay—swimming, boating, fishing. It occurred to me that my dad always got cranky in August because the sudden upsurge in dilettante fishers, even at dawn, wrecked it for the regulars. The fish all headed out to deeper water for a few weeks, scared off by the motors and loud laughter and occasional beer bottle flung their way.

Was that the only reason the dredgers would need to hide during August? Might they also be hiding from vacationers who knew them? Vacationers who would be surprised to see them anywhere near Purple Bay when they should be hobnobbing with minor royalty in overseas cities or yachting outside territorial waters? Did that mean our dredgers were rich?

Rich, and with enough pull with the board of governors to alter research at will. Everything was pointing to the Praxicopolises. For some reason, they needed something in the mud that the Purple River dumped into the bay. And they'd been searching for it for at least eighty years, maybe more. They knew when whatever it was had washed downstream, because they were only interested in new deposits, new delta mud.

What else did the Praxicopolises have of value? The Littoral Codex, of course. Were they looking for the glass tablets, then? But those wouldn't have washed downstream, they'd have sunk to the bottom of any stream they were thrown into, and stayed there.

In the *Reminiscence*, Millicent had talked about seeing a boat offshore, and flashes of light that were the same colours as the tablets. The tablets were probably known to someone back then, so why not the Praxicopolises?

I realised that with the Infonet—the exponential growth of information and ways to share it around—it must eventually have become impossible for even the Praxies to keep up with *everything*. Which was probably why Pace and Kortnoz had been able to stay out of their scrutiny for so long. But clearly those days were over.

For them. But maybe not yet for me. Nicki hadn't told her brother my name, and my only claim to fame was that two years ago, I'd tried to steal the research of the extremely high-profile Pace Garoux. As far as the university community was concerned, now that I'd been taught a lesson, I was irrelevant. For once, being in Pace's shadow was coming in handy.

I had a very strong hunch, aided by the complaints from my stomach, that it was nearing lunchtime. I placed the thesis back on the shelf. It had been safe enough here for eighty years.

I was hoping I'd see someone in the canteen who could give me an update or, better yet, a plan. Waiting around for other people to have the ideas was something I was rapidly losing my taste for, but I didn't see many options. And I sure wasn't going to hear anything all alone in the library.

But I did. I heard one of the doors click open, and two people talking in soft voices. I ducked back into the alcove and stayed very still; I was already getting into the habits of secrecy and clandestine observation. I could barely hear them for the first few minutes, but apparently they were starting to annoy each other, because they got significantly louder.

'How do we know it's sudden? No one's paid any attention to those bugs for, what? Eighty years? Ninety? It's been so long since any of those myopic dweebs in Entomology have done any field work at all—I think it was an undergrad who found them, anyway.'

'Who?'

'Have you heard of Danny Snotnose Wexler?'

'Everyone's heard of—really? You're kidding.'

'Anyway, we'd better get looking. Canteen opens for lunch soon, and I'm hungry.'

Their voices dropped again. I peeked over the brass railing to see them browsing the stacks. 'Ha!' said one. 'Here it is!'

'Great! Let's see—*Registry of Radio-Station Ownership*, from the Government Printing Office. That's it all right.'

'We already know the Praxies have owned virtually every radio station in Purple Bay since radio was invented.'

'Not quite, and this book will prove it. If we can demonstrate that they've brutally and systematically squashed diversity of media ownership, there's a chance we can make a strong enough anti-monopoly case to bring this to court. Maybe even the high court.'

I frowned. Was Danny involving them in his special project? Or had they independently been asking the same questions?

They walked out of the library, taking the book with them.

I'd thought the fight against the Praxicopolises was just Ty and Pace. But it was also an army of librarians, researchers, students, and retired professors, along with an underground labyrinth, a network of safe houses and spies, a sophisticated battle plan, and … and me.

I sat back down in the alcove, feeling a bit wobbly. But maybe that was just hunger. I made myself get back up and walk to the canteen. I didn't have too much trouble finding it again: the scent of food drew me. It wasn't long before I'd loaded a plate with pot roast, carrots, potatoes au gratin, and green beans with almonds. I glanced at the dessert section as I made my way to a table. Lemon meringue pie. This sure beat my usual Sunday lunch of peanut butter on stale crackers. I sat down and started eating enthusiastically. The pot roast, luckily, was tender enough that I could cut it with my fork, as my wrist was still killing me.

'Can I join you?' It was Joan.

'Oh—hi. Sure.'

'How'd you sleep?'

'All right, thanks.'

'Have you had a chance to look around the library yet?'

'Yes, it's fantastic!' I started to tell her about finding Millicent's handwritten draft, but it was as if Millicent had murmured in my ear, *Tell no one that this copy exists. No one!* 'Who built all this, anyway?' I said, mainly to cover my false start.

'Believe it or not, we don't know. At one point there was only one person left who knew it even existed, and he told the people who started our organisation how to get in, but not who made it, or why. He's dead now, so we just have to make our guesses. We're pretty sure it's always been used by people affiliated with the university, but you can imagine what the board of governors would do with a library collection like that. It looks like they've always been the way they are, and there's always been a group of people trying to thwart them.'

'Who was that guy? Who told you about the labyrinth?'

'That's as good a name for it as any, but we tend to call it the Sewers. A bit of verbal camouflage, as well as a touch of irony. Anyway, I think his name was Gartner.'

I tried to hide my reaction. Gartner, as in Russ Gartner? Russ hadn't been kidding about being part of an academic dynasty.

'We've managed to set up an appointment this afternoon for you to get that wrist x-rayed, by the way.'

'Another agonising crawl through the tunnels.' I was trying hard not to sound ungrateful, but it was a challenge.

'No, it's okay—we've brought in a mobile x-ray unit. You would not believe how small those things have gotten in the last few years. It's the size of a television set! We just carried it in here in a cardboard box.'

'Nobody will notice it's been borrowed?'

'Not on a Sunday. We really ought to invest in one for here, shouldn't we? If you want, we can take care of the x-ray as soon as you're done eating. I'll let Dr Compton know to meet us in the infirmary.'

'Okay.' While Joan went over to the wall phone to make the call, I concentrated on my food; eating one-handed meant I couldn't shovel it in as fast as I wanted, although as Millicent's champion perhaps I had an obligation to be a bit more genteel. It was what she would have preferred, I was sure.

I finished up and got my dessert. I didn't care if Joan had to wait for me, I wasn't going to pass up lemon meringue pie for anything or anyone. When I was done, it was only her scrutiny that kept me from picking up the plate in my good hand and licking it clean.

The infirmary wasn't far from the canteen. It was set up in what looked like a rather aristocratic and opulent old study of about a century before, or at least what I figured one might have looked like, based on movies I'd seen. There was a fair bit of heavy wood-and-leather furniture, old maps on the walls, and glass cabinets full of shells and bits of pottery. A couple of folding camp beds were set up, unused, toward the back of the room. The mobile x-ray unit stood on the massive table; in contrast it looked quite futuristic, even extraterrestrial.

Dr Compton was waiting for us. 'What took you?' she said irritably.

'Lemon meringue pie,' said Joan, with a meaningful look in my direction.

'Sorry,' I said, but I wasn't, really.

Dr Compton gave us all lead-lined aprons to wear that came up around our throats and down to our knees. She was in a foul mood, more than just the three minutes I'd taken to eat a piece of pie could explain.

She got her revenge, though, when she positioned my wrist on the x-ray machine. I yelled.

'Sorry,' she said. There was a buzz and a click, and she said,

'Done. Take a seat and I'll get this processed and show you what's going on.'

I cradled my now-throbbing wrist and sat in one of the enormous chairs. Joan sat in another.

'Tell me about the Littoral League,' I said.

She blinked. 'Oh. Um … let's see. It was founded by Norella Honeycott, an idealist who went off the rails.'

'I know she wanted to aggregate all the research on the Codex, but what's she doing now? How many people are in the League? Where do they get their funding?'

'As for that, they probably apply for grants like other think tanks. Or maybe they do contract research to pay the bills. But I couldn't tell you who's in it, or what their projects are. I try to think about them as seldom as possible.'

I was shocked: a tear was sliding down her cheek. 'Are you okay?' I said.

'Yes,' she said, and wiped her cheek in a businesslike way. 'It's nothing.' Then she frowned, and said, 'No, it's not nothing. I'm not going to say that anymore. My husband died in a car accident not long after he left the League. He'd become disgusted with their secretive ways and their amoral methods, and he'd just handed in his key card. He came home that night and told me. I was ecstatic—I'd seen how it was eating him up to work there. The next day he was dead. It was ten years ago—no, more than that now.'

'I'm sorry. That you had to go through that.'

Joan shrugged and looked away for a moment. 'Anyway,' she said abruptly, 'we got a call from Pace this morning, from a payphone in one of the little towns along the coast. They're going to try to double back and make it to somewhere we can meet them. They want you to hand over the glass tablets.'

'Hang on. They didn't want to carry the tablets around. What makes them think they can keep them any safer than they could before? And what are they going to do with them when they're on the run? No.'

Joan stared at me for a moment. 'What?'

'No, I'm not going to give them the tablets. They're just being selfish, Pace is being selfish, and I'm sick of it.' I had no idea why this anger was sweeping over me at this moment, but I knew I was right. Angry people always know they're right.

'What am I supposed to tell them?'

'Tell them Celeste says no.'

'I have to tell you, the organisation leadership thinks it's a good idea to get the tablets out of here.'

'Then let me go, and I'll take them out of here.'

'You're not a prisoner.'

'Aren't I? I'll go get my things, then, and you can show me the way out.'

'All right,' said Joan. 'But can't you just wait until after Dr Compton has seen to your wrist?'

I hadn't been expecting her to acquiesce, and it was true that I didn't want to be running around with a broken wrist and no cast. 'Yes, all right.'

We sat silently then, waiting for Dr Compton. She brought the x-ray over and showed it to me. 'Not broken, luckily,' she said. 'See?' She pointed vaguely to the x-ray, and I nodded, even though I had no idea what a break might look like. 'The brace will do you. Keep it on for a couple of weeks, and see your own doctor as soon as you get the chance.'

'Thanks.'

'You're welcome,' she said without looking at me, as she packed the x-ray machine into a plastic case and left.

'I'll just go get my things together,' I said. 'Can you please point me to the right corridor?'

'Where will you go? Do you have somewhere lined up? How are you going to keep the tablets safe and secret? It would be a disaster if the Praxicopolises got them.'

'I'll think of something. Which way back to the library, please?'

'I'll go with you.'

'No, thanks, just point the way.'

'I only—'

'Why do you want to come with me? You're making me feel like I'm under surveillance or something.' I laughed casually.

'No, of course not.' We got up and went back out into the corridor. 'That way. Second left. First right.'

'Thanks, Joan. Where should I meet you to show me the way out?'

'I can come and get you in a few minutes. If that doesn't make you feel too scrutinised.' Her voice was even, but my unease twitched a bit and became the beginnings of fear.

'Say, fifteen minutes?' I said. 'I want to make sure I'm comfortable on the trip. If you know what I mean.'

I found my way back to the library and, once I was sure it was empty, ran and grabbed Millicent's manuscript. I hurried back to the guest room and hid the book inside one of my notebooks, then put it in the backpack and shoved some of my clothes around it and on top. I put the rest of my stuff in the gym bag, and went to the bathroom (because I really did have to). When I came back out, Joan was waiting for me. I picked up my backpack—which was now quite heavy indeed, with the glass tablets and the manuscript—and my gym bag, and followed her out.

'It's Sunday, but that doesn't mean you can be careless,' said Joan. 'I'm going to have to bring you to an exit near the duck pond. We're fairly sure it hasn't been discovered yet, but you're not going to look pretty when you get out.'

'That's fine,' I said.

She took a different passage and turned off it almost right away, and turned again off that passage. Soon what little sense of direction I had was gone.

'Keep going along here. You'll be fine,' said Joan. 'I have a librarian's afternoon tea and chamber-music concert this afternoon, and mud is not accepted attire.'

There was no 'Good luck' or 'Keep us posted.'

'Thanks,' I said, and started up the tunnel.

Chapter 11
Celeste Re-emerges

I began to go uphill, and the tunnel got dirtier and rougher and narrower. The concrete floor turned to gravel and dirt, and then to mud. Soon I was on my hands and knees, trying to keep my backpack from scraping too badly against the roof, and pushing my gym bag across the mud ahead of me. I was nearly at the point of having to crawl on my stomach when I noticed daylight. The tunnel sloped upward sharply, and I looked up to see a hole framed with reeds.

Pushing my head and shoulders past my gym bag, I stuck my head up and had a cautious look around. I couldn't see anyone. I reached up and pushed the gym bag onto a clump of reeds I could reach through the entrance, then my backpack. Finally, I scrabbled up. I was covered in mud. I was glad I had some extra clothes to change into; otherwise it would have been interesting trying to explain to the bus driver why I looked like the entertainment at a seedy bar.

I saw no one, so I waded through the mud until I got to some trees (and firmer ground). I emptied my gym bag onto the grass and brought it back to the water's edge, where I swirled it in the greenish water to get the mud off. After a moment's hesitation, I ducked my head down into the water as well, and splashed and rubbed to get the worst of the mud out of it, and off my hands and face. I had to take the brace off to rinse it as well, which made my wrist extremely unhappy.

Back in the trees, I used yesterday's shirt to wipe my face, hair, and hands, and to wipe as much mud as I could off my backpack. I didn't care if my gym bag got soaking wet, but I didn't want to damage the manuscript by carrying it around in a dripping backpack. I quickly stripped off and put the clean clothes on. I'd have to shower at the gym. I checked my watch (I was glad it was water-resistant): two o'clock. The gym would be open for another two hours.

I plodded across campus. My gym bag, now heavy with wet, muddy clothing, cut into my shoulder and dripped down my back and leg. Something in my backpack was digging into my spine. My wet shoes and socks were giving me blisters. My wrist ached. I was confused and angry and scared. I knew I looked like hell.

'Celeste?'

I turned around. Oh, God. It was Russ. His eyes were wide, his expression startled and concerned.

'Celeste, what *happened*?'

I opened my mouth, but nothing came out at all.

'Come on, we'll get a cab or something, I'll take you home.'

'No—not home. It's staked out.'

He didn't even ask for an explanation. 'Your parents don't live too far, do they? We'll get you there.'

I shook my head again.

'Well, then, my place. How many people know we're together?' Again, that swooping lurch in my stomach—*we were together*.

'Pace. And my parents, sort of. And those students of yours who heard you ask me to lunch that day.' Last week, last lifetime.

'That's all right, then. You'll be safe enough at my place for a little while.'

I didn't even want to argue.

'Cabs usually won't go to Beggar's Pit,' he said. 'We can wait for a bus, or we can walk.'

I thought about walking with the scraping pain growing in my feet. Then I thought about sitting, damp, dirty, and distressed, at a bus stop for what could be over an hour. 'Walking is fine.'

Russ said, 'Let me take one of those bags.' He reached for the gym bag.

'It's wet,' I said.

'That's okay. In return for carrying it, once we get to my place, maybe you'll tell me why you were swimming in the duck pond.'

As we walked, I said, 'I thought you told me you only lived *near* Beggar's Pit.'

'Welllll, right on the edge.'

'In more ways than one.'

'The rents are very cheap there.'

'There's a reason for that.'

The neighbourhoods deteriorated as we approached Beggar's Pit. Streets had a bit more litter, buildings a bit more graffiti. There were more fences and more empty storefronts. Soon there began to be more broken windows, then a stretch where every window had bars. Finally we got to the part where nobody bothered with bars anymore, because they had nothing to steal, and the only people out on the street were the homeless.

Russ turned into a side street and took his keys out of his pocket. He let us into the stairwell of a building that had three floors. We walked up to the top floor, and he unlocked two dead-bolts on his apartment door and opened it with a flourish.

'Welcome, and be at ease. I shall for thy sustenance and repose provide.'

I stepped inside. It was a small apartment, fairly neat and clean, nondescript except for a large bronze sculpture in the corner. It was abstract, with lines of such grace and power that I couldn't take my eyes off it.

'Wow,' I said.

'Mom's pretty good, yeah.'

'What's it like, having a mom who can make something like that?'

'It gives you a lot to live up to. My dad is absolutely besotted with her, even after thirty years of marriage.' He closed the door behind us and bolted both locks.

'Tough neighbourhood, if you deadbolt the door even when you're home and awake,' I said. 'Expecting thugs to burst the door down?'

'No, but you are,' he said. 'You're a wreck. Big circles under your eyes—at least, I can see one under the eye that isn't black—all the mud, and what happened to your wrist?'

'Would you mind if I had a shower? I'd feel a lot better if I were clean and warm and dry.'

'Oh—sorry, what was I thinking? I'll get you a towel. Do you want to use my bathrobe? I could do a load of laundry so you could have clean clothes. I have plenty of coins, it's fine. Would you like a coffee?'

I suddenly felt like laughing. 'What you were thinking, can't answer that. Towel, yes please. Bathrobe and laundry … it seems a bit intimate for this stage of the relationship, but these are desperate times, aren't they? Coffee—oh, yes, please.'

Russ went into the bedroom and came back with a neatly folded towel and a bathrobe. 'Just throw your stuff outside the door and I'll wash it along with what's in the gym bag. Anything else to wash?'

I took off my backpack and opened it, and put the clothes I'd wrapped around the manuscript into my gym bag with the muddy clothes, then I put the gym bag near the bathroom door. Once in the bathroom, I stripped off for the second time that day, then stood in a torment of embarrassment and indecision—I really didn't want to put muddy underwear back on, but it seemed so … revealing to give it to Russ to wash. But it seemed coy, even ludicrous, to hide it from him. I put it in the gym bag and reached the bag out through the door before I could change my mind.

'Got it,' he said. 'I'll lock the door behind me and go and start the laundry. Help yourself to shampoo and stuff. See you in a few minutes.'

'Okay—thanks!'

The shower was wonderful. Any shower would have been

wonderful, I supposed, but the water pressure was just right, the smell of the soap was just right, the shampoo made my hair squeaky, and the towel was heavy and soft. I'd left the brace in the sink, and I washed off the mud and swamp water. Despite the pain in my wrist, I decided to leave the brace off, rather than wear it all wet.

I put Russ's bathrobe on and looked in the mirror. The shoulder seams went way down my arms and it wrapped half again around me and reached below my knees. Tying the belt was awkward with one hand, but even so I felt more comfortable than I had in a long, long time. I was also pleased to see that the black eye was fading to yellow and green—it might even be gone entirely in a few days.

I rubbed the towel through my hair a second time, just because I liked the feel of it, and came back out. Russ was waiting for me at the table, with a mug of coffee.

'You sure do scrub up good, ma'am,' he said gormlessly. 'That bathrobe looks mighty good on you.'

'Thanks,' I said. I'd thought for an instant about trying to come up with some sort of witty retort, but I was feeling too relaxed. I sat at the table. 'And thanks for the coffee.'

'I have all your clothes held hostage,' he said. 'You'll have to stay here until the dryer is done working its evil will on them. Mwa-ha-ha.'

'I've never dated an actor before. It's … very entertaining.'

'It's who we are, it's what we do,' he said. 'It's how we pay the rent, if we're lucky.'

'If it's that precarious, why do you do it?'

'A lot of us offset the uncertainty with other jobs, of course. I'm lucky enough to have a job teaching what I love, instead of shelving groceries or phoning people during dinner to sell them raffle tickets. So I'm not complaining. But …' He gazed out the window as he spoke. 'But there's absolutely nothing in the world like standing up there on stage, with thousands of people all reaching out to you, all saying, Take me somewhere magical. And you know you have the power. So you say, Come on, I know where we're going, you can rely on me. You take them to this amazing place where their dreams and their secret, desperate hopes and their loneliness and their own special powers all join with yours. And you all make a new, miraculous universe.' He took a sip of coffee. 'And two hours later they go home to their kids and their jobs and the dishes in the sink, but for once they look at it and it all seems precious and meaningful.' He looked up. 'That's why. Because it is the best feeling in the world, to do that for them, to know that you can.'

'Wow,' I said.

'Why geography?'

'Because for me, it's the best feeling in the world to *understand*. To see how the patterns all go together. To trace, I don't know, human endeavour through time and space. To marvel at how ingenious we humans are, how we solve problems and make things happen. Nobody really knows much about how we do what we do, how it all works, *why* it all works. It's a fabulous puzzle, and the more we know, the more beautiful and impossible it gets.'

'You sound like my dad.'

'You sure don't sound like *my* dad. He's a planner at Purple Bay Council.'

'I'd be hopeless at that. I'd spend my days arranging the stuff on my desk into artistic collages, and writing comedy routines based on the memos.'

'I think my dad does that anyway. He just makes sure he gets the regular stuff done as well.'

'Multi-talented.'

'Not really. The comedy routines are awful. And the cleaners keep throwing his collages out.'

'What on earth were you doing wallowing in the duck pond?'

'Ah, I thought you'd get around to that.'

'Are you going to tell me?' I didn't say anything. 'Celeste, I really care. I'll really listen. I really want to help, whatever it is, whatever you need.' He looked down, then leaned forward and stared at me intently. 'Celeste, I'm falling in love with you, for God's sake. Please, can't you tell me? I'm worried.'

The room whirled around me and took my stomach with it, and when it all settled down again, everything was different. I took a deep breath, held it for a second, and let it out again. 'Have you ever heard of the Littoral Codex?'

'Sure, everyone has. Ancient secret wisdom, woooo-ooooo.'

'That's it. Pace and Kortnoz think they've found the key to deciphering it.'

'You're joking. How?'

'They're not really sure, and won't know until they can get access to the Codex. But it's based on something they recovered from a sea cave along the coast from here.' I got up and brought my backpack over. I took out the glass tablets, unwrapped them, and set them on the table.

'That's it?' he said. 'They look like props from a bad science-fiction movie. I should know, I've been in a few of 'em.'

'Really? Which ones?'

'Don't change the subject.'

'Okay.' I gestured at the tablets. 'Pace and Kortnoz and I went and got them, and this big helicopter came and people shot at us, and Kortnoz said they were from the Littoral League, but he fired some sort of rocket at them and they went away, but then I got attacked, and you know about that, and then our office was broken into but they didn't find anything, but they wrecked Millicent Strudthorne's thesis and they squished Pace's bugs. And then I was supposed to go over to Kortnoz's for dinner with him and Pace on Friday night, but they weren't there and then when I got home I found a note from Pace that said she'd hidden the tablets up in that lava cave where one time she dangled me over the pit. She asked me to go get the tablets and take them somewhere safe and secret. And so the next day, yesterday, was the museum, that was really fun, and I went to dinner with my friend Drusy at the retirement home, and she said she'd fix up a safe place and send someone for me, and so I went to my folks' place, and then Joan Maher showed up and said, Let's go get the tablets, so we did, but we were attacked on the way and I hurt my wrist, and then she took me to this huge underground labyrinth, did you know there was a labyrinth under the campus? You should see the library! But they tried to get me to give them the tablets, or at least Joan did. So I said, Show me the way out and I'll find my own safe place. And Joan couldn't very well say no, because that would make it look like she was trying to get the tablets for herself. But I'm *not* safe, not yet. I was going to go to the retirement home and ask Drusy what to do.'

'You don't think Drusy set you up?'

I hadn't thought of that. But I couldn't believe it. 'No, I don't think so. I just don't, that's all. I don't think she knows what Joan tried to do.'

'So that's still where you want to go.'

'Drusy knows a lot about the Codex, and the Littoral League, and the Praxicopolises.'

'What do they have to do with this?'

'They have the Codex. They bought it, or extorted someone for it, or something. Are you really falling in love with me?'

'Uh-huh.'

'Even after I told you all this?'

'Especially.'

'I don't get that at all.'

'That's okay. Are you falling in love with me?'

'Uh-huh,' I said. It felt like being at the top of a roller coaster to say it. I'm not a big fan of roller coasters (not like Pace), but I said it anyway.

Russ smiled then, a beautiful, open smile of relief, and the roller coaster rushed down the slope and back up again with a terrifying and exhilarating roar. He stood up, took my good hand, and drew me gently to my feet. Then we kissed, and somehow the bathrobe became just a formality. I was losing myself in the feel of his hands on my back when he pulled away slightly.

'I don't have any …um …'

'Oh,' I said. 'Rats.'

'I wasn't really expecting this.'

'Me neither. And I haven't carried any around since I was nineteen and it made me feel cool.'

'I think we'd better stop now, because in another minute I'm not going to care whether I have any or not.'

'Yeah,' I said. 'Rats.'

'Gives us something to look forward to.'

'Yeah. No, um, no drugstores nearby?'

'Nobody's rash enough to put a drugstore in Beggar's Pit.'

'Oh,' I said.

'Rats,' he said.

I cleared my throat and pulled the bathrobe closed again. I sat down and drank my coffee. It gave me something to do other than running my hands over Russ's body.

'You don't know anything about the glass tablets, then?' said Russ as he, too, sat down. 'Other than they're supposed to be for deciphering the Codex?'

'Drusy thought they may be some kind of polarising filters, used to reveal secret writing. Millicent Strudthorne doesn't seem to have known about them, based on her *Reminiscence*, but hang on, let me show you.' I got the *Reminiscence* out of my pack and found the page that talked about the flashes of light.

Russ read it, then picked one of the tablets up and held it to his eye. Then he positioned it so sunlight from the window fell through it. He put the book in the beam to make the coloured light fall on the white paper. 'Nope,' he said. 'Nothing special. Why five filters?'

'Different layers of secret writing? Needing to combine the filters? Some sort of safeguard, so that the system only works with all the filters together?'

He shook his head as if to clear it. 'I guess we'll find out.'

'I guess I just involved you, didn't I? Damn, I was trying not to.'

'Why, because of all the guns and knives and fisticuffs?'

'Something like that, yes.' I wrapped the tablets up and put them back in my pack.

'What if I say I'm willing to risk it?'

'I'd have to say … that you're a grownup and you make your own decisions, wouldn't I? No matter how much the decisions worry me. Because I'd expect the same from you.'

'That's a pretty good way to work it, I think. Hey, there's a game on television. Why don't we watch it while we're waiting to transfer the hostages to the dryer?'

'You have a television?'

'One of my cousins gave it to me. He's in real estate, and he feels sorry for me. So when he got his super-huge home theatre—'

'You're joking.'

'I am not. When he got his home theatre, he gave me his old television. Oh. Um, it's in the bedroom.'

'So I'm supposed to go into your bedroom with you, while I'm dressed in absolutely nothing but your bathrobe, and we're supposed to *watch* the *game*?'

'Not such a good idea, huh?'

'Well, in some respects it's a terrific idea. But not until you find a drugstore.'

He looked at his watch. 'I can be back in half an hour.'

I felt all giggly. 'Okay, then.'

Another smile from Russ, this one dazzling and mischievous. 'I'll lock the doors behind me, if that's all right. They open from the inside without a key, so you're not trapped or anything. I'd just feel better if I knew you weren't sitting here with the door unlocked.'

'Sure. Don't be too long, though, okay?'

He kissed me again and my knees wobbled. 'Go *now*,' I said. 'And *hurry*.'

When the door closed behind him, I sat on the sofa for quite some time, staring into space and grinning. In spite of everything, all the confusion, injuries, and scares, this was a very good thing. This was the big good thing in my life.

I could have passed the time reading Millicent's manuscript or finishing the *Reminiscence*, but that was too sharp a reminder of all the big bad things in my life. Instead I started perusing Russ's bookshelf. There was a whole section of books by various Gartners: textbooks, collections of essays, even a couple of novels. Interspersed were books by authors with other last names; I was assuming they were on his mother's side. There were also several shelves of plays along with books on acting theory, playwriting, and stagecraft. About what you'd expect. I took one off the shelf: *Lies for Money: A Materialistic Deconstruction of the Actor's Craft.* I rolled my eyes. Inside the front cover, someone had written, 'To Russell, all my love forever, XXOO Miffy.' I felt a hot spike of jealousy. Who was this Miffy? I put it back on the shelf.

Nearby was an autobiography called *I Debuted in a Dirty Garage.* I took it to the sofa to read. The author had been a famous stage actor, no longer quite in fashion, as he had aged somewhat cantankerously. It had a lot about the Purple Bay arts scene of about twenty years ago. I turned to the index. 'Praxicopolis, Angelo' had about a dozen entries, and I started looking them up.

Angelo, the impoverished player in pit orchestras and ad-hoc chamber groups. Angelo, the composers' advocate and tireless champion of new music. Angelo, the inspired and gifted teacher. Angelo, the reluctant head of a musicians' strike that crippled Krasnian arts for months but resulted in wage safeguards that were in place to this day. Angelo, brilliant and innovative collaborator in the fields of opera and musical theatre. Angelo, amateur linguist and enthusiastic spelunker.

Looking for the glass tablets, were you, Angelo? I thought.

The index turned up nothing for either 'Littoral Codex' or any of the other Praxicopolises. As the actor himself seemed to richly deserve his reputation as a self-absorbed old curmudgeon, I soon tired of the book itself. I put it back and resisted the urge to open the Miffy book and glare at the inscription.

My wrist started to ache again, and I wished the brace were dry. I'd have to ask Russ if he had a bandage or something. How romantic.

Someone pounded on the door, and I jumped a mile; the jolt made my wrist flare into real pain. I slowly and quietly moved off to one side of the apartment, away from the door.

'Russell?' called a voice—a *woman's* voice. 'Russell, it's me, let me in. I know you're home.'

I wondered, with a sick, angry feeling, whether this was Miffy.

'Russell!' More pounding. 'You coward!'

I held utterly still, lest I brush against something and knock it over. She'd never leave if she thought Russ was in here.

'All right, I get it,' she hollered. 'You don't want to go out with me anymore. But if you just gave it another—shit.' And there was silence, except for the sound of her running down the stairs.

'That'll teach you to come around here making all that racket,' yelled another voice, querulous and with a heavy North Kras accent. 'Next time I'll bloody fire it!'

'Shut up, you stinking Northie!' yelled someone from another apartment. 'You don't like it, go back where you came from!'

Just what my poor jangled nerves needed, an afternoon of idyllic peace and quiet in Purple Bay's finest neighbourhood. I could tell one thing about my relationship with Russ right from the start: there was no way on this green earth I was going to be moving in here.

I tiptoed over to the sofa and sat there as quietly as I could, curled up with my good arm wrapped around my legs. I rested my hurt wrist, palm up, along the top of my knees. My fingers, curving softly up from my palm, reminded me of a baby bird I'd seen once that had fallen from its nest. The euphoria of just a few minutes ago was gone, and I felt fragile and frightened. And that made me feel ashamed and anxious. Russ was in love with a brave, strong, smart woman who laughed off assaults and clandestine adventures with a toss of her hair. Would he still be in love if he saw me, crouched and quivering, jumping at shadows?

I sat and stared out the window at the brick wall of the building next door. Maybe I rocked back and forth a little.

Finally, I heard the keys in the locks, and Russ bounded in. 'I took an extra minute to put your stuff in the dryer,' he said. 'Not that I'm in a hurry for you to leave—what? What happened?'

'Not such a nice neighbourhood, Russ. Someone claiming to be a former girlfriend came by hammering on the door.'

'Oh, God,' he groaned, and buried his head in my shoulder. 'How embarrassing.' I felt his lips move against my neck as he talked, which was doing amazing things toward making me feel a bit better.

'We broke up, well, I broke up with her, a few months ago. I came to a few realisations, that's all. She did not agree that this was a good decision.'

'So she's stalking you.'

'Not exactly. Not very often. Just once in a while she figures surely I'll have come to my senses by *now*.'

'And then someone in one of the other apartments came out and it sounded like he waved a gun at her, because she ran off.'

Russ laughed. 'Bruno! He's great. I don't think he even has any cartridges for that thing. I don't *think*, anyway.'

I felt better still that Bruno was not a raving mass-murderer who just hadn't found his true expressive outlet yet. 'And someone else yelled at him to go back where he came from.'

This time Russ scowled. 'Bruno gets that a lot in this neighbourhood. You'd think the downtrodden would stick together, wouldn't you?'

'So, um, this ex.'

'I don't want to talk about her. I—' he kissed me 'don't want—' another kiss 'to talk at all.'

This made me feel much, much, much better. I was almost back to my old self. 'Shall we go and … watch the game?' I said.

'Oh, yeah,' he said vaguely. 'The game.'

We didn't watch the game.

A bit later, I said, 'Unfortunately, at some point I'm going to have to go.'

'Please stay. It's good tactics, to stay in Beggar's Pit. They'd never think to look for you here. I'll make dinner. You can sleep here. Tomorrow—you're not going to teach, are you?'

'Drusy said she'd get one of the retired geography professors to cover my classes. I'm a little edgy, because I've met the guy she's sending over, and he's a bit of a wild character.'

'You can stay here during the day at least.'

I shook my head. 'I'll be a nervous wreck, holed up in here with Bruno and his gun and the ex-girlfriend and the neighbourhood bigots all at the door. But I have to admit that staying the night here is something I'd really, really like to do.'

'Settled, then, at least for the night. Where to in the morning?'

'I've got to see Drusy, she's the only one I think I can trust to give me straight information. Joan is just plain scary, and is doing things that don't make any sense. Drusy should know about that, if nothing else.'

'I'll come with you in the morning, then go teach my classes. My first one is at ten, so we'd need to leave here at eight.'

'Maybe set the alarm for seven-fifteen then.'

'Or,' he said speculatively, 'I could set it for six. Since you don't mind waking up early.'

'Actors can't wake up at six, you said so.'

'For *some* things, I'll wake up at six.'

I pondered this for a moment. 'Let's just see, first, how late we're up tonight. I doubt I'll be feeling too particularly sleepy for some time, myself. How many of those things did you get?'

'Lots.'

Chapter 12
Celeste Hears Disturbing News

We did wear each other out that night. Dinner was spaghetti; nothing special, just what Russ had in the cupboard, but we had our minds on other things. Sleep, when we got around to it, was infinitely sweet. I didn't even mind the alarm, because it meant waking up with Russ.

At some point last evening he'd brought my clothes up from the dryer. I showered and dressed in about five minutes.

'Wow,' said Russ. 'You weren't kidding—I think that's a world record for getting ready.'

'I'm not much of a primper, I'm afraid.'

'Not a problem. You're absolutely gorgeous anyway.'

I tried, just barely successfully, not to giggle. Once we were outside waiting for the bus, though, I felt all too solemn. Russ caught my mood. The bus was right on time, quarter to eight, and we rode in silence to University Park. Every now and then he would hug me or kiss the top of my head. Nothing too insistent, just a reminder that he cared.

There was yet another desk attendant on duty at the retirement home. 'My name is Celeste Carlucci,' I said. 'I'm here to see Drusy Kelso. She's not expecting me, but it's important.'

The attendant buzzed Drusy's apartment and spoke quietly with her, then hung up. 'Go ahead,' she said. At least this one didn't say it with a snarl or a sneer.

Drusy, still in her nightgown and slippers, was waiting for us in the doorway of her apartment.

'Come in, come in, I've just put the coffee on.'

'I'm really sorry if we woke you,' I said. 'Oh—Drusy, this is my friend Russ. Russ, this is Drusy.'

Drusy motioned us inside. As I followed Russ past her and into the apartment, she looked at me with a raised eyebrow and a half-smile, and nudged me with her frail, bony elbow. I blushed.

Drusy sat us down at the table and brought over a bowl of fruit before sitting down as well. 'Help yourself,' she said. 'If you'd like cereal or toast, please let me know.'

'This is great, thanks,' I said, and took an apple.

'This is an unusual time to be paying a visit,' she said. 'But I won't deny I've been worried, ever since our colleague showed up Saturday morning to find you'd already left.'

A cold wave crashed over me. 'Then … Joan Maher … you didn't send her.'

Drusy's eyes narrowed. 'Maher. From the library.'

I nodded.

'Tell me everything that happened. I'm in no rush. Neither are you.'

'But I've got to teach at nine.'

'Lenny's covering, remember?'

'Russ has to teach, too.'

'Oh?' said Drusy, her face lighting up. 'What do you teach?'

'Dramatic arts,' said Russ.

'I'll keep that in mind,' she said. She turned back to me. 'He can go when he needs to, I'm sure. Start talking, sweetie.'

I told Drusy about Joan's arrival at the house, our battle on the trail, retrieving the tablets, the labyrinth, the library, and what I couldn't help thinking of as my escape. While I talked, she brought the coffee, milk, and sugar to the table, but never interrupted. It was a surprisingly long story, and by the time I was done we'd all finished our coffee. Russ was looking at me with such admiration that I blushed again.

'Wow,' he said. 'Just … wow.'

'Celeste, sweetie,' said Drusy, 'after a story like that, if you think for one minute I'm going to let you go back to your apartment, you are just going to have to adopt a new modality of thought.'

'She can stay with me,' said Russ.

'Oh, you'd like that,' said Drusy with sly humour.

'Well, yes, actually.'

'Me, too,' I said. I was minding less and less about the rebuffed girlfriend.

'Well, I was going to say Celeste could stay with me, but if you'd rather—'

'We'd rather,' said Russ, with just enough eagerness to make Drusy laugh. 'I'll go over to your place with you so you can get some things,' he said to me. 'When and where should I meet you?' He stood up; it was time for him to leave for campus.

'I think it's best if you stay here during the day, Celeste,' said Drusy. 'I'll be happy for the company, I don't mind telling you. What time are you done teaching, Russ?'

'My last class finishes at three.'

'That will work out fine. I have an online chat with my economics buddies scheduled for five, and I'd hate to be rude and leave you sitting here while we all typed at each other. Celeste, honey, does Russ have the number of that phone I gave you?'

'Um, no, I don't even know what it is.'

Drusy wrote on a piece of paper and handed it to Russ as he and I walked to the door.

'See you later,' I said. 'I'll fill you in on everything.'

He kissed me. 'See you.'

I sat back down at the table, and Drusy poured another coffee for each of us. 'A very nice young man,' she said. 'He looks familiar. What did you say his name was?'

'Russ. Gartner.'

'Gartner! That was it! He looks just like Graham Gartner.'

'That's his dad.'

'He took an economics class from me once. Very smart boy.

Nice to see he finally put those books away and found a woman to settle down with.'

'Um. Yes.' There were no secrets at Purple Bay University, clearly. 'So … now what do I do? I don't know how to find Pace and Dr Kortnoz. I'm tired of carrying those damned tablets around and feeling like a target. Joan Maher gives me the creeps. And why does everyone care so much about those blue-headed *bugs*?' I took a drink of coffee to try to stop my own babbling.

'As for what you do now,' said Drusy, 'you try to calm down a bit. How's that wrist doing?'

I held out my left wrist. My flesh bulged out around the brace, and had turned even more colours than my black eye. I was shocked—I'd had no time to pay much attention to it until now.

'That looks absolutely horrible,' said Drusy. 'Does it hurt much?'

Quite suddenly, it did. 'Um …'

'That doctor gave you pain relievers, didn't she?' I nodded. 'Well?'

'I wanted to stay alert.'

'Take one, and have a nap. My friends and I will look out for you.' I guess my face must have shown what I was thinking, because Drusy raised her chin and said, 'So you're thinking that a bunch of old academics aren't worth much in a fight? Is that it?'

I shook my head frantically. 'No—'

'Because let me tell you something. Just because the board of governors made us retire at sixty-five, doesn't mean our *brains* retired. Maybe we move a little slower, maybe we're a little more frail. But we're *smart*. So smart, the governors are scared of us. They keep changing the staff so we don't get close to any of them—that way they close off a potential line of information for us. Our Infonet connection here keeps "failing". Same with the elevators—ever try to get a good conspiracy going when you can't manage the stairs? But we do manage. And, Celeste, if you're starting to piece together information that spells trouble for the governors, we'll keep you just as safe as you need to be until you can bring them down. And not only that, but we'll come in handy. You put us all together, and we know a hell of a lot, young lady, a hell of a lot.'

She stared at me defiantly. Finally I said, 'I … I know. I know you do. Sorry. I didn't mean—'

'So take the pain reliever. You'll be fine for a few hours. And I don't trust that doctor, we'll have Abdul or Irina have a look at it. Now, where are those pills?'

Meekly, I took the bottle out of my pack.

'Take one.' She got a glass and filled it with tap water.

'The bottle says take two.'

'Take *one*. You had a point about not getting too fuzzy. One will dull the pain enough for you to sleep. God knows you won't be getting much sleep with that young man tonight.' She set the glass down in front of me and stood there until I took the pill.

'That's better. I'll get you a blanket and you can stretch out on the couch.'

But I couldn't sleep, despite the wooziness that pressed down on my thoughts. Instead, I drifted in a sort of waking nightmare, with images flashing and fading: the puffs of dirt I saw from under Kortnoz's vehicle as the bullets hit the ground around me, the sight of my own blood soaking the napkin that I pressed to my throat, the agonising crawl through the labyrinth, Joan Maher's strange expression as I insisted on leaving, the mud coating my clothes, my skin, my hair. And, again and again, the sunlight shining through the glass tablets.

When Drusy's phone rang, I sat straight up, my heart pounding. I heard her talking from the bedroom, but couldn't make out the words. After a minute, she came into the living room. She looked worried; her earlier defiance was gone. 'I have some bad news, sweetie. Your mother didn't show up for work today.'

I whispered, 'Mom …' and jumped up from the couch.

I don't know how she did it, but Drusy managed to get between me and the door. I couldn't very well run her over, but I danced around, frantically trying to get past her.

'You just calm down,' she said sharply. 'You won't be much use to your mother if you're tied up in the trunk of someone's car, will you?'

That got through, and I stood still, even though my heart was still pounding.

'It's no secret who your mother is,' said Drusy. 'She hasn't been involved in any activities against the governors, so it's obviously bait to get you. She's all right until they do get you, is what that means, so we have a little bit of time.'

'Why don't I just give whoever it is the tablets? They were just sitting there in that cave, anyway. Kortnoz made out like it was this tremendous coincidence—someone put them there! It's all trap within a trap within a trap!' I realised I was shouting.

Somebody pounded on Drusy's door, and I choked on my words. We stood in utter silence.

'Open up, damn it!' We started breathing again: it was Dr Garrick. Drusy let him in, and he stared sourly at me. 'Oh, it's you. You call those little snots geographers? I'd be ashamed to admit they were mine if I were you. I was halfway tempted to send them back to grade school to memorise the capitals of all the North Kras provinces, that would keep 'em humble. But I made a start at fixing them up for you, don't you worry.'

There went my tenure, although that didn't seem to matter to me now.

'Lenny, hush. We've got issues. Celeste's mother, Beatrice Golden, may be in some serious trouble. Fred in Personnel just gave me a call.'

I blinked. I vaguely remembered Fred as a gentle man who sat a few cubicles away from Mom and did something with envelopes all day until he could retire. Fred was one of these … wrinkly commandoes.

'How do we start looking for my mom?'

'I told you, sweetie, she's safe for a while, as long as *you* stay safe.'

'But what if they're hurting her?'

'There's no benefit in that, no reason to. If it's the governors, I will tell you right now they never do anything that has no benefit for them. And if it's the Littoral League, they're—'

'They're just a bunch of dangerous clowns,' said Dr Garrick. 'They don't have the kind of focus you need to be deeply evil. That's not to say they don't do some real damage, but usually it's by accident.'

'What about those people in the underground tunnels, the … the Sewers? Joan Maher?'

Drusy said, 'That's what's the most disturbing of all—those people are *our* people. Joan seems to have gone renegade. We'll have to follow that up—very disturbing.'

'What about my dad?'

'Where does he work?'

'Purple Bay Council.'

'He should be safe enough, then. How many security desks does someone need to get through to reach his office?'

'I think it's up to five now.'

Dr Garrick snorted. Drusy said, 'We'll have someone check to see that he got into work all right. Do you want us to take him to a safe place?'

'Will we find my mom before he gets off work at five?'

Drusy looked at me hard. 'We could. I hope we do.'

'Then he'll be all right. He even eats lunch at his desk most days.' Making decisions made me feel capable and businesslike. 'If I can't go out after my mom, what's the plan?'

Drusy gave me an approving look. 'You've got a knack for pulling yourself together. I told you that you had real courage. We don't have any insiders in the Littoral League, which is a pity, because they're the ones most likely to do something melodramatic and pointless like kidnapping.'

Dr Garrick said, 'We could check out the League lairs that we know about, and I could get Mark listening in on radio transmissions and the cell-phone network, that might turn something up.'

Drusy said, 'That's a start, anyway. Any suggestions on checking out what the governors are up to?'

'Since they shielded their communications, it's been a nightmare.'

'Maybe Mark's made some progress there, too.'

This was no jolly lark these people were running—this was a huge operation. One that had obviously been going on for years. A century or more, if the underground library was any indication. Maybe we stood a chance.

Dr Garrick sat down on the couch and dialled the phone. 'Mark, Lenny here. We need some surveillance on the League and the governors. Yes, both. Well, get Ruby to help you. Specifically? Celeste Carlucci's mother has been kidnapped. Beatrice Golden. Yes. Yes. No. Bye.'

He beckoned me over to the couch and patted the cushions next to him. I sat obediently, but I kept jiggling my knee up and down as he talked.

'I remember Kortnoz from back when he was a slimy-nosed undergrad, like those snots of yours I taught today. He had talent even then, but he didn't have the common sense God gave a cabbage. Still doesn't, obviously. He's gotten himself mixed up in something he clearly can't handle, and I'll have to bail him out, just like I used to. Words to live by: never, ever agree to be an academic adviser to someone whose preliminary thesis research involves wire cutters and gunpowder.'

'Sweetie,' said Drusy from the kitchen, 'why don't you update Lenny on what you've been doing the past few days?'

I told the story again. I wound up with, 'So I can't help wondering whether someone planted the tablets in the sea cave for Kortnoz to find.'

'That would mean there's someone who's been hanging onto them for a while—years, decades?—who thinks Kortnoz would be a better person to have them. And clearly plenty of someones who think *they'd* be the better person.'

'Why Kortnoz?'

'Maybe it's a question of dumping the tablets on the first person who seemed altruistic.'

Drusy's phone rang again. I was really starting to hate that sound. 'Hello, Mark—have you found anything?' she said. 'How much increase? Enough to mean they're coordinating a hostage transfer? Can you get a direction? That will have to be enough. Could you keep the cans on for a while? I'll bring you a coffee in a minute. Thanks. Bye.'

Drusy brought Dr Garrick a coffee, and, to my surprise, another one for me. 'Thanks!'

'Don't sound so surprised,' she said. 'I told you we'd look after you, and that can mean a lot of things. Mark Durakovic, the physicist, has been monitoring the airwaves for us. There's some unusual radio traffic originating in two places—up in the mountains, and west of the Mud Flats, where the escarpment starts to rise. Your mother could be in either place, although that doesn't narrow it down much, or she could be in neither. But it's something.'

'How does he know all this?' I said.

'You know physicists, always with the gadgets,' said Dr Garrick. 'Fiddle fiddle fiddle. The money Mark spends on that stuff could feed the teeming masses of North Kras.'

'It's come in handy more than once,' said Drusy tartly. 'Unlike some people I could mention.'

I sipped my coffee while Drusy made another. 'Celeste,' she said, 'why don't you come up with me to deliver this to Mark? You should meet him.'

'Okay.' I drank more quickly, so as not to delay her. The coffee was hot enough to make this very uncomfortable.

'Don't you think at *all*?' said Dr Garrick. 'You can take the coffee with you.'

'I've been under a fair bit of stress,' I said. 'Lighten up.'

Dr Garrick grinned. 'Good, goooooood! Hey, Drusy, you were right, she has got some guts. Hope it's enough,' he added, as if to himself.

'Let's go, sweetie,' said Drusy, and she and I left Dr Garrick in the apartment. 'I think the elevators are working today. Let's be optimistic.' She pressed the up button, and a minute later, the elevator arrived. We got out at the fifth floor and went down to the end of the hallway, where Drusy knocked on the door of the end apartment. A large man with lots of lines around his eyes and a pudgy face opened the door. He smiled, and I could see where the lines came from.

'Come in,' he said. Once we were inside, he stuck out his fleshy hand. 'I'm Mark Durakovic. Mark.'

'Celeste Carlucci.'

'Oh, I know—I've been listening to every radio and phone in Purple Bay for your name.'

'Sorry. I didn't mean to be a bother.'

'Are you kidding? I spent my entire childhood fooling around with amateur radio, hoping the chance would come to foil the bad guys. It only took another fifty years—I had no idea when I moved in what a blast it would be here!'

'I asked him right away—well, as soon as I was sure he wasn't a plant from the governors—if he wanted to help,' said Drusy. 'We can't let skills like Mark's go to waste, now, can we?' She set his coffee on the kitchen table.

'Oh,' he breathed. He picked up the mug, took a gentle sip, and closed his eyes. 'Thank you.'

'It's just a cup of coffee,' said Drusy, but she looked pleased. 'Now: anything else since a few minutes ago?'

'No, and those spikes from the bay and the mountains have dropped off, too. Still, it gives us something.'

'We have to find my mom before my dad gets off work, or he'll go off his nut,' I said. 'And I won't be able to cope with worrying about both of them.'

'Why don't you two make yourselves at home, then, and I'll have another listen.'

I stared around the apartment. One entire wall was a series of racks with electronic equipment. A big fat rope of cables disappeared into a neat opening cut into the wall—I assumed those went to the roof.

'How do you keep all this secret? The roof must look like an antenna forest,' I said.

'The governors don't trust us, but they're too busy and too closed-minded to think that we could have a major, organised operation,' said Mark. 'At least, that's what we're counting on.' He sat down in front of one of the racks and started tweaking the equipment. *Fiddle fiddle fiddle*, I heard Dr Garrick's voice saying.

'Good,' said Mark after a while. 'I just caught a transmission that suggests they have no idea where Celeste is. Where are you staying tonight, Celeste?'

'At her boyfriend's,' said Drusy.

'Ooooooo,' said Mark. 'Do a lot of people know you're together?'

'No,' I said. 'And he lives in Beggar's Pit.'

'Wow, that's heavy camouflage,' said Mark. 'Not even those idiots in the Littoral League will go there.'

'If they're so idiotic, why is Kortnoz so scared of them? And anyway, idiotic or not, they've got helicopters and guns,' I said. I didn't like to think I'd been so scared of a bunch of clowns.

'Oh, just because they can't plan and have no internal discipline and are led by someone who's mad as a cut snake, doesn't mean they aren't dangerous,' said Mark.

'In fact,' said Drusy, 'it's exactly why they *are* dangerous.'

Chapter 13
Celeste Finds Out Way Too Much About the Littoral League

As the day wore on, the adrenaline seeped away and left me leaden and despairing. I assumed Mark was still upstairs, listening for some word of my mom, but there were no updates along the way. The despair eventually gave way to a fretful restlessness. Drusy ignored this as long as it was just a question of my glancing at either the door or the phone every few seconds. But when I finally stood up, she was at my side in a moment, reaching up to press on my shoulder with a birdlike hand.

'Sweetie, please. Just wait a while longer.'

'But nothing is happening!'

'That's better than some of the things that *could* happen.'

I sat back down on the couch and buried my head in my arms. I wasn't interested in lunch.

At three-thirty there was a knock on the door. I gasped as a spasm of shock squeezed my lungs. Drusy looked through the peephole, then opened the door to Russ.

He took one look at me, hurried over to the couch with hardly more than a word to Drusy, sat down, and put his arms around me. 'What's wrong?' he said.

'Mom,' I said. 'She didn't show up for work this morning.'

'Well, why are we all just sitting here?'

'Drusy says to wait until we have more information. But my dad is going to get off work soon, and he's going to be a lot harder to control than I am.' I gave Drusy a resentful look, which she ignored.

'I could distract you with tales of my dismal day, how's that?' said Russ.

'Okay.' It beat staring at the walls.

'My lawyer called today. There's no precedent in the Legal Record of Krasnia for my case. It seems like nobody's ever fought a loyalty provision in a contract before.'

This was so bizarre that even through my worry I said, 'Nobody at *all*? Not in the military, not *anything*?'

'Military doesn't count, they have their own legal system. And no, not in circumstances like mine. Employers, it seems, have a perfect right to put loyalty clauses in their contracts, and they can define loyalty any way they want to.'

'Is it defined in your contract? Maybe you could fight it as being too vague.'

'Maybe, but because there's no precedent, my lawyer is starting from scratch to get the arguments together.'

'So … what's next?'

'I keep teaching. I have that play to operate on, and students who are counting on me, and I don't want to disappoint my dad, and I wouldn't mind being able to pay the rent.'

'Maybe … maybe you could get a big acting job.'

'Not in Purple Bay. I'd have to move to Lilia for that—don't tell me you're trying to get rid of me already?'

'Nuh-uh.'

'All right then. And not only that, but then Miffy stopped by, you know, my ex-girl—'

'Yeah. The one who comes by your apartment.'

'I *told* you. She's nuts. And twice in the space of a few days is nutser than usual. I'm thinking I may need to see if my lawyer knows a way to keep her away from me, you know, like she'll go to jail if she comes close to me or something.'

'She doesn't happen to offer an explanation for this sudden upsurge in interest, does she?'

'No,' said Russ. But his voice sounded funny.

'You're trying to keep me from worrying about it. What did she say?'

Russ took a deep breath, and I felt his heart beating against the arm I had draped across his ribs. 'You'd think an actor would be a better liar, wouldn't you?'

'Yeah. *What did she say*?'

'She ... um ... says that if I don't start going out with her again, she'll ...'

'*She'll what*?'

'Go to the governors and get them to downsize the Dramatic Arts department to a sub-branch of the debating team.'

'Cut your funding?' I whispered.

'Yup.'

'And ... and all the department's teaching positions?'

'Yup. Except for the chair; she'd end up as the adviser to the sub-branch. Stipend only.'

'But—I don't get it. Who is she, that she can just get the governors to do whatever she wants?'

'I don't want to tell you. It's embarrassing.'

'Russ ...'

'Miffy ... um ... Wexler.'

'Danny Snotnose Wexler's ...'

'Big sister.'

'Daughter of ...'

'The chair of the board of governors.'

'Oh, no, Russ.'

'Tell me about it. My parents were never so relieved in all their lives as the day we broke up.'

'Why did you go out with her in the first place?'

'People aren't their parents. At least, I thought so. But she ended up being a chip off the old block: charming, smart, capable, but utterly controlling. She wanted to pick out my clothes, which auditions I went to, which gigs I accepted, what journals I submitted articles to, it was a nightmare. I told her it was over after she bought me one black shirt too many.'

There was a moment's silence.

'Gee,' I said at last. 'Small town, Purple Bay, huh?'

Drusy cleared her throat. 'Russ, this young woman—she doesn't know you're seeing Celeste, does she? You didn't say, "Go away, I'm seeing someone else now"?'

'God, no. The last thing I wanted was for her to start showing up on Celeste's doorstep.'

'Good thinking. Very good thinking. You just might be worthy of her.'

I blushed and stared at the coffee table. Usually, it was Pace who drew all the admiration.

But Pace wasn't here to overshadow me. Still, she couldn't bail me out, either, as she'd done so many times. Never mind that in every case, the trouble she bailed me out of was trouble she'd caused in the first place. I was on my own now.

Just then, Russ gave me another hug, and Drusy brought over a plate of cookies, and I thought: not entirely on my own.

Another knock at the door. I turned around so quickly my skull nearly dislocated Russ's jaw. Drusy looked through the peephole again, then opened the door to Mark.

'Did you find her?' I said, before he could speak.

'I *may* have,' he said. 'I'm fairly certain I caught some phrases like "more trouble than she's worth" and "got a mouth on her". Does that sound like your mom?'

I grinned. Mom didn't usually have a temper. But when she did go off … 'Yup. Where is she?'

'The coast, as far as I can tell.'

'Well?' I stood up.

'What are we waiting for?' Russ, God bless him, stood up too.

Drusy said, 'You want to go out there now, hurt wrist and all, with a couple of frail old folks as backup, and take on an entire gang of kidnappers and who knows what-all else?'

'Well, yeah,' I said, like it should have been obvious.

'Well, too damn bad, because Mark isn't going to give you any clearer directions until we have a proper expedition mustered and equipped. So you may as well just sit back down while I make a few phone calls.'

Mark sat in the easy chair in serene silence. When it became obvious that Drusy meant it, Russ and I sat back down on the couch. I glared at Mark across the coffee table.

'Pace wouldn't let you push her around like this,' I said. 'She'd be out there tracking them down.'

'I've watched that young lady work,' said Drusy as she flipped through the pages of an address book. 'She's like a tsunami trying to get through the eye of a needle. No finesse at all. It's a wonder she's still alive.'

'Doesn't that mean her way works?'

'It means she's lucky, and she surrounds herself with people who are willing to keep saving her bacon,' said Mark irritably.

I thought Pace did all the saving. Except for the time I beat up Jasper Smith-Fennel, up near the headwaters of the Purple River.

Thinking of Jasper was unfortunate—not only because in and of itself it was a nasty experience, but because it reminded me that he'd been following me around. And that he'd wanted me to steal research from Kortnoz. Could he have known about the tablets? Or was there yet another arcane project that Kortnoz was working on? I thought of Kortnoz's rapt expression when he showed me the tablets, and I thought, no, when you love a project like that, there's only room in your heart for the one. It had to be the tablets Jasper wanted.

I heard Drusy's voice behind me as she talked on the phone, but I didn't pay much attention until she called over to me, 'Sweetie, what's your dad's name?'

'Pete Carlucci,' I said, feeling a new, sickening wave of worry swamp me. 'Uh … why?'

'He's fine, but you're right to worry what he'll do when he finds out your mom is missing. We're going to send a few people over to the Council building to break it to him and bring him over here. Running around loose is as bad an idea for him as it is for you.' She went back to her phone conversation.

'This is getting to be quite a circus,' I said bitterly. There was a reason Northies were famous for flying off the handle, and even though my father had been born in Krasnia, he was a through-and-through Northie when it came to temperament.

I'd thought the waiting was agony before. Now it was genuine torture. After all that coffee, I had to pee, but getting up and going to the bathroom wasn't much of a diversion, even with the challenge of trying to wash my hands without soaking the brace or wrenching my wrist. Damn Joan—it almost looked like she ditched me on purpose so I could be attacked and she wouldn't have to pretend to fight the attacker off. She gave me the creeps even worse than Jasper did, with her sly intimidation and her sneaky ways.

When I came back to the living room, I saw that three more people had arrived. I remembered two of them from when they'd walked me to the bus stop a few days before; the third was a big kid, and I mean really big, taller than Russ and twice as broad. Someone's grandson—I think Drusy said his name was Ozzie.

Dr Garrick appeared next, saying he'd had a nap and was ready to go. The apartment was getting cramped, and most of us were looking increasingly edgy—Ozzie kept cracking his knuckles, which creaked and snapped like old floorboards. I didn't care how big he was, if he didn't stop it soon, I'd smack him. The phone rang one more time.

'The minibus is here,' said Drusy. Instantly all the residents headed for the door, followed by Ozzie. Russ and I looked at each other. He shrugged, and we followed the mob into the hallway.

'I know better than to leave you behind with no one to keep you from doing something stupid,' said Drusy as she locked her apartment door. 'We'll meet you in the lobby.'

I gestured toward my backpack, still on the floor near the sofa. 'What about the ...?'

Drusy frowned. 'I suppose they'll be as safe here as anywhere. Safer than carrying them around, anyway.'

Russ and I pounded down the stairs. When we burst into the lobby, the kid on the desk was staring at the sight of a dozen old academics piling gaily into a bland minibus. I felt more than a bit annoyed: they were treating the abduction and possible torture of my mother a bit lightly.

Russ and I were the last onto the bus. 'Mousie!' I heard a voice calling. I craned my neck to see around the mountainous bulk of Ozzie's massive chest.

'Dad!' I pushed painfully past Ozzie and stepped gingerly around fragile knees and canes and orthopaedic shoes to find Dad sitting in the back row.

'Oh, God, Celeste, I was so worried! And where's your mother?'

One of the residents shifted aside so I could sit next to Dad.

'I don't know, Dad. My friends here may know where to find her. We'll just have to wing it and hope Mom's okay.'

We clung to each other. I heard Dad muttering something in North Kras dialect. It was a prayer that Grandma Carlucci had taught me when I was little. I said it softly along with Dad, even though I didn't remember what it meant.

As soon as the van pulled away from the retirement home, everyone fell utterly silent, and their faces became solemn. That made me feel better: the jollity had only been a trick to fool the desk attendant that they were off on a trip to the museum and a nice afternoon tea.

In the silence, Drusy said, 'I'll go over the briefing formally now that we're all together. The situation is that Beatrice Golden, Celeste's mother and Pete's wife, has been kidnapped. We think it has something to do with some research into the Littoral Codex that Celeste has been helping with.' At this, several heads nodded. 'Mark has narrowed her possible location down to a stretch of coastline west of the bay. We're going to try and find where she is, and we're going to get her out.'

'Fighting?' said Russ incredulously.

'Do I look like a superhero?' snapped Drusy. 'First, we listen, then we talk. Then we trick. Finally, if we have to, we blackmail. In that order. Just like department meetings and grant applications. Now,' she said briskly, 'since we don't know what we'll find, we're going to have to be even more on our toes than usual. Bring all problems and questions to me. I'll represent us when there's talking to be done. You all know the drill. Stick together, stick to your roles, keep quiet. Ozzie, you're ready?' I saw the boy shrug, and the two academics wedged in on either side of him rose and fell like corks on a wave. 'Celeste and Pete?'

We looked up. 'Uh-huh,' I said.

'Do not *go* anywhere by yourselves. Do not *do* anything by yourselves. Do not *speak* to anyone—*anyone*—you don't see riding this bus right now. I can't even begin to tell you how important this is. It's Beatrice's life we're talking about. Are … we … absolutely … clear?' We nodded.

As the briefing was obviously over, people began hushed conversations as the minibus rolled toward the coast. Neither Dad nor I felt like talking. Every few minutes, Russ would catch my eye from the other side of Ozzie and give a gentle, worried smile.

Eventually the road narrowed and became rougher. I saw Mark sitting closest to the driver, giving directions. She nodded, and turned off onto a dirt road that led along the coast to where the escarpment just began to rise from the sand and mud. In the distance I could see a small house. As we got closer, I saw a large antenna tower near the house. This had to be it! I pointed out the window; Dad looked, and clutched my other hand so hard I gasped.

'Sorry, Mousie,' said Dad, and loosened his grip just a bit. I was glad I'd given him the uninjured hand to hold.

The bus drove closer and closer to the little house, a dirty, run-down beach cottage. Two cars were parked outside. Drusy said there wouldn't be any fighting, but I'd believe that when this was all over. The bus stopped at the house, and the driver took out a book she obviously kept handy for just such occasions and settled in for a good, long read.

By the time Dad and I got out, the others had formed a sort of phalanx. I was pretty sure it was not to storm the house, but to provide a human barrier that would keep Dad and me from doing so. Dr Garrick was closest to me, and from the look in his eye as he glanced over, I knew my guess was correct.

Up we marched: a dozen creaky old academics, a bureaucrat, a silent mountain of a boy, a maverick actor, and me. Drusy knocked on the door. To my shock, it opened.

'Drusilla Kelso!' said the woman in the doorway warmly. 'It is Drusilla, isn't it?'

'Hello, Norella.'

'But I don't need you, I need Celeste Carlucci, and she's such an altruist, she'll never let her mother languish in a kidnapper's clutches.'

I started to step forward and say, 'You've found her, chump,' but Dr Garrick grabbed the cane of the person next to him and poked me viciously in the stomach—enough to make me huff and double over, but not enough to make the woman in the door-way look around to see what the trouble was.

'No wonder your students are so *thick*,' he whispered furiously. 'They take after *you*.'

'Shh,' said the person he'd taken the cane from, and snatched it back again.

'What, exactly, do you need Celeste for?' said Drusy.

'Our sources suggest she may have access to the key to the Littoral Codex.'

'Your sources,' said Drusy. 'Who would they be?'

'People who know, that's all. You may be surprised to realise, as many people are, that the Littoral League attracts some of the finest minds in Krasnia, people with keen observation skills and a knack for discovering things.'

'Sneaks, in other words,' muttered Dr Garrick.

Jasper Smith-Fennel, in other words. It had to be. He must have been following Pace around for weeks, and he wasn't above the judicious use of a pair of binoculars when, say, she and Kortnoz might have been having a look at the tablets.

No, maybe it was Joan Maher, playing us off the League. Or Pace herself—maybe they'd captured her after all and she'd let something slip under torture. Not that that would be like Pace. Not even Sister Genesia, at the height of the hysteria over the pencil shavings and the pepper spray, had been able to break her.

Or none of the above. And all the speculation in the world wasn't going to get my mom back. Why hadn't Drusy sent Ozzie in, fists swinging, to bring her out?

'Russ?' said Drusy. He moved closer to her. 'Have you heard Celeste say anything about the Littoral Codex?'

Russ looked puzzled. 'No, I don't think so. It doesn't sound familiar.'

'And who are *you*?' said Norella in a lilting, 'hey, big guy' kind of voice. I gritted my teeth.

Russ looked down and blushed, then glanced up shyly. 'Oh, Celeste's mom and my mom have been friends for years. My mom sent me along because Ms Golden hasn't been answering her phone. She's worried. Ms Golden's all right, isn't she?' He gave a winning smile. Somehow Russ was creating the impression that he had started out doing his dear old mom a favour, but now things were getting a *lot* more interesting. He's an actor, I told myself. He's an actor, he's an actor, he's an actor. And she's a troll.

When she did step out onto the porch to get a better look at *my* boyfriend, I saw to my dismay that no, she wasn't. She was older, yes, but she was gorgeous. My suspicion that her 'source' was Jasper became near certainty.

'I'm so rude, heavens!' said Norella. 'Keeping you all standing in the hot sun. But it's such a small house. There's a carport around the back, why don't we all go back there to chat?'

Next to me, I felt Dad shift from foot to foot. I was getting impatient, too—more than impatient. But my stomach still hurt from where Dr Garrick had jammed the cane into me. I wasn't so much afraid of the pain, but it had definitely reminded me that hasty action could do more harm than good.

'I think we'll stay here,' said Drusy. I could see her point: who knew what was waiting for us back there? But neither could we do anything to get to my mom from here. I felt like my brain was about to explode.

A loud thump from around the side of the house broke the stalemate. We rushed in a bloc toward the sound. That wall had no windows, but the house wasn't very sturdily built, and we could see the clapboards bulging outwards for just an instant as another thump came. If someone's hands were tied behind their back, they might try charging the wall with their shoulder or kicking it as they lay on the floor, if they thought someone might be out there to hear. Dad and I looked at each other and nodded.

Without a word, Ozzie walked up to the wall, reached down to where the boards near the foundation had rotted out, and calmly started pulling them away and tossing them away. The academics started to cheer, and Ozzie sped up the pace. Splinters and insects showered us as the gap got bigger.

'That's fine, whoever you are, I can get out now,' yelled Mom from inside. Ozzie stepped back, and Mom wriggled, feet first, out onto the grass. Mark had a penknife out in an instant and cut the wrist-tie and the ropes around her ankles.

'Oh, thanks,' said Mom breathlessly. She gingerly flexed her arms and shrugged a few times. 'Any of you guys a chiropractor?'

Big, silent Ozzie raised her gently to her feet. He gave her a look that said, Mind if I try and help? She nodded, and he closed his eyes and pressed along the tops of her shoulders and down either side of her spine with his thumbs. I could see a look of surprised relief on Mom's face.

'Thanks,' she said as Ozzie stood back.

Russ had sidled up while Ozzie worked, and he immediately took Ozzie's place at Mom's side. He murmured something in her ear. I saw Mom's eyes slide over the crowd until she saw Dad and me, but she said nothing.

'Now why did you have to do that?' said Norella fretfully. 'Do you know how hard it is to get carpenters to come out this far?'

'Norella,' said Drusy, 'why not just stop the melodrama and simply tell us what's going on? You may have your faults, but at least you've always been straightforward.'

'We're the Littoral League. Anything to do with the Littoral Codex is our business. It's as simple as that. If Ty thinks he can keep secrets from me—' She stopped herself with a small choking sound.

'Celeste knows very little about what Ty does. Are you sure you don't want to go after him directly?'

'I can't find him,' Norella said petulantly. 'Nor that young tramp he's taken up with. Now *she'd* be useful for leverage. Celeste's mother was definitely not our first choice. Quite far down the list, in fact. But we had to do *something*, once we knew the crystal key had been found.'

From inside the house, someone said, 'Holy shit, what happened here?'

'Termites?' said another voice.

'Yeah, right, mutant termites the size of shopping carts.'

'Hey, if the blue-headed beetles can mutate, why not termites?'

'You reckon we might just possibly have *noticed* giant termites chewing on the walls?'

'*I* might have, but you were on level ten of Jaws of Dismay, which means you wouldn't notice if all the angels in heaven came down and told you that you've been elected God and it's time to fix a few things up around here.'

'There are a few things I'd fix right away, like your ugly face.'

'How can a supposed genius have such a juvenile sense of, what was it, oh yes, humour?'

My God, Norella had stacked the Littoral League with *under-graduates*. I started to relax a bit.

Now that we had my mom back and Norella's minions were turning out to be only as frightening as my Intro to Geography class, I couldn't see why I shouldn't go and give Mom a hug. But Dr Garrick saw me start to move and reached meaningfully for the cane again.

'Well, maybe we should be going,' said Drusy.

'Maybe not,' said Norella. 'Maybe you still have some information you can share with me.'

'I don't think so.' But as Drusy turned to go, she said, 'Uh-oh.' Three gawky kids, who looked for all the world like they'd graduated high school early and started college at fourteen, had let the air out of the tires. The driver, still reading her book, hadn't even noticed.

'We'll let you go, don't worry,' said Norella, surveying her kingdom of pimply children and elderly captives. 'Just as soon as we find some way for you to give me what I want. I know: you promise to tell me everything Ty, his trollop, and Celeste find out about the keys, and I'll let you go back to the city. But if I find out you're not keeping me informed—and do not doubt that I *will* find out—next time I won't be so generous. I've postponed my dreams too long as it is. The university is going to hell in a hopped-up hot rod, and it's up to me to save it. Things will be different when I'm in charge.'

She started what was obviously going to be a long ramble about restructuring and mission statements, but before she got too far along Russ smiled at her again and said, 'Maybe one of your colleagues could get us that pump?'

I'm pretty sure I saw the sparkle of drool at the corner of her mouth as she said dreamily, 'Sure. Justin? Jason? See to it.' Two of the gawky kids went around the back of the house; the third one stayed where he was and glowered with his arms folded across his narrow chest.

I saw that Dad had managed to move unobtrusively over to Mom. I wanted to be there, too, but if I revealed myself as *the* Celeste, I knew that, deal or no deal, I'd have a hard time leaving the cottage that afternoon. To distract myself, I had a look around the back of the house myself. Not much but an empty carport, I thought, until I happened to look through the kitchen window and catch a glimpse of a veritable arsenal on the wall above the sink: guns, knives, medieval swords and maces. Some of them looked like the sorts of things those historical re-enactors played with, and I reckoned Norella's troops had pooled all the stuff they used to keep in their parents' basements. Still, damaging enough if swung with adolescent angst.

'Cool,' someone murmured behind me. I turned, then breathed in relief: Ozzie. He was staring through the window at the weapons like a small kid would stare at a candy counter.

'Yeah,' I said. 'If you're into that sort of thing.'

When we meandered back to the front of the house, Russ was pumping up the first tyre. Norella was still regaling the academics with her plans, Dad and Mom were still holding each other up, and the driver was still reading her book.

I didn't like this 'arrangement' we'd come to with the Littoral League—there were already far, far too many people watching and following and poking and prying. All this, just for the tablets, and nobody even had the book. Nobody but the Praxies, and they weren't sharing. I wondered if Norella had any kind of plan for dealing with them. Or, indeed, if she ever had any plans at all, except for a vague ambition of conquering the Codex, the university, and Kortnoz—sort of a mission statement.

We got onto the bus eventually—Russ was a bit dishevelled from pumping the tyres; it looked quite alluring, really—and drove back to the retirement home. We'd protected my identity, and the tablets, for the moment. But all the unanswered questions were as much of a danger as Norella's ambitions.

Chapter 14
Celeste Starts to Think

Over my parents' objections ('Sweetie, why don't we just stick together tonight?'), I went back to Russ's after getting my stuff at the retirement home. Drusy had managed to convince my parents not to go to the police just yet.

'There's too much going on below the surface,' she said, which was literally true, if you considered the Sewers and the magnificent underground library. 'While I agree that what the Littoral League did was horrible, getting them arrested now might have dangerous consequences elsewhere that we can't foresee.'

'Like moving the bottom pickup stick,' said Mom.

'Exactly! Celeste, your mother is just my kind of thinker.'

Mom looked pleased.

The minibus had dropped them home, and Russ and I had taken my pack and got on a nice, anonymous bus. It let us out quite far from Beggar's Pit, of course—no bus would go there (I vaguely remembered the drivers' strike ten years back that had put that clause in their contract). But the afternoon was pleasant, and the setting sun was starting to turn the sky pink and orange and green. We walked casually to Russ's apartment. It was nice not to feel in a rush—or, for that matter, in peril of one's life.

I didn't have the energy for another night of cavorting. Russ didn't even suggest it; instead, he left me to rest in the apartment while he went out shopping for dinner ingredients. I resisted the morbid temptation to check more books for Miffy's little love notes; instead, I went into the bedroom and turned the television on. I settled back against the pillows to watch.

It was one of those talking-head shows, where people who were supposed to matter gave opinions on things that were supposed to matter and then argued with each other in ever-louder tones, which I guessed made it all matter even more. Being as this was a Praxie-owned station, I wasn't expecting deep intellectual debate.

Sure enough, it was the usual 'universities and their irrelevant research are sucking resources from the things that are genuinely important' diatribe. And, as expected, the argument wasn't about whether that was true, but about specifically what should suck these resources up instead. The suggestions seemed to be more highways, a reinforced border with North Kras, improved high-school sports programs, or a new sound system for the Purple Bay stadium. I snorted: the annual operating budget of Purple Bay University wouldn't even pay the power bill for one night game at the stadium, let alone an entire sound system.

That's when things started to get nasty. 'It's not even as if these academics are Purple Bay's finest citizens,' said one panellist.

'Why, what do you mean?' said the moderator, in a way that told me instantly the whole thing was carefully staged. But the pseudo-intellectuals who craved this kind of thing wouldn't be noticing that. They'd be too busy feeling pleasantly riled up and righteous.

'Well, they spend their entire *careers*—' and the word was a sneer—'approving grants for each other. Grants that you and I pay for out of our taxes. They monitor each other's research, they give each other jobs, they piss in each other's pockets, frankly. And that's as disgusting as it sounds.'

'I really don't know how they've managed to get away with it for so long,' said another. 'How are we supposed to know that all this so-called "research" they do has any basis in reality at all? It could all be like one of those elaborate role-playing games the kids play. The ones with all the dragons and things that make them go nuts.'

I was hoping this would divert the panel into a rant on unstable teenagers and fantasy worlds, but no.

'If an academic came to my newspaper with some sort of scoop,' said the editor of the Lilia *Commentator*, 'I'm sorry to say I would assume it was just some publicity stunt to gain funding for the latest "research".'

So that was it. The Praxies had noticed that the academics were starting to move, to gather their forces, and wanted to sterilise us. And they were using their media empire to do it.

I felt a shock as my conscious mind caught up with what I'd just heard myself thinking. This bizarre secret organisation of academics had obviously been around for at least a hundred years in one form or another. It had waxed and waned—at least, at one point only Russ's ancestor had known about the underground library and the Sewer network. But it was rallying again, and something, or someone, had triggered the process.

I could only trace it as far back as Kortnoz taking Pace and me to recover the tablets. But I knew that had to be just one link in a chain that went further back. Who had told him the tablets were there? And how had they gotten there, in their leaden box? Not exactly the kind of thing you take inconspicuously along on a nice beach picnic.

I was aching to ask Kortnoz, to have him answer all my questions, just as he had when I was an undergrad. And in between bouts of fearing for my own life, I was still deeply worried about Pace. Although if this discussion show was any indication of how public opinion was being swayed against academics, maybe they were right to stay hidden, and not just because the Littoral League was after them.

I wanted to change the channel, because the show was making me sort of sick, but I figured I needed to know my enemy. I wondered how many enemies I had actually collected by now.

After about twenty minutes of listening to how horrible all my colleagues and I were, I was relieved to hear Russ come in.

'I got lots of veggies and rice, is that okay?' he called.

'Sure, sounds great. You need help with anything?'

'Unless you can cut vegetables up one-handed, I'll be fine, thanks.'

I relaxed back into the pillows. I could get used to this.

'I tried to call your cell phone to see if you liked green pepper,' said Russ, 'but there was no answer.'

'Oh. Drusy told me to keep it turned off. The last thing I want is for someone to check the records and know that I'm in Beggar's Pit. I'll check for messages when I get into work tomorrow.'

'Did Drusy say it was okay for you to go back to work?' Russ appeared at the bedroom door, looking worried.

I blinked. 'She didn't say it wasn't. Russ, I'm going crazy with all this hiding and skulking. And God knows what Dr Garrick is telling my students.'

'Humour me. Check with her. Here, use my phone.' He handed me the handset from the bedside table. He stood waiting for me to dial.

'For heaven's sake, Russ, I'm a grown woman. I can decide if I'm going into work tomorrow or not.'

'Okay, then, at least phone her to let her know Dr Garrick doesn't need to cover for you. You wouldn't want him to hobble all the way over to campus, just to find out he had to turn right around and hobble back again.'

He had me there; I didn't like the thought of inconveniencing Dr Garrick like that. I started dialling Drusy's number. 'Since when did you get to know me so well?' I said peevishly.

Russ sat down on the bed. The mattress dipped under his weight, and I slid downhill a little so my head ended up on his shoulder. He put his arm around me and murmured, 'When I'm really interested, I pay a lot of attention.' I forgot completely about calling Drusy, until Russ tapped the phone with his finger. 'Dial.'

'*Okay.*' Drusy's number was already burned into my brain.

'Hello?'

'Hi, Drusy, this is Celeste. I just wanted to ask a favour. Could you please let Dr Garrick know that he doesn't need to come in to teach for me tomorrow? I'll be back at work.'

'You certainly will not. Are you absolutely insane?' Her voice was sharper than I'd ever heard it.

'Drusy—'

'Has everything you've been through made no impression at all?'

'I thought the Littoral League agreed to leave us alone if we kept them informed.'

'Norella Honeycott says whatever she needs to say to get what she wants. And if you remember carefully, she only promised to let us go, not to leave us alone entirely. Details, Celeste. They're important.'

I felt chastened and sullen.

'I'd rather face them than do all this sneaking around. I'm not a sneaky person. And none of the sneaking kept my mom safe, did it? And it hasn't accomplished anything in terms of finding Pace and Dr Kortnoz, has it? Or figuring out how to use the tablets? Or how to get the Littoral Codex from the Praxies? Or even getting me tenure?' I sat up and pulled away from Russ.

I heard Drusy take a deep breath. 'Sweetie, I can't make you do anything. If you really believe it's the right thing to do, then go into work tomorrow. But we might not be able to find you the way we found your mom. They won't be that careless again. Maybe I can make some sort of deal with Norella this evening, so that at least you don't have to worry about the League.'

Wow. Drusy was more powerful than I'd thought. 'That … that would be great. Thanks.'

'This number on the caller ID—is that Russ's number?'

'Yes.'

'You haven't turned on your phone while you've been there, have you?'

'No.'

'Well, good, then, at least you listened to that. I think I'll ask Lenny to go over to campus tomorrow anyway, as backup for you. And he'll want to update you on what he's been going over in your classes.'

I shuddered to think, but I recognised the sense in it. 'Okay, then. Thanks.'

'I just hope things don't turn out where I can say "I told you so".'

'I'll be fine.'

'Okay, sweetie.'

After I hung up, Russ said, 'Well, that went just about how I figured it would. I'm going to be a nervous wreck tomorrow, knowing you're in danger.'

'What would you do, if you were in my place?'

'I hope I never have to find out.' He went back to the kitchen to finish making dinner.

We ate, we watched television, we slept. On the surface it all looked very normal. But I hardly tasted the food, didn't remember the shows, tossed and turned. Tomorrow I was going to stop running. And there was no Pace to tell me what to do. My cheekbone, my neck, my wrist, all the scrapes and bruises burned in the night as I tried to sleep.

When Russ's clock said seven, I got up, took a shower, and got dressed. I went to the kitchen and boiled some water for coffee—enough for two. I already knew Russ woke quickly in the mornings, and that he wanted caffeine when he did. Sure enough, a minute after I poured the water over the crystals, he followed the scent into the kitchen.

'If you can wait until I'm showered and dressed, I'll come with you,' he said. 'And thanks for the coffee. Sorry it's instant.'

'It's fine. And yes, I'll wait.'

'Whew. I was thinking you'd lost all sense of caution.'

'I didn't sleep last night, and I'll need you to nudge me so I don't fall asleep and stay on the bus all the way across town.'

'At least this humble servant can be useful to madame,' he said. 'This humble servant thanks madame most profusely for the opportunity to attend to her needs and whims.' He was the utter picture of servility.

'Don't mention it,' I said casually.

While Russ showered I dished up some leftover rice and ate it cold. I hated eating breakfast, so it didn't really matter what it was. I just knew that, what with life being so unpredictable and all, it was probably a good idea to eat when I could.

I put the tablets in my gym bag, and put it under Russ's bed. Not too subtle, but at least not in plain sight. And maybe my backpack would act as a decoy as I carried it around all day.

The morning was unexpectedly chilly, and I shivered as we waited for the bus. Russ sat closer and hugged me. I fought a sudden wild need to shrug him away. His concern for me felt like a burden—just one more person who would be hurt if something happened to me today.

But nothing would happen. Drusy would make some phone calls, Pace would turn up, and everything would be fine. I could go back to worrying about tenure and teaching and—

—and Danny Snotnose Wexler. Danny, who had studied with Angelo Praxicopolis. Danny, who'd discovered the mutated blue-headed beetles. And systematically alienated everyone on campus. And was researching the Praxies' media empire for me. And whose mom was a governor and whose dad was a media despot and whose sister was stalking Russ. Brilliant, obnoxious, pathetic, complicated Danny. He was the pivot point of all of it.

'What?' said Russ. I realised I'd sat bolt upright.

'Just thinking,' I said. Something I clearly hadn't been doing enough of.

The bus ride was uneventful, except for my noticing Russ's increasingly worried expression. Finally he said hesitantly, 'Is ...is something wrong? I mean, yeah, I know there are plenty of things wrong, but I sort of meant, is anything wrong with, um, me?'

'Huh?'

'Have I said something wrong?'

'Why do you say that?'

'Just … all of a sudden, you're … kind of distant.'

'Sorry.' But I couldn't think of anything cuddly to say. 'Sorry,' I said again.

'You, um, don't have to stay with me if it's not working for you.' I looked at him. 'No, I want you with me, don't get me wrong, boy oh boy, do I want you with me. But this isn't exactly a typical relationship. Maybe you feel like we're getting too close too quick.'

I sighed. 'No,' I said, maybe a bit wearily. 'You're fantastic, you're unreal, you're incredible, you're beyond my wildest dreams. That's not melodrama, I mean it. Just …'

'Yeah,' he said.

I kept having to swallow, and all the muscles around my eyes felt tense and hot. A tear leaked out of my left eye and ran down my cheek. I was ruining everything. I couldn't even do the falling-in-love thing right.

Neither of us said much for the rest of the trip. We got off the bus at the university gates. The Geography building was first. I expected Russ to just give me a kiss and move on, but he insisted on coming to my office with me. I didn't know whether to be resentful or grateful. I ended up being both.

The police tape had been taken down; obviously Security was done with the investigation. I knew they wouldn't have found anything really useful—but maybe they would have taken away 'for evidence' things the governors would like to get a closer look at. The governors were everywhere, they knew everything. How was I supposed to defeat them? Through publishing Millicent's data on *mud*? Mud isn't much of a weapon against tyranny and brutality.

The computer was still gone, but the phone was there, which I noticed because it rang. I glanced at Russ, then picked up.

'Hello?' Usually I answered with my name, but suddenly that seemed rash.

'Oh, fantastic, you're back! Ricky, she's back!' It was, of course, Nicki. 'I was so worried! I mean, Dr Garrick is fabulous, we all learned so much, not as much as with you though, that's not what I meant, but you're back! Dr Kelso phoned me last night and told me that if you came into work today I needed to be ready to help you with whatever you needed. I am so totally fine with that! Are you all right? Is everything all right?'

'Yes, everything's okay, thanks.'

'How's your wrist? Is your wrist okay?'

It was like talking with a puppy. 'Yes, fine, thanks.'

'Is there anything I can do? To help?'

'I don't suppose Ricky has any of those cookies left …' I was joking. Sort of. The memory of cookies swirled around in my brain and my mouth started to water.

'No, he made a different batch yesterday. Coconut almond, wait until you taste them, I'll bring you some!'

Things were looking up.

'I'll be there in a half hour, Dr Carlucci, and if you think of anything you need, I can get it for you, okay?'

'Thanks, Nicki.' I was touched. She was so enthusiastic, I was pretty sure it wasn't just an assignment from the underground academics, but that she really cared. Maybe I wasn't screwing absolutely *everything* up.

'Oh. The screw-up is back,' came a thin, irascible voice from the hallway.

'Hi, Dr Garrick,' said Russ.

'Not you, *her*. What the hell are you doing in here?'

'Um, teaching.'

'Wrong answer. First of all, your students are a disaster, except for that governor's kid, that Danny Wexler. He's the only one with an independent idea in his head. Don't you teach them any inquiry skills at all?'

'The syllabus has to pass approval by the governors.'

'Okay, fine, so get it approved and then subvert it. Is it so hard?'

'I don't have tenure.'

'I know, that's your only saving grace.'

'Dr Garrick, could you please stop haranguing me? I'm not in a position to appreciate it.'

'Oh, sor-REE.'

I heard more footsteps down the hall; odd, for so early in the morning. It was one of the assistant librarians I remembered seeing at the reference desk.

'Hi, Celeste, I don't know if you remember me, I'm Martha over at the library. Drusy gave me a phone call and asked me to stop by and let you know that Joan is on a leave of absence. The official reason is a flare-up of the damage from the predatory mould. We don't really know where she's gotten to. We don't *think* she's with the League.'

'The League doesn't want her,' said Jasper, who'd pushed his way past Martha. The office was getting very crowded indeed.

'And how do you know?' I snapped.

'Because I'm Norella's second in command,' he said smugly.

'Oh, that'd be like you, wouldn't it?' I was never all that inclined to be polite to Jasper; now I was really enjoying being rude. It was a great tension-reliever. 'You creepy little brown-noser. Was it you who suggested they kidnap my mom?'

His face reddened. 'No. All I wanted was the research. Norella had … had that idea without me.' I could see that that really galled him. I was glad.

'So even in that pack of losers you're still a loser,' I said.

'Losers or not, you're supposed to work with me to bring the key and the Codex together.'

'Yeah, right. Says who?'

'Says Drusy Kelso. In return for us not kidnapping anyone. For a while.'

'So Norella can dismember the university.'

'So we can free the university from the governors. Once we have that Codex—and the key—this university will be the centre of the intellectual universe. The governors won't be able to touch us.'

Why would Drusy agree to this? It seemed like a steep price to pay for a bit of breathing room.

I looked away from Jasper and over to Martha. 'Thanks, Martha. I appreciate the news. If you hear anything else from or about Joan, could you please let me know?'

'Sure thing,' she said. 'Time to get back to the reference desk, while we still have one.'

'Funding cuts?' said Russ.

'Yup, that's the rumour. I guess we'll see when the budget comes out. See you all later. Hope it's not on the unemployment line.'

If the library was being cut, could the Geography department be far behind? I might be able to continue my research as a private citizen, but no one would publish it or pay attention to it, no one at all. I wouldn't be able to contribute anything to geographical knowledge, nothing to the life of the university. And three years of work would be wasted.

I wished the Ickies would get here. I was really wanting a cookie.

'Jasper, please leave me alone. When I find anything out, I'll tell you.' The hell I would.

He must have suspected as much, because his eyes narrowed and he said meaningfully, 'I'll be close by. If you find anything out. Or if I can help you.'

When he was gone, Dr Garrick said, 'Who was that nasty little tick? Not a former boyfriend, I hope.'

'God, no,' I said.

Dr Garrick turned to Russ. 'So, Gartner. Keeping up the family traditions?'

'Which ones?'

'Rabble rousing. Being an irritant.'

'Sure hope so, Dr Garrick.'

'It's irritating me that you're hanging around when I need to talk to Celeste, that's for sure.'

'I get the hint. Celeste, I'll be checking in through the day, to see if you need anything.' He kissed me, although I was a little uncomfortable with Dr Garrick looking on, and left.

Dr Garrick shut the office door, then sat down in Pace's chair, motioning for me to sit in mine. 'Have you thought anything through at all, even once, this whole week?' he said.

'No.'

'Do you have a goal? Let alone a plan to achieve it?'

'No.'

'Still think altruism is enough to make everything right?'

I said nothing.

'You're in trouble, deeper than you know. Kortnoz is in it so far over his head that it will be a miracle if he ever surfaces again. Same with that young woman he goes around with, that Pace. They've screwed things up even more thoroughly than you have. I'm sorry I ever retired.'

I still couldn't think of anything useful to say.

'Let's do something novel,' he resumed. 'Let's think about things methodically. What do you want to *accomplish* here?'

'I want to stay alive.'

'Worms want that. What else?'

'I want to find Pace and Kortnoz.'

'They're probably safe enough, as long as they keep their stupid heads down. What else?'

'I want every member of the Littoral League to fry in hell for what they did to my mother.'

'Now we're getting somewhere. What else?'

'I want the governors overthrown.'

'How does the Codex fit into all this?'

'Damned if I know, Dr Garrick. I'm starting to think it's a false god, myself.'

'Hooray!' he shouted suddenly, scaring me quite unpleasantly. 'Sense at last!'

'Uh … what?'

'The issue is not the damned Codex. The issue is the chokehold the governors, backed by the Praxies, have on this university. The issue is the way the Praxies are making academics the enemy. The issue is that we can't research what we want, can't teach what we want, can't even think what we want! This university, which has sheltered and nourished the best minds in Krasnia for two hundred years, is being dismantled, brick by brick, and nobody sees it but you and a handful of rickety old retirees.'

There was a timid knock.

'Come in,' I said. It was the Ickies.

Nicki handed me another of those plastic tubs, full of cookies. I looked past her to see Ricky smiling shyly.

'Thanks, guys, you have no idea what this means to me.'

'Dr Garrick?' said Nicki.

'Mmph.'

'I see it. I care. And so does Ricky.'

'See what?'

'What you said. That the governors are wrecking the university. It's not just you and a few people. There are lots of us. All of us in the Sewers. Just because I'm an undergrad, doesn't mean I don't count. And just because some people don't have PhDs, or don't have tenure, or whatever, doesn't mean they don't count. This university is more than just PhDs. And if it's threatened, well, you'd be surprised at how many people will fight for it. *Are* fighting for it. That's all.'

A slow smile spread over Dr Garrick's wrinkled face. Finally he turned to me. 'Maybe you've been doing your job after all. But that still doesn't tell me what you're going to do.'

'Wait until they come and find me. That way I'll know who they are.'

Dr Garrick snorted. 'They'll just keep sending henchmen, as they've done so far. You've been attacked, how many times?'

'If you count my mom's kidnapping—'

'Kidnapping?' gasped Nicki.

'—as an attack on me, then … um … three. No, four. Five if you count Joan trying to trick me.'

'And you still don't know who's who.'

'Well, I'm pretty sure the first one was the Littoral League. And I know the kidnapping was. The others …'

'That's what you'll find out by waiting. A big slice of nothing.'

But I had no intention of just waiting. I was going to have a word with Danny Wexler. More than a word.

And then I'd know what to do.

Chapter 15
Danny Answers Some Questions

Into the silence, Ricky spoke: 'Have … have a cookie?'

He took the lid off the tub and passed it around. 'Thanks,' we mumbled in turn, with our mouths full.

I swallowed my first cookie, and while I reached for another, I said to Dr Garrick, 'While I was gone, what did you do to my students? I mean, with them?'

'I know what you mean,' he said testily. 'Your Intro class was a disaster. These kids didn't know a drumlin from their right butt cheeks. Now …' He started listing the concepts he thought they should know by now, and I took a pen and notebook from my pack and dutifully wrote them down. We both knew I was just being polite.

'In your Riverine seminar, things looked a little brighter. I listened to what they could tell me about their projects, and encouraged them to challenge themselves. These two were there, why not ask them?'

'Your feedback was really helpful,' said Nicki tentatively.

'But man, were you mean,' said Ricky. 'Dr Carlucci's never like that.'

'Anyway, Ricky and I have to go in a minute and get ready for our Literature class,' said Nicki. 'Is there anything else we can do for you right now?'

'No, thanks. I really appreciate the cookies and all your concern.'

'That's okay,' said Nicki.

'You're our favourite professor,' said Ricky, astonishingly.

'Yours, too?' I said to him. 'Not just Nicki's?'

'Sure.'

'Wow. Thanks.'

'You're the one who likes my cookies the most.'

Well, I'd take what I could get in times like these. 'They're very good cookies. Ever consider a career as chef?'

'Really?' he said, with more animation than I'd ever heard from him. 'You really think I could make it?'

'If your cookies are any indication, I'd say there's no doubt whatsoever.'

'That's it, Nick—this afternoon I go to the registrar and transfer into food science!'

'What … what about all our research projects?'

'Come on, who're we kidding? You do all the work on them anyway. Please, Nick, don't be upset. I know geography is great—'

'It's everything!'

'So is cooking! If Dr Carlucci thinks I can make it—'

'Then you should give it a try. I understand,' said Nicki. 'Really.' And she gave him a kiss on the cheek. This was either the end of their relationship, or its real beginning.

'Okay, guys, thanks so much. I'll see you later, right?'

'Right!' said Nicki, but she was obviously finding Ricky's new-found enthusiasm unsettling. I hoped she wouldn't think I'd been trying to sabotage their relationship. I was starting to lean on this new support, this group of brave and truculent academics, and I didn't want to wreck it now. Now that they might be all that stood against the governors, the Praxies, and the Littoral League. And whatever rogue element Joan represented. The Praxies et al. were Them; Nicki and Drusy and their organisation were Us.

Pace was Us, too, and at the thought of her, the worry rushed back in. Dr Garrick could say all he liked that they were okay, but I wasn't so sure. I realised she might have left a message on the cell phone, and turned it on.

Hell's bells—eleven messages. This couldn't be good.

'Hi, Celeste, it's Pace. I got this number from Drusy. Did you get the things I left for you? Please phone and let me know.'

'Hi, Celeste, it's Pace. Don't bother phoning, Drusy's updated us.'

'Pace here. Ty and I are still undercover, but it's actually not so bad. Except that we can't use our bank accounts, so we're trying a bunch of different ways to earn cash.'

'Pace here. Whatever you do, don't give those things to anyone else. Anyone. I hear someone's gone renegade, don't know who. Trust no one!'

'Pace. You've been busy, haven't you? Look, keep your head down. You don't have much experience in these things.'

'It's me. Hope your mom's okay. Sorry I got you into this.'

'Me. Battery's getting low. Don't even bother calling now—sheesh.'

'Meet me at the River Walk on Tuesday. We need to talk.'

'Sorry, I meant to say—Tuesday at three.'

'Will you be there today? Three. Please.'

'Bring my phone charger, will you? It's in my top—'

The battery had clearly died. Pace would have made the charge last a lot longer had she texted me, but she never did have the patience. So now she needed to talk, and she needed her phone charger. Well, that was my afternoon spoken for.

Dr Garrick cleared his throat, and I realised he'd been sitting there for several minutes while I'd checked the messages. Oops.

'Sorry, Dr Garrick.'

'Mmph.'

'Did any of the students have any questions or problems while I was gone? Any messages from admin?'

'Not a one. Things seemed to go on just fine without you. So why don't you head on over to Drusy's again where it's maybe a little safer?'

'Sick of running, Dr Garrick. Sick of looking over my shoulder.

In fact, I think I'm going to spend the morning doing a little chasing myself. I have until one o'clock.'

'What's at one o'clock?'

'Geography of Art.'

'Wrath of God, the courses get worse every year. What sort of abomination is that?'

'I don't want to get into it. I need to go. Will you be all right here?'

'Girlie, don't patronise me. I've saved *your* bacon these past few days, remember?'

'Yes, thanks for that.'

'What if that movie-star boy comes around looking for you?'

'Can you tell him to meet me at my one o'clock class? He knows where it is. Thanks.'

'I'm not liking this, Celeste.'

'I'm sorry about that. I'll see you.' I grabbed my backpack, zipped it shut, and left. This felt right: deciding, doing. Not waiting or following orders.

My first stop was the library. Not so much to research the Praxies or the governors or even the League—I doubted the kinds of things I needed to know would be in books or newspapers. But I wanted to ask Martha to tell me more about Joan, and I wanted to look up Danny Wexler's email address, which I hadn't been able to do in my office because my computer had been confiscated. He and I had to talk, and it was the only way I had of contacting him. Even though there was the chance his parents would intercept the email, I had to risk it. I sat at one of the computers in the reading room.

> Hi, Danny—
>
> I need to talk with you urgently. Please find me in the reference section at the library, or meet me before Geography of Art (the seminar room, second floor, Geography building). I need your help.
> Dr Carlucci

I hoped he was lonely and geeky enough to check his emails a hundred times a day.

I logged off and found Martha's desk. She looked up as I approached, then smiled.

I leaned in over the desk so I could say quietly, 'Do you have a few minutes to chat with me about Joan?'

Martha's smile changed to a worried frown. 'I thought I knew a lot more than I really did,' she said. 'But I'll try to help. What time is it now?'

'Nine.'

'My break isn't until ten, but I think I could manage. Come on over to the reference stacks. It will look like I'm helping you with a reference question. And I am, sort of.'

We strode with obvious purpose over to the reference stacks. Luckily, the Infonet still hadn't displaced shelf after shelf of enormous, hugely expensive books.

'Okay,' said Martha, as she took a weighty tome off one of the shelves and opened it. I pretended to look with her at the pages. 'Joan came in as head librarian about five years ago. You may remember all the press there was about it. She set out changing things right away. Which journals we carried, which books got put on the reserve list, which stacks and records were locked to undergraduates—'

'What?'

'Oh, didn't you know? Why do you think they always cite the same sources, year after year? Anyway, little by little, this place became Joan's kingdom. She even had certain items placed on a watch, so whenever they were checked out, she would get an automated notification.'

So she must have known all the time exactly where Millicent's thesis—the published one—had been. Maybe she had arranged the break-in. What was all the destruction supposed to cover? And why squash the poor bugs?

'She'd started out so full of energy and enthusiasm that she fooled us all. She said all the notifications and locked stacks were to make sure she knew when the governors were trying to surreptitiously remove items from circulation. Stupidly, we believed her. We told her about the underground organisation, introduced her to some of our team leaders, showed her the secret entrances into the Sewers. But just in the last week or so we—the reference librarians—started to catch on that she was actually making things easy for the governors to control both research and researchers. At first we gave her the benefit of the doubt—maybe she was just well-meaning but incompetent. Then the mould attacked her, and we knew: the library itself was sending us a message.'

At one time I would have laughed, but I knew such things happened. Kortnoz's encounter with that sentient ooze a few years back had started the whole saga of my stealing Pace's research. She'd believed him, I hadn't. My own scepticism and—I couldn't deny it—self-righteousness were what had gotten me into trouble. So I didn't laugh now. I listened.

'We're pretty sure, based on some papers she left in her office, that she's not linked with the governors. And her style doesn't match the Littoral League's.'

'She hates the Littoral League.'

'She says that. Did she tell you about her dead husband?'

'Uh, yeah.'

'Yeah, she fooled us with that one, too. But never piss off a reference librarian, because we can find out *anything* if we look hard enough. She's never been married.'

'So …' I said hesitantly, 'she *is* with the Littoral League, or she *isn't*?'

'We don't think she is. Besides, Norella Honeycott detests her, ever since she denied Honeycott borrower's privileges because she wasn't on university staff. Honeycott considered herself a legitimate private researcher, and insisted the university should give her the privileges.'

'If she's not Littoral League, why bother to distance herself from it?'

'Feint within feint. If we start to suspect, she's assuming we'll only go that one extra step, and that the more she says she isn't League, the more we'll think she is.'

'That leaves … the governors.'

'Maybe. Or she's on her own.'

'She got attacked over a week ago—during spring break, right?'

'Yup.'

'But she showed me the—the Sewers after that. Nobody so much as glanced at her. She walked around like she owned the place.' Things would have been a lot simpler if someone had been even a little suspicious of her down there.

Martha looked down. 'We kept hoping we were wrong. I'm sorry to say that you finally saw through her more clearly than we did. And more quickly. It's hard to change your opinion about someone you've told so much to, someone you were relying on—it's humiliating and scary to be so wrong. We're only human. But—' She looked up and into my eyes. 'We're sorry. We're very sorry. And we're doing everything we can to make it right.'

My turn to blush. 'Thanks.'

'We can't tell you much right now—I said the same to Drusy. But we feel ashamed that one of us betrayed you, and that we didn't see what was happening soon enough. We're taking it very personally. Believe me, if Joan Maher so much as pokes a nose out anywhere on campus, or under it, we'll find her.'

'Thanks,' I said again.

Martha struggled to put the book back on the shelf; I helped her as much as I could with one good hand. 'Will that give you something to go on, or do you need some more sources?' she said.

'Oh. Um, no, I'll be fine for the moment, thanks. The bibliography in this one is just what I needed.'

Martha gave me a quick, approving smile. I was getting better at this.

'I'll let you get on with it, then,' she said, and went back to the reference desk.

I looked at the shelf: cleverly, she'd led me to the geography section, so that I could plausibly be seen here. And plausibly browse. Most of the reference books were works I'd read when starting my senior honours thesis: good for an overview, but not primary sources. Still, compared to the do-it-yourself encyclopaedia sites, books like these were treasure troves of ancient wisdom. I picked another off the shelf at random: a handsome book of aerial photographs of Purple Bay. I checked the table of contents, and started to get excited—the photos went back nearly a hundred years. Why hadn't I thought to check here when I needed to trace the development of the delta—or lack of it?

Out of the corner of my eye, I saw someone step into the gap between the stacks. I looked up, startled, then relieved. Danny had found me.

'Right, Danny,' I said, putting the book back. I'd know where to find it later. 'We need to talk.'

'Not in here,' he said instantly.

'Okay, where, then?'

'Out in the quad, maybe. Somewhere outside.'

'How about somewhere where they'd never think to look for a geographer?'

'Where's that?'

'The Dramatic Arts building.'

Danny laughed explosively, then quieted himself. 'All right, then,' was all he said.

We walked as calmly as we could to the Dramatic Arts building, then found a black room that was empty. The only furniture was a half-dozen large foam blocks covered in fluorescent-coloured velvet. We each perched gingerly on one.

'Start talking, Danny. And don't stop until you've told me about the bugs, about Angelo Praxicopolis, about how come you're a geographer now, about how come your sister is stalking

Russ Gartner, about your mom the governor and your dad the media biggie and you, privileged son of the privileged who's so miserable he has to piss off the entire faculty, staff, and student body of Purple Bay University. Start now.'

Danny stared at me, and kept staring. Finally he whispered, 'Are you … are you going to chuck me out of the Geography department?'

'Are you a geographer?'

'Yes,' he said, still whispering.

'Then no. If we let that weed Jasper stay a geographer, there's no way we're going to kick *you* out. Talk.'

He never did raise his voice much above the whisper, and he kept pushing his hair around and rubbing his hands along his thighs as he spoke.

'Okay—Angelo. I started violin lessons with Angelo when I was eight. I'd been playing for four years, and I was already better than my first teacher. I'm not bragging, she told my parents so herself. So they decided I should have the best. And the best player in Purple Bay was Angelo Praxicopolis. He'd already let most of his students go, and was playing a lot fewer gigs, but my mom is a governor. Governors and Praxies have an understanding. I thought that was why he took me on.

'His professional pride and integrity—funny, huh, using those words about a Praxie?—meant that even though he hated me because I was the son of a governor, he would still give me the best instruction he could—'

'Wait—he hated you *because* …?'

'Oh, yeah, see, that's important: Angelo is the brother the rest of the Praxies are all ashamed of. He's wrecked more of their plans than they like to remember. He finds it easy. Most of the time, he says, it just takes not doing something, being silent at just the right time, just one look, one concert they want you to do that you call in sick for. The little things can mean a lot.'

'Okay. Keep going.'

'I kept practising, until I got really good. I don't think he expected that. But after I started winning competitions, we started having extra lessons. When I got a little older, we'd go for coffee. It wasn't because I was winning, it was because I was trying for excellence. He liked that. We sort of got to be friends. And he started talking to me about his family. He was ashamed to be a Praxie. And I realised—I was ashamed to be a Wexler.'

I felt like I was watching the shifting patterns of the delta on the Ickies' speeded-up animation: streams joining and parting and melting into one another.

'He told me that his family had a secret. I said, yeah, the Littoral Codex. He said no, everyone knew about that, this was different. They were closing in on getting the key to understanding the Codex. And once they did, there would be no stopping them. He said he was going to ruin their plans, though. It would mean he had to disappear, we had to stop our lessons. I could tell it upset him. I was maybe almost like—it sounds presumptuous, I guess—but like a son. But he knew he had to do it.'

'What plans? What did he do to ruin them?'

'He didn't want to tell me too much. He didn't want to put me in danger. But, like I told you, I'm brilliant, and I started doing research of my own.'

'What did he tell you?' I was starting to get frustrated. I guessed he could hear it in my voice, because he got to the point.

'The Praxies had this box, this old box, and it had some glass blocks, plates in it.'

'About the size of my hand. Different colours.'

That startled him. 'Yes. And you're supposed to use them to shine different coloured light on the pages of the Codex. But none of them worked, none of them has ever worked, for as long as the Praxies have owned them, even before they got hold of the Codex, back when they were just going to the museum to have a look. Angelo told me that's because one was missing.'

'Missing!'

'Angelo said about a hundred years ago, when the box was first found, one of the professors here figured it out. The Praxies weren't quite as famous for being nasty as they became, so nobody caught on that them knowing what was in the Codex was a bad thing. Except this one professor. He stole one of the tablets while they were being stored at the museum, and he ground it into powder, and he threw it in the Purple River.'

'Okay …'

'It's been washing down to the delta ever since.'

'Can't the Praxies just do up another tablet the same colour?'

'It's not ordinary glass, that's what Angelo told me. Why do you think the bugs have mutated? That powdered glass is some sort of, well, not radioactive, but the molecules resonate or emit some sort of waves or something.'

'That's as close as you can get to explaining it?'

'I'm only a sophomore, for heaven's sake. No amount of being brilliant is going to make up for that.'

'Sorry. Go on.'

'The Praxies have spent the last hundred years—ever since they got a ship fitted out with the equipment they needed—trying to recover the grains of powder, to find some way to recast them. They thought they were being secret, until I found the bugs.'

He sounded proud of himself, but I couldn't get annoyed.

'I tried to get Entomology interested. But they didn't like me. Personality shouldn't be a factor in finding out the truth, should it? It shouldn't, should it?'

'No.'

'When I found out that Dr Garoux was the only person paying attention to the mutations, I decided I had to get over to the Geography department. But I had to make it look like I didn't want to. I'd already been chucked out of seven or eight departments by then, so I went through a couple more to make it look right, then I transferred in. It was kind of funny you got me researching the Praxies, wasn't it?'

'Yeah.' I must have sounded kind of absent. I was thinking about the disappearing delta mud. Mud that might be sucked up into a ship anchored out to sea, coming in at night to filter it, looking for glass particles that hummed or glowed, and dumping the mud back out a mile or two so they didn't keep checking the same load of muck.

Danny said, 'They've nearly got enough.'

'What?'

'They've nearly got enough grains from the glass now. They're going to try and recast it. Then they'll go get the other ones, and they'll be able to read the Codex.'

'Where are the other ones?' I said, just to see.

'The Praxies think they're hidden in the family mansion, up in the mountains. They've got a meter in the hiding place to pick up whatever they're emitting. But if you think I'm brilliant, well, you've never met Angelo. He figured out he could put some low-level radioactive material in the hiding place, and it fooled the meter. They could probably have checked the signatures, or the, what do you call it, the half-life, and seen the difference, but as long as the meter was ticking away nobody bothered.'

'Where did he get the radioactive material?'

'One of the physicists at the university. I think he's retired now. Dura … Dura something.'

'Durakovic.'

Danny smiled. 'That's the one. Angelo kept the plates in his house.' The smile vanished. 'He found out too late that whatever they radiated was just as dangerous as the normal stuff. I think he's in a hospice somewhere. He never told me what he did with the plates.'

I knew. Angelo had built a heavy lead box to protect the next caretakers. He must have hired some people to help him put the box in the cave. Then he did his research. He found an academic who was keen enough about field work to venture outside his regular research area. If everything was geography, so could this be.

He started leaving clues, hints, where Kortnoz could find them—pencilled in the margins of professional journals in the library, perhaps, or a set of what looked like lecture notes left behind in a classroom Kortnoz was just about to use. Kortnoz was naive and enthusiastic; he wouldn't question the coincidences. By the time Angelo was no longer able to get around, the trail was already laid and the hound was on it.

And the result? Kortnoz and Pace were in hiding, I was in constant peril, and in Russ's apartment there was a gym bag full of highly toxic glass plates that were the key to Purple Bay's—maybe even the world's—future. Hell's bells.

The thought of Russ made me ask, even though it made me feel superficial and selfish, 'What's this with your sister and Russ Gartner?'

Danny made a disgusted sound. 'She's a predator. He's pretty good-looking, she thought maybe he was going to be famous, and—hey, why do you care?'

I stared at Danny and raised an eyebrow.

A crooked grin spread over his face as he caught on. 'Cool,' he said, and gave me a thumbs-up. 'He dumped her last semester. I'm glad his taste has improved.' He stopped suddenly and blushed furiously.

I diplomatically ignored this last comment. 'So there's nothing between them?'

'Not a thing. She just had dreams of being a movie star's girlfriend. Then she found out he wanted to act on the *stage*—how pissed off was she!'

I found this comforting.

'So,' said Danny carefully. 'Now what?' He'd calmed down a lot once he'd started talking, but now he looked nervous again.

'I don't know, Danny. I guess you should just keep going to classes as usual for now.' But I did have an idea. If the system needed all the tablets to work, and the Praxies were nearly done recovering the lost one, what if another one got lost? That would set them back, what, another hundred years. Pulverise one and throw the powder in the river, just as that long-ago professor had done. Then make sure everyone knew what the Praxies had almost succeeded in doing. If the media would let me get a fair hearing.

But for now, I needed to check in with Russ, my parents, the Ickies, and Dr Garrick—so many people who cared about me, I couldn't decide whether I liked that or not, although on the whole I think I did—eat some lunch, teach my one o'clock, and … what was it? Something—oh. Meet up with Pace, down at the River Walk.

Now that was a surprise. I'd almost forgotten about Pace. She used to be the driving force in my life—all my decisions and reactions were in reference to hers. I guessed that had changed now. For good.

Chapter 16
Pace Pursues a Sideline

The checking-in process was a bit gruelling. Dr Garrick was sarcastic, Russ hovered, Nicki fluttered, Ricky was stoic but did not contribute much to the conversation, and the phone call to my parents did not go particularly well. Finally, Russ and I were off by ourselves eating the lunch he'd thought to pack. Peanut-butter sandwiches, but they tasted just fine. I told him about the tablets, and that now that I knew they were hazardous, I'd be getting them out of his apartment that afternoon. Where I'd put them, I had no idea.

The Geography of Art class looked to be another ordeal. We'd moved on from location-independent artistic collaboration, so Russ couldn't really shoulder any of the burden for me. I delivered my lecture (a case study of the sudden and turbulent burst in artistic collaboration when the North Kras government finally opened the border, two generations ago—three, now, I thought, looking at these children I was teaching), then asked for questions.

'Dr Carlucci, isn't there something to be said for maintaining cultural integrity?' I was surprised: the question came from a student who seldom spoke up in class.

'I'm not sure what you mean.'

'Your lecture made it sound like cultural mixing is always a good thing, but what if vibrant and unique modes of expression are muddied or even lost? Wouldn't it be better if there were some discipline about all this wild collaboration?'

I had a feeling she'd had been watching some of the pseudo-intellectual talking-heads shows on Praxie-owned stations. I didn't have to answer, though, because the other students in the class started arguing energetically in favour of the benefits of cross-border collaboration. I was proud of them, and relieved. Over the years I'd had to sit through plenty of diatribes about North Kras 'infiltrating' and even 'polluting' Krasnia. Only once did I tell my father about it, back when I was seven. He went to the school and raised holy hell, and I couldn't decide which embarrassment was worse: the bigotry I took personally, part-Northie that I was, or my dad's rampage. I kept quiet after that, but the older I got, the less that seemed like an attractive option.

I considered a class that ended with a spirited assault on parochialism a good day's work. But there was still Pace to go meet. I was tempted to ask Russ to go with me, but I was pretty sure Pace would just stay hidden if she saw him.

I took the bus down to the River Walk and sat on one of the benches along the water's edge. The Purple Bay council had finally gotten the idea that tourists would prefer to sit along a nice, clean riverbank with maybe a jazz group playing in the background, rather than picking their way through sludge and debris against a backdrop of abandoned factories—and, whaddaya know, they'd been right. Luckily, once they'd built the River Walk, the council had instantly lost interest in what went on there. As a result, it was one of the most interesting and vibrant places in the city. Not just jazz combos, but sidewalk artists, improv comedians, kids sawing away on violins or puffing wetly into recorders (cases open optimistically at their feet)—everyone who had an interest in being the centre of attention ended up on River Walk sooner or later.

Despite all the stress I'd been under lately and the edginess of waiting for Pace, I found myself enjoying the spectacle. One of the more successful performers was a clown giving out balloons and paper flowers. Occasionally he handed his supply to a dour assistant, also in clown makeup, so he could juggle brightly coloured balls with gauzy streamers trailing along. Neither of them said a word, but I felt sorry for the assistant, who clearly would rather be doing something else.

They worked their way along the wall, getting closer to my bench. Finally the cheerful one was close enough to give me a charming bow and hand me a flower. I grinned as I took it, then heard the dour clown mutter, 'Quit flirting with my boyfriend. Knock it off or, disguise or no disguise, I'll paste you but good.'

The shock was as brutal as if Pace actually had hit me.

'If you're going to be like that, you should just *stay* lost,' I snapped.

'Yeah, all right, sorry,' she whispered angrily, then got hold of herself. 'Where are the, you know, the things we left for you?'

'Safe,' I said. I wasn't feeling all that forthcoming and cooperative, after all Pace had put me through in the past few days.

'Don't be like that, Celeste,' Kortnoz said gently as he and Pace sat on either side of me. I was hanging out on River Walk with a couple of clowns. Just what I'd always dreamed of.

'What's with the getups?' I said.

'For one thing, they're pretty good disguises,' said Kortnoz. 'For another, I think Pace may have mentioned in a message that we don't want to risk accessing our bank accounts. The Littoral League has eyes everywhere.'

'So you're living off children's pennies.'

'Yeah, it's not so great,' said Pace. 'There's a unicyclist who's staked out the area around the ice-cream stand, *prime* clown territory, and things have gotten ugly more than once.' She half-turned to show me the back of her clown suit: sure enough, I could see at least one tyre track running up the back and off the shoulder.

'Yikes,' I said. 'Did it hurt?'

'It hurt a lot less after I put chilli paste on the unicycle seat,' she said. 'He wears very tiny shorts.'

Kortnoz had a funny look on his face, like he didn't know whether to be disapproving or proud.

'I'd love to discuss my life in show business,' said Pace, 'but I need a little more information than what you've given us. Besides, we hear a lot of news from people's radios out here—what's this anti-academic campaign? Kim-Hatton's all over it, of course, populist moron that she is.'

'The Praxies. They know we're onto them about the Codex, and they want to blow our credibility. Just like they did with Millicent Strudthorne.'

Pace snorted. 'That was nothing. It was eighty years ago and before television and the Infonet. Our credibility is not just going to be blown, it's going to be ground into a powder and thrown in the river.'

I almost choked. It was just a coincidence, just a figure of speech, that was all.

'Not only that, but you can bet that government funding for universities will be slashed,' said Kortnoz.

'What, from next to nothing to nothing?' said Pace. 'We already have to cover so much of the budget from tuition that only rich snots like that Danny Wexler can afford it.'

I knew Pace took this personally. Her mother had spent every cent she had to send Pace to St Basilissa's, and then to Purple Bay University—sometimes I thought Pace forgot it, remembering instead whatever it was that had driven them apart; other times, I thought maybe it was *part* of what had driven them apart. Pace is complicated.

'That's not our main problem, though,' said Kortnoz. 'We need to get access to the Codex. It all depends on that.'

Even if I did suspect the Codex was a false god, there was no point in antagonising Kortnoz about it. 'Have you made any progress?'

'Not a thing. It's hard to accomplish any serious scholarship when you're wearing a clown suit.'

'Maybe it's time to come out of hiding. You don't have the—the you-know-whats, you don't even know where they are. And you could get back to doing research.'

'But the League—they're looking for me!' Kortnoz looked genuinely upset, even panicky. 'Norella!'

'Let her try anything, Ty,' said Pace darkly.

I had to be very careful here. 'What if you didn't have to worry about the League? What if, say, Drusy made a deal where they'd leave us alone?'

'In return for what?' said Pace.

'Um, hypothetically speaking, sharing our research.'

'She wouldn't do that,' said Kortnoz instantly.

'But as long as you're hiding, you can't *do* any research. And it's not like sharing it makes you un-know it. And besides, I'm a nervous wreck taking responsibility for those things that you made me take responsibility for. Please … can't you come back? As long they're looking for you, as long as you're in danger, so am I. They'll use me to get to you.' I didn't feel like telling the whole story about how they'd already begun by kidnapping my mom.

Kortnoz looked at me and Pace looked at Kortnoz. His eyes narrowed in a way that made me suddenly very nervous. Finally he said, 'Celeste, what do you know that you're not telling us?'

I lowered my voice. 'There's another tablet. Or there was. The others won't work without it, but it was destroyed a hundred years ago, pulverised and thrown into the Purple River. Ever since, the Praxicopolis family has been extracting it, grain by grain, from the mud of the delta. When they've recovered enough, they're going to recast it. They don't know yet that the other tablets were stolen and hidden away.' I was reluctant to mention Angelo's name—if he was alive, he deserved peace; and if he was dead, he still deserved peace. 'And they've nearly recovered enough.'

'But then it's still about the book.'

'The Praxies and the governors will use whatever they learn from the book to ruin the university, all the universities, and increase Kim-Hatton's power base. That's the problem, not the book itself.'

'That's a pretty big leap,' said Kortnoz. 'Do you have any data to support it?'

I made an exasperated sound. 'That doesn't matter right now.'

'Celeste!' he said in mild reproof. 'It *always* matters that you have data to support your claims!'

'I'll be blunt. We need you to keep the League busy with research so they don't cause any more trouble—and we need whatever you find out about how to get to the Codex. You can always disappear again if you need to. Surely you haven't used up all your hiding places yet?'

'Ty, maybe she's right,' said Pace. 'Some of those hiding places have been …' She shuddered.

He looked at her tenderly. 'All right. We'll risk it. I have to face Norella sometime. I just hope I survive the meeting.' His voice was bleak. Pace reached across me and took his hand.

'Ooooookay, then,' I said, sliding out from under their arms. 'Shall I see you at, say, Drusy's apartment? Around five? I'll phone her and let her know to expect you.'

'Sure,' said Pace. 'We have some things to gather up, and I want to get this damned makeup off.' Pace never wore makeup, let alone the heavy white and red clown paint. 'It's like walking around with dried delta mud on my face. And about as attractive.'

'I always find you attractive,' said Kortnoz predictably.

'Five o'clock,' I said, and walked away.

Behind me I heard a little kid saying, 'Mommy, should those clowns be kissing like that?'

I caught the bus back to campus and headed for the Dramatic Arts building. I hadn't been to Russ's office yet—it boggled my mind to think we'd been together for less than a week—but I thought I'd be able to find him somewhere in the building. Once I got inside, I put my last few coins in the hallway pay phone to call Drusy.

'I've met up with the two people who were … on vacation. I asked them to go to your place at five. He is terrified of that woman who scares him, and I was hoping you could calm him down, reassure him that you've got an understanding with them. I hope that's okay, because otherwise they're going to stay hidden and I'm going to be a nervous wreck.'

'Sure, Celeste, sweetie. You were very clever to convince them to emerge. It solves a lot of worries for all of us. Creates others, of course, but on the whole I think we'll be better off.' I hoped so.

I walked up and down the corridors, looking for Russ. I found him in one of the rehearsal rooms, with the same three kids he'd been working with when we'd met. His face lit up when he saw me, and that made me feel significantly better.

'We're going over the first couple of revised scenes,' he said. 'Want to watch? You can tell us if it's any better than the original.'

'Okay.' I leaned against a wall and slid down until I hunkered on the floor. I was quite surprised: the script had gone from bad television comedy to witty satire, with the change of only a few words here and there. The actors were all clearly having a much better time, which helped as well. Suddenly it sparkled and amused, and gave the feeling of a sly wink and a nudge. But underneath it all was a sense of deep concern. This play was about things that mattered: trust, respect, dignity—and the lack of them. You could laugh, and think that was all, but later on, when you were washing the dishes maybe, you'd think of something the characters had said, or even just the way they'd said it, so full of meaning. And maybe you'd go and give your husband a hug, or go outside and bring your neighbour's trash bins in for them.

The run-through of the scenes took about a half hour, but I hardly noticed the time passing.

'Wow,' I said when they were done. 'Dr Gartner, I didn't know you were a playwright.'

He actually blushed. 'Well, it's easier when you have something to start with. Not like coming up with it from scratch.'

I said to the kids, 'And you guys have really got a handle on it. I can't wait to see it on opening night!'

'Thanks, Dr Carlucci.' They, too, blushed, which I found a bit alarming. I hadn't expected my opinion to have such weight.

'Okay, guys, that's probably enough for today. You're doing great,' said Russ. 'Same time tomorrow—no, wait, I've got a class to teach. You know, what they actually pay me for. How about five? Are you available?'

They said they were, bid us goodbye, and left. Once they were gone, Russ and I got reacquainted for a minute or two. Maybe longer.

'Speaking of five,' I said, 'can you come with me to Drusy's tonight? At the aforementioned five?'

'What's up?'

'Pace is coming out of hiding.'

'Oh. Um, maybe I shouldn't go. She doesn't like me much, and I'd hate to put you in that position, she being your friend and all.'

'I'm not sure we're on that good of terms anymore. If you're there, she'll distribute her rancour over both of us. Better than one copping the whole hit.'

'Okay, then, glad to help.'

I kissed him, to show how grateful I was. I was pretty grateful.

Eventually, I said, 'I should get back to my office and see if Dr Garrick is still sitting there, fuming because I left and went out into the big, bad world.'

'Well, it is pretty bad at the moment. For you, anyway. Can I come with you there, too?'

'To protect me?'

'Hell, no. To follow you with slavish devotion and desire.'

'All right, then.'

We went by his office so he could get his backpack. Like me, he shared his office. His desk was a bit cluttered, but nothing horrific. The desk on the other side of the office supported a creeping glacier of papers, folders, recording disks, pens, books, chocolate-bar wrappers, and, perched on top as a paperweight, a stone that had been painted to say, 'Fame is a state of mind'.

'Yeesh,' I said, looking at the precarious formation.

'Oh. Yeah. Georgina. Can't wait to make it big and get out of here. Every week another audition. I've stopped asking how they went. I figure once she gets a juicy part I'll know: in will come the bulldozer to get all her crap out of here, and I won't be sorry to see it go.'

He glanced at his desk, then did a double take. 'Oh … no …' he said.

'What?'

'I don't want to touch it.'

'*What?*'

'It's a note from Miffy. Georgina keeps letting her in here. I've *told* her …'

'Mind if I …?' I said, and gestured toward the pink piece of paper.

'Are you sure? It may be toxic.'

'Not to me. I need a laugh.'

'I'm glad you think this is amusing,' he said, and handed me the paper. '"Dearest Rusty,"' I read. '*Rusty?*'

'Don't ask.'

'"I'm disappointed you refuse to see things clearly. You always did need help with that. If you don't come to your senses soon—and by soon I mean very soon, like, say, Friday—it will be time to ask Mom for my birthday present a little early this year. Do I need to spell that out for you as well? Waiting for you to see reason. Your loving Miffy."'

I almost felt like the note *was* toxic. 'Sheesh. Are you sure she's not part Praxicopolis? Maybe a bastard offspring left on the Wexlers' doorstep?'

Russ shrugged and looked away.

'You're embarrassed. Because you got involved with her to begin with. I get that,' I said. 'Maybe you're worried that I won't want to be with you, if that's the kind of trouble you get yourself into, and the kind of person you get taken in by.' He nodded, but still didn't look at me.

'Russ? That's not going to happen. Not after all we've been through already. Hell's bells, we've seen more trauma in one week of this relationship than most couples see in the first ten years. If I were going to ditch you, or even think badly of you, I'd have done it by now. Okay?'

He nodded again.

'And if we can figure out how to de-fang the governors, that pretty much de-fangs Miffy, too, doesn't it?'

'I guess it does.'

'There's your motivation.'

He did laugh at that, which was a relief. Then he looked at me, finally, which was also a relief.

'Risk it,' I said.

'Risk what?'

'Risk being not perfect. After all, you saw me coming from the swamp like a creature from a horror film, and you still thought I was okay.'

'I'd never seen anyone so beautiful in my life.'

My turn to blush. 'It's probably time we went over to Drusy's.'

Russ picked up his pack and we left. My office was empty; apparently Dr Garrick had had enough of me. 'We might as well head off now,' I said.

'Time enough to walk?'

I looked at my watch. 'Should be. Why?'

'Saves bus fare. And walking helps me think.'

'Whatcha thinking about?'

'Solutions. Or the lack thereof. I'll let you know if I come up with anything.'

The sky was clouding over, and the breeze blew suddenly colder. 'Cold front coming in,' I said.

'I'll take your word for it.'

'I thought all the weather people on television were out-of-work actors.'

'That doesn't mean they understand the weather. Just that they can read the prompters.'

The breeze was becoming distinctly uncomfortable by the time we got to Drusy's. The latest receptionist let us in and phoned Drusy to tell her we were there. The way to her apartment—up the stairs and down the hallway to the left—was getting to be as familiar to me as my own.

When Drusy opened the door, Pace and Kortnoz were sitting on the sofa. Dr Garrick and Mark were there as well.

'Come on in, sweetie,' said Drusy. 'Hello, Russ, glad you're still toughing it out with us. Coffee?'

'Yes, please,' we both said.

'Just bring a couple of the kitchen chairs into the living room for yourselves. There are some cookies on the coffee table.'

Kortnoz and Pace had managed to get most of the clown makeup off, but I could still see traces of thick, white paint at their hairlines and in the creases around Kortnoz's eyes. With the makeup gone, I could see how exhausted they looked. They'd both lost a fair bit of weight, too. Not too many of the cookies were left on the tray.

Kortnoz nodded pleasantly when I introduced Russ, but neither he nor Pace seemed to be in the mood to talk. We exchanged a bit of small talk with the others—well, with Mark; Dr Garrick seemed to be giving me the silent treatment, probably still mad at me from the morning—and waited for Drusy. When I saw she was on her way over, I got a third chair from the kitchen for her.

'Thanks, sweetie,' she said. She set the coffee down and sat in the chair. I poured the coffee out, and took a mug for myself.

While everyone was stirring milk and sugar into their mugs, Drusy said, 'It's such a relief to have the two of you back.' Kortnoz smiled, but Pace did not. Uh-oh. 'Now that you're here, we can share what we know, and perhaps come up with a plan for what to do next. You know it won't be long before Norella Honeycott tracks you down, Ty.'

'Last time she tracked me down, she shot at me,' he said petulantly.

'Oh, lighten up,' said Dr Garrick. 'She missed, didn't she?'

'Now, Ty, I have to warn you, because we need to keep a very close eye on the Littoral League, we're actually, in a sense, collaborating with them at the moment,' said Drusy.

Pace sat bolt upright. 'See, Ty, I told you we shouldn't have come out of hiding. No matter how well-intentioned these people are, they have no idea of what they're getting into. Drusy, do you have even an inkling of what Honeycott is capable of?'

'Pace, honey, I have more than an inkling of what *you're* capable of, but that doesn't mean I can't work with you, does it?'

'That's different. I've got morals!'

'Honeycott's got obsessions, which are nearly as useful for predicting behaviour,' said Drusy. 'And if we can predict her behaviour, we can manage it.'

'Okay, all-seeing-eye, what's she going to do next, now that Ty is standing up and yelling "Yoo-hoo, insane stalker, over here!"?'

'First, she's going to confront him, assess whether he still refuses to succumb to her charms. Next, she'll try to blackmail him.'

'Well, that's ridiculous, because Ty hasn't done anything she could blackmail him with.'

'Then,' said Drusy, ignoring her, 'it will occur to her that she is not up to date on whatever the two of you have found out, and her need to solve the Codex and thereby seize control over the entire university—for its own good, of course—will override her need to acquire Ty. That's the point at which she'll start to wheedle, bargain, flatter. Finally, her patience will snap, and she'll try to force you to cooperate, as she tried to force Celeste.'

'What does that mean?' said Pace.

Okay, time to tell it. 'She kidnapped my mom,' I said.

Pace turned a horror-stricken face to me.

'She's all right now,' I added quickly. 'But we bargained to get her out. We share what we find out about the Codex, and she leaves my mom alone.'

I was half expecting Pace to say what a lousy trade that had been, but instead she breathed a sigh of relief.

'Besides, if we share our findings up front, that takes away her worst weapon: fear of research theft,' said Drusy.

'I was actually more afraid of the helicopter and the guns, myself,' I said. I should have kept my mouth shut.

'Yeah, we already know research theft holds no terrors for you,' said Pace.

'Hypatia,' said Drusy. 'Stop that right now. What's done is done, and you weren't exactly a shining example of noble behaviour yourself.'

'So I dangle someone over a lava pit *once*, so what? Is no one ever going to let me forget it?' she muttered. 'And don't call me Hypatia.'

'The real problem isn't the Littoral League,' said Mark.

'It isn't?' said Ty, genuinely puzzled.

'It's the governors, you idiot,' said Dr Garrick. 'And the Praxies. The Littoral League is a bunch of wannabes. They're like a roller skate left on the stairs. Sure, they can make you trip and fall, but they're nowhere near as dangerous as, say, the faulty wiring that's about to burn down the whole house.'

'That's a charming metaphor,' said Pace. 'But I think you're underestimating the League.'

'Not based on what I've seen,' I said. 'It's Honeycott with a bunch of undergrads, and presumably a helicopter pilot.'

'Again with the helicopter! Is that all you ever think about?' said Pace.

'No,' I said, as mildly as I could. 'I also think about saving the university from the governors and breaking their chokehold on us and everything we research, publish, or imagine.'

'I'd like to postpone the personal squabbles for a bit,' said Drusy. 'Celeste, you probably have as good an overview of the situation as anyone. How would you summarise it?'

Pace started to talk, but Mark reached over and put a hand on her arm, then held up his hand in a 'wait a minute' gesture. She stared at him, but stayed quiet.

'The way I see it, there are four main players, or groups of players,' I said. 'First, there's us: you people here in the retirement home, and those of us who work with you to thwart the governors and the Praxies.' The older academics nodded. 'Second, there are, of course, the governors and the Praxies. We can probably consider them as a single entity for now. Third, there's the Littoral League. And fourth, there's Joan Maher, the loose cannon.' I'd avoided mentioning the Sewers, because there was probably a reason the academics hadn't told Pace and Ty about the complex. 'Joan scares me the most, in a way, because I have absolutely no idea what she wants out of all this. She tricked me to find where you'd hid the tablets, she set me up to be attacked, she tried to get me to surrender the tablets, but couldn't or wouldn't take them by force, and she used to be part of our gang here, but now she's not—who *is* she? What does she want?'

'It's true, you have to know what someone wants before you can defeat them,' said Drusy. 'We may need to wait until she reveals more. Meanwhile, can we do anything about the League, the Praxies, or the governors?'

'The governors want to quash all unrest and opposition across the university,' said Mark thoughtfully. 'Therefore, the way to defeat them is to ensure that there is more unrest and opposition than they can cope with at once.'

'Riots?' said Russ. 'People will get hurt.'

'Not riots. Something more intelligent than that. Subversion,' said Dr Garrick. 'You're a drama boy, Drusy says. Tell me, drama boy, are you producing a show this semester?'

Russ looked startled. 'Well, yes, we do one every semester, but—'

'Original script? Or old standby?'

'Original.'

'Fantastic!' said Dr Garrick, thumping his bony fist on the arm of chair. 'The power of art,' he intoned solemnly, 'can bring down empires and crumble fortresses.' He stared at Russ intently. 'Do you see?'

Russ nodded slowly.

'And you!' Dr Garrick said, pointing suddenly at me. 'You've got your deadheads in Intro to Geography. Two hundred sleeping minds that you can *WAKE UP*!' We all jumped. 'Not to mention the students of actual quality in your other classes. No telling what they'd do with a little guidance. This is a university we're talking about here, not a branding corral! Teach those kids something they can actually use. Teach them to fight! Teach them to use their *minds*.'

'If it's that simple,' said Pace, 'why hasn't anyone done it before?'

'Oh, there have been plenty of isolated battles, skirmishes really,' said Dr Garrick. 'Like drama boy's contract dispute. And the things we do here. But no one's pulled it all together before. The governors have been very careful to set up an environment where it's hard to cooperate.' I thought of Pace's struggle with Entomology over the bugs, the antipathies between departments over scheduling conflicts, the way untenured teachers had to fight like rats for resources and attention and the chance to live a decent life. And how once they got tenure, suddenly everything was easy, through the bounty of the governors—and what the governors gave, the governors could take away. And always the unspoken threat of the jackbooted security guards.

'Are you saying all that's *deliberate*?' said Pace. 'Calculated?'

Dr Garrick just raised an eyebrow.

'But the reappearance of the tablets has drawn a lot of people together who ordinarily never would have met,' said Drusy. 'Why not take advantage of that? Why shouldn't this be the time for action—concerted action?'

'I'm in,' said Russ. 'As long as it's non-violent. Like I said, I don't want any kids getting hurt.'

'I'm in,' I said.

'You bet I'm in,' said Dr Garrick.

'Me, too,' said Mark. 'And we can probably assume Ruby and the others here will be in as well. What about the librarians, any guesses?'

'They're in,' I said. 'Martha's mortified that they let Joan slip through. They're looking for her now so they can minimise the damage.'

'Each of you knows others who will be happy to help, I'm sure. Just be careful how much you say right off. Ty? Pace? What about you?'

'What about *us*? What about the Codex?' Ty was visibly distressed. 'What you're talking about will delay our research by years. And how much funding do you think we'll get if the university is in chaos?'

'Ty, you haven't been *thinking*,' said Drusy. 'How much good will all your research do you if the governors are still in control? Whatever you find out, they will know immediately. And so will the Praxies. Who will dare to publish you independently, if the governors suppress your research? And they will.'

'But—of course they—I—'

'Ty,' said Pace quietly. 'She's right.' He turned to her, shocked. 'First, the governors,' she continued. 'Then the research. We're wasting our time any other way.' She turned to Drusy. 'So. Now what?'

'We've bought you some time with the Littoral League. There shouldn't be any more stalking or kidnapping, as long as Norella thinks there's research going on that she wants. Use that time. Celeste, I'd like you to be our link with what's happening on campus. It's probably safe to turn your phone back on now, so phone me any time, day or night, whenever something comes up or something unusual happens.'

Pace frowned, clearly puzzled.

'Yes?' said Drusy.

Pace glanced at me, then said, 'Nothing.'

I said, 'What if it wasn't just the Littoral League that was stalking and kidnapping?' The still-healing cut on my neck suddenly itched.

'It's not the governors' style, frankly, and the Praxies work through the governors when it comes to the university. I think we can risk it.'

I felt like a whiner, but I had to bring the point up, if only for completeness' sake: 'And what about Joan Maher?'

'That *is* a problem,' said Drusy. 'We have no experience dealing with her, no patterns we can work from.'

'We know she's not entirely on her own,' I said. 'Otherwise, there wouldn't have been anyone on the path to jump me. And how did she find out that the tablets were up in the cave, anyway?'

Ty's distress increased audibly. 'I'm … I'm sorry about that, Celeste,' he said, near tears.

'What!'

'She … she was so helpful, finding me rare books, ancient treatises about what the Codex might contain, clues to its origins and how to use the tablets. She guessed a lot based on what I was asking for, and … and we got talking, that's all. She was so helpful, so interested … I'm sorry.'

'Kortnoz,' said Dr Garrick, 'no one can deny you've got talent as a geographer. But you are so damned naive it's a wonder you got tenure.'

'What do you mean?' said Kortnoz. 'I just signed a contract, that's all. It was years ago.'

'Hmm. Did you read it?'

'I must have. Of course I did. I think. It was a while back. I was very young.'

'What it comes down to,' said Drusy, 'is that we don't know what Joan Maher is going to do, or how she's going to do it.'

'Moreover, we don't have any firm plans for destabilising the university,' said Mark. 'It's going to be down to your imaginations and your improvisation skills.'

'At last,' said Russ, 'I can actually be useful.'

'Well, you did save my life last week, and … everything.' I'd been about to say 'You let me move in with you,' but I just didn't want to get into all that in front of Pace.

'Meanwhile, we'll be monitoring comms in shifts,' said Mark. 'When should we meet up again?'

'Thursday, I think,' said Drusy. 'Perhaps we should choose another place, rather than draw more attention here.'

'Much as I'd rather never see the place again, there's a picnic area on the River Walk,' said Pace. 'So many people milling around, a few more won't attract any notice. Unless it's raining, in which case we'll look like idiots sitting out in the rain.'

'How about the picnic area if it's sunny, but the food court in the mall next door if it isn't?' said Mark.

'Thursday, five o'clock,' said Drusy. 'Until then, go out and destabilise!'

'I think I'll be doing a bit of that myself,' said Dr Garrick as we stood up. 'I got the taste for it again, teaching for Celeste. Ah, you know you're alive when you rile up a room full of undergraduates! Just like a charging herd of badly dressed, headphone-wearing wildebeests, they are.'

'Dr Garrick, just exactly what did you say to my students while I was gone?' I said.

'You'll be amazed at how much more energetic they are,' he said, patting my arm. 'Absolutely amazed.'

Chapter 17
Destabilisation Begins

Even though Drusy had implied it was all right for me to go back home, I still stayed at Russ's. We both just felt better that way, despite the neighbourhood. We spent the night quietly again, both of us thinking of ways to 'destabilise'. Problem was—for Russ much more than for me, although we both felt it—we were used to thinking of the university as unchangeable, monolithic, the backdrop to our entire lives. It had been the backdrop to Russ's whole family for generations.

Russ said he had some ideas about how he could use the department chair's play, but aside from that, he felt as flustered as I did. It would take more than one play, the premiere more than a month off, to wreak the kind of disintegration Drusy and Dr Garrick wanted.

As for me, I pictured the sea of drowsy faces I'd be looking at tomorrow morning and quailed at what it would take to inspire them. But what had Dr Garrick meant about riling them up? On second thought, maybe I'd have less work than I thought.

We woke the next morning and got ready for the day. I felt glum and overwhelmed; I could tell Russ felt the same. We were hardly the great battle leaders who, by sheer charisma, could rally our troops to battle the forces of evil. But we were all there was. I wondered if all generals felt like this as they went into battle. Maybe none of them had actually liked war. Maybe they commanded with the leaden burden of duty and the terror of incompetence, not the fire of inspiration. I sure hoped so, because otherwise we were dead.

Russ left me at the Geography building. After I'd gone to bed the night before, he'd spent a bit of time editing the script of the department chair's play, and he seemed eager to show it to his cast.

At least he had a plan. I had none. I stood in front of my Intro class and said nothing as they stared at me. And stared. And stared. Finally, I took a deep breath and said, 'You don't want to be here, do you?'

A few of them protested politely, but the vast majority shook their heads. I saw Danny in the back of the room, a slow, open-mouthed smile of realisation taking over his face.

'You don't want to be here. This class is boring and you don't see how it's useful to your future. You're tired of the bland readings and the tedious assignments. You sense that I don't like being here either. Don't you?'

This time there were no protests, just two hundred heads nodding.

'Well, we're going to change the way we do things in here. In fact, we're going to change the whole university. Problem is, you could all be kicked out of here if it doesn't work out. But if it does, I'll be able to teach you real geography: adventure, travel, excitement, really understanding the world and how we shape it—and it shapes us. Let's start now. How does the physical layout of this university shape how we move around in it, how we learn, how we interact?'

'There are levees, disguised as regular land contours, so that the governors can selectively flood areas of the campus, put them under siege, cut them off from each other.' It was Danny. We grinned at each other across the room: he got it. He knew what I wanted to do, and he was with me. 'The pump house is over near the gym.'

'Of course,' murmured one of the kids in the front row. 'Why should this be the only spot in the floodplain that has all these low hills? Only on campus? Why didn't we see it?'

Oh, I thought, feeling breathless. She actually used the word 'floodplain'.

I pulled myself together. 'Good start,' I said in a ringing voice. 'What else?'

'Some of the paths are lit at night, and some of them aren't,' came a voice.

'So we tend to choose the lit paths,' said another. 'What happens along the dark paths at night that they don't want us to see?'

'You can't get to the pub without walking past a security station.'

'The departments that ought to be collaborating are spaced way far apart, with tons of other buildings between. Like Math and Engineering, or—'

'Or Geography and Sociology.'

'The bookstore is too small for everyone to get their books at the beginning of the semester.'

'Right!' I said, cutting through their excited talk. The silence was immediate, rapt, and complete. 'Divide into groups of five or six.' There was a buzz and rumble as they arranged themselves. 'Which group wants to do some, uh, further investigation into the pump house?' Three groups raised their hands; I chose one. 'The unlit paths? Okay. Storming, I mean accessing, the pub? Setting up communication lines between departments? Opening out the bookstore?' There were plenty of groups left over. 'The rest of you—independent study! Identify, analyse, and propose solutions to a geographical problem on campus. Are you all ready?'

'Yes!' they thundered.

'Spend the rest of this hour sorting out how you're going to start, who will do what to begin with, and when and where you're going to check in with each other. Needless to say, this research is not necessarily appropriate for discussion with your housemates or drinking buddies. Okay?'

'Yes!'

'Go!'

I watched them huddle in their groups, their faces shining. I caught Danny's eye again, and we gave each other a thumbs-up.

Towards the end of the hour, I called for their attention again. 'From what I've been hearing, you are all making good progress. Remember: this research is embargoed, not for release or discussion outside your study group. Now go and be geographers!'

I stood at the front of the room until they left, then I sank into a chair as the adrenaline started to seep away. Danny had left with his study group, and I thought I was alone until I heard Dr Garrick's scrabbling footsteps as he walked stiffly to the front of the room.

'Quite a show,' he said, leaning on the chair next to mine. He bent toward me. 'Well done.'

'Thanks.'

'What do you have planned for your stars in the seminar?'

'I improvised here; I suppose I'll do the same with them.'

'Uh-uh,' said Dr Garrick. 'Not that group. Improvising is all right for the wildebeests. But they're your elite troops. Think of something better.'

Terrific, I thought. Like what?

'By the way, has drama boy mentioned his plans to you?'

'He's editing the script for the play his students are rehearsing. Aside from that, no.'

'He's one of the Gartners, isn't he?'

'Yup.'

'What's his mother's name?'

'I don't know. Why?'

'Just wondering the degree to which genetics plays a role in these long-running university dynasties.'

'I'm the first PhD in my family on both sides, so I'm proof that genetics doesn't play a role.'

'But families can. Almost the same thing. Suppose your parents were professors here, and their parents had been, and theirs and theirs and theirs? You wouldn't know any other way of life. At least you, being a mongrel, chose to be here. Oh, don't take offence at "mongrel", it's a compliment. At least that's how I mean it.'

'The Strudthornes are one of those dynasties. Millicent to Talbot to Todd.'

'Poor bugger. He keeps to himself, mainly. Never really did recover from what the Praxies did to him. Or to his father and grandmother. He always took it very personally.'

'What about Talbot? What happened to him?'

'He taught math. Something very safe and predictable and not likely to get him noticed, he thought. He was a detail person, like Millicent. But math includes statistics and probability and pseudo-random algorithms, which all have lots to do with voting. Voting for governors, and voting for Purple Bay officials, and voting on public referendums about, say, media ownership. He wasn't as strong as his mother, and they managed to co-opt his research pretty effectively. It broke him. He wasn't much of a father to Todd. His wife left him as soon as Todd was out of high school.'

Chalk another one up to the Praxies.

I said, 'I want to go to the library, talk with a friend there. Do you want to come along?'

'I don't actually walk very … That is, I'm not much for rushing around.' For the first time, Dr Garrick sounded less than arrogant.

'That's fine,' I said casually. 'Let's go.' And we walked very slowly, but in pleasant silence, across campus.

Martha came toward us the instant she saw us walk through the library door. 'Come on,' she said. 'We need to talk. Hi, Dr Garrick.'

'It's Mary, isn't it?' said Dr Gararick.

'Martha.' She led us to a meeting room behind the reference section and unlocked it. We went inside and sat down. It was stuffy, and a layer of dust made the table and chairs look faded.

I hesitated to sit down. 'What does toxic mould look like?' I said.

'Oh, don't worry,' said Martha as she and Dr Garrick sat. 'You'll know it when you see it. And you won't see it unless it means business.'

I didn't really want to know what business it might mean. I sat gingerly.

'What's up?' I said.

'Joan. We think we've located her. She's underground.'

'In hiding? Or literally underground?'

'Literally. The volunteers in the canteen have noticed food disappearing. They've got a new cook. He can only do a few meals a week—he's got classes and assignments, but everything he touches turns into the best food you ever ate. And he's all over what goes on in the kitchen, knows where every packet of sugar and every piece of pie goes. He's the one who spotted it.'

Looked like Nicki had brought Ricky into the family business at last. Things must be getting serious between them. I also suspected she'd waited until Ricky demonstrated aptitude at something—when you're part of an academic dynasty, maybe you feel a little funny about bringing an academic dud into the fold, unless he's got some sort of blazing talent that compensates.

'So she's skulking. Waiting for an opportunity? To do what? Or is she just hiding from our wrath?' said Dr Garrick.

'She wants the tablets and the Codex,' I said.

'Why didn't she just take the tablets from you?' said Martha. 'Why the elaborate scheme to get them, and you, and then just let both go?'

'I'm betting it's because she still wanted the run of the Sewers—can't you people come up with a better name than that? I feel so stupid saying it,' I said. 'Anyway, she didn't want to blow her own cover.'

'What changed?' said Martha.

'That I don't know. She showed me the tunnel to the duck pond, and I haven't seen her since. As far as I knew, she was just a slightly odd and uncomfortable member of the team. It was only when I had time to think about it that I figured out she wasn't a team player. I feel like an idiot for not seeing it sooner.'

'*You* feel like an idiot?' said Martha. 'We worked with her every day and *we* never saw it.'

'I take it you've set up a buddy system underground,' said Dr Garrick.

'Yes, of course,' said Martha.

'And you've locked off most of the exits?'

'I assume so.'

'Assume?' said Dr Garrick sharply.

'I'll double-check,' said Martha meekly.

'You do that,' muttered Dr Garrick. 'Pity we don't have access to the university surveillance recordings. We could see which exit she's using.'

'Why should she be using any exit?' I said. 'There's food, shelter, plumbing, books even. But why does she want the tablets so badly? They're just pretty glass without the Codex.'

'Maybe …' Martha spoke in a horrified whisper. 'Maybe she's got the Codex.'

'If she has it, then she has it underground, and won't leave it,' Dr Garrick said. 'It means we have to start sending search parties down there, looking for her and it. What a pain in the ass.'

'Can the tunnel network be sectorised?' I said. 'Gates, barriers, piles of rocks? So she can't sneak into an area once a search party has passed?'

'We'll work something out,' said Dr Garrick. 'I need to talk to the Sewers coordinator and get that happening.' He got carefully to his feet. 'I'll see you two around. Obviously there's work to be done that it takes a geographer emeritus to do.'

I thanked Martha for the update, and started back to my office. I wondered how Pace and Kortnoz were doing. I didn't see either one as being much of a rabble-rouser. Pace, in particular, was more like a guerrilla soldier.

Or a ninja, I corrected myself when I got back to the office. Because, sure enough, she'd summoned her martial-arts club, and they packed the office from wall to wall: when I managed to open the door a few centimetres, all I could see were a jumble of muscly backs and shoulders and legs before Pace saw me, hollered, 'Give me a minute,' and had one of her buddies shut the door again.

I waited in the hallway until they all came out. Every one of them was adrenalised; I could see it in the slightly tense way they moved and in how their eyes were wide and dark. I realised this was the day they'd been training for all their lives, the moment when they actually got to use their skills to combat evil. The comic book had come to life.

I went into the office, which suddenly seemed cavernous. 'What have you got them doing?' I said.

Pace grinned, an animal grin that made me want to step back. 'Don't click on that if you don't want that screen to come up,' she said.

'I wonder when we're going to get our computers back, speaking of clicking,' I said.

'When hell freezes. They're doubtless going over those disks with an electron microscope, looking for seditious documents. Ironic, isn't it? The very act that is supposed to repress us is actually the one that guides our feet into the way of sedition. There's something poetic in that. Is this just the fruition of plans laid down years, decades, a century ago? How much choice do any of us have? Are we just the pawns of the forces of history?'

'Nope,' I said.

'You're probably right. Want to get some lunch?'

'Do you have any money?'

'Um, yeah, a bit. I have tenure, remember? And I can get to my bank account now. Let's go.'

Tenure. I'd forgotten all about it. That was odd; it used to consume my days and nights.

'You seem to be quite a favourite of the retirees,' Pace said as we walked.

'Maybe. I like them, anyway.'

'They seem to tell you a lot of what's going on.'

'Maybe,' I said again.

'Did you know there's a network of tunnels under the university?'

'I'd heard about it, yeah.'

'Just heard?' Pace sounded suddenly hostile.

'What's wrong?' I said.

That set her off at last. 'You think you're so special. Ever since St Basilissa's. I was smarter, I was always smarter, but everyone liked you better, even the nuns, and most of them didn't like anybody. You had the nice, kind, involved parents and the two incomes and everyone liked you. And then you stole my research—*stole my research*—and nothing happened to you at all. Shut up! I said nothing. Nothing serious, anyway. And all your students loooooooooooove you. And now the academics and the librarians and even the bloody Littoral League, they all think you're fabulous, they tell you everything, take you everywhere, like you're the key to everything. Well, you're still not as smart, not as special as I am. I'm not going to be your bloody second in command. And I'm not hungry. Go to lunch by yourself.'

I stood absolutely still and watched her go. When she was quite some way away, I saw her lift a hand to wipe her eyes, just once.

I wasn't hungry either. I found myself turning around and heading for the Dramatic Arts building. I wanted Russ. I wanted to be with someone who wasn't going to turn on me. Someone who wanted to believe the best about me. All these years I'd stuck with Pace, listened to her, tagged along, picked up the pieces, calmed the cops down—it all meant exactly, precisely … nothing.

Outside Russ's door I stopped. He had someone in his office with him. Someone distraught, by the sound of it. Damn. Right when I really needed him, he was counselling a confused undergraduate or something.

Through the door I heard, 'Miffy, for God's sake.'

Right. I pounded on the door. 'Russ?'

Silence behind the door. Then, 'Yes, Russ, let her in. It's her, isn't it? The woman I've seen you walking with—and doing other things as well. Let her in, Russ, don't be rude. Here, I'll do it.'

The door opened. I saw a woman, slight but intense, expensively dressed, with long hair that flowed in waves.

'Hi,' she said with the warmth that the rich can muster at will. 'I'm Miffy. Russ's girlfriend.'

'Ex-girlfriend,' I said coolly. After Pace's theatrics, I was in no mood for hers.

'We'll see about that,' she said.

'You're nuts,' I announced. There didn't seem to be anything more to say, so I shoved past her, pushed her out into the hallway, said, 'Buh-bye, now,' and closed the door behind her. Then I locked the door, and it made a very satisfying click indeed. The sound of Miffy pounding on the door was even more satisfying. I hoped she broke a nail. Several.

Russ's jaw hung open. Over the pounding of Miffy's fists, he said, 'I can't believe you just did that.'

'Problem?'

'No! No no no no! Absolutely not.'

'See? It's been that easy all along.'

'I … I guess it has.'

I lowered my voice to a murmur, even though it made it hard to hear over the pounding and shouting in the hallway. 'So. What have you done today to advance our goal of world domination?'

'Version three of the first act is done,' said Russ quietly. 'I've shown it to the actors—they can't wait until this afternoon's rehearsal. The chair hasn't seen it yet, but hopefully she'll be so swept up she won't notice how much we've changed it. And I've got my Intro class doing performance art in the quad.'

'You … think that's a good idea?'

'Are you kidding? They're having the time of their lives.'

'But are they any good?'

'They wouldn't have signed up for the class if they didn't want to act. This is not just learning to act, but changing the world through acting. It's—it's bringing out the best in them. I have to admit even I was surprised at some of the ideas they had in class. Want to go see them?'

The noise from outside had stopped. 'I guess it's safe to leave,' I said. 'But what if she's waiting in the hallway with a meat cleaver?'

'Nah. That dress cost a fortune, I remember when she bought it. Silk, too—impossible to get blood stains out of silk.'

'What if she were very meticulous, and wore a smock over the dress?'

'Then we'd have to worry. But … listen!'

I held my breath. In the utter stillness, I heard the slight rustling of fabric.

'Silk, my left butt cheek,' I said loudly. 'That was the sound of synthetic!'

There was a gasp of outrage from the other side.

'Well, I'll be,' said Russ. 'Looks like someone's been eavesdropping.' He yanked the door open, but Miffy had already taken off.

'How much did she hear?' I said anxiously.

'We were being quiet, and she was being loud for most of it, but the doors are pretty cheap. But anyway,' he said cheerfully, 'the plans are already set in motion. Come on, we'll go see.'

The quad was buzzing. The normal lunchtime crowd was not spread out, as usual, but gathered in clumps around the brick plaza. I heard laughs, gasps, applause.

The group nearest us was improvising based on random words from the audience. 'Book!' 'Mango!' 'Intellectual!' (I wondered if that last one was a plant.) The kids started right away.

'So, uh, what's that book you're reading?' said one.

'Why do you always ask that? Why can't I keep my brain to myself? A brain isn't something you share—like a mango or something.'

'No. You're not a mango. You're an intellectual, and I need to make sure you're not misusing your very expensive education.'

Behind me, I heard the crackle and squawk of a security radio. I spun around to see a half-dozen security guards slowly spreading out around the edges of the quad.

'I hope you gave your kids some guidelines about how to avoid getting their heads beaten in,' I murmured to Russ. He nodded, but as more and more people noticed the security guards, the crowd became quieter. I saw people start to wander casually away.

A few of the actors were giving each other nervous glances, but they kept going. The mango-versus-intellectual debate escalated into a stage-combat fistfight that got more wild and acrobatic every second. Finally, the two actors broke apart, panting. One of them said, 'This form of conflict resolution is less than effective.'

'Yeah,' said the other. 'Maybe we should go back to playing chess.' Most of the people in the audience chuckled.

'Not bad for improv,' I said to Russ. 'I can see what they're try-ing to do.'

'And they're being very professional, too,' he said. 'They're not letting the environment thwart their artistic vision. If you see what I mean.'

The next group along was teaching their crowd a song. The melody was a North Kras drinking song I remembered hear-ing my father and his cousins sing. The words, though, were in Krasnian, not Northie dialect.

Gather round the table, friends!
Though the wine is scant and sour,
Still we'll sing to cheer ourselves
And light this dark and chilly hour.
Way hey, pass the bottle!
Way hey, share the bread!
Northie, Kras, or wandering loony,
All are welcomed, warmed, and fed!

'"Wandering loony"?' I said. Russ shrugged. The tune was catchy, though, and already plenty of people were singing along and clapping.

The security guards were absolutely immobile, waiting for the instant one of the students would go too far, say or do something that could, at a stretch, possibly look like they were starting a riot. Or thinking about it. Or scratching their nose—it might be a signal to form a mob. I was disgusted.

Russ's face was shining, though—he only had eyes for his students, heedless of danger, doing what they could to make the university an entirely different place. We wandered from group to group. The jugglers were risking what looked like serious bodily harm to amaze and delight their audience. A performance-poetry competition was gaining momentum over near the bicycle rack. And—yes, there he was—a mime, whiteface and all.

'And every one of them has a reason, a goal, for each performance,' I said, wondering.

'Yup,' said Russ. 'I just had to start them off with a few examples. They're teaching the other students new ways of thinking—by *example*. Fantastic!'

'You'll call them off once the lunchtime crowds thin, won't you?' I said quietly. 'When there aren't so many witnesses, I don't like to think what the security guards will do.'

'Guards?' he said, and noticed them for the first time. He swallowed.

'Yuh,' I said.

'I'll … um … I'll call them off at the end of lunchtime.'

'Yuh.' I looked at my watch. 'I have to get ready to teach my one o'clock.' I was going to say, 'I have to think of some sort of mayhem for them,' but realised in time that saying that out loud in a plaza filled with really mean security guards was, at best, rash.

Russ gave my hand a quick squeeze, and I went back to the Geography building. My first stop was the mail room. I was hoping that anyone who didn't get an email reply from me would remember I had no computer and just leave me a written note. Did anyone remember how to write a note anymore?

There were two in my mailbox. The one from Jasper I threw out unread, just out of habit. And there was one from Pace. I went cold as I recognised the handwriting, and I fumbled as I unfolded it.

Celeste—

The office is yours. You might as well have that, too.
If you need me for anything, tough. I'm sure all your friends will help you out.

Pace

Her side of the office was completely bare. Had she always been this childish? And how would she teach, let alone do research, without an office? 'Office hours will be held in the parking lot. Students are advised to look both ways.'

I sat heavily and took out my lecture notes for the Advanced seminar. I'd worked in this office by myself a thousand times; this time the silence was desolate. Pace wasn't just out, she was gone.

I read over the notes and did some fine-tuning of how I'd present the concepts—every group is different, and I'd realised early on they can always tell if you're doing lecture-in-a-can. It was hard to focus, though, with the bare desk and cold chair just an arm's reach away.

I left a few minutes at the end for some subversion. My Intro class needed the whole hour to get the point and start producing ideas; this group would only need a gentle push and they'd be on their way. No need to set their education back a whole day. Despite feeling upset and—I had to admit it—guilty about Pace's tantrum, I couldn't help also being excited about what the students would come up with.

They caught my mood right away, and we all got the lecture out of the way as quickly as we could. Finally, I closed my notebook and stood in the tense silence, trying to think of how to start.

Suddenly, Nicki said, 'It's time, isn't it, Dr Carlucci?'

'Time for what?' said another student.

'Time for things to change,' she said. 'What we've all been preparing for, for—oh, generations!' The other kids looked puzzled, but eager.

'She's right,' I told them. 'How many of you have had questions about how this university seems to run? Things that didn't seem right, but you felt you couldn't do anything about it? Books you needed that you weren't allowed to see, places you wanted to go but found out you were always being watched?'

They nodded.

I lowered my voice. 'We … are … changing … things,' I said intensely. 'And we need you. You are the best researchers the Geography department has. Go out and research. Find the information we need to find to bring down the governors.'

'Like what?' said one in a whisper that was part horror, part giggle.

'Find the truth about how they've been altering and suppressing research. I've already got one case, I need more.'

'What case have you got?' said Nicki.

'Millicent Strudthorne—'

Several students gasped.

'But she—'

'She was—'

'Nobody could trust her—'

'Aren't you people listening?' I said. 'She was discredited on rumour and falsified research. Do you watch the news at all these days? The same thing is happening to us, right now. Listen to the talkback radio. The university is in danger.'

'Funding cuts …'

'Worse than that,' I said. 'The governors are whipping up anti-intellectual fervour. God knows they've picked the right time. Kim-Hatton is having no problem manipulating public opinion. Soon it will get to the point where the brightest kids are afraid to come here and the rest wouldn't be caught dead here.'

'Why would the governors destroy their own university?'

'They're trying so hard to keep us controlled because they're about to get the result that was the reason they've kept the university going—the reason they've had for the last hundred years, anyway. The whole reason we're here is so the governors can identify the talent and keep track of the research to solve the Littoral Codex. I don't think the Codex is going to give them ultimate control over the universe—still less the university—but they think so. Up to now they haven't been in too much of a hurry, but a couple of things are making them very nervous and wanting to get the show on the road. First, they've probably realised by now that the key to decoding the Codex is not where they thought.'

'Where is it?' said one of the students.

'Don't you worry about that,' I said. 'Second, they know that we've caught on to their evil ways—not just the loyalty clause in the tenured contracts, but how they're falsifying research, slandering dissidents, designing everything about the campus and the curriculum to keep us separated and in line. And third, they're just weeks, maybe days, away from completing the missing part of the key that's kept them from solving the Codex.'

'And you want us to stop them.'

'You're not the only ones working on it, but yes. You're the ones who can go and find the facts. I don't care where you look. Anywhere can hide a clue, anything can turn out to be important. And time is of the essence.'

'In that case,' said one, grinning, 'I'm out of here.'

The others left as well, except for the Nicki. She said uncomfortably, 'Dr Carlucci, I hope you don't mind, but Ricky and I already have tasks. Will you be all right if we're doing them? We're still helping, I promise. It's just that other people are counting on us, too, and they asked first. Sorry ...'

'No, that's fine, I understand completely.' I was not happy about losing Nicki's research skills and keenness, but Ricky could probably be more help in the canteen.

It had been a good day's work. I couldn't wait to hear what Pace's ninja buddies were planning—oh. My elation collapsed into an achy feeling in my stomach.

I made up my mind. We weren't going to win if we were suspicious of, embarrassed around, or fighting with each other. I had to confront Pace and sort all this out. If I ever managed to catch up with her again.

On the way home I stopped by the Biology building and tracked down an old friend. Delia had lived down the hall from Pace and me in our freshman-year dorm; these days she was a lab technician. She'd never been much of a troublemaker, but I'd always thought that was because she hadn't found a cause worthy of getting in trouble. Sure enough, when I took her to the vending-machine room, bought her a soda, and explained the situation, she was happy to help, and immediately gave me two lead aprons. They made the walk from the bus to Russ's place a bit of a trial, but now I could wrap them around the tablets so we weren't being nuked while we slept. I took the further precaution of dragging the bag over to the closet, figuring that would be a bit better than under the bed.

I was a little surprised that neither Russ nor I really wanted to talk about our plans. I think Russ felt, as I did, that we had set the avalanche in motion and it was stupid to discuss how the snow was going to move. We didn't know, we couldn't know. We just had to keep doing what we thought we should do, and hope it would all work out in the end.

Chapter 18
The Battleground of Ideas Becomes Something More Literal

The retaliation started the next day. Security guards appeared on every corner. Card-readers all over campus started to mysteriously have trouble reading students' identification cards; they couldn't get into their dorms or the cafeteria or charge out books. Anyone needing paperwork handled anywhere on campus suddenly had a two- or three-hour wait, or longer. Emails disappeared at random, and the university servers were blocking Infoweb sites as fast as we could try to get to them. Nobody was in actual physical danger, not yet, but getting anything done—legitimate scholarship or subversion, it didn't matter—was impossible.

Most of the professors still gamely showed up for their classes and taught as best they could. I felt bad for them, suffering in a battle not of their choosing. But they'd suffer a lot worse if we failed.

We counterattacked, of course. I was pretty sure my Intro students, for example, were doing a fair bit to weaken the defences that had been built into the very geography of the campus. I was betting the levees would no longer reliably hold a moat's worth of water, and that the pump house itself was now a bit of a dodgy proposition. I noticed, too, that a lot of the boom-gates and road barriers that had appeared on campus over the past few years were out of order—usually in the open position.

The mood had altered all over campus. Discussions I overheard as I walked around were no longer about television shows, bands, or alcohol. Instead, people were talking about social systems, ideas of freedom and responsibility, stories from both Krasnian and North Kras history. Russ's actors had been doing their job as well. I even heard that drinking song here and there.

My mom was still at home. I'd spoken to her last night, and she was more than happy to keep using her sick leave. It wasn't that she was avoiding the fight; she just didn't want to deal with her boss.

'I'm convinced she set me up to be nabbed,' she said. '"Oh, Beatrice, will you go to that meeting for me please?" And wasn't it on my way to the meeting that they grabbed me?'

'Mom, that was the Littoral League, not the governors.'

'Maybe the governors help the Littoral League once in a while because the League is a nuisance to you. I'll bet that's why they've been tolerated all this time, because they keep you people from really cutting loose. When are you and Russ coming over for dinner? He's a very nice young man.' That was Mom, resilient to a fault.

The disturbing thing about Mom's boss setting her up was that it pointed out just how horrible a risk we were taking every time we brought someone new into the fight. Would they be a true ally, or a traitor? In a way, it was less stressful to deal with Norella, Jasper, and their pathetic minions. At least you *knew* you had to watch your back with them.

Still, it was risk it or surrender. We could already see how badly we were worrying the governors, and that was after less than twenty-four hours.

My Geography of Art class greeted my call to action with surprising gravity. I would have thought it would rouse their revolutionary fervour. Instead, they were sober, almost sad. I asked them why.

'Artists always suffer in a regime change.'

'But … that's okay, right? Suffering for the sake of art?'

'Oh, in theory …'

Our forces had already started the counterattack. At twotwenty-three, every computer on the campus network started playing the tune to that drinking song, and everyone working at one of those computers discovered that the power-down and reboot functions had been disabled. At three o'clock, the library had to be evacuated because of a particularly nasty and widespread outbreak of predatory mould. I caught up with Martha at the evacuation point. She was grinning.

'We got enough of a warning that we could get nearly everyone out in time,' she said. 'One or two refused to believe us, but even they moved fast enough that the damage wasn't too severe.'

'Warning?'

'The predatory mould is on our side,' was all she said.

At three-twenty-five a convoy of black four-wheel-drives rumbled through the gates and spread out through the campus. They all had darkened windows and four or five big antennas and the kind of exhaust pipes that stuck up like a snorkel, up by the roof.

By four o'clock, most of the day's classes were over, but the campus was still buzzing. Word had spread quickly, despite telling our students not to say anything (who had we been kidding?), and no one wanted to go home now. Like everyone else, I started drifting toward the quad.

I walked past one of the black four-wheel-drives. I tried not to react as I saw a hand sneak around from underneath the back and carefully let the air out of one of the tyres. I guessed that was happening all over campus. Was it the ninjas? It was the sort of sneaky thing they were supposed to be good at. But a moment later I saw a scrawny undergraduate walking past me, brushing gravel from the front of his rock-band t-shirt. It was one of the League boys. Jason, Justin, Jayden, something like that. I caught up with him.

'I thought you were League,' I muttered.

'They're *boring*. Whine, whine, whine, Codex, Codex, Codex. I'm so over it. This is where things are happening. Besides, I'm tired of doing what that twerp Smith-Fennel says all the time. Just because he has a master's degree, he thinks he can order everyone around. But I heard he doesn't even format his references correctly. Anyway, gotta go.' He gave a quick glance around, then said, 'Those tyres won't deflate themselves, you know.'

I hoped things in the quad were going as smoothly. I did my best to keep to a casual saunter, but, looking around to see that everyone else was hurrying, I picked up speed. Pace was right about one thing: the worst way to look inconspicuous was to try to look inconspicuous.

The quad was packed. There was a small circle in the middle that was open; in the centre stood a student with a bullhorn. Sudden fear made me cold all over: it was Danny.

This was suicide. There was no way the governors would let the child of one of their own make them look bad. Danny must have known this, must have known that being his mother's son not only wouldn't save him this time, it actually made his danger all the greater. But he didn't care. His face was shining, his body was energised. He stood in the midst of people who, before today, had had nothing but contempt for him. And now, they couldn't look away.

'Yes!' he was shouting. 'That's exactly what I'm saying: *interdisciplinary* collaboration! Apply for those grants! Work on those projects together! Walk across campus and say hi to the people in a department you've never even thought about before!'

'You're nuts,' hollered a grad student.

'Maybe so,' Danny shouted back. He glanced my way; he'd spotted me. 'I know it's a revolutionary idea. But imagine if geographers worked with artists! What if mathematicians and poets collaborated? What if philosophers and physicists shared their insights? What new ideas could we come up with? Right now, there's someone standing next to you whose research area could combine with yours to ignite like a star! Go on! Introduce yourself!'

Most of the muttering was along the lines of, 'He really is nuts. You'd never get a grant for an interdisciplinary project. What does he think this is, Fairyland?'

But slowly the tone changed. One or two brave people did introduce themselves. The ones around them followed their lead, until, in a glorious chain reaction, people were talking all over the quad. I pushed through to get to Danny.

'You … were … *fabulous*,' I told him.

He grinned and ducked his head. 'Mom's going to kill me, though. And Dad. Did you see the *Backwash* reporter?'

'No.'

'There's no way Dad's going to let any of his stations or papers carry this story, what's happening here today. So the *Backwash* is going to scoop him something awful. People are going to ask why he's not covering it.' The grin turned from shy to wicked. 'It's going to be fun at the dinner table tonight.'

'Danny … do you think it's a good idea for you to go home tonight?'

He frowned for a second. 'Oh. You're thinking they'll ship me off to the relatives on the ranch near the North Kras border, where there's no phone, no Infonet, and no way I could make more trouble. Except maybe politicising the cows.'

'Something like that, yes.'

'You may be right, Doc. But what are my options? I don't have a dorm room, I don't have any—'

Any friends, was what he'd been about to say. In the awkward pause, I said, 'I know what we can do. Come with me.'

I took him to the library and introduced him to Martha. I asked her to come with me to the little conference room we'd used before.

'Danny needs to go underground,' I said. 'Underground.'

After a second, Martha said, 'Okay. Danny, we're trusting you on Dr Carlucci's word. Don't let her down. There's a carrel outside. Look like you're studying until I get off work in an hour. Then you'll come with me.'

'Doc?' Danny said to me, puzzled, yet trusting.

'It's okay, Danny,' I said, then lowered my voice: 'Wait until you see the underground library—it's every geek's dream come true.'

He tried to smile. The adrenaline of his reckless afternoon was wearing off, and he was finally starting to feel nervous, I could see.

I left him at the carrel, looking through a huge book of satellite photographs of the North Kras plains. Before I went, I pointed at a tiny pastoral town, along the Boulder River.

'That's where my dad's folks came from,' I said. 'Half Northie, that's me. That song everyone's singing? My dad sings it with his cousins when they come over and the bottle opener gets a workout. I'll catch up with you soon, Danny. Thanks for everything.'

Back outside, I sensed that the tension on campus was starting to ease. I knew it wasn't that the students had given up; rather, they'd dispersed to spread dissent like a virus. Hopefully their activity—and their energy—would be small-scale enough to avoid a confrontation with the security guards. So far the guards hadn't been able to catch anyone doing anything that was specifically against the law or university rules. But once they did, I knew the university would be locked down so fast and so thoroughly people would have trouble getting permission to close the toilet door when they needed to pee.

I'm still kicking myself, to this day, that I let that lull in tension put me off my guard. I'd gone back to my office to get some papers, and was most of the way to the bus stop when I felt someone grab me. Here we go again, I thought, as I felt a stab and a searing heat in my arm. The bastards had injected me with something. That was the last thing I thought before a wave of goo surged through my skull and I, as they say, knew no more.

I woke up in a room with one wall boarded up. I got unsteadily to my feet and walked very carefully over to the window. The view seemed familiar … Oh, crap, this was the house the Littoral League had taken my mom to. What losers! Didn't they think my friends would come and look for me here? And didn't they think I had things to do back on campus? Not to mention I'd planned on a nice evening with Russ. This was so *annoying*!

I paced around the room, and occasionally stopped by the plywood to see if I could kick or pull it loose. No luck; the undergraduates had used every nail in the box in a chaotic line around the edges. Most of the nails were bent (one had a stain around it that looked like the result of a harsh disagreement between a finger and a hammer), but there were enough nails that that didn't matter.

I wasn't troubling myself to be quiet, so it didn't surprise me that pretty soon I heard footsteps in the hallway.

It was Jasper. Of course. I sat with a thump in one of the three wooden chairs that were the room's only furniture.

He wasted no time on pleasantries or gloating. 'Where are the glass tablets, Celeste?'

I just snorted.

'What?' he said defensively.

'You're so small-minded. Do you really still think the tablets are important?'

'With them, I control the university.'

'They're useless without the missing tablet, stupid. Not to mention you have to get hold of the Codex.'

'I've got the Codex.'

'Right. Let's see it, then.'

'I know where it *is*.'

'So do I.'

After a moment of blinking and gaping, he said, 'Not anymore, you don't. We moved it.'

I sighed, and muttered a North Kras phrase my dad always used when some idiocy pushed him beyond the bounds of what Krasnian could express. 'You know, it's not your referencing that's kept you from your PhD all these years. You know that, don't you?'

Jasper looked very confused.

'It's the fact that you have no *imagination*. You can't think of things in new ways. You can't let go of the ways you've been thinking. Give it a try, Jasper. Try to picture what the university would be like if the governors actually had some sort of accountability. If the students and faculty actually had a say in what went on. Imagine the research that could flourish in an environment of cooperation, not competition! Imagine—'

'I'm imagining a heaving pit of chaos and intellectual flailing,' he said.

'Yeah, well, whatever, because I'm not going to help you, and you can't stop what we've already started on campus.'

'Stupid undergraduate posturing,' he sniffed. 'I would have thought you'd come up with something a little more sophisticated than that. And you will help me, because the League threatened your family once, and we can do it again.'

'Maybe, but now we're onto you. And I thought Norella Honeycott agreed to leave them alone. Does she know you're doing this behind her back? What will she think of your loyalty now, you sneaking little toad?'

'Name calling isn't going to help you any. I want those tablets.'

'Oh!'

'What?'

'You and Joan Maher! You've been double-crossing everyone! That's it, isn't it? The two of you! Has she no taste at all? What did she promise you?'

'The only thing I want to hear from you is where you've got those tablets. Other than that, shut the hell up.'

'Temper, Jasper. That's another thing that's been hurting your academic career. No one wants to have to sit through a staff meeting with a cranky pants like you.'

'You'll see,' he said, his voice getting louder and more strained. Idiot. He was falling for it.

'What will I see, exactly?'

'Joan and I are going to make the university what it always could have been—a haven for intellectuals, a calm, welcoming place for people who want to live the life of the mind—'

'And only the mind. Brains in bubbling beakers, that's all you want. All you are. Real learning that *means* something demands your whole self, not just your brain!' I was surprised at how emotional I was getting, and tried to calm down. I needed to stay alert, watch for opportunities. 'Where are all your minions?' I continued. 'All those undergrads following you around like puppies?'

'Busy,' he snapped.

'Or gone. Sick of the hierarchy-obsessed, soulless world you're offering them. You're here by yourself, aren't you? Trying to make me think you've got dozens of people at the snap of your fingers.'

He smiled then. 'Not entirely by myself. Ozzie? Could you come in here for a minute?'

Ozzie, who'd helped my mom—but had also been so enchanted with the weapons. I stared at him, aghast, when he came into the room.

'Could you please phone Dr Maher and tell her we'll be a bit longer?' said Jasper as he sat in one of the other chairs. 'Dr Carlucci is not being helpful. Although that shouldn't surprise her.'

Ozzie nodded and left. But … from the hallway I could hear him start to whistle the North Kras song that had spread across campus like fire. Taunt, reassurance, or coincidence?

I was hoping Jasper would leave me alone, like they do in movies, so that an unsuspected helper could sneak into the room, set me free, and take me back to the action, where I would arrive just in time to stop the mass slaughter of hundreds of idealistic undergrads. Instead, we sat, glowering at each other, as the minutes ticked by. I'd never been so bored and frustrated in all my life, even during staff meetings.

'How much time have you got, really?' I asked him after a while.

'More time than you. I'm not a revolutionary. It's revolutionaries who are always in a rush. And look where it's gotten you. What's your hurry, anyway? The governors have been running the university for so long, what's the difference if they run it for a month or two, even a year or two, more?'

I didn't want to tell him that the missing tablet was nearly recovered. I didn't want to say that once the governors recovered the tablets and the Codex, and their hold on the university was complete, there would be no chance ever again to overthrow them.

I stood up and walked over to the window. Jasper stood up, too, but made no move to stop me. I looked out at the headland, green and lush in the spring sunshine. I grinned to myself as I wondered how Danny was doing. What a surprise he'd turned out to be! It only took one person to give him a chance, and he revealed himself as a hero in training. The exact opposite of Jasper.

Why was Jasper still at the university? Why did he persist, why was he *permitted* to persist? Even Pace did nothing to chuck him out.

In the silence that settled on us once again, I heard Ozzie still whistling from another room. I was going to risk that it was a signal: he wouldn't chase me if I decided I wanted to leave. In fact, it was entirely possible that the academics had asked him to come here as a plant.

Abruptly, I pushed past Jasper and walked out the door. He was scrawny, and afraid of a physical fight. It was easy.

'Ozzie!' he cried, his voice cracking. 'Get her! Stop her!'

There was a set of car keys casually left on the table by the door. It would hurt my wrist to drive, but not as much as it would hurt my brain to stay cooped up with Jasper. As I picked up the keys, I glanced over my shoulder. Ozzie was in the kitchen, the water in the sink running loudly. He winked at me.

As I hurried toward the car in the driveway, I heard him saying, 'What, Jasper? Oh. Sorry. Gee, I didn't hear a thing.' I got in and turned the key and drove way too quickly toward the university.

I got back to the city just as darkness was falling, and went straight to the retirement home. I ran past the reception desk and up to Drusy's apartment, and pounded on the door. 'Drusy! It's Celeste!'

'Oh—thank God,' she said as she pulled me inside. 'But now that we know you're not dead, there's a lot of work to do.'

Chapter 19
Celeste Returns Underground

'One of the students found your pack and brought it to Lenny, who was leaving the quad,' Drusy said. 'The student apologised for looking at your wallet, but everything's still here. Lenny's beside himself. There are too many people who want to see you hurt or killed.'

'Why me? What did I do?'

'Oh, sweetie, what didn't you do? You're researching Millicent Strudthorne, for a start. Todd is very flattered, but he told me what it might mean for someone to make her research public. Even he wasn't told about it as a child, because it would have put him in danger. He doesn't know what you've found, but he's sure it's dangerous for the governors. Which makes it dangerous for you.'

'But I haven't told anyone what I've found. No one at all.'

'Just the mention of her name is enough to make the governors put their pencils down and start wringing their hands. They have long memories, and they pass their worries on to each new governor. The ones these days have been told so many things to be afraid of that they jump at shadows. Millicent may be only a shadow now, but you're not. And that's just the start. Word's gotten round that you know where the tablets are. And you're a known rabble-rouser. Now that you've burst on the scene, it seems you've had more of an impact than you realised.'

'But Pace—'

'Sweetie, Pace is hating the competition. She's been the wild child for so long, she just can't stand letting someone else have a turn. She's doing her bit to destabilise things, but she doesn't consider herself part of the team. And poor Ty is just sitting still, wondering how things got so out of hand. All he wanted to do was win the Delmarva Geography Prize. No, it's up to you. The students will follow you.'

'And the governors want me dead.'

'Mm.'

'And Jasper won't stop badgering me. Hell's bells, he had me sedated and kidnapped, despite the truce. I don't think he's League at all. I think he's allied with Joan Maher. Martha told me Joan is hiding out in the Sewers, and I think she's swiped the Codex. I'm the only one who knows about the pulverised tablet, though. Me, and Danny Wexler.'

'What pulverised tablet?'

'The one someone ground into a glowing powder and threw into the Purple River. Mutant bugs, disappearing delta mud, flashing lights on the horizon, it all fits in. It means, though, that while the tablets have been useless up to now, the Praxies, or the governors—same thing really—have recovered just about all the powder. It took them a hundred years, but they did it. And they're ready to recast the last tablet.'

'Have a seat. I need to phone Russ, he's been out of his mind with worry.'

'Can I talk to him?'

'Of course, sweetie, but not for long. I need to keep the line free.'

Drusy handed me the phone, and I dialled Russ's number frantically. I hadn't realised I'd memorised it.

'Hello?'

'Russ, it's Celeste—'

He let out a wordless cry of relief that brought tears to my eyes.

'Russ, I'm so sorry.'

'What for?'

'Worrying you.'

'Don't be stupid.'

'I'm here at Drusy's for the moment. Can you phone my folks and let them know I'm okay?'

'Yes, of course.'

'I have to get off the line. I love you.' The words came easily.

'I love you, too. Bye.'

'Step one,' I said to Drusy as I handed the phone back to her. 'Immobilise Jasper. Or I'm not going to be able to set foot out of this apartment ever again. Question is: how?'

'What if we captured him for a change?'

'What, go back to the cottage?'

'If you're not there, and Pace isn't there, and the tablets aren't there, and the Codex isn't there, I doubt he'll still be there.'

'Where, then? And how are we supposed to capture him?'

'I'll bet Lenny has some ideas about that. You leave it to us. Now, what would you like for dinner?'

My stomach roared at the thought of dinner. I was embarrassed, but Drusy just laughed. 'How about spaghetti with garlic bread?'

'Yes, please,' I said. 'Thank you so much.'

'My pleasure. While it's cooking, I'll phone Lenny and ask him to join us. He'll be happy to know you're safe.'

'He thinks I'm an idiot who can't teach properly.'

'Sweetie, have you learned so little about him?'

I let that one go by. 'Can I help with dinner?'

'No, thanks. It's a question of boiling water, opening a jar, and heating the bread from the freezer. You just relax.'

I took Millicent's *Reminiscence* out of my pack and sat on the sofa to catch up with my reading.

The work on my thesis progresses slowly. I have begun to suspect that I am being deliberately hampered in my quest for the truth—it shouldn't surprise me, all things considered, but it does. Even to the extent of finding sand in my ink bottle—such childishness! What next? A frog down the back of my shirt? Rude comments about me on the toilet wall?

Oh, Millicent, I thought. If only they'd done that instead of trashing your research, your character, and your child's future.

The tone of the book was definitely getting darker, presumably as Millicent tried to get her thesis finalised and submitted. I wondered what had happened to her, what she did after getting her PhD. Would the governors have let her teach? I doubted it. How did she provide for her child? It's not like you could set up a geography shop where people could come in off the street and buy geography from you.

Dr Garrick arrived just as Drusy was draining the pasta. 'Dish it up, Dr Kelso, dish it up! This old academic is hungry!' He went into the kitchen and got himself some pasta and sauce. Drusy brought out the bread and a dish of grated cheese.

We ate, Dr Garrick and I with the same sort of gusto that had always gotten me in trouble with Sister Genesia, Drusy with more refinement.

'So,' said Dr Garrick after he'd devoured a large piece of garlic bread, 'you want to get rid of that little shit Smith-Fennel. Not before time—why has everyone been letting him hang around?'

'I don't know,' I said, exasperated.

'He knows something about someone,' said Dr Garrick.

'Oh, Lenny,' said Drusy. 'You don't know that.'

'You just add it to the list of things I've said that have turned out to be true.'

'When it turns out to be true, I'll add it.'

'How can we catch him to get rid of him, though? He's going to be on the lookout for me, and I don't want you getting hurt in the unlikely event that he decides to fight back for once. Maybe if we lured him to where we can slam a door shut behind him or something.'

'What attracts him most of all?'

'Pace.'

'He's an optimist,' chuckled Drusy.

'But Pace hates me now and I bet she won't help, particularly with something like this.'

'You just let me chat with her,' said Drusy.

'I don't even know where she is.'

'Oh, most likely she's over at Ty's place. I'll just give her a ring.'

'I don't know if—

Drusy ignored me. 'Hello, Ty? Yes, fine, thanks. Everyone is fine. Yes, she's here, safe and sound. Ty, I'd like to talk to Pace, if I may. Thanks.' There was a pause, then, so loudly I jumped, '*Hypatia*! Now you listen to me! No, I mean it, be quiet and listen! You've thrown one tantrum too many this time. Do you think it matters one bit whether your feelings are hurt because you're not the centre of attention? Do you think, in fact, that you matter at all? Now you just pull yourself together, because I need your help. Something only you can do. What was that? Don't get smart with me— you matter when I say you matter, and you don't when I say you don't. I need you to phone Jasper, what's his name? Smith-Fennel, yes. *Yes*, tonight. And ask him to meet you for an important discussion. It doesn't matter what about. He doesn't need to know, and neither do you. What's the place where people go these days to have important discussions? No, not on campus. All right, that sounds good. What's the address? Tell him eight o'clock. Never you mind what's up. If you don't know, you won't give anything away. He's cunning, and he'll notice. Eight o'clock. *Yes*, it's important. Now, could you put Ty back on the phone again, please?'

Her voice went suddenly gentle again. 'Ty? I've asked Pace to do me a favour tonight. I'd like to make sure you know it's just for her to do. We'll be taking care of her, don't worry. Don't *worry*. All right, thanks, Ty. Bye.' She hung up the phone. 'That girl has cornered the melodrama market. Well, she can make herself useful. Her having disappeared for a few days will make Jasper all the more curious about what she has to say, there's that at least.'

'I thought we were going to try and lure him somewhere we could just slam the door on him. If he's in a pub or something with Pace, how are we going to do that?'

'She's only the primary lure,' said Drusy. 'Just to get him to a place, and a time, of our choosing. After that, we leave him bread-crumbs, until he follows them into the cage.'

'What do I do?'

'Are you nuts?' said Dr Garrick. 'Nothing!'

'You have other things on your mind,' said Drusy.

'Um. Like what?'

'Like, the students who are still on campus,' said Dr Garrick. 'And we're hearing that the security guards are getting restless.'

'For God's sake,' I said, 'why have we been sitting here eating dinner, if kids are getting bashed?'

'Nobody's been bashed yet. And you were hungry. You can't do good work on an empty stomach. But yes, it's time we got you over there. Ozzie should be back soon, he can take you.'

'I'm just one person. And it's going to be dark soon. Even if I knew what to say, nobody could see me, nobody could hear me. This is insane. I don't have tenure—this will be all they need to fire me. And there goes all my work, all my research, and no one will ever know what happened to Millicent Strudthorne.'

'What did happen?' said Drusy.

'The governors made her adviser fudge her data on the Purple River delta to cover up their dredging activities.'

'You can prove it?'

'Yes, I have her original manuscript right here.'

'What, you're *carrying it around*?' said Dr Garrick.

'Well, it's not like I'm *telling* everyone, so they can come up to me and say, "Hey, Celeste, hand over that manuscript", I said.

'Where did you find it?' said Drusy.

'The underground library. I found it by accident, and I took it because I thought Joan Maher might think to look for it, and better I have it than Joan. She was starting to give me the creeps right about then.'

'You're probably wise not to talk about it,' said Drusy. 'But I'm afraid you're going to have to risk your job if you're going to stop the governors.'

'How am I supposed to do that?'

'Wing it!' said Dr Garrick. 'Ask yourself, "What would Dr Lenny Garrick do?"'

'And then do exactly the opposite,' said Drusy.

'You guys are a lot of help.'

'Finish your dinner, sweetie.'

'Not hungry,' I said, feeling sullen.

Dr Garrick let out an exasperated sigh, but said nothing. I wondered if Drusy was going to blow up at me the way she had at Pace. I didn't care. It wouldn't matter a bit if I went over to the campus and rallied the students or overthrew the governors or convinced the security guards to enrol in mime classes. I would still end up losing everything I'd achieved, and ruining my chances of achieving anything more. And my wrist hurt.

The silence went on and on. Dr Garrick started to say something, but Drusy held a hand up. Finally, she said, 'Sweetie, no one is going to make you do anything. But just think of this: what good is tenure, and publications, and the Delmarva Geography Prize, if all it means is that you're good at being part of a bad system? There are people who love you, and that won't change. There are students who look up to you, and they'll only admire you more if you return to rally them. You have parents who will never desert you, no matter what you do for a living. And if you can't be a geography professor at Purple Bay University, who says that's the be-all and end-all of creation?'

'Everything is geography,' I murmured. But her words were buzzing in my head.

'We don't want to gloss over the very real possibility that the security guards will hit you with big sticks, though,' said Dr Garrick. 'That would be naive.'

'Sweetie, we can't do what you can. We'll keep helping you, and I don't think we've done too bad a job so far. But we've been waiting for someone like you for a long time. Someone who can stand up and be seen, someone the entire campus will follow.'

I took a bite of spaghetti. 'I'm the one who stole Pace's research,' I said with my mouth full. 'I'm an object of scorn.'

'You're the one who thought you were saving the Purple River,' said Drusy.

'I haven't done anything. I'm just a … a leaf in the current.'

'Can you really believe that, after the past few days?'

'I—' And I realised I didn't have anything to say.

'Settled,' said Dr Garrick. 'Drusy, when's that big ox supposed to show up to take Celeste to the university?'

'What?' I said. 'Did I actually just make a decision here, or did you have the whole thing arranged?'

'Just trying to be efficient,' said Dr Garrick. 'If you'd chickened out, we could have always just fed Ozzie some spaghetti and sent him on his way, and you wouldn't have been any the wiser. This way, we don't have to wait around for Drusy to phone him, and for him to battle rush-hour traffic to get here, and everything.'

'Purple Bay has distributed centres of manufacturing and white-collar work,' I said automatically. 'Even the usual barriers to the flow of traffic, such as the bottlenecks that occur at bridges, are less of a factor here—despite the Purple River and the mountains to the north and west—because of the historical development of industries along the entire—'

'And just whom do you think you are instructing in basic principles of urban geography, girlie?' snapped Dr Garrick.

'Oh. Sorry.' Oops. To cover my embarrassment, I resumed eating. I figured Drusy was right: if I was going to lead a revolution that evening, it would ruin the effect if my growling stomach was picked up by the media microphones.

I was just about done when there was a knock on the door. Drusy let Ozzie in and sat him down with a plate of spaghetti.

'Eat up quickly, Ozzie, the clock is ticking,' she said. He nodded, and polished off the food with remarkable speed.

'Okay, then, off you go. Celeste, are you sure you want to take your backpack with you?'

'Yes.'

'All right, then, we'll be taking care of Jasper—'

'Can I help with that?' said Ozzie.

'Sorry, Ozzie, but your main job is to look after Celeste.'

'Okay,' he said reluctantly. 'But it would be so sweet. He drove me nuts.'

'Don't do me any favours, Ozzie,' I said. 'If you'd rather not—'

'No, it's okay,' he said. 'Sorry I gave you that impression. Hey, what's wrong with your wrist?'

'Sprained it. Why?'

'Give it here.'

Puzzled, I reached my hand over to him.

'Mind if I take the brace off for a second?'

'I … guess not.'

He took the brace off very gently, then held my wrist between his two hands. I looked at his face; he'd closed his eyes and was frowning. He poked carefully at various places along my hand, wrist, and forearm, then pressed with his fingertips at a couple of the spots he'd poked. He kept the pressure on while he breathed very slowly: two, three breaths. Then he opened his eyes, smiled, and said, 'There.'

'There what?'

'It's fixed. Try it.'

I moved my hand just a little. There was a bit of stiffness, sure, but the searing agony I'd been feeling whenever I'd bumped into something or carelessly picked something up was gone. 'How did you do that?'

He shrugged. 'I like fixing things. No reason for things to hurt if they don't have to.'

'Words to live by,' said Dr Garrick. 'Now get out.'

Ozzie and I took the elevator down and walked through the lobby. The kid at the desk didn't look up. When we were in his car and buckled up, I asked, 'What were you doing out at Jasper's cottage?'

'A bunch of his kids deserted. He had a labour shortage. My grandma asked me if I could keep an eye on him—she had a feeling, she said. Having feelings about stuff runs in my family. Plus, I wanted to get a closer look at all those cool weapons.'

'Did you have a feeling about how you fixed my wrist?'

'And your mom's back, uh-huh. Grandma's descended from the tribespeople of the North Kras steppes. So, so am I.' As if this completely explained his powers. 'Maybe I'll go back there some-day. Why should it all be one-way, people coming here?'

'Well, there are computers and plumbing and jobs in most places in Krasnia, whereas I think they are in short supply on the steppes.'

'Mm.'

I sort of figured that would be the end of our conversation, but after a while, he said, 'You're part-Northie, too, aren't you?'

'Not from the steppes, though. My dad's family had full-on grazing lands.'

And *that* was the end of the conversation. I was hoping there wasn't some sort of generations-old grudge about pastoralists versus nomads that his race-memory was dredging up. Family is a funny thing that way. Geographers know this—maps, conflicts, resources, sharing, grabbing, most of it comes down to family, sooner or later. Us and them. The Praxies knew it, too: look how they stuck together, except for Angelo.

Ozzie parked near the quad. There weren't many parking spots available; ordinarily at this time, the lot would have been close to empty. Uh-oh, Drusy hadn't been kidding. Trouble was brewing.

I walked warily to the quad, Ozzie shadowing me. There were hundreds of kids there, and not just kids. Professors, secretaries, cleaning staff. And security guards—the entire quad was ringed with them. Someone had set up some lighting and a genera-tor—presumably taken from Dramatic Arts, a sign that Russ was involved—and people were staying more or less clear of the lit space. I couldn't see past the crowd, though, to catch what was happening inside. There was a sound system, but I couldn't make out the words over the noise of the people near me.

I was about to shove myself through the line of guards when Ozzie put a hand on my shoulder. 'Let me,' he said.

He said, 'Excuse me,' very quietly and politely to the guard just in front of me. 'Excuse me, I need to get through.' The guard ignored him. 'Excuse me,' he said a bit more insistently, and started to step forward. I kept close in his wake, and by the time the guards noticed he wasn't just trying to get a better look, we were both through. Ozzie instantly pushed me in front so that he was between me and the guards; his bulk shielded me easily.

'Thanks, buddy,' I said.

'No problem.'

I made my way to the lit area. Sure enough, the three students I'd met with Russ were doing the play. They still held their scripts—there was no way they could have memorised all that material so quickly—but the play was still working. The people who could hear what was going on were rapt, and the ones behind them were nearly as interested. The dopey sitcom scenario had become a metaphor, full of grace and meaning. The banal interactions had become a channel for the actors to express real fears and dreams. Each line rang. As I listened, I realised the message was: Things may be normal, expected, even boring, on the surface. But underneath is passion, glory, daily heroics in the face of daily evils. Go, therefore, and be a hero.

Without turning around, I knew Russ had come to stand behind me. I leaned back and he put his arms around me and said, 'Hello, Danger Woman.'

I couldn't think of anything to match that, so I just said, 'Hello.'

'Just a few more minutes until they're done,' he murmured. 'Then the audience is going to want the next act.'

The kids finished to wild applause. 'Like I told you,' Russ said, and pushed me toward the open spot where the kids were taking a bow.

'Are you nuts?' I cried.

'Go on! There's a microphone on the ground near the speaker. Just switch it on and start talking. Why else did you come here tonight?'

My heart slammed in my chest and my knees felt like they were vibrating, but I stepped into the light, found the microphone, and turned it on. Silence rippled out from where I stood, until hundreds of pairs of eyes were locked onto me.

'Hi,' I said into the quiet. 'I'm Celeste Carlucci.'

The entire quad erupted in cheers. It was at that moment that I lost all sense of consequences. Now was our chance to overthrow the governors and save the university—and who knew how many generations of students and professors to follow us. It was time for the bravest and most desperate of attempts, and it just didn't matter anymore what happened after.

I took a deep breath and continued: 'Welcome to the moment when everything changes. If we refuse to live under the old rules, if we demand new rules of intellectual freedom, respect, and the true adventure of learning, we can have them.'

I had no idea where these words were coming from, but I could feel them waiting to rush out.

'Step one: is there a reporter from the *Backwash* here?' There was no answer; I didn't expect any. No non-Praxie reporter would be rash enough to draw attention. 'Have a word with the people around you, and make sure you are never, ever alone, and never, ever near a security guard. People near the reporter, your job is to make sure that reporter gets back to the *Backwash* office safe and able to write our story.

'Step two: any of you who, at any time, have ever gotten the feeling that something isn't right—a controversial reserved reading disappears from the library, or your professor suddenly takes sick leave after giving you a really interesting and challenging assignment, anything at all—post it on the Infonet. Start one site, one blog, one do-it-yourself encyclopaedia—start the do-it-yourself encyclopaedia of the Resistance at Purple Bay University. And start it tonight. I know you can coordinate yourselves so that people outside don't have to waste a lot of time trying to find all your stories in a thousand different places. The rule is, though, that you can only post what happened to you—not what you heard about from a friend. Got it?' There was a murmur of assent.

'Finally, I need you all to keep your heads. Do you see those people standing around edges of the quad? The ones with the guns and the big boots? They're just waiting for an excuse to bust you up pretty bad. Do—not—give—them—one. Now: go and pool what you know and tell the world!' I turned off the microphone and stepped back into the crowd. The cheering died away, and the cleared spot disappeared as people began to mill around, finding their friends and sorting out who was going to do what.

Still the security guards did nothing, but I knew it would only take one slip before the brutality began. I was relieved to see the quad becoming emptier as the groups began to leave.

Russ had just put his arm around me when one of the security guards approached. I remembered her—the one who had taken my statement after I'd been knifed. She remembered me, too, and she looked apologetic.

'I'm afraid you'll have to come with me,' she said.

'What? I haven't done anything!'

'You've incited riot.'

'I have not. And you know it.' I sounded like a five-year-old, but I didn't care.

'I'm sorry.' She gripped my arm with a steel clamp of a hand, and three of her buddies joined her to surround me.

As we started to move off in a bloc, Russ said, 'I'm coming, too!'

'No—then no one will know,' I cried. I didn't want to tell him out loud who to tell; I was hoping he'd figure out he should get word to Drusy.

I said to the guards, 'Where are you taking me?'—just to make light conversation. None of them said anything, surprise surprise. We left the main campus, and started along one of the unlit paths. 'No, really,' I said. 'Where? To the governors? The Littoral League? Joan Maher?' There was a slight tightening of the guard's grip. I could feel my pulse pounding under her fingers, like getting my blood pressure read.

I heard a rustle from the foliage beside the path. The guards heard it, too, and held cudgels at the ready. Too late—we were surrounded by a dozen lithe and agile people dressed in black and keeping spookily silent. In a second, they'd disarmed the guards and pried me loose from the one who held me.

'Run!' she hollered at the other guards, but—again—too late. The ninjas threw them heavily to the ground and knelt on their necks.

'Hey, Dr Carlucci!' said one of them cheerfully, and I recognised one of my Intro students. 'Does this mean I get extra credit?'

'Sure,' I said.

'When I told Dr Garoux—she's in our martial-arts club, did you know that?—when I told her my group wanted to check out the unlit paths, she said, "Take a few of the lower-belts with you, they could use the practice." Good thing, too, huh? I don't think I could have handled four security guards on my own!'

'Not on your own, turkey,' said two more Intro students, who emerged from the bushes conspicuously dressed in normal clothes. 'Sure, you dragged some of your thug buddies along, but who decided which path to stake out?'

'Oh, yeah, like *you* can fight,' the ninja leader said. 'What was your sport in high school? Chess?'

'Debating,' said one of the non-ninjas. 'So what?'

'So you were going to argue them into submission?'

One of the security guards grunted, 'Can we get up now?'

'Let them up,' I said. 'They can take me to Joan Maher.'

'What!' said the first ninja, my Intro student. 'After all we did to save you?'

'There's a big difference between being dragged somewhere as a prisoner and walking in under your own steam with a body-guard of highly trained martial artists.'

That worked.

We kept going along the path, the ninjas in sleek silence, the security guards with the grace of tanks, and the Intro students and I stumbling determinedly along with them. We were in a part of the campus I hardly ever visited, let alone at night. They could have been leading me to the very gates of hell and I wouldn't have known the difference. So when the guards stopped and unlocked a small stone building that looked like it might be one of the uni-versity's oldest surviving structures, I just shrugged and followed them inside.

One of the guards pulled an iron grate up from the stone floor, and we climbed down a rusty ladder. I went last, mainly because I didn't want anyone stepping on my fingers. If that happened, I would probably burst into hysterical tears, and that wouldn't be good for the Fearless Leader thing I had going. Just when I was getting the hang of it, too.

Another trip along endless tunnels, this time lit by the fero-ciously bright flashlights of the security guards. Down, down— but at least I didn't have to crawl.

The guard who knew me stopped in front of a metal door. I felt stupid and somehow vulnerable not knowing her name, and it occurred to me to look at her nametag: Sergeant Greta Funk.

'Hey, Greta,' I said, stopping her arm as she reached up to knock on the door.

'Please call me Sergeant Funk.'

'Why did you ditch the governors to work for Joan Maher?'

'Not all of us did,' she said. 'But—'

The door opened so suddenly I felt my hair moving in the breeze. Joan stood in the doorway.

'Come in,' she said. 'Happy to see you again, Celeste. And how wonderful that you've brought so many friends.' I'd never heard sarcasm that smooth. You'd almost think she meant it sincerely.

'Mm,' I said, and waited for two ninjas to go ahead of me. Two more stayed close behind, and one completed the formation behind me. The room, a plain office, was empty except for Joan, a desk, and a chair. The desk was piled with books.

'Where's Jasper, your toy boy?' I said, with maybe a little disgust in my voice. Certainly my question did nothing to improve Joan's mood.

'He doesn't even know how to format an annotated bibliography. He doesn't matter.'

'Not like Tyrone,' I said carefully. I had a hunch.

Her eyes narrowed. 'No.'

'You're not after the Codex at all, are you? At least, not for its own sake.'

'Why?' she said quickly. 'Have you found it?'

'N-n-o-o-o,' I said. 'But it wouldn't matter if I did. One of those glass tablets is missing. Has been missing for about a hundred years. The rest of them are useless without it.'

'And so is the Codex, is that it?' She waved a hand dismissively.

'What you really want is Ty Kortnoz.'

'If I had the book and he had the tablets ...' Her voice trailed off.

'He would see that you are meant to be together.'

She said nothing.

'But he loves Pace,' I pointed out.

'He just thinks he does.'

'And Norella Honeycott is after him, too.' No wonder Pace was so territorial. She must have to deal with this sort of thing all the time.

'Norella is not his type,' said Joan flatly. 'I did need you to get the tablets and keep them safe, if only from her and her pathetic Littoral League. But if you ended up giving them back to Tyrone, so much the better. Then, once I found the Codex ...'

'The Praxies have the Codex.'

'Everyone who knew about the tablets thought the Praxies had them, too. I thought perhaps you knew where the Codex was, but weren't telling. So I watched you, kept track of your research and your borrowing record—'

'You sneak! No wonder the mould went after you.'

She raised a hand to her scarred face.

'And you're the one who had my office trashed. And did they have to squash the bugs? That was just sick.'

'She made us!' cried Sergeant Funk. 'We didn't want to!'

'No, we didn't,' murmured the other security guards.

'But noooooooo, she specifically said, "Make sure you squash those bugs." It was a job, and a way to stick it to the governors while earning extra money. That'd teach them to cut our benefits down to nothing at the last contract negotiation—at least that's what we thought. I didn't think anyone could be worse to work for than the governors. But at least with them we didn't get beaten up!' Sergeant Funk's voice rose with wounded outrage. She turned on Joan. 'You told us it would just be a matter of—how did you say it? "Intimidating doughy academics and pimply undergraduates".'

My students scowled.

Sergeant Funk sounded like she was just getting started, but I needed to go back over something.

'Hang on, Sergeant,' I said. 'Joan, you knew about the bugs? And the powder in the silt? Did you know that the Praxies were trying to recover enough powder to reconstruct the missing tablet?'

'I knew it all, yes, of course,' she said impatiently.

'But you didn't want to stop the Praxies, or reform the university, or thwart the governors? Nothing like that?'

'Oh, I suppose I wanted all those things, eventually. There was plenty of time—at least, I thought so. But Tyrone found the tablets, and Norella came out of seclusion—I have no idea how that vapid fool ever got a PhD—and, well, the chase was on. Revolution had to wait.'

'Guys?' I said to the ninja band. 'Can you please make sure Joan doesn't try to hurt any of us? I can't leave her here, God knows what nooks and crannies she knows about down here, and what she's got hidden in them.'

Sergeant Funk stepped toward Joan, who actually shrank away. 'Don't worry,' said Sergeant Funk. 'We're sick of her. We'll make sure she doesn't do anything.'

I needed to figure out what to do next: search for the Codex, go back above ground to fight the governors, make sure the Littoral League was behaving itself, look for a way to undermine the Praxies' hold on the intellectual life of Purple Bay, or go home and go to sleep. Unfortunately, personal preference didn't figure as a decision-making tool.

'My problem is,' I said, 'that in order to do *anything*, I need to get to the part of the complex I know. Sergeant, any of your people know the layout down here?'

She shook her head.

Suddenly one of my students sniffed. 'Is that … cookies?'

'If it is, it's the best cookies I've ever smelled,' said another.

God bless Ricky! 'Follow those cookies!' I cried.

Chapter 20
Things Escalate

It didn't take us long to follow Ricky's cookie-beacon to the canteen. Luckily both the ninja band and the security guards were disciplined enough to take turns at the cookie plate so that Joan didn't slip away.

Nicki was overjoyed to see me.

'Dr Carlucci, this is *great*! I was so upset that I was missing the big night in the quad, but this is so cool, it's even better, because here you are, and I can help out after all!'

'How did you know this was the big night in the quad?'

'I think I've sprained my thumb with all the text messages going back and forth,' she squealed.

I took my fourth cookie from the plate. 'Miraculous as always, Ricky,' I said, and he beamed. I put three on a napkin and handed them to Joan. 'Not that you deserve them,' I said. But if I were to be scrupulously honest, no human being, flawed as we all are, deserved those cookies. If I didn't share, I might not get any next time. Fate was like that.

'Ricky, you legend!' called someone from the hallway. 'Did you make another batch of cookies?' Danny came into the canteen, saw me, and smiled so brilliantly I was embarrassed. 'Hi, Doc. How are things?'

'Oh, you know, little of this, little of that. You?'

'This place is *incredible*! I could be happy my whole life in that library.'

'Yeah, I thought so.' We sat at one of the tables.

A thought occurred to me. 'Sergeant, just how many of you took that second job with Joan?'

'About half, I guess.'

'And there's really no way of telling which ones—no, I don't know, secret signal, badge, handshake?'

'We all keep to ourselves. It's a useful habit when you're dealing with the governors to never say a word more than you have to. To anyone.'

She was talkative enough now—maybe Ricky's cookies really were magic.

'So if there were trouble—say, an actual uprising, rather than the nonviolent stuff we've been doing—there's an even chance that a particular guard might have already decided the governors aren't looking after his or her best interests.'

'That's right.'

'You're not actually planning violence, are you?' snorted Joan. 'Even those idiots in the Littoral League stopped short of that.'

'I'm not planning anything yet. Quit distracting me or no more cookies.' I'd sort of meant it as a joke, but she shut up all right. Those were some cookies.

How important was it to find the Codex? If we had it instead of the Praxies, that might hinder—but probably not stop—their quest for media coverage, political support, and global domination. It wasn't my highest priority.

What about returning above ground to fight the governors? I figured all the destabilisation (including Joan's unwitting contribution of subverting the security force) would probably continue just fine without me now, as long as the kids kept their heads.

Drusy had assured me she'd be taking care of Jasper, so that he couldn't keep pestering me. That really left only the major question mark of the Littoral League. I spared a fleeting thought for Pace and Kortnoz, but I figured they could probably take care of themselves. I yawned, and checked my watch. Only nine o'clock. It felt a whole lot later.

Suddenly every security guard and ninja was on the alert. I was too tired to figure out why at first, then I heard it too: feet thundering along the hallway. Many feet. As they got closer, I could hear voices: 'Quit shoving, asshole!' 'You quit shoving, dickhead.' 'Hey, do I smell cookies?'

Yup. Norella Honeycott and her army of undergraduates. I guess not all of them had abandoned her, or else she'd found some new ones. I'd set my pack on the floor next to me; I put it on again, in case I needed to make a run for it.

The rabble swept into the canteen. Bringing up the rear was Norella, resplendent in army fatigues and a black turtleneck. She carried a large gun. When she saw Joan, she stopped in her tracks and raised her chin just a little. The muzzle of the gun swung in Joan's direction.

'How did you find this place?' snapped Joan.

'Are the governors the only ones who can set up cameras?' said Norella. 'And are you—' she rounded on me, and I jumped—'the only person who can inspire people?' Her undergraduates giggled. Mine made exasperated noises.

I decided to take the direct approach. 'Norella, just exactly what are you hoping to accomplish here?'

'I want the Codex, and I want the tablets.'

'Well, tough luck, because neither of them is here. The Praxies have the Codex, in fact, as far as I know.'

'They never did,' she said irritably. 'That was a myth that they themselves spread. It's here, it's in the library! I know it! All the clues lead here!'

'What clues?'

'Well, for one thing, if you want to find an old book, where do you go? An old library.'

'Hardly compelling logic,' I said. 'But go on.'

'*She's* here,' said Norella, pointing the gun savagely at Joan. 'Who knows more about books than a librarian? And the tablets are here, we can detect their signature. The tablets are being drawn toward the books. By fate.' She swung the gun back to me.

'Poor thing,' said Joan. 'For your information, the tablets *aren't* here.'

'Where, then?'

'I—I don't know. But I saw them taken from here just a day or two ago. What you're reading is a cold trail.'

'What about the Codex, then?'

'You don't deserve to find the Codex, you hypocritical hag!'

'Hypocritical! Me!'

All the undergraduates began to fidget—except for the ninjas, who I assumed were maintaining martial focus and discipline. I felt like fidgeting, too. No wonder it hadn't worked out between Kortnoz and either of these two women. Each was interested in only two things: herself and Kortnoz. Neither subject interested *him* in the slightest—only learning, only the latest research puzzle. (And maybe the Delmarva Geography Prize. Everyone has a weakness.)

'I'm tired of this bickering,' said Joan.

'Then if you'll excuse me, I'll be off to the library.' Norella turned to her minions. 'Which of you said you know where it is?'

'Um, Pete did,' said one of them.

'I did not, you're such a liar!'

'Be quiet, then—if we found our way here, we can find the library.'

'There aren't any cookies in the library,' muttered one of the minions sullenly.

The ninjas arranged themselves across the doorway. I knew this was my cue to say something like, 'Nobody's going anywhere,' but I felt so out of control I knew it would sound hollow. A fight was brewing, kids were going to get hurt, and I had no way of stopping it. Unless …unless we just went to the library, got it over with. Even if Joan and Norella found the Codex, what could they do with it until they had the tablets? And what use were the tablets without the missing one?

I said to the ninjas, 'It's okay, guys. It won't do any harm to bring them to the library. You can come with us, or you can stay here, whatever you want. No cookies allowed in the library, though.' Their shoulders slumped, but duty came first. The security guards had no such compunctions, and sat happily drinking coffee—real coffee, I knew Ricky would never permit instant in his kitchen—and wolfing down cookies.

I led the way, followed by the strangely quiet Danny, then Joan, then Norella and her entourage, then the ninjas. When we entered the library, even Norella's minions were impressed. They wandered, gaping, staring up at the carvings. One of them actually backed into Joan. Her angry rebuke was drowned out by a loud electronic squeal from his pack. The faces of Norella and every one of her minions snapped toward the pair.

Norella slowly walked toward Joan. 'What's in your purse?' she said.

'Nothing that would interest you.'

'Oh? Let's see.' Norella lunged for the bag and yanked it off Joan's shoulder. She opened it and cried out. Very, very carefully, she reached in and withdrew a tablet of deep, deep blue crystal.

'That explains why the readings suddenly got so funky,' said one undergraduate wisely to another.

'Mm, yes,' said the other, nodding.

'Where did you find it? How?' gasped Norella.

I was less interested in the logistics of it than in the fact that it now made the danger much less, shall I say it, academic. There was no more waiting for the tablet to be remade. Even the 'any minute now' assumption we'd been going on had given us the comforting feeling that there was still time to find things out, to make a good decision. That buffer zone was gone.

Norella gave a panicky look around at the thousands upon thousands of books, uncatalogued, many even unlabelled. 'Get to work,' she said to her minions. 'Find the Codex.'

'Um,' said one.

'*What?*'

'What does it look like?'

'It's really old. And you won't recognise the alphabet.'

They spread out, Norella tucking the tablet into her pocket as she went.

I heard a noise from behind the stairwell, near the door to the guest room. I looked over and nearly shouted in shock: Russ was looking at me over the top of a gargoyle head that formed one of the carved banisters. He had his finger to his lips, which was the only thing that kept me from chewing him out right there in front of everyone. I was pretty sure he could tell I was angry, though. I looked away before anyone else could notice and follow my gaze to spot him.

I tried to think of some excuse to go over to the staircase, but if I was to maintain the image of someone who was convinced the Praxies still had the Codex, I couldn't very well look like I was searching for it here in the library.

I sat glumly at one of the heavy tables, the ninjas dutifully arranging themselves to safeguard me. I'd have to get rid of them, too, if I was going to manage a chat with Russ. In desperation, I said, 'You guys stay here and keep an eye on things, okay? If they do find the Codex, don't let them leave with it. It'll probably be pretty big, and all sealed up in something, tough to sneak out with, but I don't know for sure. I need to, uh, find the bathroom.'

I left the library and walked toward the canteen as slowly as I dared. It didn't take Russ long to sneak out and catch up with me. I waited until we were nearly at the canteen to whisper furiously, 'What the hell do you think you're doing? And how the hell did you get here?'

'Family secret. The Gartners have known about this place for generations. At one point, a Gartner was the *only* one who knew, apparently.'

'I heard about that, yes, but what made you come here now?'

'Pace. She found me over at Drusy's, and told me where the

guards had taken you. Nearly a dozen people go into a building not much bigger than a refrigerator, and with only one door, but they don't come out again.'

'She must have been following us the whole time up there. Why didn't she—'

'Reveal herself and give you a great, big hug? Based on the way she was talking at Drusy's: guilt.'

'What? No, never mind, no time. Russ, the missing tablet—'

'I saw. We have to bring everything together before anyone else does, and—and what, exactly?'

'Give them to Kortnoz. Angelo Praxicopolis was right, Kortnoz is the one who deserves to solve the Codex, the only one who won't use it to dominate the university or expand control over the media or whatever it is everyone else wants it for. He's completely guileless.'

'We need to get that tablet away from Norella Honeycott, then. Hey, didn't she have the hots for me, back where we rescued your mom? Maybe I can use that.'

'She has the hots for every good-looking guy. And just how far are you planning to go to "use that"?'

He shuddered. 'Not very. Just until I can get her off her guard. Maybe get her to take off that jacket—didn't I see her put the tablet in the pocket? Then one of those ninjas can sneak the jacket out to you while she's making eyes at me.'

'You're convinced you can distract her?'

'You keep forgetting. I'm an actor. It's part of the job to have an absolutely accurate impression of how good-looking one is, or isn't. Anyway, um.' He blushed; I could tell even in the dim hallway.

'I'll wait here for one of the ninjas to bring me the jacket, then,' I said, trying not to laugh at him when he was about to go into such mortal peril.

Russ gave me a quick kiss, and strode back into the library.

'What the hell?' I heard him shout. 'Can't a man get any *research* done around here? The place is crawling with undergraduates—if I'd wanted that I'd have just gone to the campus library, but that place is a hellhole, and you can't turn around without the predatory mould getting a jump on you. You, over there, dressed in black. Get over here. What the hell are you doing in here?' There was a pause, during which I assumed he was giving the ninja a surreptitious briefing. Then, 'Oh. Hi. Yes—yes, I do remember you. But I'm afraid I can't quite recall—Norella, of course, that was it. That lovely cottage by the seaside. What a lovely day that was, yes. You're quite right …' His voice got too low for me to make out the words. I did my best to wait patiently.

After what was probably only a few minutes, I was startled when a slim figure in black appeared out of nowhere, handed me the jacket, and faded away. I checked the pockets through the fabric; even though it made no difference either way, I felt funny about touching the crystal directly when I knew it was pumping out some kind of emissions that no one really knew about.

I heard Russ again: 'Well, it's been lovely catching up with you, but with all this racket in here, I won't be getting any work done. I'll have to go back to my office and try and work there. What a nuisance. Bye, then. Yes, bye. Toodle-oo.'

He met me in the hallway again, and together we went back to the canteen. A moment later, Danny came in as well. 'I can't stand watching them crawl all over that beautiful library like roaches,' he said. 'Hi, Russ.'

I was a little startled at his informality to a professor, but then I realised he must have seen quite a bit of Russ while Russ had been dating his sister. I couldn't help it, the whole thing was a little embarrassing.

'Hi, Danny,' said Russ. 'How are things?'

'Better than they used to be, thanks,' he said, then turned to me. 'Do you really think the Codex is in there?'

'No,' I said. 'Angelo made the tablets easy for Dr Kortnoz to find, didn't he? If he'd been able to get the Codex from his family, as he did the tablets, wouldn't he have made that easy to find as well?'

Ricky brought a plate with more cookies over. 'Secret stash,' he said. 'But that Norella woman, the one with all those dopey guys following her around, she said it was a myth that the Praxies had it.'

'No, they had it, all right. Angelo told me,' said Danny. 'You wouldn't keep a thing like that underground anyway, would you? These strata are relatively porous, and so close to the river, I'm surprised there isn't mould on everything. They must have one hell of a ventilation system.'

'So it's probably a good bet that the Praxies do still have the Codex,' I said. 'And in order save the university from their tyranny, as exercised through the governors, we need to get it to Dr Kortnoz, along with all the tablets. Question: do we choose the safe route of keeping the restored tablet separate from the others, or do we choose the quick route of keeping them together and shoving them into Kortnoz's hands?'

'Either way, pretty soon Norella is going to notice that her jacket is missing,' said Russ. 'We'd better go.'

'Ricky, thanks for the cookies. You're a magician, you know that?' I said. 'When the ninjas come back, could you please tell them I got called away, and thanks very much for all their help?'

'Sure,' he said cheerfully. 'Hey, tomorrow night I'm making stewed spicy chicken and roasted peppers for dinner. I could set a few extra places. Man, this is the best work-study job *ever*.'

'We're going to have to leave that open, I'm afraid,' I said. 'But if we can't make it, I'll take a rain check for when things calm down, okay? Bye, guys,' I called to the security guards. They raised hands in lazy farewells and went back to their coffee.

Neither Danny nor I remembered the way out, but Russ seemed to know the tunnels quite well. 'Do you spend much time down here?' I asked him.

'Nope, this is my first visit. Great-Uncle Johan showed me the map after he swore me to secrecy. There wasn't supposed to be a map at all, but apparently we've always kept just one, carefully hidden.'

'You're doing all the navigating from … your memories of a map.'

'Actors memorise. Lines, blocking, where the techies keep the props. It's a useful skill. The exit I'm making for should take us out near the Gutierrez building.'

'Did you know that used to be called the Strudthorne building?'

'Why'd they change it?'

'As part of a campaign to discredit Millicent and render her outcries against censorship and disinformation ineffectual. The governors put pressure on her adviser to falsify the data in her thesis.'

'Yikes.'

'Yeah, I may have stolen Pace's research but at least it was all still true.'

The night air was warm and damp as we emerged; summer was definitely on its way.

'Pace was at Drusy's?' I said to Russ.

'Yup.'

'Maybe that's where we should go.'

'It's as good an option as any.'

'Who's Drusy?' said Danny.

'Dr Drusy Kelso, retired economist and academic,' I said. 'And charismatic paramilitary leader.' He started to laugh until he saw I was completely serious.

For once, the student working at the reception desk did pay attention to us. 'Hey, Snotnose,' he said nastily. But Danny walked past without a glance.

'Well done,' I murmured when we were well down the hallway.

We had to knock on Drusy's door several times before anyone heard us, and when Mark opened the door, the roar from inside made Danny step back in alarm. There must have been twenty people in there, all talking excitedly. Drusy was on the phone, shouting over the noise. Pace and Kortnoz were sitting on the sofa, looking utterly exhausted. And over in the far corner, on one of the kitchen chairs, sat a hopeless and horrified Jasper. Next to the chair, Ozzie stood calmly. You would have thought he was just daydreaming, but when Jasper fidgeted, Ozzie's hand came down on Jasper's shoulder and gently pressed him to be still.

We pushed carefully through the crowd to the sofa.

'Hi,' I shouted to Pace. 'Thanks for the ninjas.'

'Yeah, they're good, aren't they?' She looked away uncomfortably.

Kortnoz looked up and smiled but made no attempt to converse above the noise. I handed him Norella's jacket and pointed to the pocket. He frowned, then reached inside. At the sight of the blue tablet he was transfigured. Enraptured, he held it up to catch the light.

'Holy shit,' said Pace, as far as I could judge from reading her lips.

Slowly the room fell silent as, one by one, people noticed what Kortnoz was holding. Soon only Drusy's voice could be heard.

'Thanks for the update. I've got to go, though. Bye.'

She came over and sat on the arm of the sofa. 'Well,' she said. 'That explains a lot.'

'Like what?' I said.

'The Praxies have released a statement that they're the victims of industrial sabotage, that a proprietary experimental substance has been stolen from their laboratory. They're saying it's exceedingly dangerous—is it?' she asked Kortnoz.

'Not in the short term. I don't think. I was pretty sure they were emitting something, because why else had they been put in a lead box? So I devised a scanner that could measure it—no regular equipment even twitched, so they won't do any of the normal damage.'

This was not comforting.

'The bad news is,' continued Drusy, 'that the governors have been told the trail leads to the university. The whole campus is being locked down.'

'Convenient, isn't it?' said Dr Garrick. 'Just when the kids are doing something useful with their time.'

'Any violence yet?' I said.

'No,' said Drusy. 'But it's probably a matter of when, not whether.'

'Anything in the media about the kids' stories?'

'Nothing on the airwaves, of course—they're Praxie territory,' said Mark from across the room. 'But there is a website up, and according to the tracker it's getting a fair number of unique visits. And climbing. I'm looking forward to seeing tomorrow's *Backwash*, for once.'

'Dr Kortnoz, do you have any idea at all where the Codex ought to be? If we can bring you together with the other tablets, and this one, and the Codex, you'll have the attention of the world, won't you?'

'Well, of course, that's not why I want the Codex, I just—research—academic inquiry—I just—yes, I will.' He looked extremely uncomfortable. 'But I always thought the Praxies had it. Don't they?'

'Norella and Joan are looking for it in the underground library, but I don't think it's there—the conditions are not the best for ancient manuscripts, and there aren't any hermetic storage facilities that I know of down there,' I said.

As no one had any suggestions, the conversations resumed, albeit more soberly (and quietly). I took the opportunity to say to Pace, 'How come you don't hate me anymore?'

'Your friend Russ here tore strips out of her, with Drusy cheering him on,' said Kortnoz. 'What department are you in again?'

'Dramatic Arts,' said Russ.

'I'd been thinking maybe it was Entomology; they have a bit of a grudge against her for some reason. And they're kind of nuts.

Almost as bad as the physicists. One of them has come up with some new conjecture that parallel universes can intrude into this one not only in dreams—lots of people think that, God help them—but through the behaviours of large, mindless systems.'

'Like universities,' said Danny, and looked pleased when there were a few chuckles from nearby people.

'So somewhere in a parallel universe there is another university, and we're influencing each other without knowing, is that it?' I said.

'Apparently,' said Kortnoz.

'Could I have a cup of coffee, please?' called Jasper in his nasal, whiny voice. 'Or even a glass of water—that is, if it's not too much trouble?' Hell's bells, he could sound obnoxious no matter what he was saying.

'How'd they catch him?' I asked Pace, nodding towards Jasper.

Pace snorted. 'When he arrived at our meeting place, Ozzie showed up and just took hold of his wrist, and he was too scared to even struggle.'

'Who is he?' said Danny. 'Why do you all look like you're … gloating?'

'Jasper's been trying to get his PhD for, oh, nobody knows how long. But he keeps thinking he's entitled to it, and so he doesn't put in the work,' I said. 'Also, he's coordinated or committed several attacks upon my person in the last week or so. So I'm happy to see him brought to heel. But it's not nice to gloat. I should stop it.'

'Me too,' said Pace. 'I should.'

Danny went over to where Ozzie still stood guard over the glowering Jasper. Someone had given him a coffee, but that had done nothing to improve his temper. Out of curiosity, I got up to get a coffee for myself, so I could listen.

'You're going to be sorry,' Jasper was saying. 'You think they're wise and kind and wonderful, and they'll help you and encourage you, but you'll find out. They'll do to you what they did to me. What did you say your name was?'

'Danny Wexler.'

'Snotnose? You're kidding me.'

'You've heard of me,' said Danny dryly.

'Everyone's heard of you, the obnoxious, conceited son of a governor, the kid who thinks he knows more than everyone.'

'Yup, that's me,' said Danny.

'Which governor?'

'Anthea Fulton, if it makes any difference to you.'

'Is it true she's got a huge portrait in her office of President Kim-Hatton?' said Jasper mockingly.

'You know, I'm glad I met you,' said Danny. 'I was on my way to being you. Now, though, I'm more sure than ever that I've had a very narrow escape and I'm on the right track at last. So thanks for that, you disgusting, weedy, whiny twerp. And my mom does *not* have a portrait of Kim-Hatton in her office. She has a photo of my sister and me, a massive globe, a North Kras nomad's sword, and a collection of rare documents in a big safe.'

'Danny, what?' I said instantly. 'What has she got? That last thing.'

'A … big safe,' he said hesitantly.

'Danny, is it climate-controlled? Hermetically sealed?'

'Yes,' whispered Danny, his eyes wide and dark. 'Yes, it is.'

'She hasn't by any chance given you a swipe card or access codes or anything, has she?'

'No. Sorry. It really pisses my sister off, but Mom keeps all that stuff to herself.'

'Pace! Do you have any ninjas left? We need to break into the governors' offices.'

'Even they can't defeat those locks,' said Pace. 'They've tried.'

'That leaves us just one option: to try and find a rogue security guard.'

'Are you nuts?' said Pace.

'No, discipline has broken down. There are a few rogues. I wish I had Sergeant Funk's phone number.'

'Greta Funk?' said Pace.

'Um, yeah,' I said. 'She was underground a little while ago, but I was thinking maybe if she'd emerged I might be able to get her to help. She's as sick of the governors as we are. You're not telling me you have her number, are you?'

'Remember when our office was trashed? I was in such bad shape over the bugs that she gave me her card and said she knew of a good grief-counselling group. I was sort of touched that she'd take the trouble, so I kept the card. Wait a minute.' She rummaged through her bag and a few pockets before coming up with the card. 'Here you go.'

I realised I was still wearing my pack. I took it off and got out the phone I'd nearly forgotten I had. I turned on the phone, and dialled Sergeant Funk's number. Mercifully, she answered.

'Sergeant, hi, it's Celeste Carlucci. Are you back outside again?'

'Yes, why?'

'I need a favour. Where can I meet you to talk about it?'

'Well, I'm over near the quad at the moment, near the statue of Papa Purple.' Nobody ever bothered to remember the real name of the patriarch of the Purple family.

'Can you hang out for a few minutes until I get there?'

'Sure.'

'Thanks—see you soon.'

I turned to the room. 'Can anyone drive me over to campus?'

Kortnoz said, 'I'll take you.' He put the tablet back in the jacket pocket, bundled the jacket up, and tucked it under his arm. He wouldn't be letting it out of his sight, I was betting. Drusy frowned.

'It's fine,' said Kortnoz. 'I'll just drop Celeste off and go straight home. The tablet will be safe.'

'I'll go, too,' said Pace.

'And me,' said Danny.

Russ took a step to stand next to me. 'I'm not going to sit here worrying anymore. I'm going too.'

'Dr Kortnoz, can you fit all of us in your four-wheel-drive?'

'You bet I can,' he said.

'While you're over there,' said Drusy, 'see if you can spot Lenny. He said he'd stay on campus to keep an eye on things, but he should have been back by now.'

It was a quick drive over. Maybe someday I'd own a car. Kortnoz parked in his usual spot, and we walked toward the quad.

I didn't want to spook the Sergeant Funk with a gang after what had probably been a hard day for her, so I said, 'Could you guys wait for me near the west entrance to the quad? Thanks.'

She was standing at the feet of Papa Purple, as promised. I sat beside her. 'I'm going straight to the point: I need to break into Anthea Fulton's office, and then I need to break into the safe that's in there. Possible?'

She nodded. 'Not even the governors know how many passkeys and swipe cards we carry around. And how good we are at improvising when we don't quite have the right one. I'll admit I'd like the chance of doing a number on her office—she was one of the nastiest ones during the contract negotiations. Ha! Negotiations! That implies the other person has a say.'

'When can we meet you there?'

'Fifteen minutes. Don't be late, because not all the security guards see things the same way.'

I checked my watch. 'Okay. Thanks.'

'No problem.'

I caught up with the others, but I saw right away something was wrong.

Russ said, 'I just heard a couple of people talking. Seems a cranky old man with a cane started insulting the security guards, and one of them took a swing at him.'

'Dr Garrick—is he okay? What happened?'

'It was bad enough to start things deteriorating. A few of the students recognised him from when he taught their geography class, and their outrage is boiling over. Have a look.'

I stepped through the west entrance into the quad. It was a nightmare scene. Someone had started a small fire in the centre, and as people came to it and dumped chairs and papers on it, it started to blaze. The smoke, sharp and bitter-smelling, was filling the quad. The guards were just about to come in swinging, but the kids didn't care. Someone started singing that North Kras song, and they all took it up until the quad felt like it was shaking with it.

'We have to stop this!' I said.

'Too late. There's no way you could make yourself heard now,' said Russ. 'The only way to stop it is to finish it.'

'Where's Dr Garrick?'

'Some kids apparently took him out of the quad, and I'm hoping they called an ambulance for him.'

I couldn't do any thing to help him, then. Not directly, anyway. There was only one thing left to do. 'Danny, can you please take us to your mom's office?'

'Sure,' said Danny, and we followed him as the sounds of singing and bonfires and breaking furniture continued behind us. I hoped to God we wouldn't hear gunshots.

Chapter 21
Celeste Finds that Victory Is Not Sweet

As we hurried across campus, I started to notice that while there were dozens of security guards all over the place, none of them were rushing to the quad. Most were clustered in small, nervous groups, looking over their shoulders. One or two seemed to be trying, unsuccessfully, to draw their guns. More than a few were clutching their backsides and complaining in loud, frightened voices.

Pace laughed out loud. 'They did it!'

'Who did what?' said Kortnoz.

'My martial-arts club! They've been aching to try out these techniques for years! Gargantua Glue carefully squirted into a gun holster while the guard is distracted by a disturbance. Air let out of vehicle tyres. That one's quite popular; I'm told there are a lot of copycats out there doing their bit. And, the *pièce de résistance*, a little innovation of my own: close-range throwing stars, on a little tether of fishing line. Once they bite the quarry on the butt, a little yank of the line both exacerbates the damage and removes the weapon from scrutiny. Phantom butt-bites—very demoralising! Petroleum jelly smeared on the surveillance-camera lenses doesn't hurt, either. It won't stop the guards who are already in the quad, but it will keep these ones from wanting to run into an even worse situation than the one they've got out here.'

Danny took us to the office building that everyone called 'the new tower', as it had only been built about ten years ago.

Sergeant Funk was waiting in the lobby. 'Okay,' she said as she pushed the elevator button. 'We'll make this quick and I'll be on my way.' The elevator opened. We were about to shuffle inside when she held up a hand and reached around with the other to swipe a card on the elevator panel. 'Security setting five,' she said. 'Disables the cameras. You have no idea how handy that is.'

The ride to the top floor was quick, and I swallowed and swallowed to clear my ears as we rose. We stepped out into a lobby of unimaginable opulence. To compare the office Pace and I shared to this was sickening. I glanced over at Danny, but this was all he'd ever known. He walked steadily to his mother's office, quite used to the carpets and chandeliers, the carved woodwork and stone sculptures, the designer furniture and classic paintings. I wondered if he realised he'd be giving all this up if he kept on with us.

At Anthea Fulton's office door, Sergeant Funk waved the swipe card at the lock, then strode inside to scowl professionally at the safe. She handed me her flashlight, took a small toolkit off her belt, and spent about fifteen seconds fiddling with the lock until it clicked, and the door opened smoothly and slowly.

'Man,' said Danny. 'Is my sister ever going to be pissed that it's this easy.'

'It's not easy, kid. The trick is making it *look* easy,' said Sergeant Funk. 'Glad I could help. You never saw me here. Keep the flashlight, it's personal, not issue. Just wipe my prints off, okay? Bye.' And she was gone.

Kortnoz peered into the safe and took a long, shuddering breath. Then he set down the swaddled tablet and reached into the safe with trembling hands. He lovingly removed a box made of what looked like glass, but was probably some sort of advanced, inert, and incredibly tough plastic. Inside was a book. That was all. An old, old book, bound between two wooden slats. But even I could sense that it pulsed with meaning. Maybe that was wishful thinking, or maybe meaning was there because we put it there. Or maybe it really did hold ancient wisdom that would help us live braver, wiser, kinder lives. I felt my heart beating faster, and I knew that whatever I was feeling, it was nothing compared to what Kortnoz was going through.

I said, 'We'd better go. Dr Kortnoz, do you have anything to wrap that up in?'

'I have the jacket.' It lay at his feet. 'But what will I do with the tablet?'

The lights in the office snapped on, blinding us all for a second.

'I can suggest something,' said someone. We all turned and froze.

Danny said, 'Hi, Mom.'

'Danny, get out of the way, please.'

'Mom—Mom, you don't have a *gun*, do you? Is that a gun?' He sounded amused.

'Danny, move.'

Danny stepped in front of Kortnoz.

'Danny—'

'Go ahead, Mom. If that's how much I mean to you, then shoot.'

'Don't be stupid.'

'You're the stupid one!' he said. 'You're the one who does whatever the Praxies say. Angelo told me about what they're like, and you're too stupid to see it! Unless you *admire* them, unless you want to be like that, too.'

'Angelo,' said Fulton softly. 'I see. Hello, Ty. Pace. And Russ. Good to see you again.'

'Hello, Anthea,' said Russ.

'Miffy came to me with some wild story that you were planning something. I figured, better safe than sorry, and I came in tonight to keep watch. I'm not on my own, either.'

'What, the security guards?' said Danny. 'Lots of luck.'

'What do you mean?' said Fulton.

'Mutiny,' said Danny. 'They're not doing what the governors say anymore. At least, enough of them so that you can't have your way. It doesn't pay to mistreat the help, Mom.'

Anthea did not respond to this. I wondered if she'd ever responded to his efforts to get a reaction from her. Instead, she pointed at me. 'Danny, who is this?'

'I'm Celeste Carlucci,' I broke in. 'Maybe you've heard of me.'

'*You're* Celeste Carlucci? You don't look much like an amoral, publicity-hungry spider.'

I glanced over at Pace, who looked down. 'That was years ago,' she muttered.

'She's my geography professor,' Danny said loudly. Uh-oh.

'Oh, really?' said his mom, still speaking only to me. 'And you're the one who taught my son to ruin his life, waste his intelligence, and cause me quite a lot of embarrassment?'

Danny grinned at this.

'And now you're robbing my office. What a lovely role model.'

'And you're a better one?' I said. 'Coercion, repression, propaganda—'

'Danny, did you know your mentor stole someone else's research and published it as her own?'

Danny looked confused.

'No, go on,' said Fulton. 'Tell him. He should know exactly what sort of person he's decided to idolise.'

'All right, then. It's true, Danny. Dr Kortnoz and Dr Garoux had made some important progress in understanding what was happening when the Purple River got so murky a couple of years back. I … I thought something was wrong, I thought someone was maybe doing it deliberately, and I wanted to bring attention to it. But nobody noticed the research at all. Nobody …'

I stopped, because I felt cold and dizzy. Because I finally got it. Any attention drawn to the sediment entering Purple Bay would be bad attention for the governors and the Praxies. There was no way it would ever, ever have gotten the coverage it needed. I'd ruined my career, destroyed my friendship with Pace, hurt the trusting and generous Ty Kortnoz—all for nothing.

To top it off, Danny was looking at me, mouth open. I didn't want to meet his gaze, lest I see the contempt I'd seen on so many other faces.

'I'm not going to try to justify myself,' I said. 'Not anymore. I did what I did.'

'Now that Danny has heard it straight from you, I don't need to prolong this. Everyone keep still. Believe me, there will be no repercussions at all for me if I happen to shoot one—or more—of you while defending precious artefacts against theft.' She kept the gun pointed in our general direction and reached into her jacket pocket. 'I've just paged the security guards. Ty, put the box down please. There are still feet, hands, a shoulder I can see that my son isn't blocking. I'm a very good shot, and I think you'd prefer to keep all your limbs.'

'Mom, call the guards off.'

'Do you still think your friends are so wonderful, Danny? Now that you hear how they lie and backstab each other? Do real friends treat each other like that?'

'At least they don't—'

Five security guards walked into the room. They bristled with weapons.

'Leave my son alone, but cuff the rest of them.'

'No!' Danny yelled. 'Cuff me, too! I'm not her son!'

But the guards left him alone as they wrenched our arms behind us and bound our wrists with plastic ties that tightened if we struggled.

Danny started to cry. 'I hate you!' he screamed at his mother. But it didn't sound like the tantrum of a child; if I'd been Anthea Fulton, I'd have had the guards cuff him right there.

'Oh, Danny, don't be stupid,' was all she said, and glanced down to put her gun away.

At that instant, as though he'd been waiting for it all his life, Danny grabbed the plastic box and ran. A voice from the hallway yelled, 'Hey, kid!' I heard the stairwell door slam shut and imagined Danny running, running.

'Danny!' shouted his mom.

Sergeant Funk burst through the doorway. 'I saw the pager message.'

Fulton rounded on me. 'Where's he going?'

I shrugged, which was unwise, as the movement of my arms tightened the wrist-tie.

'Hey, guys,' said Sergeant Funk to the other guards. 'Haven't you heard? Down tools until the governors restore our benefits.'

'I didn't know they were reopening the negotiations,' said one of the guards.

'They just heard about it back at base.'

'Oh. In that case …'

'What—' spluttered Fulton.

The guards left us with our wrists tied and walked out the door. As they left, Sergeant Funk cast a glance back and winked at me.

That made things a little more even, but Fulton still had the gun, which I noticed she'd taken back out of her pocket. With her left hand she reached into the other pocket and took out a phone.

'Monitor all cameras. My son is running away, and I want him back.' The very ideal of concerned motherhood, yeah. She hung up. 'As soon as they get back to me with a sighting, we'll know where he's going, won't we? And he's going to lead us right where we need to go. He's just a boy, he hasn't learned much yet.' I reckoned Danny had learned a lot more than she thought.

It only took a minute before the phone rang. 'Thanks. Can you send people over there? What, all of them? All right, I'll take care of it.' She put the phone away. 'You're all coming with me to find Danny, because I can't have you damaging this university any more than you already have. I know you'll cooperate, because none of you wants to see any of the others—or all of the others—shot on the spot, do you?'

'Shooting people who have their hands tied behind them isn't going to look so good,' said Pace.

'It's the work of a moment to cut the ties off and put a rock or a letter-opener in your hand,' said Fulton coldly. 'And it will be my word against that of any survivors.' Still keeping the gun ready, she moved over to the jacket and tucked the bundle under her arm. Then she retrieved the flashlight a security guard had grabbed from me and tossed it away. 'Out to the elevators. Then over to the old stone shed. Nobody runs, because even if you scatter, I can still shoot at least one of you.'

'In the back,' snorted Pace. 'Figures.'

The five of us crowded into the elevator. I was next to Russ, and we leaned against each other, saying nothing. Pace and Ty did the same across the elevator. Fulton glanced from one pair to the other, sneering. When the elevator opened, she motioned with the gun for us to get out.

'Old stone shed. Go on, you know where it is.'

This part of campus was far enough from the quad to be deserted. We walked, stumbling over breaks in the path. When we got to the shed, Fulton carefully opened the door. There was just enough moonlight coming through the windows to see that the shed was empty.

'Okay, where did he go?' she said. None of us said anything. Fulton alternated glancing at the walls, the floor, and us. Eventually she found the grate on the floor. She knelt and lifted it with one hand; the guards opening it earlier must have loosened it.

She peered quickly into the hole. 'A ladder. Shit. All right, just get down there as best you can. And remember, I can shoot faster than any of you can run. Pace, you first.'

Pace glared and stepped carefully onto the ladder. I saw she stayed on the very tips of her feet, so that she could lean in at least a little. If she started to tip backwards, there'd be nothing she could do to save herself. I tried to remember how much of a drop there was; hopefully only a couple of metres. I heard Pace's feet stepping carefully on each iron rung. Seven, eight, nine, ten. Then the sound of her feet hitting the ground together.

'You next,' she said to Russ. Then Kortnoz, and finally me. I pushed my cheek into the side of the ladder. It hurt, but it kept my weight a little better balanced as I made my way down. Now that my eyes were getting used to the dark, I could just see people as dim figures.

Fulton switched on the flashlight. 'Ty, you go first. Take me to the most likely place that Danny would go.'

'That would be the library,' said Russ carefully. 'Go on, Ty. Third turn on the left, then first on the right.'

Joan and Norella were probably still in the library, searching for the Codex. They wouldn't like seeing Kortnoz bound and threatened by another woman.

'He's right, Dr Kortnoz,' I said. 'Please, let's go to the library before this lunatic shoots us all.'

We started walking. 'Left here,' said Russ. And a few moments later, 'Now turn right.

I remembered the metal door. When Ty pushed it open and saw who was in there, he recoiled in horror.

'Don't be stupid,' I heard Russ mutter. 'Go on!'

'You don't underst—' Ty gave a cry and stumbled into the library as though Russ had shoved him. We all came after.

'There he is,' shouted a voice I recognised as Danny's. 'Dr Kortnoz! I saved the Codex, look! And everyone here is helping guard it.' Suddenly his voice became harsh. 'Everyone, Mom. No more secrets and plans and lies.'

'Ty!' said Norella. 'Ty, baby, what's wrong?' She rushed over to him and started running her hand up and down his arm. She turned on Fulton. 'What have you done?' she said in horrified tones. 'You've hurt him! Look at his face. Have you ever seen such terror?' She darted toward Fulton, hands up and in fists.

'Back off!' cried Fulton. 'Do you think I'd hesitate to shoot any of you—oh!'

Joan had snuck up behind her during Norella's theatrics, reached around, and yanked Fulton's gun arm out to the side. The gun went off, the bullet presumably burying itself into a book on the shelves. Joan tripped Fulton and landed on top of her, still keeping the gun arm stretched out to the side. Norella ran up and stomped savagely on Fulton's wrist, and the gun slid out of her now limp hand. A helpful ninja stepped in and kicked it out of her reach, and two more tied Fulton up as Joan slowly stood. Joan and Norella gave each other an exultant high-five before remembering to glare at each other suspiciously.

'Wow,' said Danny. 'Where did you learn to do that?'

'You'd be surprised what you can pick up in a graduate seminar,' said Joan. Norella nodded knowingly.

Norella's undergrads were awestruck, but the ninjas were more practical, cutting the plastic ties off our wrists with throwing stars.

Ty went over to Fulton's prone, but struggling, form and gently slid Norella's jacket out from under her. 'The blue tablet,' he said.

'How did you—it was—just over—' Norella finally noticed that the jacket was no longer where she'd set it several hours ago.

'It's okay,' said Kortnoz courteously. 'Academics can be so single-minded when they're involved in crucial research.'

'You, there,' said Joan to Danny. 'What did you mean, "I saved the Codex"? Are you telling me that box you've got contains the Littoral Codex?'

'Yup.'

'Why didn't you say so?'

'I wanted to wait for Dr Kortnoz. He's the one who ought to have it, anyway.'

Kortnoz, Norella, and Joan all started talking at once. Danny coolly held up a hand, and such was his confidence that they all stopped.

'Angelo wanted Dr Kortnoz to have it. Didn't he?'

'I—I don't know,' said Kortnoz.

'You kept finding clues that led you to the tablets.'

'Um, yes, but how did you know about that?'

'Angelo told me he would choose the right person to fix what his family had done. But it looks like he accidentally chose a bunch of people. Including—including me.'

'Danny, I'm guessing he chose you a long, long time ago,' I said.

'And all that time, I was paying him for your violin lessons,' said Fulton disgustedly from the floor. 'Had he no loyalty?'

'He did, Mom, just to something more important than you. As incomprehensible as that concept may be for you.'

'Now what?' said Pace. 'We have the Codex. We have the missing tablet. We know where the other tablets are.'

Joan and Norella both swivelled their heads toward Pace. 'We do?'

'What, do you think I dropped them down a storm drain?' I said, annoyed. 'Give me *some* credit.'

Pace said, 'I hate to say it—you have no idea how I hate to say it—but Norella's idea of a research consortium makes sense. Just—no secrets. And lots of accountability.'

Norella squawked.

'No, but wait,' said Pace. 'This gaggle of governors is clearly incompetent—look at how the campus has just completely gone to pieces over the past few days. So the federal government— which, after all, is the source of most of the funding—is going to want to see an all-new, all-singing, all-dancing board of governors. And you and Joan have both shown such dedication to the university, such commitment to its higher aims, well …have you updated your resumes lately? You may be wanting to send them in. And of course as governors you'd have access to all the Codex research as it happened.'

They both looked thoughtful at that. What were a few months on the lecture circuit when they could control the entire university? I quailed a bit when I thought of the changes they might wreak, but then I realised we'd made it so that neither the students, nor the faculty, nor the security guards would be so easy to dominate again.

'Um,' said Russ. 'We should maybe go see about those tablets, really. There are still other governors, not to mention the Praxies, and eventually they'll figure out how to scan for that radiation, like Ty did. Lead aprons notwithstanding.'

'Makes sense,' said Kortnoz. 'Where are they?'

'Beggar's Pit,' said Russ.

'Wow. That *would* be the last place I'd look,' said Kortnoz admiringly. 'Good thinking. Is there a safe place I can leave this tablet? Somewhere,' he said meaningfully, 'where I can find it, safe and sound, when we get back?'

One of the ninjas said, 'There's a room back by the big stairwell. We'll get the key from—what was her name? The chirpy one?'

'Nicki,' said another ninja. 'I'll get it.'

'Danny, I'll let you oversee getting the blue tablet locked up, okay? Maybe put the Codex with it.' He handed the wrapped tablet to Danny. The remaining ninjas who weren't actively involved in guarding Fulton gathered protectively around Danny. He looked at his mother tied and humiliated on the floor. His lower lip trembled. 'Sure,' he said quietly.

Fulton looked up at him, but I couldn't tell anything at all from her expression. 'Now,' said Kortnoz cheerfully, 'what's the best way back out?'

I suddenly wanted nothing more to do with this whole business. Maybe it was fatigue—it must have been about two in the morning by now—but it felt more like despair. Ruining my career and my closest friendship had seemed worth it to save the river, the university, and the entire city of Purple Bay. Even though I'd been wrong in the end, and neither my career nor my friendship with Pace had ever recovered, I'd told myself all this time that I'd done my best to do something worthy. But now I knew I'd been naive and stupid and selfish.

Feeling dull and shamed, I followed Russ, Pace, and Kortnoz out through the tunnels and up to the exit behind the gym. There was no need for subterfuge now. Before long we were off campus and walking toward Beggar's Pit.

'Shouldn't we have gone to get my car?' said Kortnoz nervously as the neighbourhoods grew increasingly menacing.

'Not if you wanted to drive it back out again,' said Russ.

Pace, of course, looked utterly at ease. Russ walked with the businesslike coolness of a local. Me, I simply didn't care. I guess all that passed for toughness, or else the residents decided the four of us were too many to threaten efficiently, because we had very little trouble. One drunk threw an empty bottle after us and it crashed on the footpath, making Kortnoz jump, but that was it.

Russ went first into the building. A few steps into the foyer, he said, 'Aw, no. Miffy, come on now.'

The old Northie opened his apartment door and hollered down the stairwell. 'This lady, always banging on your door. Maybe you should tell her to stay away. I am just coming out here to say shut up, like I always do, when she waves this machine around and says, "I know they're here!" So I say, "What's here, you noisy lady?"'

'The tablets!' Miffy broke in. 'I took the monitor and tracked them here. I thought Mom would manage to keep you away so I could break into your apartment in peace!'

'Then what?' said Russ. 'You'd take the tablets to Mommy?'

Miffy sneered. 'Like I owe her anything. There's a whole family of Praxies who really, *really* want the tablets.'

'And once you show up with them, they start to see you're more than just your mother's pretty daughter, is that it?' Russ sounded more contemptuous than angry. I was all right with that.

Miffy tossed her hair and said nothing. Kortnoz pushed gently past Russ and peered at the device she was holding. 'My monitor. How did you get it?'

'It was in your office on a shelf labelled "monitor". Easy enough to take. Your security procedures are laughable.'

'What are we going to do about her?' said Pace, pointing at Miffy.

'Let her go,' I said wearily. Everyone, even Bruno, turned to stare at me. I sighed. 'How much damage could she do, really?'

'Plenty!' Miffy snapped.

Pace said, 'Maybe Celeste is right. Maybe we should let her go. If she's double-crossing the governors, that can only be a good thing for us.'

Russ moved aside. 'Go on, then, Miffy. And if you come here again, I'll call the cops. I mean it, I'm tired of this. Of you.'

Miffy strode down the stairs and out the door without a glance at any of us.

'And stay out!' hollered Bruno as the door to the street slammed shut. He muttered something in North Kras that I assumed was not polite, and went back up to his apartment.

Russ said, 'I hope I don't live to regret that.' Maybe he was waiting for me to assure him that no, it was all fine. But after a second's silence, he shrugged, and let us into his apartment.

My battered gym bag was still in the closet, wrapped in the lead aprons. After seeing how easy it was to monitor the radioactivity, I didn't have much faith in them. But I supposed they were better than nothing. Kortnoz apparently felt the same, because he took the tablets out and rewrapped the aprons directly around them, then put the heavy bundle into the gym bag.

'Do you remember how to get back underground?' I said.

'I can take them,' said Russ. 'But don't you want to come, too? Your triumphant journey, bearing the spoils of battle?'

'No. It's all right. Can I just stay here, please?'

'Well, sure, but …'

'Thanks.'

Russ gave me a brief kiss, and then I was alone in the apartment. I sat on the sofa and let my eyes glaze. Soon, they closed, but that was only exhaustion, not the sleep I ached for. Images and voices roiled in my brain: from the past week, from two years ago, from my undergrad years. Again and again, I watched myself make mistake upon mistake. I traced the path my choices had made for me, and saw it lead me into futility. How sad, how pathetic I'd become.

I imagined what Russ would think of me if he knew. I remembered my parents' disappointment. But through my self-loathing and despair, I suddenly heard one bright voice: my mother's, telling me what she'd always told me at my darkest hours.

You'll feel better after you've had some sleep and a hot breakfast. Now quit whining and go to bed.

All right, Mom.

My toothbrush was still in Russ's bathroom. I brushed my teeth, took a shower, staggered into the bedroom, and fell asleep. Maybe I *would* feel better in the morning. Or maybe not.

Chapter 22
A Few More Secrets Are Revealed

The days seeped past, indistinct and dull. After the one night at Russ's, I went back to my own place, where I spent each night listlessly reading geography journals before sinking into sleep. I rose sluggishly in the mornings and went through the motions of teaching. My students didn't seem to mind; I got a standing ovation that week from each class when I walked into the room.

Things had definitely changed on campus. It took a while for the undergrads to settle down and start turning in their assignments again, but that was only the least of the changes. The security force was now the 'Campus Safety Support Service', and their uniforms included far less hardware. A lot of books had started reappearing on the library shelves, and the position of head librarian was being advertised. For some reason, nobody bothered to call the exterminators about the predatory mould, but there were no further attacks.

Danny moved out of his parents' house, of course. He found a place in a squalid group house and started playing jazz gigs to earn money. It didn't take long before he acquired a modest local following. He still kept turning in assignments, good ones, and I kept my deal with Russ: I gave him the grades he deserved. Kortnoz figured he was a shoo-in for the seminar next year. Danny told me he'd never been happier, but something about the way his voice sounded made me think otherwise. Or maybe it was just my own dark mood.

Russ's students performed the full version of the doctored

play to packed houses. The department chair was in raptures, as the *Backwash* not only gave it great reviews, but did a full-page spread—with photos—on her and 'how her philosophy of dramatic arts had galvanised the student uprising'.

'Everything is drama!' she told the reporter. In her case, it was more than usually true.

Kortnoz publicised the finding of the tablets and the recovery of the Codex internationally, and announced the formation of the new research group. Even before the reporters had packed up and left the media conference, offers of grant money started pouring in. Not to mention invitations to speak on the lucrative private-sector lecture circuit, which paid about ten times more than the academic one. The Delmarva Geography Prize committee phoned and said he was in consideration for this year's prize.

'Strictly speaking,' they said, 'it's not a geographical research question. But of course, if you look at it with the sort of broad, inquiring mind the Delmarva Prize seeks to honour, *everything* is geography!' Kortnoz could only agree.

Pace's prediction about a new board of governors had come true in its entirety. Joan and Norella fought like jungle beasts, but that was a good thing, as it slowed down the governors' meetings and drastically limited their ability to actually influence what went on day to day. On the whole, a very good result, although Russ, in particular, did wish they'd get around to abolishing the loyalty clause so he could get tenure. I'd stopped hoping for mine. I'd pretty much stopped hoping for anything.

Russ told me in so many words he was worried about me. He tried to get me to talk about what was wrong, but how was I going to tell him that I was moping around because I detested myself? I'd been clinging for two years to the consolation that in stealing Pace's research I'd been making a noble and brave attempt to save the Purple River. But the moment I realised, that night in Danny's mother's office, that there had *never* been any chance for my plan—I knew in that one crushing moment that what I'd really wanted was to get one over Pace, to prove her wrong, to be the smart one, the famous one, the *right* one. So noble, so brave.

I kept to myself, mostly. When I did spend time with Russ, I had to keep telling him it was nothing he'd done, that I was sorry, and it all got so leaden I just started staying away. Pace moved back into our office, but I did most of my research at home now, spending time on campus only to teach and hold office hours. With the governors dethroned, there seemed little urgency in getting Millicent's original figures analysed and published. Not to mention it had gotten pretty much impossible for me to look Pace in the eye—even worse than when the research theft had first happened.

My mom wasn't on campus to look out for me anymore. She'd decided that a boss who would set her up to be kidnapped deserved to be left in the lurch, and she quit without notice. She spent her time these days over at the University Park retirement home, recording and transcribing oral history from the academics. Most of them had never learned to type, being of a pre-computer vintage, and several had arthritic hands anyway; it was easier for them this way, and Mom thought they were all fantastic. She'd also discovered a new fascination for amateur radio, and she and Mark and a few of the other gear freaks spent hours staring at oscilloscopes and listening to faraway crackly voices with unusual accents.

'You have no *idea* the setup they've got,' she gushed to me. 'And the stuff the biologists are doing in the basement—but I'd better not say too much before they're ready to release the results. The negotiations with the new life forms are a little tricky.'

I'd been hoping that with all her new projects, Mom wouldn't notice that I wasn't doing so well. But no mom is ever so distracted that they can't worry about their child. Especially when the mom is my mom. I got a phone call every other day or so, inviting me for dinner, for a video, for a session of cleaning out the garage. I turned all the invitations down.

The adulation of my students, Russ's concern, my parents' increasingly worried phone calls—all only made me feel more of a fraud. The final crisis came when Kortnoz stopped by during my office hours and told me, 'You know, it's about time for you to be resubmitting your tenure application.'

I looked up from my new computer. 'You're joking,' I said. 'You … are … joking.'

'Um, no,' he said mildly. 'Why would I be?'

'Dr Kortnoz, do you know why I stole Pace's research? The real reason?'

'You thought you were saving the Purple River.'

'That's what I used to tell myself. But I've had to think a lot about people's motives and goals these days, what with all the trying to keep myself alive and everything. As an unhappy by-product, I've taken a good long look at my own. And I'm not noble. I'm just as sickeningly self-absorbed as any governor, any Praxie. Every day I've got to face rooms full of kids who think I'm a hero. But what I've done over the past few weeks doesn't change who—what—I really am. And what I did this semester wasn't even that big a deal anyway. I don't know why everyone's so impressed.'

'If they really knew what you were like, they'd leave you alone, is that it?'

'Yes,' I snapped.

'So … you don't deserve tenure?'

I laughed bitterly. 'Tenure is the least of it. I don't deserve parents who keep thinking I'm wonderful, I don't deserve a boyfriend who tells everyone I'm wonderful, I don't deserve students who tell each other I'm wonderful—'

'And you don't deserve friends either, do you?' said Pace from the doorway.

I looked at her for a long moment. 'I don't think I do, no.'

'Ty, could I borrow your four-wheel-drive, please? Celeste, I need you to come with me for something.' Kortnoz handed her the keys.

I stood up to go. I had no energy to argue. We went out to the parking lot and got into Kortnoz's vehicle.

'Any helicopters and guns this time?' I said.

'Missing the excitement?'

'No. No.'

After a few minutes I saw that Pace was driving up into the mountains. 'We're not going to the lava cave, are we?' I said.

'Sure are,' said Pace. 'Best place I know when you don't want to be disturbed.'

'Are you finally going to drop me into the pit?'

'If I were going to do that, I'd have done it two years ago. You and I have to have a talk.'

'Couldn't we have it at the pub?'

'Don't worry, I brought a bottle of wine. And a huge chocolate bar, really immense. I didn't want you to feel deprived.'

'That assumes I have wine and chocolate as a matter of course.'

'I'm as poor as you are. Ty sprang for these.'

'Oh. I guess I'm not missing much not having tenure, then.'

'That's one of the things I want to talk about when we get to the cave.'

My uneasiness grew as we parked and started pushing our way through the brush that blocked the path.

'Here's where I was ambushed,' I said. 'I'm surprised I'm not more jittery, coming through here again. About being ambushed, at least. I'm jittery enough about this "we gotta talk" thing.'

'Post-traumatic stress is an unpredictable bastard,' said Pace. 'That's another thing I want to talk about.'

By the time we stepped into the cave, I was a nervous wreck. Pace sat against the wall of the cave, where the heat from the lava pit wasn't quite so uncomfortable. She brought out a bottle of red, two plastic cups, and the largest chocolate bar in captivity.

'Better get started, before the wine gets too warm and the chocolate starts to melt,' said Pace. 'No point in being genteel.' We ate and drank.

'Feeling better?' said Pace after a few minutes.

'No. Just less hungry. And with the start of a buzz.'

'Could be worse. You could be miserable *and* hungry *and* sober.'

'What did you want to talk about?'

'Ohhhhh, lots of things.'

'Pace, please.'

'All right. First of all, I wanted to say you should cut the crap and stop feeling so damned sorry for yourself.'

'Um, you don't think that's a little presumptuous?'

'Not remotely. You feel like crap exactly why?'

'You didn't hear what I told Dr Kortnoz?'

'No, I came in on the end of your speech on why nobody ought to love you. Why, what did you tell him?'

'The real reason I stole your research.'

'Because you wanted to stick it to me. I know. I've known that the whole time.'

'What—'

'*And* because you wanted to save the Purple River. They're not mutually exclusive, and I suppose you get some credit for trying to stick it to me by doing something noble, rather than just straight-out villainy. Also, as I recall, you saved my life as part of that little incident.'

'I have to ask you something about that, since this is True Confessions Afternoon on the Lava Cave Channel.' I guessed the wine was relaxing me a little after all. 'You kept letting Jasper hang around, even though you knew he'd wanted to kill you. What's the story there?'

'That sort of brings me to that other thing I mentioned earlier. About tenure. I don't really have it.'

'*What*? How in hell can you fake having tenure?'

'I read that stupid loyalty clause, and I forged a copy of my contract that had that line in gibberish and I signed that instead. The department never checked, it looked the same as all the other contracts, so they have me listed as having tenure. During that time when Jasper was stalking me, he broke into my files and saw the doctored copy of the contract. He threatened to tell the governors, which would have meant I'd have to leave Ty and go work in Lilia or something, in disgrace, as a high-school geography teacher.'

'Nothing disgraceful about that. Remember Sister Grace Sackbutt? She was awesome.'

'Do you really think I could herd rooms full of adolescent girls like Sister Grace Sackbutt did? I'd do murder before the first week was out.'

'Mm. But if everyone thinks you have tenure, why aren't they paying you like you have tenure? You're not paying your extra money to Jasper, are you?' I was shocked.

'Not exactly. You know how they are over in Payroll. This one pay officer checked the contract as well, and she refuses to update my records so I could get the bigger salary. She could blackmail me, too, I suppose, but I told her it was a printer glitch, and, like a lot of rigid people, she has no imagination, and believed me. But she's damned if she's going to update the records until she has a proper contract with no gibberish. Did I think I'd be getting special treatment? Not while *she* was working in Payroll, thank *you*. Et cetera, et cetera. So bureaucracy wins after all. At least they think they can't fire me. And Payroll doesn't talk to anyone else on the entire campus, so as far as I know my secret, and my job, are safe. And I didn't sign that stupid loyalty clause.'

'But Jasper could spill the beans at any time.'

'Yup. I'm stuck with him. For now, anyway.'

'Pity. So what were you going to say about post-traumatic stress?'

'I was wondering if it had ever occurred to you that this depression you refuse to snap out of may be at least in part due not to your own moral failings but to post-traumatic stress? It does tend to deplete one's resilience, or so I've heard.'

'What, you've never had it yourself? After all the traumas you've been mixed up in?'

'When you *cause* the traumas, you don't feel as out of control. Which diminishes the stress. See how it works?'

I took an excessively large mouthful of chocolate, and chased it with an equally large mouthful of wine. 'So, what you're saying is, even though you know I'm a selfish creep, you don't hate me.'

'I'm saying exactly that. And might I add that you've known for years what kind of person I am, and you don't hate me either.'

'What kind of person are you?'

'The kind who would never collaborate with you on any research because I was afraid everyone would think I just coasted on your brilliance.'

'But you're the brilliant—'

'The kind who would make sure you were there when I got into trouble, because I knew the nuns would never punish you as much, and they had to give us both the same punishment to be fair.'

'Oh. Yeah. That.'

'The kind who kept hanging around for hours and hours every day after school at your house, because of how everyone was always nice to each other there.'

'Mm.'

'The kind who always wanted to be you, creep or no creep, because you were always kind and encouraging, and your teachers always loved you, and your students always loved you—everyone loves you, and it's really pissing me off that you don't care about that!'

I couldn't think of a word to say. So I drank some more wine. Then something did occur to me: 'I'm going to have a hell of a time getting down that trail again.'

'Don't worry, I've had hardly any wine, I'll help you.'

'Pace?'

'Uh-huh?'

'I do care.'

'Then act like it.'

'How?'

'Teach. Research. Be kind and encouraging. Keep me out of trouble. Or at least keep the punishments from being so bad. Do the stuff you've always done. Do it because people love you and need you. There's a whole campus full of people who look to you when they're trying to figure out how they should deal with their screw-ups and their flaws—not because they think you're perfect, but because they see that you take those screw-ups and flaws that everyone has, and you turn them into energy and direction. So quit moping, because it's tiresome, wasteful, and most unattractive. Russ is a saint.'

'I thought you detested him. Dramatic Arts and everything.'

'Well, he's certainly no mime—he had plenty of words for me in Drusy's apartment. And he's good with maps. And undercover work, I can see where acting would come in handy for that. He should join the martial-arts club, we could make something out of talent like his.'

'I'll suggest it to him.'

We sat in silence, watching the light from the lava pit through our plastic cups of wine. The chocolate was nearly gone, and really starting to get soft now. I divided the last piece in two and gave a chunk to Pace while I ate the other. We licked the melted chocolate off our fingers.

After a while, I said, 'I don't know if I can turn despair and shame on and off like a tap.'

'But at least you're agreeing that you're more than just your despair and shame. Or else there'd be no one to turn the tap.'

I grimaced at the strained analogy, but I had to admit she had a point. 'I suppose I could take it one bit at a time.'

'That's the only way that ever works. How did you save the campus? One bit at a time. If you'd known at the beginning all the stuff that was going to happen to you, you'd have frozen. This way, though, you started a revolution! And you kicked the backsides of the Praxies as well! Millicent Strudthorne would be proud. That reminds me: I read about a call for papers for a conference on fluvial geomorphology this summer. Something on the recovery of Millicent's original research would be perfect.'

I found myself getting interested. 'What's the conference called?'

'I think they're calling it "Sediment Research: Paradigm Shift or Just Another Mudslide?"'

'Perfect.'

Acknowledgements

I would like, first, to thank the academics who have taught me, been my colleagues, and employed me. This book is, above all, a fond valentine to the glorious, ancient, and threatened institution of the university, and much of my love for it springs from my respect for them. I would also like to thank those who continue to be my indefatigable cheerleaders, my comforters in dark days, and my comrades in the fight for justice and good art. They are many, but I single out in particular, and always, Cathyann Sweeney, comrade in arms, in scholarship, and in revelry; the SWISHErs, many of whom are academics and all of whom are jaw-droppingly fabulous; my NaNoWriMo Coffee House buddies, who were with me during that long-ago November that saw the birth of this book; Jack Dann, Janeen Webb, and Richard Harland, who have been a help in many times of need (including during the writing of my PhD thesis); Russell Kirkpatrick, writer, academic, and geographer; James Patrick Kelly, best accomplice ever; Shauna O'Meara, writer and encourager; my fellow Odyssey authors, who are a daring company of bold and swashbuckling writers and fit companions for any adventure; and the wonderful team at Odyssey themselves, who (as I have noted elsewhere) see my idiosyncrasies as strengths, and my weaknesses as manageable. Finally, I wish, once again and always, to thank the three most important people in the world to me: my mom, Dr Elspeth Goodin, who was so amazing a parent that she took tiny me with her to her classes while she was getting her bachelor's degree, thus instilling in me a lifelong love of the wonderland that is a university campus; my brilliant daughter Margaret, who may (or may not) decide to follow the family business and become an academic herself; and my beloved husband Houston, who has a surfeit of degrees (really, five could be considered wretched excess). They enthusiastically encourage me in everything I undertake, and I love them beyond measure.

About the Author

American-born writer Laura E. Goodin has been writing professionally for over thirty years. Her stories have appeared in numerous publications, including *Michael Moorcock's New Worlds, Andromeda Spaceways Inflight Magazine, Review of Australian Fiction, Adbusters, Wet Ink, The Lifted Brow,* and *Daily Science Fiction,* among others, and in several anthologies. Her plays and libretti have been performed on three continents, and her poetry has been performed internationally, both as spoken word and as texts for new musical compositions. She attended the 2007 Clarion South workshop, and has a PhD in creative writing from the University of Western Australia.